T0207892

WILFONG THE
WIZARD

Wilfong the Wizard

Charlton Clayes

iUniverse

WILFONG THE WIZARD

iUniverse books may be ordered through booksellers or by contacting:

iUniverse
1663 Liberty Drive
Bloomington, IN 47403
www.iuniverse.com
1-800-Authors (1-800-288-4677)

ISBN: 978-1-5320-0081-2 (sc)
ISBN: 978-1-5320-0080-5 (e)

Print information available on the last page.

iUniverse rev. date: 07/13/2016

Ye elves of hills, brooks, standing lakes and groves.
And ye that on the sands with printless foot
Do chase the ebbing Neptune and do fly him
When he comes back; you demi-puppets that
By moonshine do the green sour ringlets make,
Whereof the ewe not bites, and you whose pastime
Is to make midnight mushrooms, that rejoice
To hear the solemn curfew; by whose aid,
Weak masters though ye be, I have bedimm'd
The noontide sun, call'd forth the mutinous winds,
And 'twixt the green sea and the azured vault
Set roaring war: to the dread rattling thunder
Have I given fire and rifted Jove's stout oak
With his own bolt; the strong-based promontory
Have I made shake and by the spurs pluck'd up
The pine and cedar: graves at my command
Have waked their sleepers, oped, and set 'em forth
By my so potent art....

William Shakespeare
The Tempest
(Act Five, Scene One)

THE FIRST CASTING

THE WIZARD AT WORK

Wilfong the Wizard sneezed.

Ordinarily, a sneeze was the product of one of three things: a respiratory disorder, an allergy, or – in Wilfong's case – an overly sensitive nose. The act of sneezing represented a peculiarly human gesture which separated mortals from both the gods and the beasts; it was as spontaneous as, say, a hiccup and thus unavoidable. The hapless individual must either bottle it up (leading to all manner of unintended consequences) or let fly full blast and suffer other unfortunate consequences. By and large, however, since sneezing was so commonplace, one was as liable to be ignored as he was to garner a polite "Xenox watch over you" from his neighbors.

This writer, during a browsing expedition at the Library of the Metropolis of Atlantis in researching the present work, stumbled across an obscure treatise written by an equally obscure philosopher who lived some one hundred and twenty years ago, one Xelax by name. In fact, he was so obscure that many mistook him for an attendant at one of the public baths. Apparently having a great deal of time on his hands, Xelax decided to classify the various types of sneezes by sound patterns; and, after a year of painstaking observations (and not a few annoying experiments on unsuspecting passersby), he settled upon seven major forms (and thirteen minor forms), ranging from the Thunderclap to the Whimper. All in all, the treatise occupied forty-one sheets of papyrus which might otherwise have been better used on some other project. This writer does not recommend it as contributing to a greater understanding of the human condition.

In any event, the illustrious Wilfong sneezed. In Xelax's classification system, it was a Drumbeat; that is to say, it was a short series of respiratory discharges, a *rat-a-tat-tat*. Moreover, it was the minor form called a Little Drumbeat (as opposed to the major form, a Big Drumbeat), whereby the discharges occur in rapid sequence (as opposed to a slow sequence). Something had irritated the Wizard's overly sensitive nose, and he was unable to discharge the sneeze in a single blast, e.g. the Thunderclap. Wilfong was most annoyed that his whole body quivered while he was in the throes; yet, being a natural body function, the sneeze was immune to a Spell of Magick, and he had to endure as best he could.

This was no ordinary sneeze, however, for it produced a most astonishing effect. The first inkling of it that Wilfong received came while he was wiping his nose. He heard several loud, frantic thumps emanating from his bedchamber; these thumps were concurrent with equally loud, frantic cries for help. The Wizard rushed into his bedchamber and immediately sought out his manservant, the loyal Murkol, whom he had instructed to pack his winter clothing in a storage trunk. Murkol was nowhere to be seen.

"The Cosmos take the fellow!" Wilfong muttered. "Has he slipped out for a mug of beer again? I'll cast a Spell of Paralysis over him!"

The thumping and the bellowing now increased both in frequency and in intensity. Wilfong was startled to learn that they were coming from *inside* his trunk. He snapped open the clasps and threw back the lid, not knowing what to expect. Instantly, up popped the missing manservant, gasping for air. His brown face had just begun to turn a sickly yellow, and his hairy ears twitched uncontrollably as panic gripped him. Murkol leaped out of the trunk in a single bound and went to his knees before his master; and before the Wizard had time to react, his hand was kissed repeatedly.

Murkol was a member of the primitive race known as the Zarelor, who lived in a land beyond the Great Western Ocean. Zarelor were noted for two extremes of behavior: absolute indifference to any living creatures (except when they wanted something), and canine slavishness toward anyone who inadvertently showed them a kindness (a reaction which was often exploited, as Wilfong had done). On a previous visit to Zarel, the Wizard had rescued Murkol from a lynch mob, and the latter had repaid him by following him everywhere and assisting him without being asked to. Wilfong was forced to take the brute into his service.

"Oh, Mashter!" the Zarelor sputtered between slobbers, displaying his race's difficulty with Atlantean sibilants. "Dou hasht shaved me again!"

"There, there, Murkol," Wilfong soothed, attempting to extricate his hand. "Everything is all right now. You're safe. But, tell me, how did you happen to be *inside* my trunk?"

"I cannot shay, Mashter. I wazh going to unlock it sho I could shtore dy chlodezh. When I heard dou shneezhe, I turned to shay 'Zhenoksh blessh dee.' But a horrible trembling came over me den, and all wazh darknesh. I had a great fear."

He seized Wilfong's other hand and bathed it in a similar fashion. The Wizard finally had to push him away. Murkol bowed his head in embarrassment over his presumption.

"Well, this is very queer and strange," Wilfong mused aloud. "I wonder if you were somehow seized by a Spell of Transition. Unfortunately, I have no time to ponder the question now. I must leave for the School. Finish packing here, then scrub the floors and walls. The apartment appears a bit grimy these days."

"Yesh, Mashter. Hasht a nishe day."

It may be fairly said that Wilfong, if he did not live in the best of times, certainly did not live in the worst of times either. According to the *Histories* of Ceppid the Wise concerning the Middle Fourteenth Dynasty of the Kingdom of Atlantis, its "Golden Age" four centuries before the Wizard's day, high and low alike prospered beyond their wildest dreams. The King then was Cimmalute IV ("the Magnificent"), and he had inaugurated a vigorous program of public works which provided a job for anyone who was able to work. He had also encouraged industry and agriculture so that there was plenty of consumer goods to keep money in circulation. Those unable to work by reason of age or ill health or disability were given vouchers with which to purchase the necessities of life. Yet, all good things must come to an end; and, in Atlantis, an economic slump forced the monarchy to scale back governmental largesse. In succeeding reigns, public-works projects decreased, a more lackadaisical attitude toward the economy set in, and greater restrictions were placed on the voucher system. While some few were now left adrift, the majority of Atlanteans found no specific reason to complain about their lot in life and so went about their business in complacency.

Wilfong counted himself among the majority. He lived in the Third Ring of the Metropolis, that which had been assigned to the professional and commercial classes of society. Specifically, his apartment was located on the west side of the Ring where others of his sub-class could also be found. By profession, he was a teacher of writing at one of the handful of scribal schools; for ten hours a day, twenty days in the month, he attempted to tutor the children of the wealthy class in the rudiments of language so that, one day, they would be able – as he often phrased it – "to butcher it at their leisure." For his efforts, he received a monthly stipend sufficient to rent a three-room apartment on the top floor of his building and to purchase the necessities of life. On occasion, he also indulged in some private tutoring of the children of the professional and commercial classes in order to obtain some extra silver coins for a luxury or two. The Wizard was neither rich nor poor as those things went, and he muddled along just as the majority of Atlanteans did.

A person of routine, he followed his usual path to the School. He passed the shops of the craftsmen – goldsmiths, potters, wainwrights, weavers, glass-blowers, and the like – in the southern section of the Third Ring and observed his surroundings with a practiced eye even as he maintained an outward demeanor of indifference. The everyday hustle and bustle of the district was in full bloom that day; shopkeepers vied with one another to catch the attention and the patronage of the hordes of would-be buyers. Many in the crowds were trusted servants of the upper classes seeking some novelty for the further aggrandizement of their masters/mistresses, although one or two of the high-born could be seen dragging their menials about and piling heaps of merchandise into their arms. If not for a quirk in fortune, Wilfong himself might have been relegated to the status of a menial. His talent with letters had caught the eye of a wealthy patron who steered him toward the teaching profession, a decision for which he thanked his lucky stars daily.

Always standouts in any crowd were the hordes of tourists from a score of distant lands as they pushed their way haughtily through the streets, gawking at the sights the Metropolis had to offer but more likely than not searching for some over-priced trinket to take home and impress their neighbors. If the craftsmen and merchants earned less than a comfortable living from the local trade, they compensated handsomely for it by sharping the tourists who had not the least idea of how to haggle with a retailer. It was this tourist trade, in fact, which had shaken Atlantis out of its economic slump and made it once again the envy of the Known World.

Not everyone on the cobblestoned streets was in pursuit of an honest coin, however. As individual fortunes fell, an army of thieves, beggars, pickpockets, and prostitutes arose to prey upon those witless tourists (and not a few Atlanteans if the opportunity presented itself) to keep themselves solvent. Wilfong at this time came within two meters of such an encounter. As he passed by a notable silversmith, he spotted a tourist from far-off Hyperborea – a rough-looking fellow with a craggy face and a shock of unruly blond hair, dressed in animal skins and an elaborate headdress of leather and bones (no doubt the latest "fashion" in his part of the world). In a land of woven fabrics, he stood out like a facial wart.

He was eyeing the handiwork of the aforementioned silversmith with a none-too-keen eye, trying to decide if some of his treasure should be spent on a plate or a jewel box, when a boy dressed in rags slammed into him. The Hyperborean turned and expressed his outrage with a bit of growling. Wide-eyed, the boy apologized profusely for his clumsiness and genuflected several times; then he ran off and disappeared into the crowd. A few seconds later, the tourist discovered that his money bag was missing and uttered (in halting Atlantean and in his own tongue) a round of curses. He collared a local person and demanded to be directed to a law-enforcement official; the passerby, intimidated by the fellow's appearance and demeanor, stammered out some hasty directions and scurried away.

Wilfong merely shook his head in bemusement. He had seen the boy's hand expertly detach the Hyperborean's money bag from the belt upon which it had been hanging and slip it under the boy's rags. It was a daily occurrence, he knew, but it seemed that tourists never learned from either their own experiences or those of others. If the youthful pickpocket were ever caught, he would most likely be subject to a willow branch on the buttocks and a brand on his brow to denote him as a thief. And, in that, he could count himself fortunate; in the days of the present King's great-grandsire (a strict law-and-order type), thieves, regardless of their age, lost a finger for each offense, starting with a thumb.

As the Wizard approached the Gate of Sighs, which led to the eastern section of the Second Ring of the Metropolis, he spotted a familiar face, that of a well-known Egyptian courtesan. Though in her middle years, she yet held onto her beauty with a firm grip; although her dark hair was starting to be streaked with gray and her face was becoming rounder, she was still able to turn a male head and interest its owner in a delightful hour or two. Wilfong, in his days as a student seeking to gain experience in the wider world, had spent a few precious coins sampling her wares. Nowadays, he exercised more self-control; a Disciple of Wynot the Wise was expected to concentrate on more esoteric matters. He did catch her eye, however, and received an inviting smile. It was doubtful that she recognized him; one customer was much like another in her profession. Her expectation of employment turned to disappointment as Wilfong hurried on to his own employment.

He strolled through the Gate of Sighs but had to leap aside at the last moment in order to avoid being trampled by a team of oxen pulling a huge four-wheeled cart laden with Cosmos-knows-what. "Gate" was a misnomer, but it was the term in vogue. The stone wall which separated this Ring from the next consisted of shaped slabs held together by pressure, with a bit of mortar to fill in the cracks to form a true arch. There were four Gates in each Ring, staggered every thirty degrees as a defensive measure. While the Gates to the First Ring had been richly decorated, there was no attempt to embellish any others; yet, this Gate had been "decorated" in a fashion by centuries of graffiti scribbled upon every conceivable surface by those who could not afford to leave any other permanent mark of their drab existence.

As soon as he had passed into the Second Ring, the Wizard was aware of the not-so-subtle differences between his middle-class world and that of the upper classes, as reflected in the architecture and the landscaping. This region of the Metropolis was reserved for the great merchants and traders whose business was the economic lifeblood of the Kingdom, the priests of the temples of Atlantis' pantheon, royal advisors, and others of wealth and influence. Here were the multi-story, multi-room private residences with ornately carved and gaudily decorated facades, surrounded by expansive courtyards filled with statuary, gardens, hanging vines, trees, flowers, and fountains. Here too could be found the only grass in the entire city, a green "collar" between the "head" of the Metropolis and its "body." The streets were broader – and cleaner. Further along, one would encounter squads of City Sweepers (one of the few public-works programs still extant), plying their brooms and scoops on the rectangular paving stones.

Despite the generous thoroughfares, traffic was lighter here. Haughty young men cruised by on their gilded chariots. Slaves carried litters fashioned from mahogany and brocaded silk, bearing some lord or lady to a business appointment or a shopping spree. The only commercial vehicles allowed in this Ring were hired liveries depositing their cargoes of purchased goods at the rear entrances of the grand estates. If anyone took notice of any pedestrians, he gave them at best a cursory glance. In the Wizard's case, no one questioned his right to be there, nor would he be detained by the City Guards for any reason; so long as he wore the badge of his profession – a pin representing crossed quills – upon his left shoulder, he was allowed free passage.

The School where Wilfong taught lay in the southeast quadrant of this Ring, nestled between the private chapels of two international traders who each owned a fleet of ships and who thus could afford to indulge themselves rather than rub elbows with the lower classes in a public chapel. The School was an unpretentious two-story building made of bricks which stood it in sharp contrast to the quarried stone of its surroundings. In point of fact, it had been one of the original structures in this area, having been at that location for over two millennia, before the new wealthy class began to appropriate the land for their own use; and, as it served a useful purpose, i.e. teaching the scions of that class the rudiments of language, it was tolerated despite its lower-class appearance.

Wilfong himself had matriculated at this School and might have spent his life teaching the children of the middle class at another school had he not graduated with the highest honors the School could offer. The Headmaster himself had recommended him for a position "more worthy of your talents, my lad." In the beginning, the Wizard had been required to live on the premises (in the upper story) as an apprentice to the older tutors; when, after five years, he had demonstrated his worth, he was awarded a stipend by which he could afford private quarters. During the next ten years, thanks to his prowess, the School's own reputation was increased – and his stipend rose proportionately – and more of the wealthy class chose it for their sons (or daughters if they had no sons to inherit their estates). Were it not for the fact that he belonged to a secret society under sanction by the King, Wilfong might have led a grander life; but, of necessity, he had had to keep a lower profile.

He entered the School and immediately turned to his right. Set in a niche in the wall sat a votive figure about twenty centimeters high. It represented Caxeot, patron of learning and the arts. No self-respecting Wizard of the Order of Wynot believed in Caxeot, or any of the Atlantean pantheon for that matter, for Wynot had replaced them all as a Teacher of Harmony and Wisdom. Yet, it behooved the prudent man to pay lip service to the *official* gods while he was in public view. Thus, Wilfong bowed his head and moved his lips (though no thoughts were formed and no words were spoken) in imitation of prayer. The obligation completed, he quickly moved on to his classroom.

His students were already at their desks, standing at attention until he gave permission to be seated. Some wore eager faces, ready to learn and to use their learning wisely; some wore anxious faces, worried about not learning well enough and about the consequences of their failure. The majority, however, looked bored and sullen, wondering why they had to endure this nonsense and wishing they were elsewhere having fun. A teacher's lot was not an easy one. Every day, Wilfong watched these young louts go through the motions and wished he had a classroom full of bright children. Someday, when he could afford it, he would establish his own school, picking and choosing students based upon their willingness to learn. Until then, the rent had to be paid....

He took his place at his podium and studied his charges briefly.

"Good morning, gentlemen," he intoned gravely.

"Good morning, Master Colxor," all responded in unison.

He motioned them to be seated, adjusted his papers, and scanned the class once again.

"Zorpac," he said, singling out a rough-hewn youth with dark curly hair and sleepy eyes, "will you begin please?"

The designated individual reacted as if he had been asked to clean out the stables. And, on a subconscious level, the Wizard had deliberately selected him first for the very reason that the boy was his *worst* pupil – an arrogant pup who made no secret of his contempt for any "Middle Ringer" who presumed to teach his betters – and he hoped to make an example of him. Zorpac, thus taken by surprise, got awkwardly to his feet, papyrus in hand, and cast his teacher a brief look of defiance. Then, remembering his place, he began to recite the assigned lesson.

This was the "advanced" class (if any of them could be said to be "advanced"), and Wilfong had chosen a volume of Xallog's *History of Atlantis in the Fourteenth Dynasty* as a teaching aid. The previous day, he had read a lengthy passage from the florid, dry-as-dust prose, and the students had written it down word for word, hopefully accurately. Today, they would reveal just how accurately. Haltingly, Zorpac read what he had written and stumbled over every fourth word. Not a few snickers issued from those who held themselves in higher esteem; the levity died instantly at the teacher's stern gaze and sharp rap upon the podium. Soon, the object of their derision ground to a halt, unable to make out his own writing.

By Wynot's flame-red beard! the Wizard thought. *I wish I could tie this lout's tongue literally!*

9

He moved from behind the podium and walked over to Zorpac's desk. Tension filled the classroom; given the boy's reputation for ill-disguised contempt, an expectation of verbal combat gripped the students. Perhaps there would be *physical* combat as well, though it would hardly have been an even match. Wilfong, as Atlanteans went, was on the short, frail side; he would not have survived as a common laborer. Nevertheless, he fearlessly faced up to the tall, husky youth and held out his hand. Zorpac worked his jaw a second or two, considered his options, decided he had none – at the moment – and placed his sheet of papyrus in his teacher's waiting hand.

The Wizard glanced at it and winced. Undoubtedly, it was the worst penmanship he had ever had the displeasure to read. Written Atlantean was phonetic in nature, and each of the characters represented a specific sound. This lout had done the assignment in so sloppy a fashion as to render many of the characters ambiguous, and one who was less adept in the language than Wilfong might have misconstrued the essence of the passage entirely.

"See here, young sir." Wilfong pointed to the current stumbling block. "You've made a left-hand hook when it ought to be a *right*-hand one. Now read it as if there were a right-hand hook."

Zorpac obeyed as instructed and received a nod of approval from his teacher, a gesture calculated to infuriate him further. Wilfong returned to his podium, motioned Zorpac to be seated, and called upon another student at random to read the next passage. One by one, each pupil demonstrated his skill (or lack of it); one by one, the teacher pointed out the obvious errors. When the last student had had his turn at offending the teacher's sensibilities, the latter requested the class to re-write the entire assignment. While they did so, he adjourned to the privy behind the School and contemplated.

Shortly before mid-day, as soon as his intermediate class had finished its session, Wilfong departed the School to take his lunch. Formerly, he would have been required to eat on the premises; now that he was a Junior Master, he had greater privileges. As was his custom, he walked down to the Port of Atlantis. On a previous venture in search of unique cuisine, he had discovered an out-of-the-way inn, owned and operated by the most unique woman he had ever met who served the most marvelous baked halibut, and he made a point of patronizing it every fourth day.

Besides, he enjoyed the ebb and flow of international traffic – even in a rough and bawdy area – a prime source of the latest news from distant lands. Atlantis was surrounded by lesser civilizations – some of which had only begun to take the first tentative steps to explore beyond their borders (when they weren't quarreling with their neighbors) – and an ancient royal edict had decreed that a greater understanding of them was a wise and prudent thing; if one could not have cordial relations with the barbarians, then at least one might have some idea of what to expect in case of attack. In any event, knowledge for its own sake was a very desirable goal for the cosmopolite. And Wilfong, the epitome of cosmopolitanism, sought to acquire as much knowledge as it was humanly possible to do.

It may be fairly said that the Wizard's soft features and relatively fine clothes posed an incongruous sight in that part of the Metropolis where hard, back-breaking labor left harsh marks on men's bodies and in their minds. And it may be also said that his presence might cause much resentment amongst the rough-necked and coarse-minded denizens of this sub-world against one who dared to flaunt his airs before them. Yet, the fact of the matter was that his own lower-class origins had been made public by a boyhood acquaintance who had not had the good fortune to escape the drudgery of his socio-economic status. Consequently, the "wharf-rats" – a term of derogation by the "civilized" citizens of the Metropolis and one of sarcastic endearment by the dock hands themselves – tolerated his visits (if they did not exactly welcome him with open arms) and made him the butt of many a practical joke. For his part, the Wizard took everything in stride and attempted (mostly unsuccessfully) to match his tormentors joke for joke.

He was more welcome by the children of the workers who haunted the wharves and who regarded him as a prime storyteller. Invariably, whenever he put in an appearance, he drew a crowd of urchins, earning him the sobriquet of "Colxor the Child Collector." The children were an unpretentious lot, eager to be entertained if only for a short while in order to escape the misery of an otherwise drab existence. And the unwritten rule was that no one was to pick his pocket or to run a scam on him. Because of that, Wilfong preferred their company to that of snobbish scions of wealth who did not appreciate some acculturation. He would sooner teach the wharf-rats to read and write (if he could afford it), but that notion was much too radical in that day and age – not when the King's agents were everywhere seeking "deviants" to persecute and to prosecute.

The first thing he noticed when he stepped onto Pier Twelve was the total lack of activity. Not a worker was to be seen, nor any of the children. Neither did he spot the usual crowd of hangers-on – drunkards, scroungers, whores – whom he avoided like the plague. Even though it was mid-day and most of the wharf-rats would likely have gone off in search of their own lunch, a skeleton crew was always on hand in case of an arrival whose schedule did not correspond to anyone else's. Even the skeleton crews were missing. There was absolute dead silence; no arguing, cursing, or insulting broke the stillness. To all appearances, the docks were deserted. Wilfong looked about in perplexity, then peered at the neighboring pier. It too was deserted. He moved on, slowly, cautiously, searching left and right for some sign of life.

"Colxor! Hey, Colxor!" a gruff voice sounded off to his left.

The Wizard swung around to confront a small bull of a man. Though shorter in stature than the average Atlantean, the newcomer was considerably stockier; he possessed arms and legs which resembled branches of a tree and a barrel of a chest, and his huge head seemed to be attached to his body without benefit of a neck. His hair and beard were thick and reddish-brown which complemented his ruddy complexion. He stared at Wilfong with black, deep-sunken eyes. The short man's name was Hamilton, one of the crew bosses on Pier Twelve. Rumor had it that he originally came from an island far to the north, liked what he saw in Atlantis, and settled down permanently.

"Greetings, Ham. Where *is* everyone?"

"Over on Pier Eight, I'm thinkin'," the other replied in his queer accent. "There's a big commotion there."

"When *isn't* there a big commotion on Pier Eight? It boasts the rowdiest crews in all of Creation."

"Aye, that it does. But somethin' new is brewin'."

"What?"

"Dunno. I was just on me way over there meself when I spotted you. Come on, we'll have a look-see together."

This odd couple strode off toward the opposite end of the wharf district. When Atlantis had been but a small city-state centuries earlier, its trading capacity had necessarily been minimal; traders seeking new and exotic goods for sale or barter were forced to collect them at considerable risk to their persons and money pouches. The barbarians which inhabited the Known World (the northern and southern coasts of the Great Inland Sea and the eastern and western shores of the Great Western Ocean) had once taken offense at the intrusion of strangers and either expelled or killed them. Survivors of these encounters usually had horrific tales to tell. Eventually, the barbarians acquired some small appreciation for civilized behavior and the benefits of international trade; they learned ship-building and navigation skills, formed trading companies to service Atlantis, and sent their merchants abroad by the score. Atlantis was forced to expand its harbor in order to accommodate the increased traffic, from the original four piers to eventually twelve – with new ones under construction – as befitted a bustling metropolis and economic empire. There was always work to be done. A half dozen or more work crews scuttled to and fro on each wharf eighteen hours a day, loading or unloading veritable mountains of goods. Some of the wharves had begun to specialize, i.e. receive or ship out only certain types of commodities, in order to create some sort of order out of a potentially chaotic situation. Specialization never reduced the work-load, however.

Pier Eight was just a specialized wharf, and the nature of its trade had given it a certain notoriety. The merchant who leased it (at a very favorable rate) dealt only in slaves. An economic superpower required prodigious amounts of labor to keep it functioning efficiently – labor for the factories, the mines, the agricultural estates, and bodies for the "personal" needs of the upper classes. Atlantis' native-born population could not have filled all of the slots, even had it been so inclined; and voluntary immigration had not been able to keep up with the labor demands. Therefore, slavers roamed the Known World, gathering herds of human beings from the hinterlands and shipping them off to the Kingdom, where the poor devils were auctioned off to some entrepreneur in need of replacements or to some lord or lady for amusement. Many of the wharf-rats were slaves under the thumb of the merchants; the remainder were ex-slaves who had no other skills and thus were forced to remain where they were, toiling for subsistent wages. (The crew bosses, like Hamilton, earned slightly more but were no less driven by the demands of the merchants.)

Not unexpectedly, the trade in humans had its peculiar problems. After all, the "cargo" arrived in Atlantis against its will and exhibited all the symptoms of resentment, hostility, and/or outright violence. When someone reported a "commotion" on Pier Eight, he spoke in terms of gross understatement; the "commotion" more likely than not was an insurrection by a "cargo" against maltreatment by either the ship's crew and/or the dock's workers, the latter of which had earned a grim reputation for brutality, despite the fact that most of them had once worn the slavers' chains. Not a day passed that a wharf-rat did not pummel someone – and usually many someones at a time – for the sheer pleasure of it; if he wasn't beating on the slaves, he was beating on the workers of another pier or of his own.

Wilfong did not frequent Pier Eight at all, and subsequently he was not as well-known there as he was elsewhere in the district. This had been a deliberate decision on his part. Wynot the Wise had taught the dignity and self-worth of all individuals, regardless of their station in life, and urged his disciples to disavow all relationships in which the parties were not equals. Above all, he had abhorred slavery and, during his time on Earth, railed against it, risking the wrath and condemnation of the Powers-That-Be. Even had the Wizard not been a faithful adherent of his master's teachings, he still would not have had anything to do with that wretched institution. For, it was in his nature to reject it, having himself arisen out of a potential situation where he could easily have been one of that number. Still, he was known to that rough crowd, such was his reputation amongst the general wharf population, and they regarded him in the same manner as they did anyone else, with contempt.

As soon as Wilfong and Hamilton stepped onto Pier Eight, they immediately realized that the "commotion" was of a very different sort than the usual occurrences. It seemed that all the wharf-rats had gathered here; the Wizard quickly scanned the assembly and noted representatives from every other pier. Some he recognized by distinctive clothing, others by personal knowledge. They numbered nearly two hundred and jammed and pushed and crowded against each other in order to get a clearer view of whatever had attracted them in the first place. None of them evinced any violent tendencies, a rarity on any given day, but were merely curiosity-seekers. Hamilton began to jump up and down in order to see over the crowd, gave it up as a lost cause, and fell to muttering under his breath.

"Hamilton! Colxor! How the hell you are?"

A bear of a man, sinewy and muscular, with shaggy blond hair and blue eyes which were set too close together, waved at the pair from three rows of human beings over. Upon seeing him, Hamilton broke out in a toothy grin.

"Hiya, Trimon! What's the drift?"

"Scuttlebutt is there a slaver from a place no one ever heard of just arrived. A cargo he has, full o' strange-lookin' folks. Ain't seen 'em yet. Close enough can't get."

"Let's work our way around," Hamilton suggested. "Mebbe we can find an opening, or at least a higher spot."

It may be fairly said that Wilfong's curiosity was piqued, despite his aversion to the institution of slavery in general, by the possible discovery of a new species of humanity. Over the years, he had seen a wide spectrum of beings, from the dark-skinned peoples the Egyptians called "Nubians" in the southernmost parts of the Known World to the pallid Hyperboreans to the far north to the Zarelor on the western edge of the World. Yet, he supposed he had not seen all of the varieties which existed; many of the lands beyond the Great Western Ocean and those of the southern continent had never been fully explored, and only the Cosmos knew what lay further east of the Great Inland Sea. Perhaps these newcomers were natives of one of those faraway places. In any case, the Wizard desired to catch a glimpse of them, if only to satisfy his natural curiosity. And, if he could also learn something of their culture, so much the better.

The trio edged around the perimeter of the crowd until they were actually within the confines of Pier Eight, though they were no closer than they had been before. Despite its unique trade, this wharf looked no different than the others. The pier extended a hundred meters into the man-made harbor of Atlantis; it could easily accommodate four ships at a time (two on either side) and often did. At the head of the pier sat two long, low brick buildings, five meters by fifteen, which normally served as transitional warehouses, one for incoming goods, the other for outgoing. Since Atlantis never exported slaves, however, Pier Eight's warehouses were segregated according to gender. Which was which was of no importance; the "cargo" never stayed there very long but was moved out as soon as an auction could be set up. Naturally, there were no amenities attached to this temporary "residence"; the buildings had been constructed for goods, and people were co-incidental.

Luckily, several large amphorae stood at the side of the nearest warehouse. All bore the mark of the former lessee who had moved on to better facilities on Pier Twelve and not bothered to take all of his possessions with him. The short man turned two of the amphorae upside-down, gingerly climbed onto one, and stood on its bottom. Awkwardly, Wilfong followed suit. Even if they were not close to the source of the "commotion," still they had a better view than most of the assembled workers.

And what a view! The Wizard discovered what had pulled all of the wharf-rats away from their jobs at one time: a shipful of women. Ordinarily, the slavers carried a "mixed" cargo, often an equal number of each gender, depending on the demands of the day. Not so this ship. And the women were of a species Wilfong (or any other Atlantean, he was willing to wager) had never seen before. They were, on the average, taller than most Atlanteans, dusky-skinned, sloe-eyed, and slender; and they were all scantily clad, some wearing only a breech-cloth to cover their privates. Generally speaking, they were some of the most beautiful women the Wizard had ever laid eyes on; and while the precepts of Wynot concerning self-indulgence of the pleasures of the flesh were ever-present in his mind, he found his heart beating rapidly and his breathing shallow. He closed his eyes and whispered a Spell of Tranquility.

"Be damned!" Hamilton was muttering. "Wouldja look at that, Colxor? I ain't seen so many nekkid women in one place in many a moon."

"Nor I, Ham. It's…quite a sight."

"Sure, an' they'll not be goin' into the fields, I can tell you. Some high-born will be gettin' hisself a *harem*."

Unpolished as he was, Hamilton nevertheless had a gift for driving straight to the heart of a matter, regardless of the subject under discussion. Some of his opinions were so uncanny that it seemed he had intimate knowledge of the events and people concerned. Even as Wilfong had a reputation as a story-teller, the short man had one as a settler of arguments without resorting to his fists (though he did use those when the occasion warranted). He could be crude at times, but he was an accomplished conversationalist – which is why Wilfong enjoyed his company so much.

"Undoubtedly. I wonder where they're from?"

"As soon as this party breaks up, I'll be after nosin' around and see what I can dig up."

Wilfong remained there for a while longer, drinking in as much of the fabulous "cargo" as he dared. Abruptly, his stomach reminded him of why he had come down to the wharves in the first place. He shielded his eyes and peered obliquely at the Sun. He still had time for a quick bite before having to return to the School and his gods-awful students. Just as he was about to lower himself to the ground, however, he spied a calamity in the making. In the hasty rush to Pier Eight to ogle the new shipment of slaves, some careless worker on Pier Nine had done a sloppy job of securing one of the loading booms. A bale of goods still depended from it, but the line which held it had been improperly tied; the knot was slipping loose, and the bale was inching downward. If the knot slipped completely, the load would come crashing down on the heads of the workers who were standing beneath it.

Wilfong was in a bind. He could shout a warning, but he might not be heard above the clamor of the wharf-rats trying to catch the attention of the slave women. And, given the rate of slippage, he might not be timely. Clearly, he had to take action himself, though what he had in mind was potentially dangerous for him to do so in public. He eased himself off the amphora and sidled along the side of the warehouse until he reached its corner. Fortunately, no one – not even Hamilton – was paying any attention to him. Gazing up at the boom, he saw that the knot was slipping faster now. He had to cast a Spell of Protection quickly.

He became perfectly still, both in mind and body. In his mind's eye, he visualized the scene of potential disaster: the boom, the bale dangling precariously, the knot loosening its grip. He placed the tip of his left index finger against his left temple and murmured:

> "There once was a rope unbound
> That slipped with nary a sound.
>   If it fails, it will dash
>   Many people into hash.
> Oh, Wynot, turn it around!"

Had anyone been noticing, he might have seen a marvelous sight, one which would have caused him to lie awake at night pondering the why and wherefore of it. Unperceptively, at first, the boom began to swing around; no one was operating it, but it was moving all the same. Wilfong observed anxiously. The boom was moving much too slowly to suit him. It was going to be a near thing. Gradually, however, the boom picked up speed and completed a ninety-degree arc just as the knot slipped entirely. The bale plummeted downward and crashed onto the mid-section of Pier Nine with a loud thud. The impact split the outer covering of the bale, and its contents – raw cotton from Egypt – spilled in all directions (mostly into the water). Those closest to the crash site shouted and cursed, and a dozen workers scrambled to gather up the mess before it was all lost. The Wizard breathed a sigh of relief to know that no one had been injured.

He peered about. Still, no one had been looking his way. The casting of Spells of Magick was punishable by death in Atlantis, and whosoever turned a Practitioner over to the King's agents was promised a fat reward. A wharf-rat would have jumped at the opportunity to pocket a handful of gold coins, and it would not have mattered to him who suffered – even a mild-mannered school teacher whom he had known for years. Quietly, Wilfong returned to Hamilton's side so that it would appear that he had not left at all. It was a futile gesture.

"Where the hell did you disappear to, Colxor? You missed all the excitement."

"Um, call of Nature," the Wizard replied as nonchalantly as possible. "And, no, I didn't. I saw the bale drop as I was coming back. Thank Xenox it fell where it did, or someone might have been killed."

"Aye. But that's a risk we all take down here. In some cases, it's a mercy. Hmmm. All this excitement has made me thirsty. I'll be after headin' for Lymatan's. The Chief'll have ten kinds of fits, but what the hell – he does it all the time hisself. You comin'?"

"Yes. I was going there anyway for lunch."

"Great. You can buy."

If Wilfong had bothered to look several millennia into the future, he would have learned that there is One Immutable Law: a tavern must never change its appearance. By some unwritten rule passed down through the ages by countless generations of innkeepers, a tavern had to be (1) dingy, (2) ill-lit, (3) noisy, (4) smelly, (5) willing to accommodate anything on two legs that chanced to wander in, (6) equally willing to water down the liquor and short-change the customers, (7) well-prepared to face the consequences of (6), (8) ready – often eagerly – to crack some skulls if (7) got out of hand, (9) suspicious of the law and its enforcers, and (10) easy to find. If an establishment failed on even one of these counts, it suffered eternal pariahship in the eyes of the Brotherhood of Drunkards, Layabouts, and Brawlers.

Happily, Lymatan's inn would have received five stars from the Brotherhood, if such a rating system existed and if they were sober long enough to do the rating. Of all the inns which dotted the fringes of the wharf district, it "enjoyed" several well-earned reputations, all of which would have satisfied the Ten Points admirably. If one wished to get roaring, falling-down, stupid drunk, Lymatan's was *the* place to go in Atlantis (and possibly all of the Known World). Never mind the fancy parties the high-born threw; you didn't have to be rich to get potted – only glib-tongued. If one wished to observe and/or brawl with the motliest collection of riff-raff in all of Creation (including some indeterminate strangers), by any and all means he went to Lymatan's.

And yet, these "reputations" were quite negated by a lesser-known but more appetizing reputation – the main reason why a genteel individual like Wilfong was attracted to the place – and that was the serving of very delicious and well-prepared meals, often under the personal direction of Lymatan herself. Food service had never been a requirement for any tavern, though many innkeepers saw the benefits of accommodating those who liked a little food with their alcohol. Lymatan went a step further by making her food palatable.

Ordinarily, the Wizard would never have entered such an establishment, even on a bet, except that Hamilton had once found a gold coin carelessly dropped by a high-born and suffered a fit of generosity by buying him a meal. A free meal to one of limited means had been too great a temptation to pass up, and so Wilfong had taken a deep breath (and made a hasty apology to Wynot) and walked into this den of iniquity. And, once he had sampled the "specialty of the house" – baked halibut – he was instantly hooked. Lymatan bought fresh halibut every day, personally scaled it, and soaked it in beer for two hours before baking it in her special batter. Even after he had been informed of the dish's "secret ingredient," Wilfong shut his eyes to the implications and feasted.

By and large, the other patrons did not molest him as they were too absorbed in the business of getting drunk to pay much attention to some "Middle Ringer." And, if they had ever had a mind to molest him, they would have had to go through the feisty wharf-rat who guarded the "little teacher" like a mother hen. In the end, it was Wilfong's own reputation as a story-teller which had put him in good stead with the denizens of Lymatan's; he was constantly badgered to "entertain" the crowd with a tale or two, and no one wanted to eliminate such a source of amusement.

This day, the inn was no less busy than on any other day, and perhaps a little busier. The Wizard noted that Hamilton was not the only wharf-rat using the extraordinary event on Pier Eight as an excuse to sneak off for a quick beer or two. While dock workers made up the majority of the clientele, they seldom frequented it by day. During the day, the clientele was more likely to be the crews of the ships being loaded or unloaded. Because of the additional influx, Wilfong and Hamilton had to wait a few minutes for a table (minutes that the former really couldn't spare unless he wolfed his lunch down). Presently, a bosun's mate and four of his shipmates from a Phoenician freighter staggered off in search of Cosmos-knows-what, and Hamilton quickly staked a claim to the vacated table.

"Master Colxor!" a husky but feminine voice boomed from across the room. "You've graced my humble inn again!"

There were mountains on Atlantis, in the northern region of the main island, beyond the central plain which was the geographical center of the Kingdom. Those mountains were not very imposing as mountains went but were high enough to form a natural barrier against potential invaders from that direction. The present speaker might have been carved out of those mountains. Lymatan was the most enormous woman Wilfong had ever encountered; through some fluke of birth, she stood two meters tall and measured nearly a meter at the shoulders. Yet, she was not a *fat* person, merely large-boned; she possessed all of the seductive curves of a woman half her size and flaunted her charms when it pleased her to do so. It was rumored that one of her ancestors was a Hyperborean who had passed this way and dallied with one of the local tarts (though no one made such a remark in *her* presence unless he was desirous of a huge fist planted in the middle of his face).

Lymatan did bear distinctly northern features: long, flowing blond hair, clear blue eyes, a light complexion, and a well-muscled frame. Atlantean clothing seemed ludicrous on her, and so she had taken to wear the garb of her alleged ancestor. How she had come to operate an inn was another interesting story, one which must be told on some other occasion. Suffice it to say that she did a thriving business despite the nearly hourly brawls which broke out. Like the semi-couth Hamilton, she also had become endeared to the frail and gentle scholar who seemed so out of his element here, and she seldom passed an opportunity to give him a good-natured ribbing. And, while others might offer him a round of drinks, she usually made him an offer of a different sort, one which reddened his face right to his ears.

The Wizard craned his neck around to gaze at this pretty she-mountain and smiled warmly. Whether or not anyone had enjoyed her charms was a point he would rather not dwell upon, although the idea of having intercourse with her provoked an intriguing (if perverse) line of thought. One could easily be smothered by and/or crushed under all that soft flesh. He hadn't heard anyone brag about conquering her and concluded that either her lovers were afraid to admit the deed and risk her ire or the giantess was actually still a virgin.

"Greetings, Lymatan. You're very kind, as usual."

"'Kind'?" Hamilton hooted. "Sure, an' you shoulda been here two nights ago, Colxor. This 'kind' person broke some Greek sailor's arm – in *three* places!"

"Xenox take the bastard!" she retorted. "He wouldn't pay his bill. Claimed someone else was buying." She leaned down to scrutinize each of them. "Which one of you is buying?"

"I guess I am," Wilfong replied weakly.

Lymatan stared at him grimly for another second or two. Then her face split into a huge grin, and she stroked his face gently, a gesture which embarrassed him greatly.

"Ah, dear Colxor, I wouldn't charge you a copper if you'd consent to come to my room tonight."

"Uh, sorry. I, uh, have another engagement tonight."

"Who is she, Colxor?" the giantess wailed. "I'll tear her hair out by its ugly roots!"

Wilfong had no doubt that she was capable of such a threat, if her threat had been a serious one. But, the twinkle in her eye belied the jealousy in her words.

"'She' is a he, dear Lymatan, a shopkeeper's son whom I'm tutoring privately."

"Tsk, tsk, Master Teacher. All work and no play is bad for you. You need a bit of comfort – which I could provide, if you so desired."

"Perhaps. Um, do you think I could have something to eat now? I haven't much time before my next class."

"I hear, and I obey, Master," she responded, bowing deeply. "I've got a nice fat fish for you."

As soon as she had departed, the Wizard noticed that Hamilton was regarding him with perplexity.

"*Boyo*, I woulda taken her up on that offer – with or without a free meal attached. Half the wharf-rats in here talk about takin' a tumble with her, and the other half just dream about it."

"And which half are you, Ham?"

The short man grinned wickedly and waggled a finger.

"I ain't sayin', friend. You can guess until Atlantis sinks into the sea."

THE SECOND CASTING

THE WIZARD AT RISK

In the past, Wilfong had taken great care in casting Spells of Magick in public. If he had to use them, he always tried to choose a moment or a place when and where he was alone; failing that, he would choose to cast a Spell at night or in the shadows so that no one could see his face. The King's agents were everywhere, searching out Practitioners of all sorts, and they could always enlist the assistance of any rogue out to earn a quick reward. The incident at Pier Eight had been the first time he had cast a Spell in broad daylight in the presence of a huge crowd. Granted, the crowd's attention had been diverted elsewhere, but there couldn't have been any guarantee that *all* eyes had been on the slave women. If not for the urgency of the situation, he would have allowed that bale to crash onto the pier and not given much thought to the matter. Yet, he could hardly have stood by and watched a fellow human being – even a wharf-rat – being crushed to death if it was in his power to prevent it. Wynot had taught better than that. Therefore, the Wizard had taken a calculated risk for a greater good. He hoped his humanitarianism would cause him no regret.

Practitioning had not always been a risky business. Once, Practitioning had contributed a valuable service, both for private individuals and for the Kingdom. On any given day and on any given street in the Metropolis, one might have observed at least half a dozen wizards, diviners, sorcerers, astrologers, seers, palm-readers, witches, warlocks, and magicians employing their allegedly arcane skills in the open and in perfect bliss (except when someone had "misread" the portents and erred in his predictions); and all of them had no end of customers who flocked around them and importuned them to provide some relief from misery and woe (real or imagined). Did you need a Love Potion to win over the object of your affections? Visit so-and-so in such-and-such a shop. Did you need an astrologer to plan your daughter's wedding? Consult so-and-so two streets over. Did you want a wizard to cast a Spell of Money-luck? Go to this or that house and ask for so-and-so. There were so many Practitioners operating at any time of the day or night that one could shop around for bargain rates (so long as one knew he was getting exactly what he was paying for!); and, because there were so many in the field, specialization had sprouted up, making it that much easier for the potential customer to find the right Practitioner at the right price.

The only interference from the Kingdom in those halcyon days was the imposition of excise taxes. Where large sums of money exchanged hands around the clock, the King – or, rather, his Minister of the Treasury – wanted a percentage for the "public good." Treasury agents roamed the streets and the backroads almost as frequently as the Practitioners, armed with record-keeping forms (and occasionally a troop of soldiers) as they diligently carried out the King's edicts. For the benefits which accrued to the Kingdom, it was a small price to pay. Yet, as all good things under the heavens, the freedom of Practitioners was a fleeting thing.

This writer has relied heavily on Xorzist the Elder for the following account of the Great Persecution, which occurred three hundred years before Wilfong's time. His *Chronicles of the Golden Age of Atlantis* has been regarded as the seminal work concerning the late Thirteenth Dynasty, the more so because of the difficulty he had in uncovering supporting documentation. As one might suppose, palace officials were reluctant to bare the deeds of their predecessors and expose them to criticism lest the criticism rebound upon themselves. Those in possession of private eyewitness accounts had been equally reluctant on the grounds that they might be liable to reprisals from the descendants of the persecuted. Thus, Xorzist struggled for twenty-plus years in assembling his *Chronicles*, and they may now be read in public without fear of contradiction.

Like all momentous events in human history, the Great Persecution stemmed from a most innocuous source, centering about the activities of a minor astrologer named Ecipad (self-styled "the Erudite"). Ecipad's reputation was well-known throughout Atlantis, and it had little to do with his ability to read the stars. The plain fact of the matter was that he was a consummate braggart who loved to regale whoever would listen with tales of far-off lands and of the powers he had acquired in them. Subsequently, he was not in much demand as an astrologer and eked out a meager living casting natal charts for unwary tourists who had not yet been apprised of his reputation.

The King of Atlantis in Ecipad's day was Curtelic I, the eight-times-great-grandfather of the King in Wilfong's time, also known as "Curtelic the Vengeful" for reasons which will be shortly explained. This King was a handsome man by all accounts, rather taller and lighter-skinned than most Atlanteans but nevertheless possessing the chiseled features and wiry frame of our race. In his youth, he spent as much time in learning the arts of statecraft as he did in pursuing sports and hunting. It was a time of peace in the Known World, the Kingdom having defeated decisively a Phoenician attempt to establish a colony on the southern satellite island several years before Curtelic ascended the throne and thus extend its empire to the far reaches of the Known World, and no one (including the future King) gave much thought to extending Atlantis' dominion eastward.

Even so, it was said that Curtelic ought to have been more temperate in the affairs of state ere he assumed the reins of power. But the old King, his father, had contracted a severe case of food poisoning from eating a rancid piece of pork and, due to his advanced age, was unable to purge himself completely. The new King pledged to continue the generous and progressive policies of his predecessors, and the whole Kingdom breathed a collective sigh of relief and returned to its comfortable routine.

In due course of time, Curtelic took himself a bride, a princess from the land of Meshico on the western coast of the Great Western

Ocean. He had become acquainted with the lady on a visit of state early in his reign and been instantly smitten by her charms. The customary arrangements between Curtelic and her father were made, and the royal pair returned to Atlantis amidst much pomp and circumstance. For the first year of their marriage, all was bliss, and the King spent his waking hours entertaining his Queen and allowed the affairs of state to run by themselves. Yet, since all things under heaven are transitory, the bliss came to a tragic end. One who has visited the land of Meshico will realize that the climate there is radically different than that of Atlantis; specifically, it is much warmer and drier, dominated as it is by a high desert, and its inhabitants have difficulty adjusting to wetter and cooler climes.

And so it came to pass that the new Queen of Atlantis caught a chill and developed pneumonia. Despite the efforts of the Royal Physician – who daily incurred the wrath of a distraught King – her condition deteriorated, and each report from the Palace concerning her health was more dispiriting than the one before. It was an anxious time in the Kingdom, and Atlanteans went about with bated breath.

And, in his temporary madness, Curtelic I made a very fateful decision.

The King had consulted the Royal Astrologer from the first day his Queen took ill, wishing to expedite the aid of the stars in affecting a cure. This worthy was clearly in a precarious position. On the one hand, he could not predict a rosy future, for the lady's natal chart had had a fatal element contained in it; to present this finding to the King in his current state of mind would have meant a dire end for himself. On the other hand, if the Royal Astrologer had attempted to put a happy face on the outcome and the Queen died, he would have suffered death just as surely. In the end, he resorted to ambiguity which pleased Curtelic not at all, and the astrologer was executed anyway. Thereafter, the astrologers of Atlantis were called upon to "patriotically assist in restoring the Queen's health and the well-being of the Kingdom." The fate of the Royal Astrologer uppermost in their minds, all but one of them chose another line of work – at least until the uproar had died down.

The lone exception was Ecipad the Erudite, who saw a chance to do what his colleagues refused to do, a chance to cease his catering to the trivial demands of strangers and make a name for himself, a chance to be truly an Astrologer for All Times. And, despite the warnings by his few friends against enmeshing himself in court politics, Ecipad showed up at the North Gate of the palace one foggy morning and demanded an audience with the King on the grounds that he "possessed earth-shaking news" for the royal ear alone. On any other occasion, the braggart might have been chased off at spear point and told not to show his face again. This time, however, the King was at his wit's end as he watched his beloved Queen wasting away, and he seized upon the least little hope by permitting Ecipad to enter the Palace. And what Ecipad relayed to the royal ear was great hope indeed – too much so, as it happened. Curtelic followed the astrologer's counsel to the letter and, for a time, the Queen's health stabilized.

But her health failed again, and this time the inevitable occurred. The Kingdom bore witness to a royal funeral most notable for the loud lamentations of the King-widower. All of Atlantis held its collective breath. The hammer blow was not long in coming. In his despair and anguish, Curtelic cursed those who had had a hand in taking his Queen from him and swore vengeance on *all* of the Practitioners of Magick. The first victim was, of course, Ecipad, who stood trial and was immediately dragged to the misnamed Square of Contemplation (long the place for public executions), where he was drawn and quartered. The King then issued a grim Royal Edict: all who practiced Magick of whatever form would, upon discovery, share the same fate. "Dabblers in devilment" were declared "corruptors of the body politic and civil" and forever outlaws in Atlantis; the liberties which they had enjoyed were rendered null and void, and all loyal Atlanteans were encouraged to turn in any they knew of (failure to do so earned life imprisonment and forfeiture of all their assets). For good measure, a bounty of five gold coins was offered for each Practitioner turned in (which led – and still leads to this day – to many abuses). Even the mere suspicion of one's practicing Magick was sufficient to bring an accusation by the King's agents, the defense against which was as likely to fail as not. In the months and years that followed, the Great Persecution took in the innocent and the guilty alike, and the name of Ecipad was roundly denounced by both Practitioners and non-Practitioners. There arose the expression: "May the wisdom of Ecipad guide your path."

Those who escaped the purges (if only temporarily) went underground, figuratively and literally. A demand for divination in Atlantis still existed – tradition and custom were hard to stamp out – and many there were who were willing to risk the Dread Edict in order to ascertain some magical aid. Both for self-protection and the protection of their clients, Practitioners organized into clandestine groups known as Orders, and each Order had its own specialty. If one wished to contact any Order, one went to the marketplace, bought a single item of produce associated with that Order, and ate it on the spot. On the way home, whispered instructions at one's back took the seeker to the next phase; and, by a roundabout method, the transaction was completed. The Order sent out the next available member for the consultation. Fees collected for services rendered were shared equally by all the members – minus a percentage for the general expenses of the Order. An ever-present danger was a King's agent posing as a customer, and the contact ritual grew ever more complex. Yet, there was little talk of quitting Magick altogether, and the Orders actively recruited (after taking the usual precautions) new members whenever a youth showed promise and trained them to replace those who took a tour of the Square of Contemplation.

Now we must speak of Wynot – whom his disciples called "the Wise" – the greatest of all the Practitioners who walked the streets of Atlantis. For this part of the tale, this writer has not only the *Chronicles* of Xorzist but also the records kept by the members of Wynot's Order. In the latter case, one is cautioned to keep an open mind and not to take any of the material too literally. Freely supplied for the benefit of posterity though it may be, the temptation toward self-aggrandizement still exists. Be that as it may, even a born skeptic like Xorzist had nothing but praise for – in his words – the "Compleat Sorcerer."

No one knew whence came Wynot, neither the date nor the place of his birth. He simply appeared in the Metropolis twenty-five years after the advent of the Great Persecution. Though he bore certain Hyperborean features in the face, he always disclaimed any natal connection to that frozen land; no taller than the peoples who populated the areas surrounding the Great Inland Sea, he spoke Atlantean with none of their accents. To all who listened (and there were some in those early days of his ministry), he declared that he was there to "do good works and to improve the lot of all humankind." It was not long, however, before Atlanteans began to take notice of this unprepossessing stranger, for Wynot demonstrated the most astonishing feats of mental gymnastics the Known World had ever witnessed. His specialty was Spell-casting, and it seemed that his knowledge of sorcerous incantations was second to none. Upon request, he would conjure up both animate and inanimate objects, become invisible, place whole crowds in a trance, produce illusions, or levitate to the highest roof-top. He could divine the future by several different methods and concoct potent potions for all occasions. But his clientele preferred Spells.

Unlike other Practitioners, the Compleat Sorcerer never charged a set fee for his services but accepted whatever token of gratitude a client thought best. (It was rumored that, given his powers, those clients tended to fall on the generous side lest their attempts at miserliness provoke an adverse reaction and color any future requests.) Many of the Orders sought to prove fraud and/or deceit (though they denied yielding to professional jealousy), but any such attempts were fruitless, despite the most rigid examinations of the evidence. Wynot lived up to his reputation and, after a few years of residency, he acquired a sizeable following of young men (and some women!) who begged him to teach them his secrets. To a select few, he did, but they seldom matched the skills of their master.

The reader may well ask: how was it possible that Wynot the Wise was able to perform Magick in public and escape the consequences of Curtelic's Dread Edict? According to Xorzist, the vengeful King never re-married, believing that no other woman was worthy to kiss the buttocks of his late Queen. Thus, he had no children to succeed him on the throne. When he crossed over to the shores of Eternity because of a broken heart, the rule of the Kingdom fell to a younger brother,

Cimmulate VI. The new King had held to the old ways and felt that his brother had made a colossal mistake in condemning all Practitioners because of the foppishness of one individual. While he reigned, the Dread Edict was seldom enforced; only if some very important person complained was any action taken, and usually banishment from the Kingdom was the severest penalty, after which complacency once more ruled. It was in this relatively benign atmosphere that Wynot lived and worked. And, it was rumored, he often entertained the King himself with his Spell-casting; and thus few dared to move against him, even if they could, and proceeded with great caution lest their actions rebound upon themselves.

Unfortunately, Cimmulate VI had always been a sickly sort, and he too inevitably crossed over before his time. The succession fell to his son, Curtelic II, long an admirer of his uncle, Curtelic the Vengeful. The new King also believed that Practitioners were worthy of death and champed at the bit as he watched his father turn a blind eye to the alleged danger. As soon as he assumed the reins of power, he began to enforce the Dread Edict with a vengeance; those Practitioners who had dared to surface during the benign period immediately went to ground again. Curtelic II thus had only one public target against whom to move (not that he didn't try to overturn the Kingdom looking for others). Whether Wynot believed that hiding was a cowardly act and that one ought to declare himself boldly, or whether he believed that he was immune to the Dread Edict, no one could say for certain. He had founded his own Order, and hordes of would-be Practitioners enrolled in it; however, they met in secret in all parts of Atlantis and, despite their entreaties, he refused to skulk about like a common criminal.

Curtelic did not move against Wynot immediately. He was not so zealous that he sought to catch the "biggest fish" in the first cast of his net. He knew well Wynot's powers, having been in attendance when the Practitioner performed at his father's court, and the Compleat Sorcerer's popularity, and he was willing to bide his time until the proper moment. Meanwhile, others kept their "appointments" in the Square of Contemplation as the King invoked the Dread Edict as he could and put a proper scare into all of his subjects.

For the first ten years of Curtelic's reign, there was played a curious game, much like that which the peoples on the eastern shore of the Great Inland Sea called "chess" – except Curtelic played it with live human beings rather than with carved ivory pieces. The King made a move – either a feint or a set-up or an attack – and Wynot countered with a move of his own. All of Atlantis walked on eggshells as this duel progressed day after day, month after month, and rumors flew like the gulls in the harbor (many of which were started by the King's agents). Most of these rumors were quickly dispelled by either Wynot or by some sympathizer.

In due time, after the most elaborate of preparations, the King launched his "master campaign" to rid Atlantis of its Practitioners – including its most prominent one -- once and for all. Previously, when each victim had been executed, the routine of the burning of the body had been followed precisely. This routine was replaced by a new one; the body was hung on a pole in the Square of Contemplation for a month after which it was removed, chopped up into small pieces, and then burned. The King's agents were ordered to concentrate on Wynot's Order for the supply, and the Order eventually lost a third of its membership. The Compleat Sorcerer escaped capture time and again, thanks to his tremendous powers, but he feared for his disciples' well-being. He tightened up the requirements for admission to the Order, stiffened the examinations for promotion through the thirteen levels, and placed numerous checks and balances on the lesson plans in order to trip up any infiltrators. Thereafter, the numbers of executions decreased dramatically.

Once he had safeguarded the integrity of his Order, Wynot the Wise bade his followers farewell and disappeared from Atlantis altogether. Curtelic the Vengeful cursed his bad luck for having missed his opportunity to destroy his greatest enemy. The Compleat Sorcerer has never been seen since.

*   *   *

Of all the Orders of Practitioners which existed in Atlantis, that of Wynot was the most egalitarian. In an age when only the high-born were accorded a formal education by reason of their socio-economic status, he took in all whom he believed were qualified, regardless of their lot in life. It was a radical concept – some said it was a *scandalous* one – to admit the "common people" into the halls of learning, and only Xenox knew what would become of Atlantean civilization if these were treated like their betters. It may be that the very reason Wynot insisted upon culling his students from all classes – and females as well, which was even more scandalous in some eyes – was to teach the Kingdom a great lesson in humility and charity.

Thus it was that Wilfong, son of a common laborer, became a high-ranking member of Wynot's Order – the highest rank, in fact – rather than a mere drudge like his ancestors before him. Thus it was that he too had to be circumspect in his public life, lest someday he too made an "appointment" in the Square of Contemplation.

On his return to the School, the Wizard was feeling the after-effects of his hasty meal. Lymatan had indeed served him a "fat fish" – too fat, in fact. He had had to give half of it to Ham (who accepted it without any qualms), wolf down the remainder like a common laborer, and risk indigestion and flatulence instead of savoring it as was his habit. Walking through a crowded street at mid-day and making embarrassing noises was a sure guarantee of unpopularity.

Passing gas, however, was the least of his problems, he soon discovered. Just before he arrived at the Gate of Tears in the southeast section of the Second Ring, he spotted one of the King's agents dogging his tracks. The regular police force of the Metropolis, the City Guards, had no need of stealth; they were meant to be a visible presence in order to demonstrate the King's intent to protect his subjects (or arrest them should the need arise). The special uniform – short scarlet robes with two black stripes crisscrossing on front and back – made them stand out in any crowd. Whether they were effective was quite another matter. This fellow was dressed as a City Sweeper, with a plain brown breechcloth and tunic, torn in many places and filthy to boot. He moved about as if he had nothing better to do that to gape at the tourists. It was a ruse which might have fooled the average Atlantean but which Wilfong, through his special training, had learned to recognize.

Certain of the fellow's facial expressions and body language gave him away and fairly announced him as a hunter of men instead of the oaf he pretended to be.

The question was, *why* was this spy following him? Had he at long last been so careless as to invite suspicion to himself? He mentally reviewed his movements of the day so far but could not pinpoint any specific moment when he had dropped his guard, including when he had cast a Spell at Pier Eight. Perhaps the fellow was in training and had been directed to trail a citizen at random. Whatever the reason, the Wizard meant to discover it. But not now – he had to return to his classroom.

Once Wilfong had passed through the Gate of Tears, he looked back surreptitiously. The spy had halted just on the other side of the Gate, looking very dejected even while he continued to gape at the tourists. The Wizard smiled to himself. The badge of his profession assured him of entry into the Second Ring without raising any suspicion from either its inhabitants or the City Guard. A lone City Sweeper, on the other hand, dared not walk those streets lest he be stopped, interrogated, and possibly arrested for trespassing, loitering, and/or creating a public nuisance; he would have had to reveal his true identity or give up his mission. Wilfong was sure he'd encounter that fellow again; but now he was alert to his presence, and he could plan several interesting counter-moves. Meanwhile, he had to warn his Order about this new development. Using a meditative technique to relax his mind, he projected his thoughts outward into the ether and aimed them at a specific individual.

-- Wembly? Are you free?

-- Wilfong, dear chap. How good of you to 'cast. We haven't heard from you for days and feared you were lost to us. Yes, I'm free.

-- Excellent. I've been pursuing some leads as to the Master's whereabouts. I'll report on them at the next meeting of the Inner Nest. Right now, I have to tell you that I seemed to have picked up a 'shadow.'

-- *What!* Are you sure?

-- Quite sure. I can spot one of the King's agents a *stadium* away with one eye shut. This fellow was good, but not *that* good.

-- The Cosmos preserve us all! What shall we do?

-- Listen carefully. I'm transmitting an image of the spy. [*A pause*] Have you got it? Good. Pass that image along to all of the Clutch who are able to cast Spells. Tell them that, if they see this person in the future, they are to cast Spell #260.

-- #260? The 'itching disease'?

-- Correct. That fool will be too busy scratching to do any spying.

-- I'll see to it, Wilfong. In the meantime, watch your step.

-- Don't worry about me, old friend. I'll see you soon.

His warning given, the Wizard turned his attention to more mundane matters, specifically facing his first class of novices. Senior Master though he may have been, he still hadn't enough seniority to avoid having to teach beginning students. He needed to advance to the rank of "Exalted Master" first. On the other hand, he had enough seniority to recruit a "volunteer" from the advanced class to assist him. Had he been the vindictive sort, he might have selected Zorpac for this "honor"; it would have been a pleasure to watch that young lout squirm under the grammatical onslaught of youths just as stupid as he was. He might have learned something about responsibility if he expected to carry on his father's business when the time came. But Wilfong was not the vindictive sort, and he did not want to inflict Zorpac on innocent students. He usually selected one of his better students who deserved the experience and would be able to use it to obtain a teaching position if he so desired.

Presently, he stood before his first group, most of whom regarded him with varying degrees of boredom. Few of them had the intelligence to master the alphabet – least of all the rules of grammar – and, after two months of (barely) patient instruction, they were displaying their ignorance admirably. How he would love to cast Spell #576 and watch them parade through the streets of the Metropolis, naked, singing at the top of their lungs. A little public embarrassment ought to have put them in their places. The one or two here – and a few in the next group – who showed some promise would advance; the rest were doomed to be sent back to irate parents who would send them to yet another School, which was not as strict in its standards, thence to be turned loose upon an unsuspecting society armed with ornately wrought "certificates of excellence" and no more understanding of the Atlantean language than a wharf-rat. Where was the love of learning these days? Wilfong lamented daily. What would become of Atlantean culture if this lot became "pillars of the community"? Better to dwell amongst Murkol's people than to endure such a decline!

Wearily, he pointed at one of the novices. The youth went wide-eyed with shock and scrambled to his feet.

"Young sir," the Wizard grumbled, "what is the eleventh character?"

The youth hemmed and hawed for five seconds – during which only the clacking of the water clock outside was the only distinct sound – then blurted out an answer. It was the wrong answer, of course, and it provoked a smattering of titillation in those who knew the right answer. The youth, realizing his error, compounded it by changing his mind and making another wild guess. More titillation issued, halted instantly by a stern look from the teacher. The youth was about to make another stab at it, thought better of it, and lapsed into a chagrined silence. Wilfong stared at him for the space of two seconds (which, he hoped, would seem like two *lifetimes* to this fool), then ordered him to be seated.

"You there, in the back row," he announced, pointing at a fresh victim, "you appear to have some intelligence." And it was true, for Wilfong had observed this one carefully since his enrollment. Unlike the rest, this one possessed an aura of eagerness about him; he would be gently nudged along the right path. And perhaps the lad would not disappoint him by falling in with his so-called "peers." "Tell the class the eleventh character."

The pupil stood up quickly and smartly and barked out the correct answer.

"Very good, young sir. Now, will you step forward and point it out on the chart?"

The chart was an oversized piece of papyrus onto which all twenty characters of the Atlantean alphabet had been printed with large, bold strokes, four rows of five characters each. Atlantean had once had a pictographic form but had long ago evolved into a more stylistic one which could convey much more information than the crude stick-scratchings of lesser races. The only language the Wizard had ever seen which even approached the sophistication of Atlantean was Phoenician on the eastern shore of the Great Inland Sea – only because those pirates had copied the original pictographic form wholesale and adapted it to their own needs. Someday, he supposed, other languages in the Known World would achieve the same level. By that time, of course, his native language would have evolved even further.

The bright boy padded to the head of the class with an air of supreme confidence (the Wizard imagined it was the same air *he* had displayed in similar circumstances years ago). After a curt bow to his teacher, he ran his eyes over the chart and pointed to the character in question, repeating its name for good measure. Out of the corner of his eye, Wilfong noted several sneers, sure signs of jealousy on the part of those who would *not* be advancing to the next level. Would they then translate their jealousy into cat-calls and taunts outside of class (as another youth had been victimized long ago)? Or a pummeling?

"Well done, lad. Now, if you please, recite the entire alphabet."

The youth complied at once. He pointed to each character in turn and spoke their names in a clear, authoritative voice. He did stumble at the fourteenth character (admittedly, the most difficult one in Atlantean) but corrected himself and finished with a flourish. Wilfong thought he was overdoing it a bit but otherwise harbored satisfaction for having gotten through to at least one of this group.

"Excellent. You're excused for the rest of the day. Report to Master Laxot for further instruction." He took down the chart and rolled it up. "The rest of the class will practice writing the alphabet until the end of the session."

He could sense the silent groaning and cursing without having the ability to read minds.

*   *   *

Wilfong did not take his customary route home (which was merely the reverse of the one he used going to the School) but instead passed through the Gate of Smiles. This detour would take him out of his way by a *stadium* or two, but he was anxious to learn if the noon-time spy were still lurking about. If he was, then it meant that he was targeting him specifically.

This section of the Third Ring, close as it was to the harbor, was given over to the produce vendors, the bakers, and the confectionaries. The streets here were filled with open-air markets, carts, and stands, piled high with the output of Atlantis' agriculture and imported foodstuffs from other lands in the Known World. Fruits and berries of all sorts there were, and the strange but wonderfully sweet, long and yellow fruit from a southern land whose inhabitants called it a *banana*. Vegetables abounded, from the leafy greens to the cruciferous, from the tubers to the roots, including the tuber from Meshico called a *potato*. Bread of all colors and shapes; sweet cakes, with or without dried fruits and nuts, with or without icing; fruit pies and custards; a meat and cheese "pie" the Etruscans called a *pizza* (not their word for it, but one which they had borrowed from their peasant laborers) – all competed with each other for the attention of the shoppers and especially the tourists.

The hawkers of these wares were loud and opportunistic as they sought to sell their inventories before they spoiled under the Sun. Many, selling essentially the same foodstuffs, fell into price wars, enticing potential customers with a promise of a "real bargain." These tactics were designed to hook mainly the tourists; the locals knew that the wares were over-priced to begin with and had learned the art of haggling early on. One could buy a quick lunch for a single individual – as Wilfong often did when he wasn't in the mood for baked halibut – or the raw materials for a banquet of a hundred. The streets now were crowded with shoppers with their evening meal in mind, jostling and shoving in order to seize the best pieces (and the best prices!).

Even if one were not looking for food, the open-air markets were a fertile ground for observing the human condition. In a give-and-take atmosphere of bargaining, one witnessed all sides of human behavior: on the one hand, the pleasure in making the best deal and/or fulfilling the expectations of the customer, the camaraderie of friendly rivals, feigned flattery toward all passersby, or the cautious banter between strangers; on the other hand, anger over some alleged fraud, disappointment over a lost customer to another vendor, the rudeness displayed by buyers who wanted thus-and-such and nothing less, or the greed of a vendor who refused to participate in haggling. Wilfong the Wizard was nothing if not a keen observer of the human condition. Wynot had taught that the casting of Spells was an exercise in futility if the would-be Practitioner was ignorant of human emotions; without this knowledge, no Spell could ever be fully effective and, indeed, might be counter-productive. As a True Disciple of the Master's teachings, Wilfong took every opportunity to refine his own store of knowledge, and every trip through the Metropolis did double duty.

Now he wondered if he ought to pick up something for supper. In all likelihood, Murkol (if he wasn't drunk!), had secured the basic ingredients, but it couldn't hurt to have a special treat. Since the Zarelor liked to surprise him with his culinary skills – and sometimes, Wilfong wished he weren't so surprising – turning the tables would be quite in order. A pastry then? Murkol preferred sweet cakes thickly covered with chocolate icing. In this respect, he had as great a sweet tooth as Hamilton, who simply devoured any confection he could get his hands on and, frequently, it got the better of his reasoning. Still, an overweight Zarelor was preferable to an inebriated one; the one could do more work than the other.

As the Wizard approached one of the tables laden with sweet cakes (and the baker rubbed his hands in anticipation of a sale), he caught a flash of brown rags hovering on the opposite side of the street. As he pretended to compare the wares of the vendor toward whom he had been walking with those of a neighboring seller, he confirmed the fact that the noon-time spy was back on his trail. If anything, the fellow looked more bedraggled than ever; if he had been wandering about all this time while staying out of sight of the City Guards, until his target had re-appeared, then the psychological wear-and-tear was beginning to show. Not that Wilfong cared a whit for the physical or mental well-being of a King's agent – he had no use for spies in general and for tools of persecution in particular. At the moment, the fellow was pretending to drool over an array of pies and to wish he could afford one; to all but the keen observer, it was an effective tactic. Had *he* been a City Guard, Wilfong certainly would have been motivated to order the miscreant to move along and stop annoying his betters with his scurvy presence – or else! The spy did not know it yet, but he was about to receive more than he bargained for and would soon regret having been given this assignment.

Wilfong purchased two sweet cakes (one with chocolate icing, one without), now more of a perfunctory act than a pleasurable one. Slowly, deliberately, he wandered the streets, continually checking behind him and allowing his pursuer to keep up with him. When he had reached the Gate of Pains in the eastern section of the Third Ring, he turned abruptly and passed through into the Fourth Ring. This section of the Metropolis contained the light industry which produced the locally-made household goods – furniture, draperies and tapestries, carpeting, crockery, dishes, and tableware, etc. Most of the businesses employed between five and ten persons, all apprenticed to a Master Craftsman, who attended to "special" projects even while he oversaw the work of his underlings. Further on were the stonemasons who created monuments, statuary, and tombstones. It was not unfamiliar territory to the Wizard. Some of his private tutoring occurred here in the persons of the sons of the Master Craftsmen; if they could not afford to pay him as much as the great merchants and the nobility, still the extra silver coins eased his life considerably. Besides, he enjoyed teaching willing students, more of whom could be found amongst the middle class. Now, he knew exactly where he was and where he wanted to go.

His specific destination was the workshop of a sculptor of statues of animals in various poses which the high-born purchased by the score and plunked them in the middle of their estates to demonstrate their perspicacity in matters of art. The Master of this factory would not be on the premises; after a hard day's nagging at his apprentices to work more efficiently, he would have departed for his modest house a couple of streets over. The workers, after cleaning up the area, would have retired to their little cubicles on the upper floor. No one would be around to bother Wilfong in the performance of his wizardry on the unsuspecting spy.

Without hesitation, he pulled open the heavy wooden gate which led to the courtyard where most of the preliminary work was done and eased himself in. The yard was littered with slabs of granite and marble in various stages of configuration. In one corner were heaped the bits and pieces which had been chiseled off; the Master Craftsman called it his "votive pile" since some of the pieces were large enough to fashion small religious figures for the more pious Atlanteans to set in their homes.

The Wizard sat down on a semi-completed lion in a crouching position and relaxed himself. He placed the tip of his right index finger against his right temple and chanted:

> "There once was a spy most fell,
> Who thought he was a spy most swell.
> But his clumsiness betrays him
> And evilly repays him.
> Oh, Wynot, this fellow compel!"

In a few moments, the gate swung open again, and the spy marched in. Perhaps "marched" was not quite accurate, for the fellow was clearly not acting under his own will. He walked ram-rod stiff with his arms pressed tightly at his sides, and each step he took was taken woodenly as if he were a puppet on a string. In his stupor, he made no effort to avoid the chunks of granite and marble but collided with or stumbled over any number of them; and, whenever he did so, he merely righted himself and continued to move in a straight line in Wilfong's direction. Presently, he jerkily halted before the Wizard and ceased all motion altogether. One might have taken him for just another statue in the yard. Wilfong regarded him with a mixture of bemusement and contempt.

"Identify yourself," he commanded softly.

"I...am...Aloxam," the spy replied in a monotone.

"State your rank and function."

"I...am...a...Second...Stripe...in...the...Circle...of...Friends. I...seek...out...the...enemies...of...the...Kingdom...and...destroy...them."

Wilfong's hackles raised immediately. He knew well the Circle of Friends – a deceptively harmless-sounding name for a group of specially trained assassins. Once, they had been strictly free-lancers, working on commissions paid for by those who could afford the Circle's rates; nowadays, they worked exclusively for the King to enforce the Dread Edict against Practitioners. The tales told about this elite organization were not conducive to a good night's sleep. It was said that, to become a Friend, an initiate had to put away all notions of conscience and morality, that one had to obey and to act without hesitation or question, that one had to take an oath in one's own blood never to betray the Circle upon pain of a hideous death. How true these tales were, only the Cosmos knew for sure; the few facts which had surfaced in the collective consciousness merely fueled more rumors. And, it may be said, the Circle itself fed on these rumors as well, the better to instill fear in both its membership and the general population.

"What is your current assignment?" the Wizard asked through clenched teeth.

"I…am…to…monitor…the…activities…of…Colxor…the…teacher…of…writing."

"For what reason?"

"He…is…suspected…of…being…a…Practitioner…of…Magick."

"What evidence is there to support the charge?"

"I…am…not…privy…to…the…evidence. My…sub-Circle…Leader…gave…me…my…orders…and…I…am…carrying…them…out."

Now there was a curious admission. Even the lowest rank in the Circle was given a reason for doing what he was ordered to do; to be completely ignorant of the aim of one's assignment did not ring true. This admission had all the marks of political intrigue and of a grand conspiracy in the making. Wilfong was back at the beginning of his original question: why him? Who in the higher ranks of the Circle of Friends suspected him of being a Practitioner? Obviously, this new development called for a thorough investigation. He was not likely, however, to get any more information out of this fellow – best to get him out of the way, quickly.

"Listen carefully. At my command, you will walk out of here. While you are walking, you will count to sixty; when you reach sixty, you will awaken and remember only that you lost your suspect in the crowd. Do you understand?"

"I…understand."

"Furthermore, the next time you see a City Guard, you will go up to him and kiss him on the mouth. Now, go!"

Stiffly, the King's agent pivoted and marched off toward the gate. In a loud, clear voice, he began to count. Wilfong remained where he was until the spy had disappeared from sight, then walked quickly to the gate himself. He spotted the agent taking the direction from which he had come; therefore, he departed in the opposite direction. By the time the count of sixty had been reached, the Wizard should have put considerable distance between him and the would-be spy.

He checked the position of the Sun. It was just an hour before sunset. Undoubtedly, Murkol (if he were still sober enough to notice and to care) would be worried that his master was not yet home at his accustomed time. Wilfong himself disliked breaking his routine, but the current circumstances had dictated a break. The member of the Circle of Friends he had just put under a Spell of Compulsion might not cause him further trouble, but his superiors who had given him his assignment might be suspicious as to why he had been so careless in the assignment; they might even send another member to take the fellow's place and/or dispose of the careless fool. The Wizard had every confidence that he could confound anyone the Circle sent after him – his skill with Magick was sufficient to hold a large crowd in check – yet, all potential defenses consumed time and energy for their execution, time and energy he could use instead to discover the reason behind this sudden interest in him.

As the Tenth Dynasty philosopher Nylleot had once declared: to be forewarned was to be forearmed. Wilfong the Wizard was now forewarned.

THE THIRD CASTING

THE WIZARD AT BAR

Later in the evening, Wilfong retired to his personal library to meditate, his usual routine when he was not engaged in tutoring. In fact, he retired before finishing his meal and left the uneaten portion to be thrown out or consumed by Murkol as the latter pleased. The Zarelor was pleasantly surprised to learn that he might have *two* sweet cakes for dessert that night, and he greedily crammed them into his mouth before his master could change his mind. He cleared the table with one hand and ate with the other, saving the cake with icing for last so that he finished the day with the taste of chocolate in his mouth.

The Wizard's library was originally a third sleeping room. A large family had once lived in this building and required the extra space; when they had left the Metropolis to live with the man's brother's family in the countryside, Wilfong promptly claimed the apartment for himself. The rent was more than a teacher might otherwise pay inasmuch as the average teacher did not need that much space. This teacher, however, was not average, and he had great need of extra space. Thanks to a recent increase in his stipend, he could just barely afford it, the bare necessities being paid for by the fees he charged for private tutoring.

To the casual observer, the room was a shambles. It was the one place where Murkol was not allowed to ply his housekeeping duties "on pain of the direst punishment imaginable." Wilfong guarded his *sanctum sanctorum* jealously. Books and charts and scraps of papyrus and various odds and ends were strewn from one corner to another in seeming reckless abandon; and, had anyone but the Wizard been allowed inside, he might well have believed that he was walking into a jungle. And yet, this room was a *cultivated* shambles. Despite the confusion, Wilfong knew exactly where everything was and, given a moment to visualize the room, he could lay hands on a desired object unerringly.

There was a good reason for the shambles: Wilfong was an information addict. And not just any information either – though his knowledge of the physical world was considerable, he collected everything which had been written in whatever language, from whatever land, on the subject of Magick. He knew the myths and legends, the rituals and sacred symbols, of three score or more religious systems, from the Parsi in the east to the Meshicoan in the west, from the Hyperborean in the north to the Kush in the south. One of the reasons he spent so much time lurking about the harbor was to acquire some new scrap of information about Magick; and by now, Ship's Masters had found in him a ready market for whatever they chanced to possess in order to earn an extra coin or two. These dealings, of course, had to be conducted in the utmost secrecy. Should the King's agents learn of trade in "contraband materials," both buyer and seller would quickly visit the Square of Contemplation. But, once he had his prize in hand, the Wizard cast a Spell of Illusion; and to any prying eyes, it appeared that he had purchased pornographic materials which were not illegal to buy or to possess (although it was rumored that one had to compete with the King himself for such materials, the more illustrated the better).

Wilfong also possessed a special collection of arcane writings: every single word that Wynot the Wise had ever put down on papyrus, an enormous body of work though it was the merest fraction of the Compleat Sorcerer's knowledge which he had deigned to share with his disciples. The Wizard, believing himself to be a True Disciple, had committed all of it to memory. As a consequence, he had mastered all of Wynot's teachings – including the 997 Special Spells of Power – which had allowed him to rise through the ranks of the Order in record time. Whatever information he had gleaned from other lands contained only bits and pieces of Wynot's teachings, and he collected it only for the sake of comparing it to the Truth. Perhaps Wynot had sought to enlighten others even as he attempted to enlighten Atlanteans; if so, there had to be True Disciples elsewhere in the Known World – as slim a percentage as there was in the Kingdom – and someday Wilfong would have to seek them out.

The Wizard waded through this jungle of information and came to a two-meter high, four-legged stool which commanded the exact center of the room. Whatever else might be moved around here (if at all), this piece of furniture never was. It was his Meditation Stool, and it was as sacrosanct as the room itself. He heaved himself up on it and sat cross-legged on its seat. He relaxed body and mind, placed his hands on his temples, and entered a trance state.

*   *   *

Wilfong the Wizard dreamed:

i am walking along the streets of my home town. on either side, i see familiar buildings, familiar signs, familiar scenes.

i am in no particular hurry. i am just out for a pleasant stroll. all is well with the world.

i have been down these streets many times. and, while most of the landscape is familiar, there are significant differences here and there. often, the differences i see are never the same ones twice in a row; always, the scenes re-form into something else.

once, when i entered the central city, i saw the streets filled with water, as if a great flood had overtaken everything. the people passed from building to building by means of specially constructed walkways high above the water.

on another occasion, i saw that some of the bridges which cross the river that splits the city in two had collapsed and were nothing but rubble, as if a great earthquake had overthrown everything. the one bridge which remained intact was itself in shaky condition, and people trod upon it very carefully.

yet again, I saw a tall building that reached nearly to the abode of the gods, a slender pyramid which seemed to sway with the wind. and no one could enter it save by a great curving ramp as fragile-looking as the building itself.

though i have seen structures where none like them had ever existed and no structures where they ought to have been, the general appearance of the city seldom changes. it is as familiar to me as the back of my hand.

why then are there these glaring differences?

i have two possible explanations:

one, i am seeing the city as it will exist in the future.

two, i am seeing it as it might have been had those who built it taken its development in a different direction.

both explanations are utterly fantastic, because they are beyond the ken of mortal man. yet, what other explanation is there?

more disturbing than the scenes of change is the manner by which i can perceive them. it is as if someone – perhaps the gods themselves – has (have) cast his (their) mind(s) across a great gulf of time and space and placed these images in my mind. assuming this is so, for what purpose does it occur? to tantalize me with impossible things? to show me all the wonders of the Cosmos? or to provoke me toward a greater understanding of All-That-Is? it is a matter for much thought.

i am walking yet again through familiar-but-unfamiliar surroundings. i see as though through another's eyes. now, without warning, a great wind blows out of the west and roars down the streets, scattering everything before it. the wind screeches like a thousand demons escaped from the pits of hell. but, wonder of wonders, i am not affected by this tempest; i am not swept away like some scrap of papyrus, nor am i deafened by the hideous noise. i seem to be in the eye of the storm, safe while all about me is devastated.

when, at last, the wind subsides, I see that the city has changed yet again. where once there were bridges across the river, now there are large earthen dams upon which the streets run, and tunnels in the dams for the water to flow through.

i cross the river and behold a tiny park of green grass and tall trees and trimmed hedges and flowers of all colors and scents. in the center of the park lies a rock garden and a miniature waterfall. small animals scurry to and fro in search of food and ignore me altogether.

near the rock garden, a sign has been posted. the words on the sign are in a language i have never seen before; and yet, i know instinctively what the sign says. it says: 'keep off the grass.'

while I am marveling at this sign, a stranger approaches and beckons to me. i am greatly alarmed by his appearance, for he wears my face as it had been in my youth. and, yet, that is not the most wondrous thing about him. the most wondrous thing is that he ages before my very eyes, one year for every passing minute.

the man with my face salutes me in the manner of the Order of Wynot, and i reflexively return the salute. wordlessly, he commands me to follow him. i obey, for i know that it is right and proper that i should.

the man with my face marches off toward a small wooded area at the edge of the park and enters it unhesitatingly. he winds his way through the slender, dark-barked trees. i hear the song of many birds.

in the center of the wooded area, there is a clearing and, in the clearing, stands a colossal oak tree. it is easily two meters in diameter and twelve meters in height. its branches and leaves overhang the clearing to form a natural roof.

the man with my face circles around the oak tree, and i follow. on the far side, there is an opening which has been carved out of the trunk. it is twice the height and width of a human being. the man with my face motions me to step inside the opening. i obey. i see that the interior surface is not the wood of the tree but rather some sort of metal. i turn to ask the man with my face about this.

before i can speak, however, he fades from view, like fog before the heat of the sun. and before he disappears altogether, i observe that he has become a young man again.

while i marvel at this sight, a great tingling overcomes me, touching every fiber of my being. a powerful, blinding flash of light then engulfs the opening in the tree. i blink furiously. and, when the light subsides and my vision returns to normal, I discover –

i discover that i am no longer in the tree nor in the clearing of the wooded area!

i discover that i am in a tremendous cave, a tremendous cave of metal!

the walls, the floor, the ceiling are all metal. what few pieces of furniture there are are also metal – plus some shiny material i cannot identify. to my great relief, i see tapestries on the walls which are woven fiber, rich in color and delicate in texture. some of them depict a variety of geometrical shapes, while others show scenes of fantastic vistas populated by strange beasts and peoples.

bisecting this cave of metal is a long, golden-yellow carpet, approximately a meter wide. on either side of the carpet, a row of rigid figures stretching to the nether end of the cave stand. these figures are strangely garbed; they wear bulky tunics and breeches, granite-gray in color. tucked under one arm of these figures is a translucent globe with a metal ring at its opening.

as strange as the garb is, it is nothing compared to the faces of the figures who wear it. i peer at the nearest one. it is like no other face I have ever seen; it is not a face that has a place in the world of human beings. it is pig-like, gray-green, with bright red eyes. and yet, I feel no fear of it. i know that this Being — and its fellows — will not harm me but will accord me all the respect and honor which is my due.

for, this is a Holy Place, and the Spirit of my Lord and Master abides here and fills me with grace.

the figure nearest me now faces me and smiles an inhuman smile. it raises its hand and salutes me in the manner of the Order of Wynot. i do likewise. then it gestures me to walk down the golden-yellow carpet to the nether end. i do so with great joy and confidence. and, as i pass each figure in its turn, it salutes me, and i it.

as I walk the length of the golden-yellow carpet, i am aware of a low droning sound like the buzzing of a thousand bees. it seems to come from beneath my feet, but i cannot determine this for sure. in a Holy Place, it is not wise to appear too curious, and so i dismiss the droning sound from my mind.

as I approach the nether end, i observe a colossal metal throne, a meter above the floor. and the throne is occupied. now, i begin to tremble, for i know Who sits upon that throne. though i have never seen Him in the flesh, i have seen His image many times. my pace begins to falter, and i have difficulty breathing.

at last, i stand before Him Who is Lord here: a slightly-built figure with reddish-brown hair and beard, a paunch, and a lop-sided skull. He is not the prepossessing sort, and one might ignore Him in a crowd. but, it is His eyes that marks Him as a Being of Power. they penetrate to one's very soul or gaze upon the furthest reaches of the Cosmos. they are Harmony and Wisdom everlasting.

He Who occupies the throne smiles down upon me and salutes me in the accustomed manner. i am so giddy at standing before the Presence that i nearly forget to return the salute. then i throw myself onto the floor and abase myself.

in a low, throaty voice, i hail the Presence.

'o, Wynot! great art Thou, and lowly am i! strong art Thou, and weak am i! wise art Thou, and stupid am i! may Thy glory shine forth forever and ever! bless me, Thy humble disciple, and guide me down the path of Harmony and Wisdom!'

'arise,' says the Lord.

shakily, i get to my feet and gaze reverently upon my Master. He smiles yet again, showing a gap in His teeth. nervous though i am, i wait expectantly for His teaching. i know that Wynot has called me to this Holy Place in order to bestow upon me a Great Truth.

'who are you?' He asks.

'i am wilfong, Master, of atlantis.'

'atlantis? atlantis? Oh, yes, i've been there, haven't i?' He turns and continues to speak as if to some invisible being. 'i've been to so many places, i've lost count. so, wilfong, what do you do in atlantis?'

'i am a teacher of writing, Master. i have taught many the skills of language.'

'very good. a most noble profession. now, tell me, how do my teachings fare in atlantis.'

'alas, not very well, Master. the persecution which Thou didst experience when Thou wert among us continues unabated. Thy disciples still must hide themselves and meet in secret.'

'even after – how long has it been? – two hundred and fifty years? i'm really disappointed, wilfong.'

'no more than i, Master. how i long to walk freely about and preach Thy message without fear. yet, not all is dismal. the Order which Thou didst found still recruits new members and trains them in the ways Thou didst establish.'

'but my message, *wilfong? what of my message?'*

'we cling to it faithfully, Master. though the days be dark, it remains a light to our eyes.'

'and you personally? are you worthy to be my disciple?'

i swallow hard.

'who among us is truly worthy even to kiss Thy buttocks? but, i am steadfast in my devotion to Thee and shall follow Thy teachings all the days of my life.'

'i am pleased to hear that. for, if you remember what you've seen here and measure its significance and bury that significance deep in your heart and in your very being, then you are on your way to being a True Disciple.

'i tell you truly, wilfong, where i go, few can follow. if you would follow me, take the One True Path to Harmony and Wisdom and be One-with-the-Cosmos.'

now the Lord salutes me again, and i do likewise. He touches His forehead with His left thumb. instantly, there is another blinding flash of light, similar to the one that had engulfed me in the opening of the giant tree. when the light has dissipated, i observe that Wynot has vanished. i turn and discover that the Host along the carpet have also vanished.

i am all alone in that cave of metal.

i do not fear to be left alone, but i am fearful of having been left behind. for, i have longed to join my Master in His Holy Place and bask in His glory forever. my trial upon this plane apparently has not yet run its course, and i must abide a while longer.

nevertheless, on the off-chance that i had been invited to follow Wynot to where He has gone, i leap up onto His throne to be also consumed by that brilliant light. alas, i leap into thin air. the throne and the cave of metal have vanished in their turn, and i fall to the ground at the base of the huge oak tree.

i return to the city, filled with wonder and awe. yet, the Spirit of my Master is within me, and i am filled with Harmony and Wisdom.

*   *   *

Ordinarily, Wilfong would have set his mind to analyzing the dreams and visions which came to him, minutely examining each facet for its symbolic value and comparing his conclusions with previous analyses. It was best to do this while the images were still fresh and vivid;

with the passage of time, memory – even in those with as sharp a mind as his – tended to dim. The Wizard, it must be said, had no difficulty in recalling his dreams and visions, as some trick of his brain allowed him to retain images longer than most people could; even years after the event, he could remember selected, significant sequences. And ordinarily, he could review them with dispassion. One could not approach symbolic messages with a load of emotional baggage; otherwise, one could misinterpret the message and take the wrong course of action. While persecution of Practitioners continued unabated, the wrong course of action usually proved to be fatal.

In the present instance, however, Wilfong was so overcome by emotion that he had to spend a few moments relaxing himself before proceeding. Clearly, this had been no ordinary dream. He had never had the like before. For the first time, since achieving the highest level in his Order, he actually had received a vision of the Compleat Sorcerer in all his glory, surrounded by the trappings of his awesome power; for the first time since he had begun to record his dreams, he had received a direct message from his master. To say the least, it had been an extraordinary experience, and Wilfong shook with excitement. His face was flushed and covered with perspiration, and his breathing came in shallow gasps. He required a longer time to regain his equipoise.

Wynot's message, he soon realized, was unmistakable. It *was* an invitation – a Summons, if you will – to join him, wherever he had gone, to leave this plane of existence and explore new realities. Wilfong was thrilled beyond belief. So far as he knew, no other in the Order had been called by Wynot; on the other hand, no other in the Order had run through the rigorous training schedule with the ease he had had or completed all thirteen levels of instruction in a record time. Though he had sought to be a person of modesty, the Wizard possessed no *false* modesty and knew his own abilities. If anyone deserved to be called to Wynot's presence, it was he. The Summons was the hope and dream of all who wore the Sign of the Owl – Wynot's personal symbol and Wilfong no less fervently harbored that desire. Now that the Summons had been issued, it remained to seek a means by which he could respond.

The key to understanding, of course, lay in the elements of the vision. Wynot would not have called him without leaving some clue as to the path he should take. All he had to do was to recall all of the symbols and correctly interpret them – a simple enough task, was it not?

The most significant symbol had been the individual with Wilfong's face who had aged so rapidly but then returned to youthfulness. Now, what was there about his face which might serve as a map and a guidepost? To answer that question, he needed a reflective surface. A bowl of water in a dimly-lit room would do the trick nicely.

Just as he was about to slide off his stool to implement his plan, he received an urgent mind-cast.

-- Wilfong! Respond please!

-- Yes, Wembly. What's the matter?

--You must come to the Temple right away. A most alarming thing has occurred.

-- Can't you tell me what's wrong now?

-- No, no. You must see for yourself.

-- Very well. I'll be there within half an hour.

-- Thank you, Wilfong.

The Wizard pondered the communication for long moments. If there had been anything "alarming" involved here, it had been the note of hysteria in Wembly's "voice." As long as he had been a member of the Order, Wilfong had always considered its Chief Elder the most level-headed man he knew; Wembly would no more yield to panic than the sea yield to a wall of papyrus. Whatever had occurred had to be colossal in nature.

Wilfong had planned to attend the Temple in any event. Tonight was his night to oversee the study groups, their training, and the Ritual of Communion. Visits to the Temple were wholly inadequate in his opinion since there was so much work to do, but the Order was constrained by both political circumstances and space considerations to be as invisible as possible. A large gathering of people when and where none was expected on a frequent basis was sure to invite the suspicion of the King's agents. Subsequently, Wynot's work was performed agonizingly slowly. Yet, better slowly than not at all.

The Wizard's part in that work was the same for all upper-level Practitioners: a teacher. Wynot had required that each level should teach the next lower one so that there was continuity and integration. Of all of the Clutch, only Wilfong occupied the lofty thirteenth level and therefore was especially obliged to take an active part in the functioning of the Order. Not that he would have shirked his duty in the first place – he was, after all, a teacher by profession and by avocation.

He exited his *sanctum sanctorum* and sought out Murkol. He found the Zarelor bent over a cooking pot, scrubbing it furiously with sand and muttering to himself in his native tongue. At Wilfong's approach, the hulking servant straightened up, then bent low awkwardly.

"What izh dy wiss, Mashter?"

"Murkol, I'll be going to Temple earlier than usual – now, in fact. When you've finished your chores, you may have the rest of the evening off."

"Dank dee, Mashter."

"*But,* you may *not* get roaring drunk as you usually do. I have a special task for you in the morning, and I want you sober."

"Yesh, Mashter. I will have only *one* mug of beer dish evening."

The biggest one he can find, I'll wager, the Wizard thought wryly, *even if he has to search all of the taverns in Atlantis to find it.*

"Very good. Then I'll see you in the morning."

"Yesh, Mashter. Be-esht well."

THE FOURTH CASTING

THE WIZARD AT ATTENTION

Famously, one of the ironies of the Great Persecution was that the most notorious of the Orders of Practitioners lay practically under the King's nose. No matter how many agents were sent out or how diligently they searched, all of them overlooked the obvious. And the obvious was that, far from being a "model" citizen and reporting all "criminal" acts to the authorities, one of the high-born in the Second Ring of the Metropolis actually aided and abetted Practitioners; one Caznat, first cousin to the reigning Queen, defied both his King and the Dread Edict by making part of his estate available to the Order of Wynot. He himself was not a member nor even a potential Practitioner, but he had heard the message of Wynot, believed it, and done what he could to propagate it. Caznat's estate was located in the northern section of the Ring, a modest affair by the standards of the day, covering a mere twenty hectares of land. It consisted of an "L"-shaped villa with a courtyard and a large lawn, the whole surrounded by a three-meter-high stone wall. Two entrances were visible – one at the front for high-born visitors and one at the back for deliverymen and servants – and a third was *invisible*. The latter was made invisible by a thick layer of clinging vines which festooned the western wall; one had to part the vines at just the right spot in order to gain access to a small wooden doorway.

Once through that doorway, a secret visitor turned to the left, walked twenty paces at a forty-five-degree angle to the wall, and halted near a piece of statuary depicting an owl and her clutch. (The owl was Wynot's mark which he doodled on every page of his writings; this was the reason his disciples affectionately called themselves the "Clutch.") When the statue was rotated half a turn, a trapdoor beneath a layer of sod slid aside to reveal a stairway leading to a series of underground chambers. This elaborate subterfuge had been designed and constructed by an ancestor of Caznat, also a sympathizer; the secret of the hidden chambers had since been passed down from father to son.

The Temple of Wynot was, by no stretch of the imagination, a place one might associate with a Practitioner of his great power, despite the fact that his disciples spoke of it (if they spoke of it at all) in glowing terms. Rather, it was as humble a place as one could find in the Known World; and, had the Known World been aware of its existence, it would have concluded that the Compleat Sorcerer and/or his disciples had fallen on hard times to meet in a hole in the ground. The Order's rivals/enemies, on the other hand, might have said that a hole in the ground suited them. Be that as it may, the group assembling here every night had little choice in the matter; either they conducted their business in the most opportune location available, or they conducted it not at all. And all were loath to choose the second option. Thus, they picked their way surreptitiously to the Second Ring and disappeared into the bowels of the Earth.

Only one in the Order did not need secrecy to enter this estate. Wilfong entered the front entrance with impunity, and no one challenged him here at night any more than in the daytime; as long as he wore the badge of his profession, he could claim that he was on his way to a tutoring lesson. Given his frequent appearances in the Second Ring, his claims were readily accepted. And, in point of fact, he did have *official* business here, for Caznat's grandchildren were some of his private pupils. Tonight was not on his teaching schedule, but few there were who were cognizant of all of his appointments and simply took it for granted that he was where he ought to be.

Before leaving his apartment, the Wizard had cast a Spell of Far-Seeing in order to assure himself that no one was on the street near Caznat's estate. Assured, he then had cast a Spell of Transition and whisked his way to the front entrance in a split second. After shaking off the after-effects of transitioning (a slight dizziness), he strolled through the gate nonchalantly. Relatively speaking, the gate was as modest as the house it fronted. The lesser nobility – even those related to the Royal House – had not that much gold to spend on elaborate sculpture. This gate boasted of the unicorn-and-gryphon motif which was then in vogue and very little else (though Caznat's ancestor had added several miniature owls amongst the cavorting beasts).

As Wilfong stepped foot on the grounds, a private guard leaped in front of him to bar his way and ask for identification. This individual was a burly fellow – for an Atlantean – and might have been right at home on the piers. One leg was noticeably shorter than the other, and he hobbled rather than walked; and his face gave evidence that he was no stranger to brawling. The guard held up a torch to view the visitor more clearly and recognized him instantly. Bowing low, he greeted Wilfong profusely. The Wizard returned the greeting, putting the correct note of haughtiness in his voice (though it galled him to do so), and continued on toward the house.

Halfway up the stone-paved walkway, he halted and peered over his shoulder. The guard had returned to whatever diversion kept his boredom at bay, and no other eyes were looking this way. At once, Wilfong turned aside, walked briskly across the lawn, and accessed the secret entrance to the Temple. At the bottom of the underground stairway stood an identical owl statue. The Wizard gave it half a turn, and the trapdoor closed over him. He was now in a small antechamber, lit by a single torch, facing a large stone slab. He struck his palm against a specific spot on the slab which released a hidden spring, and the slab rumbled laterally on a set of rollers. He stepped through the new doorway and reset the spring. The slab slid back into place.

The next chamber before him measured twenty meters by five. Paving stones covered the dirt floor, and a single layer of bricks formed the walls. Oil lamps sat in niches in the walls at three-meter intervals; yet, the chamber still seemed gloomy and sinister, and shadows flickered constantly. This chamber had been subdivided into seven distinct areas by waist-high partitions, three small ones on either side and a larger central one. Each partitioned area held three to five individuals; there, they focused on a specific skill. Displayed prominently all about were engraved plaques containing Wynot's more poignant quotations which served to remind one and all of the Grand Purpose for joining the Order in the first place. In the central area, a pit with a log fire provided heat against the chill and dankness and additional light against the gloom. At the opposite end of the chamber, the brickwork had been covered with a thin layer of plaster, sanded down to a fair degree of smoothness.

On this surface, a list of names had been inscribed, beginning at the left-hand margin, to form several columns. Currently, there were twelve full columns of names from ceiling to floor and a thirteenth nearly halfway down. These names represented the members of the Clutch who had been martyred, in chronological order. Near the bottom of the seventh column, written in characters twice as large as the others, was the name of Wynot himself. No one knew if the Compleat Sorcerer were dead or not; after the third attempt on his life and his ultimate disappearance, his disciples had added his name to the Honor Roll to pay homage to their master.

The Order of Wynot currently numbered one hundred, at various levels of skill, and all of them were ever on the look-out for new recruits. Obviously, not all of the membership could have fitted into the limited space of this chamber; they would have quickly consumed the oxygen and asphyxiated, bringing the Order to an ignominious end. Attendance then was on a thirteen-day rotation, based upon the membership of the Inner Nest, one of whom oversaw each evening's proceedings, and attendees arrived in more or less equal numbers each evening, depending upon their level of attainment. A schedule for each new cycle was posted in the antechamber at the end of the old cycle, subject to the usual emergencies (e.g. illness or execution). The training – slowed down considerably by the drawn-out schedule -- was further slowed by the capabilities of the trainees themselves. As Wynot had often said, enthusiasm does not a Practitioner make. One had to be receptive in mind as well in spirit; great enthusiasm could not compensate for an inadequate mental environment.

Consequently, not all candidates achieved the highest level but rose to their level of incompetence and no further. Yet, this failure to advance did not automatically disqualify anyone from continued membership in the Order. Wynot had taught that, one, each individual had his specific part to play in the Cosmic Scheme of Things and therefore ought to be allowed to play it and, two, it was the height of cruelty to toss otherwise valuable people to the tender mercies of the King's agents because they hadn't "measured up." Once a member, always a member, and all were expected to perform the tasks of which they were capable.

This evening, the entire Inner Nest was in attendance, a rarity since it normally convened only every thirteen cycles (five months in Atlantis' lunar calendar). Wembly, the Chief Elder for this current Grand Cycle, had called an emergency session, the nature of which was known (apparently) only to himself. The Inner Nest consisted of those members who had achieved Level Twelve (although, occasionally, the Order had to dip into Level Eleven to fill vacancies). Elders were distinguished from common members by the wearing of gold pins in the form of an owl's head; Tens and Elevens wore silver pins, while all others wore bronze. Elders served for life but could retire whenever they chose to – though few ever did.

Wilfong spotted his colleagues easily enough and could have done so even if they hadn't been wearing their gold pins. They were the ones more nervous than the ordinary members who had never seen more than one Twelve at a time; they stood in small knots, whispering loudly and gesturing frantically. At his entrance, the Chief Elder detached himself from his knot of people and hurried over to greet him. Wembly was tall and muscular, the sort who might have been a competitor at the Annual Games (and, in fact, he had been such in his youth – a distance runner, specifically). Streaks of gray ran through otherwise ash-blond hair, and crow's-feet played around his gray-green eyes. His face projected pleasure at the Wizard's arrival, but his eyes betrayed his anxiety.

"Wilfong!" he declared in a basso voice. "Thank the Cosmos you're here!"

"I came as quickly as I could, Wembly. What's the urgency?"

"Wait until we've convened. I don't want to alarm the lower levels unduly."

So saying, he pivoted and strode off toward the opposite end of the chamber. Wilfong's level of puzzlement rose considerably, and he fell in behind Wembly. They gathered up the remaining Elders as they went, as a ship gathers flotsam in its wake. The procession passed through the rank-and-file and served to disrupt the latter's training. The Grand Purpose of Wynot was hardly uppermost in their minds as they gaped at all the Elders wearing grim faces. And, if truth be told, they were particularly in awe by the presence of Wilfong, who – in their minds at least, though *he* would deny it – was one to rival the Compleat Sorcerer himself.

Wembly halted before the Honor Roll. Instinctively, he saluted it with both hands. The others followed suit. Then, he struck his palm on a designated spot on the plasterwork; as before, part of the wall slid aside to reveal a third chamber. The Elders passed through and closed the door behind them.

This chamber was half the size of the large chamber. Its principal use was the holding of plenary sessions of the Inner Nest. Here, when the training session was completed, the trainees assembled for an all-too-brief Communion. The section nearest the entrance contained another fire pit around which the Clutch gathered to listen to words of encouragement from the session's Elder and to share observations and anecdotes of their own. The farther section contained a simple semi-circular table and thirteen chairs. Many more quotations decorated these walls as well. But, the dominant feature of the Chamber was a huge, richly-textured portrait hanging on the wall directly behind the table, a life-sized – and highly idealized – representation of Wynot. The founder of the Order looked down upon his progeny with an air of bemused benevolence.

The thirteen men took their places, Wembly in the center position. Traditionally, the rest sat in order of seniority; that is, the most senior sat at the Chief's right, the second most senior at his left, and so on down the line. By unanimous consent, however, the motion that the one Thirteen amongst them should be at the Chief's right had been approved as soon as that one had achieved that exalted status, despite the fact that he had less seniority than others in the group. It had also been proposed that Wilfong be the Chief Elder permanently, a notion he rejected immediately on the grounds that Wynot would not have countenanced such a potentially tyrannical situation.

Before taking their seats, all faced the portrait of Wynot. Wembly intoned:

"Colleagues, let us pay homage to Him Who has brought us to the Truth."

He saluted with both hands again, and the assembly followed suit. Wembly then chanted:

"There once was an underground hall,
   Where men studied matters great and small.
      They serve Him Who taught
      That which they desperately sought.
   Oh, Wynot, bless them all!"

A moment of silence ensued as each individual meditated in his own fashion. All saluted the portrait a second time, then took their seats. The Chief Elder stared at the table for a long moment while the others waited patiently.

"Gentlemen," he said at last, "we'll dispense with the usual formalities and get right to the point. The Order is under attack."

The announcement was greeted with stunned silence and a few exchanged startled glances. Yet, their surprise was not that of learning new information but that of wondering why Wembly was belaboring the obvious. The junior member of the Inner Nest, a portly man just entering middle age with close-cropped hair and too-wide eyes, took it upon himself to put the puzzle into words.

"That's hardly earth-shaking news, Wembly. We've been under attack for two-and-a-half centuries. As long as that damned Edict remains in effect, we'll always be under attack."

"Wofford is correct, Wembly," Wilfong said softly. "I myself came under surveillance this afternoon." Tersely, he recounted the spotting of the King's agent from the Circle of Friends and the actions he had taken to deal with the fellow. This last point received a nervous chuckle all around. "But, I suspect you have something else in mind."

"Indeed I do, Wilfong. By now, the upper levels of the Order can spot a King's agent a *stadium* away with one eye shut. This new threat is entirely different and much more sinister, and I have no idea who's behind it. Winsley, show Wilfong the writing."

A frail-looking man with a perpetual squint and stringy black hair two chairs to Wembly's left reached into the folds of his robe and produced a single sheet of papyrus. Wordlessly, he passed it along to the Wizard, who carefully smoothed it out and read the writing minutely. There were only five lines, all written in a small, crabbed hand. The professional teacher of language in Wilfong *humph*ed to himself; the author had a lot to learn about spelling and punctuation. Basically, the message read thusly:

"There once was a Wizard named Wynot,
Who put me into a terrible spot.
He went to Zarel
But soon will go to Hell,
And his Order will then go to pot.
SC"

Of all the Practitioners who had dwelled in Atlantis, only Wynot the Wise had couched his Spells in this unique form. He had had a term for it, but no one in living memory could recall what it was. So long as the Spells worked, the name of the form was immaterial. The Compleat Sorcerer had used this form as a mnemonic; the rhythmic nature helped the novice to learn the Spells more easily. (And, when there 997 different Spells to learn, any aid in committing them to memory was most welcome!)

That the author of this wretched writing knew the form of Wynot's Spell-casting meant but one thing: he had been a member of the Order at one time. Furthermore, since Spell-casting was not taught until Level Five, the unknown Enemy had been exposed to considerable training in Practitioning. How long he had remained in the Order was a grand mystery and boded ill for the Clutch; for, in terms of danger to their existence, a rogue member represented a graver threat than an army of King's agents.

The last two characters of the message were a curiosity in and of themselves. Obviously, they represented the name of the unknown Enemy. Yet, their usage did not conform to Atlantean practice – which could mean the author was a foreigner. And he could have come from anywhere in the Known World (or the unknown world, for that matter), since Wynot had traveled far and wide and taught wherever he went.

A parade of questions marched through the Wizard's mind – an *orderly* parade, however, as it served to gain an insight on the person who called himself "SC." He had not been trained to yield to blind panic; the questions he now posed for himself were part of a check-list designed to take him from Point A to Point B to Point C and so on. Carefully, he handed the papyrus back to Wembly.

"How did you come by this?" he asked quietly.

"Well, that's the damnedest thing. I arrived earlier to work on the training schedule for the next cycle, and I discovered it nailed to the Master's portrait."

Wilfong pursed his lips. Was the rogue then one of the *current* membership? He concentrated on the one hundred individuals and their ethnic origins. Save for half a dozen, the Clutch were native-born Atlanteans, and that half-dozen were second- and third-generation. One of the latter, who had difficulty in spelling and punctuation, could be working under a false name – which meant that the Order's screening process needed to be re-evaluated. On the other hand, if the rogue were an outsider, then either there was a weakness in the wards around the Temple or the Enemy was powerful enough to slip pass them. Whichever the case, it was cause for concern. What might happen if the fellow decided to publicize the Order's whereabouts and the identities of its membership in order to claim the standing reward? The Square of Contemplation might suffer from overcrowding in the near future. The entire Order would have to flee Atlantis altogether – if they could. Yet, Wilfong did not think it likely that "SC's" motives were strictly venal; rather from the tone of the message, he was seeking revenge for some personal grievance.

"Winsley," he addressed his colleague, "what vibrations did you pick up from the papyrus?"

The frail man cast his eyes down at the table and wrung his hands.

"I'm ashamed to admit, Wilfong," he replied in a squeaky voice, "that my so-called skill in gleaning images from objects which have been touched by human hands has availed me of nothing in this case. I drew a blank, no matter how hard I concentrated."

"Most queer and strange. If the Enemy can neutralize all traces of his presence, he is at least a Level Nine." Briefly, he related his thoughts on the possible identity of "SC." "I suggest we double-check those members who have foreign heritage -- and Level Nine status and above. Once we can eliminate them as suspects, we can start looking outside our ranks."

"Does that include me as well, Wilfong?" Wofford asked. "My grandparents came from Egypt, though I have taken an Atlantean name."

"Nothing personal, Wofford, but yes. We trust you'll co-operate fully."

"Wynot knows I am a True Disciple. I'll match my loyalty with anybody's."

"Thank you, Wofford. We'll make it as painless as possible. Wembly, this 'SC' has mentioned Zarel for a reason. Since I've been there before and have a Zarelo servant, I think I ought to check out that angle personally."

"My very sentiments exactly, Wilfong. Besides, as the Master's greatest pupil" – murmurs of assent circled the table – "we feel you are the best qualified to meet this new threat. I regret you must shoulder most of the burden, but it seems to me that there is something at work here the rest of us may not understand."

"You're closer to the truth than you realize. Earlier, I had a vision." He described it detail. Reaction by the senior members of the Inner Nest was one of great admiration for the recipient of the vision; the junior members simply sat there slack-jawed at such a revelation. "I think the Master is calling me to Him. This message may be part of a test of my worthiness. If it is, I will leave the Order and join Him."

"Wilfong!" Wembly exclaimed. "We'd never see you again?" He clutched at the Wizard's sleeve. "I can't begin to tell you what a great loss to the Order this would mean. You've been as much a spiritual force for us as Wynot was. Surely, He can't mean to take you from us."

"Who knows what the Master has in store for any of us, Wembly? He was as above us as we are above the insects. Whatever He purposes, however, it is for our greater good."

"Yes, of course. You're right – as always. Still… Well, it's settled then. Our prayers are with you, Wilfong. May the Cosmos give you Harmony and Wisdom."

A chorus of "amens" circled the table, and the Wizard was actually quite moved by this show of confidence. Before, he had worked diligently to keep the Order functioning, asking for neither praise nor thanks; and, if it seemed that his fellow Elders relied upon him overly much, he had dismissed the notion as pettiness. In these trying times, the welfare of the Order was supreme and that of the individual members was sublimated. Wynot had taught that "from each according to his ability, to each according to his need." All other paths were selfishness incarnate.

"There is one more thing I need to bring up," Wembly said hesitantly. "While you're in the field, will you please make periodic reports to Zondar?"

A dark cloud passed over Wilfong's face, and he began to drum his fingers on the table.

"Zondar? Is that bundle of gripes still alive?"

"Very much so, and still bundled up in Cimmeria. I do wish you'd be more tolerant of him; after all, he is our best eidetic and the Order's Librarian. That should entitle him to a little respect."

"Hardly compensation for his coarseness and impudence. But, for the sake of the mission, I'll hold my ire in check."

"Thank you, Wilfong. If there are no other comments, we'll adjourn. I will admonish you that, in the days ahead, we all may be called upon to perform extraordinary service. Don't make any long-term plans."

He stood up and faced the portrait of Wynot. The others followed suit. As one they saluted double-handedly, and Wembly chanted the standard homage to the Founder. One by one, the Elders slipped away toward personal concerns.

Although the general rule was that each level in the Order teach the next lower one, there was one exception, and Wilfong the Wizard was it. Strictly speaking, he ought to have confined himself to instructing Twelves so that they might in their turn achieve Level Thirteen. And he did instruct them when they were scheduled for training. And he ought to have acted the part of proctor to the teaching assistants during his scheduled evenings, handing out the lesson plans, answering any questions the TA's might have, interpreting Wynot's words in the light of present-day circumstances, and generally assuring that the training sessions ran smoothly. By personal and professional inclination, however, Wilfong was not content to play such a passive role. He was a teacher too, and he wanted to teach. Consequently, he often took an active part in the proceedings. No one took any umbrage in his "meddling"; rather, TA's and trainees alike were in such awe of his abilities and reputation that they considered it the greatest privilege and the highest honor to be taught personally by him. If he was aware of this adulation (and he no doubt was), he did not let it deter him. A lesson well executed was a teacher's best reward for his efforts, and he sought no other.

Except that, on this night, his mind was not entirely on teaching or on the lesson plans in progress. Instead, his mind was many worlds away, contemplating the implications of the declaration of war against the Order of Wynot by the mysterious "SC." That it was war could not be denied. The declaration – poorly written as it was – was most clear: the unknown Enemy had vowed to destroy all who wore the Sign of the Owl, perhaps to destroy even Wynot himself. Whether the fellow was capable of such a deed was immaterial; the fact remained that he was going to attempt it, come what may. And, if he failed to achieve his wanton goal, he still could wreak enough havoc from which the Order might never recover. While "SC's" abilities remained a mystery, Wilfong was essentially powerless; his own talents were useless if he had no idea how they should be employed. This feeling of impotence disturbed him the most. He had to wait until the Enemy actually attacked before he could counter anything the fellow threw at him, and he hated waiting.

Waiting wore one down psychologically and permitted the foe to exploit weaknesses.

Such was the Wizard's distraction that he failed to notice the Level Ten TA standing at his side respectfully until she *ahem*ed for his attention. He had been staring at the fire in the main chamber, nearly putting himself into a trance, and reacted with a start. He peered at the young woman with the chestnut hair fashioned into ringlets, the pale complexion, and the intense gray eyes with a momentary lack of recognition.

"Yes, Winona," he said at last, "what is it?"

"Forgive me, Master Wilfong," she murmured. "I desire a clarification."

"Concerning?"

"One of the students raised the question of, uh, seduction, and I was not sure how to respond."

"Seduction?" the Wizard asked incredulously. "Why in the world would a Practitioner want to know about that?"

"My very question as well, Master. Apparently, the student had taken it in his head that the King might send out female agents in an attempt to seduce suspected Practitioners and trick them into revealing themselves, um, in more ways than one."

Wilfong regarded Winona – now red-faced with embarrassment – his face twisted into a grimace of disbelief. Of all the things for a trainee to ask! What were his experiences that he should be worried about seduction and the possibility of entrapment? Perhaps he required a stern lecture on the perils of self-indulgence....

"Wynot spoke of many things," he began slowly, "not the least of which were matters of the heart. Basically, He said that, even in this realm, rationalism rather than emotionalism ought to prevail. 'Treat others as you would want them to treat you,' or words to that effect. While He wasn't too specific about, um, male-female relationships, I should judge that His maxim would apply there as well.

"As for a deliberate attack by a female agent of the King, one must counter it in a similar manner as any other form of attack – recognition, understanding, and negation, or RUN. That," he added wryly, "and a little common sense."

"A wise course, indeed," Winona responded, her eyes shining. "Thank you, Master Wilfong. Again, I apologize for disturbing your meditation."

He dismissed the woman with a casual wave of the hand. If she had been aware of his uncharacteristic distraction, she had been polite enough not to mention it. Now that he had a new goal to concern himself, he needed no inane distractions from anyone, including the Clutch.

Not all distractions were inane, however. The next time he was aware of someone hovering over him, he was surprised to observe all of the TA's and trainees watching him with much anxiety. He hadn't seen a bunch of nervous ninnies since he had announced an impromptu examination to his beginning students at the School. Still, that they were gathered around meant something important.

"Yes?"

"Pardon again, Master Wilfong," Winona said respectfully. As the Senior TA for this session, she had appointed herself as the "spokesperson" for the group. "Will we be having our Communion this evening?"

The Wizard kicked himself mentally. Of all the people who ought to have known better, it was he. The primary reason for the founding of the Order had been to provide a safe haven (however temporary) for the persecuted Practitioners of Atlantis and to allow them to let down their guard and be themselves. Once the serious business of honing their skills was completed, a time of fellowship commenced. When he had been in training, Wilfong had looked forward to these periods of relaxation and camaraderie when all of them sat around the fire as equals, when anecdotes and experiences were shared, when tears of happiness commingled with tears of sadness, when no one was ashamed to be what he was. To suggest that the time of Communion was less worthy of consideration flew in the face of everything Wynot had ever taught. And, if he, Wilfong the Wizard, was supposed to be the Compleat Sorcerer's "greatest disciple," why, he had better start acting the part and stop his damned daydreaming, hadn't he?

"Of course we will." He got to his feet. "I fear I owe you all an apology. I've had a lot on my mind recently, but that's no excuse for neglecting you."

"You needn't apologize to us, Master," Winona declared, glancing left and right as if to seek affirmation. "We're honored to be in your presence." A murmur of assent rippled through the group. "We're strengthened by your example, whether you speak to us or not."

"I'm flattered that you think so. And it behooves me to do better in living up to your expectations. But, now, let us seek Communion."

The trainees followed close on his heels as he strode toward the innermost chamber. Winona directed two Level Ones to carry several skins of wine which she had procured earlier with funds from the Order's treasury (funds which were replenished by donations of one piece of silver per month per member, plus a generous donation of five gold pieces per month from Caznat). Once gathered around the fire, Wilfong signaled for attention.

"Friends, colleagues, let us pay homage to Him Who has brought us to the Truth."

The company faced the portrait of Wynot and presented the double-handed salute. The trainees sat down, but the Wizard remained standing. The wine-bearers offered the skins to each member. Wilfong allowed himself a rare long swallow. When all had drunk and were relaxed, they fixed their attention on him.

"If you don't mind," he said boldly, "I'd like to start things off by sharing with you a vision I had last night. It's been bothering me ever since. Perhaps I can enlist your help in unraveling its meaning."

Later, when Wilfong had departed the Temple, he replayed in his mind the expressions of shock and surprise which the assembly had taken on at his request. That a Level Thirteen would ask for help from his inferiors was unthinkable; that he would ask it for a *personal* reason was incredulous. A few there had been who were moved to say aloud that, while the request was intriguing, it was beyond their poor powers to attempt such an analysis. And one very brave soul went so far as to suggest that Master Wilfong was surely playing a joke on his juniors. Interestingly enough, he thought, Winona was not among this skeptical group but held her piece and regarded him with an air of pensiveness. Even after he had assured the group that he was quite serious, two remained unconvinced and chose not to participate for fear of being made fools.

The Wizard realized two object lessons here. The first was that he personally had a long path to travel toward the breaking down of barriers surrounding people who, steeped in an atmosphere of paranoia and persecution, were afraid to open up to anyone regardless of the circumstances, including the Order's time of Communion. It was not enough to teach these future Practitioners the techniques that Wynot had instituted long ago; they must also be immersed in his *philosophy* so that they had a better understanding of their place in the Cosmos. Skill without understanding led to amorality, and understanding without skill led to futility. The Compleat Sorcerer had placed equal emphasis on both. Wilfong's task therefore was to restore a balance in the minds of the timid lest they inadvertently betray the Order and themselves.

The second lesson was the other side of the coin. Once he had involved his students into more practical applications of their training, they were bound to appreciate what was being taught. He had had no great expectations when he asked for assistance in interpreting his vision; yet, he had been most gratified when the majority enthusiastically plunged into the exercise. Very little positive production had come of it, but he had succeeded in strengthening the group's sense of self-assurance. And that was more precious than mere ideas. One might expect to see much feedback in the future as the trainees tackled other practical problems. If the Wizard had been the boastful sort, he might have said that Wynot couldn't have done better. But, considering what the Founder had been capable of tended to be an effective antidote to pride.

One useful idea had arisen out of the impromptu brainstorming, however, and significantly it had come from the pensive Winona. She seemed to have an instinctive understanding of symbolism and had launched into a lengthy, dispassionate analysis of the various elements in Wilfong's vision. Upon cross-examination by both him and her fellow trainees, she had held her ground and provided additional arguments in her rebuttal. Wilfong was quite impressed and made a mental note to monitor her progress in the future. Again, he marveled at Wynot's foresight in including women in his Order. He had been the only Practitioner to have done so – amidst the jeers and snide remarks of his nominal peers – on the grounds that the female perspective was just as valid as the male one, that the two often complemented each other. This Level Ten was the living proof of the Master's wisdom.

Wilfong could have dismissed most of her analysis as mere speculation, and he could have given half a dozen explanations himself. But, what really piqued his interest was Winona's views on the symbolism of the figure with his face and its aging and re-juvenation. She argued (masterfully, he thought) that the figure represented Time and the aging face its passage. Therefore, the events in the vision were to occur sometime in the future, quite possibly the distant future since the face had aged to that of an old man, whereupon Wilfong would be re-born (spiritually, that is) after his encounter with Wynot as shown by the "de-aging" of the face. The Wizard was almost persuaded to accept her explanation as the most logical.

Almost, but not completely. Winona had not viewed the second part of the vision – the actual meeting with Wynot in the cave of metal – as a symbol for a real event but as the event itself. Either a dream was symbolic through and through, or it wasn't; it couldn't be both at the same time. Certainly, he had never heard of a vision doing double duty. Though he had pointed out this anomaly, she was adamant in her position – an admirable stance, showing conviction and self-assurance. He could hardly fault her attitude even as he doubted her logic.

Refreshed though he had been by the camaraderie of Communion, he was still devoid of any new insights. He was still a blind man, stumbling around in unfamiliar territory without guides along his path; and, the more he realized his lack, the sooner frustration returned. His newly acquired problem, the identity and purpose of the being known only as "SC," was of paramount importance now, and only the sure knowledge of what the Enemy hoped to accomplish would serve to retard frustration's progress. Whoever or whatever "SC" was, he should not trust in having an easy fight of it. A Level Thirteen was no push-over!

Late though the hour was, Wilfong did not return to his home immediately. Too much filled his mind, and he needed to clear it out before retiring. Otherwise, he was doomed to spend his sleep period tossing and turning; and the next day, he would be so owlish that his students would be even less tolerable than they already were. Subconsciously, he wended his way down to the harbor.

He had a favorite spot to which he went in times like this, having discovered it as a child. A huge outcropping of rock squatted on the north shore of the mouth of the bay which formed Atlantis' natural harbor, a mighty sentinel which guarded against all intruders -- or so the legend went. The legend had it that, when Xenox created the World out of the corpse of his brother, Zonnilep, whom he had slain in a fit of jealousy, he took one of Zonnilep's molars and placed it before Atlantis as a reminder to mortal men of the might and wrath of the King of the Most High. In the ages since Creation, the great rock had served primarily as a place of sacrifice – first of humans, later of animals – as the ancestors of the present generation of Atlanteans sought to appease Lord Xenox and to seek his aid in their endeavors. With the acquirement of knowledge of architecture and engineering, humans constructed more elaborate temples, temples which reflected *human* mastery over the natural world (though few ever recognized the irony of the situation).

The Tooth of Zonnilep was thus abandoned by all except a small corps of puritans who held to the old ways. When it was not being used as a site for sacrifice, the rock was a place for more secular (and crude) activities. Lovers had pledged their troth (and often consummated it). Wise men had meditated upon the Mysteries of the Cosmos. Criminals had attempted to hide from the City Guards (though it was not the most invulnerable spot in the Kingdom). But, chiefly, the jetsam and flotsam of generations of Atlanteans had used it as a lavatory and/or a vomitorium.

The Wizard went to the furthermost part of the Tooth where it overlooked a one-hundred-meter cliff which fell to the sea and against which the sea battered furiously. A familiar "chair" – actually a crevice between two small boulders – awaited him, and he took his seat easily. From this vantage, he could gaze far off to the East. The only sounds were the lapping of the waves below and the shrill screech of gulls searching for a late-night snack. The Moon was rising now, a slender crescent in the last phase of its current cycle. The Moon was also known as the "Watchman"; if one looked closely, one observed the face of a man, a fat-faced man with a lopsided grin. It was said that this "man in the Moon" was a sign to mortals by Xenox that he would not interfere unduly in the affairs of humans, so long as they did not abuse the Holy Places. On a more esoteric level, certain philosophers claimed that the Moon was just another smaller world that circled the Earth. They were generally hooted down as soon as they opened their mouths.

The Wizard had no sooner settled down than his ever-alert senses detected a slight scrabbling sound off to his left. He focused more attention upon this disturbance. Someone else was clambering up the outcropping, and he was not bothering to be quiet about it. Wilfong jumped to his feet and slipped behind one of the boulders which formed his "chair." He peeped around it and discovered a colossal surprise.

It was Lymatan!

Even if the dim moonlight made facial features too difficult to make out, there was no mistaking the figure of the giantess. One would have had to be blind! Wilfong at once breathed a sigh of relief; he had had his share of being followed by the King's agents for one day. Still, he wondered why she was here, alone by the look of things. Or would some other party be along shortly for a rendezvous? A lover perhaps? If so, what brave soul had risen to the challenge to woo her? More to the point, who had so charmed her that she would agree to this out-of-the-way tryst? Furthermore, ought he to remain to spy on her or to withdraw and allow her her privacy? Stealth was not an option; once he left the cover of the rock, he would be exposed to the whole world. And, unless he cared to stay where he was all night (or however long Lymatan stayed), he would just have to brazen out a public appearance. Boldly, he stepped out into the open.

"Hello?" he called out in an innocence-laden voice. "Who's there, please?"

"Colxor?" the giantess gasped. "Is that you?"

"Lymatan? You gave me a start! What are you doing up here, away from the inn?"

"I might ask you the same, little teacher. As for me, I have to get away from the racket once in a while. This seemed as likely a spot as any."

"What a co-incidence! I often come here myself to clear my head."

"Really? That's very interesting." She had now reached his position and stood but half a pace away. Wilfong could smell her easily and not all of her scent was due to the ambience of her place of business. She stretched out her hand and brushed his cheek with her fingertips. "I wish I knew when you came here. We could…meditate together."

The Wizard did not care for the direction this conversation was heading, for it was the same direction that Lymatan always took her conversations with him. He was not in the mood for her flirtations tonight; and, even if he were, this was neither the time nor the place for them. Too many expectations were associated with the Tooth of Zonnilep, and Wilfong could not meet with any of them in his present state. He had to ease himself out of this uncomfortable situation and do so gracefully without angering the giantess. He suspected that angering her was foolhardy at best and dangerous at worst. The *least* she could do was to refuse to serve him in her inn – farewell, baked halibut! – and eject him from the premises. The *worst* she could do was to break every bone in his body while ejecting him.

"Um, well, I don't know…"

She continued to stroke his cheek. His body temperature continued to rise.

"I have to tell you, dear Colxor, that, strange as it may sound, I really am attracted to you. I put on a show of it for the benefit of those filthy wharf-rats. But, deep down, I'd really like nothing better than to share a bed with you."

"Gods above, Lymatan," he croaked, "this is so…sudden. But, I confess that I've had…certain feelings toward you as well. Yet, I…"

Without warning, the woman gripped his shoulders, drew him close to her, and pressed his face against her breasts. Large as melons they were, but soft as pillows. The Wizard now experienced conflicting sensations: a tingling coursing through his body, and the desire to escape this overwrought female.

"Take me, Colxor!" Lymatan whispered. "Make me feel like a woman!"

He groaned inwardly. Either he made love to her – which he clearly did not want to do (at least not here and now) – or take a drastic step to escape her clutches. Earlier in the day, he had taken a gamble by casting a Spell in public in order to save lives. Now, he had to cast another one to save his reputation. He closed his eyes and sent his mind out into the ether as a fisherman his net into the sea. Excellent! No other living being was nearby to witness what was about to happen. As well as he was able while in the giantess' powerful grip, he placed the tip of his left index finger to his left temple and chanted:

> "There once was a woman who towered above
> And considered me her little turtledove.
>   She whispered a plea
>   To be intimate with me.
> Oh, Wynot, show her some love!"

"What was that you said, darling Colxor? I didn't –"

Abruptly, she released her grip, and her arms hung loosely at her sides. Wilfong stepped back, saw her eyes glaze over as his Spell of Illusion took effect, and grimaced in self-reproach for this unseemly action he had been forced to take. Lymatan sat heavily on the ground and slumped against the Tooth.

"Mmmm, mmmmm," she began to murmur. "Oh, you're a hell of a kisser, little teacher. Ah! yes, kiss those as well. Wait, dearest, let me take off my shirt. There, my sweet bird, have you seen any larger than mine? I swear to you that you're the first man to touch them who I wanted to touch them. Oooh, lick my nipples some more! Gods above, it feels so *good*!"

While the giantess was in the throes of imagined ecstasy, the Wizard surreptitiously slipped away and put considerable distance between himself and the Tooth. The Spell of Illusion would continue for half an hour; when Lymatan awakened, she would remember the experience as a pleasant dream. Later – much later – he would make amends to her. For the moment, his strongest desire was to get a good night's sleep. He had a hunch that he was going to get precious little sleep in the days to come.

THE FIFTH CASTING

THE WIZARD AT BAY

O Man! I have written these words as they were given to me by the Most High so that thou mayest know thy purpose in the Earth.

I am Noxonarp, son of Xoidin, son of Ceppid, and I was born in a lowly state. I was a herder of swine from the time I could walk, and never did I know any other life. But the ways of the Most High are beyond the ken of mortal men; neither their ways nor their purposes do we understand before they are revealed to us.

Thus, it was given to me, a lowly herder of swine, to be the receptacle of the words of the Most High, to be their Prophet and teach the sons of Men the things that they should know.

While I was in the fields, tending to my herd, I heard a horrible hissing sound, a hissing as of a thousand serpents, all around me, and I grew fearful. I fell to my knees and prayed to the Most High, each in their turn, to deliver me from evil. At once, the hissing ceased, and a ball of fire appeared before me; its light was greater than that of the Sun, and it hurt my eyes to look upon it. I cried out for mercy.

Then did the Lord Xenox speak unto me, saying:

'Hear me, Noxonarp the swineherd, for I have chosen thee to be my Prophet. Remember my words and give them to all the world.'

Then did I swoon and fall into a deep sleep. And, when I awakened, the night was upon me, and my herd of swine had wandered astray. Yet, from that hour hence, I was no longer Noxonarp the swineherd but Noxonarp the Voice of the Most High.

The words of Xenox that He had given me whilst I slept I now speak unto thee, o Man, that thou mayest know the Will of the Most High.

In the Beginning, there was only the Most High. They dwelt in the Void and drew pictures of light for each other. Many pictures did they draw of surpassing beauty and detail, and they vied with one another for the honor of the most beautiful and most detailed picture.

Then it came to pass that Caxeot, the youngest of the Most High, halted in the middle of His drawing and asked:

'Why do we draw?'

And Xenox replied: 'To amuse ourselves.'

'Are there not other ways to amuse ourselves?' Caxeot asked further. 'Are there not other things we can create besides pictures?'

And Xenox said: 'Let us create a world then.'

And Zonnilep, the second oldest of the Most High, Who amused Himself with pictures of things unimaginable, said: 'Verily, let us create a universe instead.'

Then did the Most High debate amongst themselves over the course they should take, and some were for the one path, and others were for another. Zonnilep wearied of the debate and, without leave, drew a picture of majesty. And in the Void, there appeared lights shining cold and steady; He drew again, and the lights were set in motion.

Xenox, the oldest, grew wroth because He had not been allowed to draw His picture first and also because Zonnilep had drawn a thing not agreed upon. In His wroth, Xenox slew Zonnilep and commanded the others to harken to His words.

Yet, the Most High did not destroy what Zonnilep had created, so taken by it were they. Instead, they let it stand so that they could shape it as they would. And the first day ended.

Xenox then drew His picture, one of exquisite beauty, and near one of the smaller lights, there appeared the Earth. He drew again, and the Moon came into being. He drew yet again, and the Earth and Moon were set in motion. And the second day ended.

Oconoc then rose and drew a picture of grandeur and might. The dry land separated from the waters of the Earth, and mountains arose to form valleys and plains. He drew again, and the rivers, lakes, and seas took form. And the third day ended.

Now Esos drew, and His was a picture of marvelous serenity. Upon the dry land, there appeared grasses and trees and flowering shrubs. He drew a second time, and the trees bore fruit. And the fourth day ended.

Now came Rinsilac, and He drew a picture of meticulous complexity. Then there swam the creatures of the waters. He drew again, and the creatures of the land walked abroad. He drew once more, and the creatures of the air took wing. And the fifth day ended.

Then the Most High gathered together to gaze upon what they had wrought, and they were pleased.

Yet, Caxeot was unhappy, for He had not drawn a picture of creation, and He remained silent. And Xenox spake unto Him:

'What troubles thee, my brother? Hast thou not been pleased by our works?'

And Caxeot replied: 'I have not yet drawn my picture, but there is nothing left about which to draw. I am unfulfilled.'

'Nay, it is not so, for thou shalt create Man, a creature in our own image, and thou shalt imbue him with reason and understanding so that he may worship us and give us service.'

Thus it was that Caxeot drew a picture of unsurpassing joy, and the First Man was formed from the rocks of the Earth. He drew a second time, and the First Woman appeared in the foam of the sea. He drew once more and brought the pair together, and they became husband and wife and knew each other. And the sixth day ended.

Then did the Most High gather again and gaze upon what they had wrought, and they were very pleased.

And they gave unto the man and the woman stewardship over the Earth and bade them to make use of the land and the seas as they saw fit. And they bade them to keep certain commandments in their hearts that they might live in peace and serenity....

...And it came to pass that, in the thirtieth generation of Men, the people were filled with apathy and complacency and comfortable living, *and they took their lives for granted. And they forgot to pay tribute to the Most High for their prosperity.*

Now the Most High forbore this behavior, for the pictures they had drawn in the Beginning, the pictures of Creation, amused them still, and they were loath to chastise their creation.

But one came among the people, and he was full of guile and sweet words. Lyton he was called, that is to say, 'glib of tongue,' and he stirred the people and caused restlessness among them and whispered lies in their ears.

'Why must we toil and not receive fair payment for our labor?' Lyton asked. 'Why must we be slaves to the Most High, never to choose our own paths?'

The words of the deceiver fell upon many eager ears, and the people's hearts were filled with rebellion; and they would not toil unless they were paid fair wages for their labor. And it came to pass that few lifted their hands to pay the Most High their tribute.

Then did the Most High look down upon the Earth and grow wroth, for they had no experience of rebellion and thus no understanding of it. They took counsel amongst themselves, and their options were divided.

Xenox, Whose picture had created the world, wished to undo all that He had created and to draw a new picture to create a new Earth.

But Caxeot, Whose picture had created the First Man and the First Woman, had grown to love His creatures and was loath to see them utterly destroyed. He beseeched His brother Xenox to spare them; but the Lord's heart was hard, and he demanded that punishment be meted out.

Whereupon Caxeot threw Himself at the Lord's feet and begged for the lives of His creatures, crying out:

'Destroy me instead, I who have created them, if blood must be shed. I offer myself as a sacrifice.'

Then was Xenox's heart softened, and He looked upon His brother with favor. Now He declared:

'We will not destroy the Earth and them who walk upon it. But neither will we suffer their rebelliousness. Therefore, we shall send them a punishment which will teach them the error of their ways. We shall cause the Heavens to open up and pour out mighty rains, for Man has never known

rain, and he will be afraid when it comes. Then will he know our wroth and return to the path of righteousness.'

And it came to pass that, in the thirtieth generation of Men, the heavens did pour forth a deluge, and the people were sore afraid and cried out to the Most High for mercy. And, when the prophets spoke to them that the Most High had sent a punishment for their wicked ways, they returned to their former ways, forsaking all evil and giving the Most High their tribute.

This then is the Covenant which has been given to mortal men, as it has been told unto me. I, Noxonarp, say unto thee, o Man, hear these words and repent!

*   *   *

Wilfong hated rain. For one thing, rain prevented him from going places and meeting people and participating in desired activities. For another, if he absolutely had to go somewhere, rain soaked him to the bone and gave him chills. He supposed, on a purely philosophical level, that rain had its uses – e.g. watering crops and replenishing drinking and cooking water – but, on a personal level, he could quite do without it, thank you very much. If he had his way, he'd ban rain within the limits of the Metropolis and restrict it to the countryside where it would do the most good. Unfortunately, as extensive as his knowledge of Magick was, he had no power over natural forces. Wynot's many Spells effected only material objects, animate and inanimate. The gods (Atlantis' or any others), if they existed, alone had control over natural forces such as the weather, and Wilfong and his fellow human beings had to endure as best they could the vagaries of the natural order.

In the present instance, the natural order was bestowing upon the Kingdom the grandfather of all thunderstorms. Having begun in the wee hours of the morning, the rain descended by the amphora-full; it fell so quickly that the streets were transformed into small rivers. Though the Metropolis had a public drainage system, a gutter on either side of the streets, the downpour simply overwhelmed the system, spilling out of the gutters and over the cobblestones. The City Sweepers might have appreciated this bit of unplanned sanitation, but there was always the danger of household flooding. Typical of most thunderstorms, this one had its advantages and disadvantages.

The Wizard stared out the window (the only window) of his apartment and shook his head in disgust. He had classes to teach, but he risked personal injury if he were to attempt to travel the streets in this weather. He could just picture himself being bowled over by a sheet of water and sent cascading until he was pitched into the harbor like a drowned rat. He hoped that the Headmaster of the School had had the good sense to cancel all of the classes or that the parents had had the equally good sense to keep their progeny at home. He would lose a day's pay only if his absence was *his* fault; his contract with the School stipulated that "acts of the gods" constituted no breech of the terms of his employment and thus would not affect his stipend. While he would rather have been in a classroom teaching, there was a bright side to this downpour; the extra time on his hands would provide him an opportunity to mull over plans for countering the threat of the mysterious "SC."

This writer has already mentioned the Master Historian, Xorzist the Elder, whose recounting of the events of the Great Persecution has no equals. This sage had a nephew who, when he grew to manhood and took up the profession of history-writing himself, went by the name of "Xorzist the Younger." This individual hoped to emulate his illustrious uncle; yet, if truth be told, he was not the scholar the old man was. Still, he diligently applied himself and set down the *Chronicles of the Early Fourteenth Dynasty*, which described events up to the time of Wilfong the Wizard. This work has not been as highly regarded by present-day historians because – it was said – of dubious or unreliable documentation. Yet, there has always been that element in any historical document where the affairs of men were concerned, and it has ever been the scholar's task to separate the wheat from the chaff, as it were, and to put forth the best effort he could. If not his uncle's equal, Xorzist the Younger still possessed enough talent to serve him well.

According to the *Chronicles*, during the days prior to the birth of Wilfong, the Kingdom of Atlantis enjoyed its sixth "Age of Splendor," although it has often been more referred to as the "Second Age of

Decadence." However one cared to label this era, Xorzist maintained that the splendor of the Kingdom was due mainly to the continued presence of the Library of Atlantis. An imposing edifice in the First Ring of the Metropolis, it was dwarfed in magnificence only by the Royal Palace and the Temple of Xenox (adjacent to which it was sited). No expense had been spared in its construction over four hundred years prior to Wilfong's day, and each year witnessed new restorative work somewhere on the premises and new collections of materials and additions to old collections. Next to the Palace itself, the Library constituted the largest public-works project in the royal budget, employing the labor of hundreds of workers and artisans.

Originally, the Library had been a personal whim of the then King, a repository for his private collection of books, both fiction and non-fiction. Later, a succeeding monarch was persuaded to store papers of state and the records of the various ministries. Still later, works of science, history, the arts, economics, and other disciplines found their way onto the shelves. Works of fiction soon followed. Finally, the Library was persuaded to accept donations from private collections (for "safekeeping"). In due time, all of the materials were made available to the general reading populace, although most of those who used the Library were scholars conducting some research/experiment. The true importance of the institution was readily understood when foreign tourists made a point to include a visit to it in their itineraries. They came, they saw, they marveled, and they told their friends back home of the splendor of the building, which in turn brought still more tourists (and, not co-incidently, more revenues for the royal coffers and merchants of the city!). And foreign scholars who visited to study there enhanced its reputation even more.

The Library was a three-story affair, neatly divided into distinct sections. The lower-most level consisted of all the Royal Edicts issued since the early days of the Kingdom, reports from the various government ministries, other writings concerning the public life of the Kingdom, and the histories of all the dynasties (if they existed). The middle floor housed all of the scholarly works – subdivided into the physical sciences, the biological sciences, invention and engineering, mathematics, economics, and the social and psychological sciences – written by the foremost thinkers of the Known World and used as references for would-be scholars. The upper-most floor held works of fiction, drama, poetry, and Atlantean- and foreign-language grammars and dictionaries; the writers represented here rivaled in reputation those of the middle floor and were read almost as often.

Each floor had a Conductor whose task it was to retrieve requested materials. A patron requested a specific title from a Master List, and the Conductor (or one of his apprentices) fetched it. For obvious reasons, no materials were permitted to be taken out of the building; one read the book desired in one of several reading rooms, then returned it to the Conductor. If one wished to make notes for a research project, the research also had to be done on the premises in one of several study rooms; all in-progress work was left with the Conductor to be recalled on the next visit. In short, the Library was very jealous of its possessions and sought to prevent their being scattered to the four winds by careless and/or sinister hands.

By no mean co-incidence, the Conductor for the upper-most floor was Wembly, the Chief Elder of the Order of Wynot. He and Wilfong had joined the Order at the same time when the former had been a mere apprentice at the Library and the latter an honors-class teaching assistant at the School. Both had risen through the ranks to their present positions, both public and private. The only difference between the two was that Wilfong had achieved at a faster rate. Nevertheless, due to their long association, they remained the best of friends and each other's confidante. Wembly's position had the added benefit of having direct access to all of the Library's materials, whereby he could supply needed information on any given subject in a day or two without having to go through "normal channels." Since Wilfong's private library consisted mostly of works of Magick, he had to rely on Wembly's expertise for material on some other subject.

Thus, it happened that, instead of staring out the window at the pouring rain, the Wizard took advantage of his enforced leisure and 'casted his old friend.

-- Good morning, Wembly. Are you free?

-- Good morning, Wilfong. Yes, I'm quite free. This thunderstorm is keeping everyone away. I wouldn't be here myself if we Conductors weren't required to live here as a condition of our jobs.

-- Lucky you. I'm staying in, even though I hate idleness.

-- Well, *I'm* not idle. The Librarian has taken it into his head to inventory all of the materials and update the Master List. He says it should fill the day nicely.

-- And it's no more than you deserve.

-- Thank you so much, my friend. I appreciate your concern for my plight. But, you didn't call just to chat.

-- No. I'm acting on the assumption that the mysterious 'SC' is not an Atlantean. I need to study the foreign dictionaries you have there and correlate their spellings with those of the message he left us. If I can determine his country of origin, I can narrow down the list of 'suspects' in the Order. Then, using Zondar's fabled memory, I might learn his true identity.

-- It sounds like a formidable and – if I may say so – a hopeless task.

-- Perhaps. But, we can't afford to overlook any lead. We have to be prepared for 'SC's' next manifestation. I have a bad feeling that he's going to toy with us for a while.

-- Well, your hunches have usually paid off in the past, Wilfong, though the Cosmos knows I wish *this* one wouldn't.

-- I share your wish, Wembly. Now, how soon can I have those dictionaries?

*   *   *

The downpour ceased early in the afternoon, finishing off as a slight drizzle. The clouds parted, and the Sun warmed the air again. Steam arose wherever there was standing water – which was to say, everywhere – and formed great, white, wet billows in all parts of the Metropolis. Pedestrians soon found themselves just as soaked as if they had taken a stroll in the rain itself.

Wilfong ventured out in the late afternoon when it was relatively comfortable to do so. Even then, the air was still clammy, and his clothing tended to cling to his skin. He was determined, however, not to let this day pass without some constructive activity. His destination was the Library, where he expected to read whatever books on foreign languages Wembly had been able to locate. Murkol had been instructed to shop for the evening meal; and, for a short while, the two walked together, the Zarelor dutifully trailing his master by two paces. Their passing provoked stares only from the tourists who had never seen a Zarelor before; the locals were quite used to the sight of the slight Atlantean and his hulking servant together.

Despite Murkol's cloying, slavish behavior, his presence served one useful purpose: the Wizard was not likely to be molested by thieves or ruffians. Though the Zarelor was the gentlest of souls, he *looked* mean, especially when he peered blankly at someone. His presence was sufficient to deter even a gang of wharf-rats. At the designated market, master and servant parted company, but not before Wilfong repeated his requirements so that Murkol could make no mistake in the purchase. The Wizard passed through the Gate of Sighs – nodding dutifully to the Egyptian courtesan at her usual post – and entered the Second Ring.

Ages ago, during the Sixth Dynasty, in a frenzy of "urban renewal," the kings decided to re-design the Metropolis from its haphazard and sprawling appearance to the current concentric-ring motif. The renewal had resulted in a great deal of displacement and even more grumbling, but it proceeded unabated. Old buildings were razed to make room for the walls of stone and brick and mortar which demarcated the city into its five socio-economic segments. The walls increased in thickness and height the further one moved toward the heart of Atlantis, i.e. the Royal Palace and the buildings of State in order to hinder would-be invaders as much as possible and give defenders time to regroup. As an additional precaution, the Gates between the Rings had been staggered; one was forced to travel laterally before reaching an access to the next Ring. To go from the outer ramparts to the Palace required a zig-zag course, akin to traveling through a maze. To newcomers (and a few lazy locals), the arrangement was a colossal nuisance; but, in the two thousand years since the Metropolis had been re-designed, no successful invasion had been suffered. The city might have been confusing, but at least it was safe.

For Wilfong, the configuration of the walls proved to be a boon that day. For, as he was approaching the Gate of Joys to the First Ring, he spied a furtive movement out the corner of his eye. Because of the Order's outlaw status in Atlantis, its members had learned to exercise their peripheral vision more than usual; such extension helped to spot potential agents of the King and to surveil *them*. What the Wizard observed, however, was not so much a figure of a man as a distortion of space in the shape of a man. Someone was employing a Spell of Invisibility – and clumsily, he noted wryly – to track his prey. The shimmering in the air resembled that produced by the intense heat in a desert, but the distinct shape betrayed its unnaturalness. A Level Eleven Practitioner would have been able to limit the distortion to the bare minimum so that the casual observer might believe he had merely seen a trick of the light.

Wilfong searched his surroundings and found no other traffic in this neighborhood. He relaxed and called up a counter-Spell to reveal the clumsy fellow.

> "There once was a shifter of light,
> Who cloaked himself from visible sight.
> He shimmers and shakes
> And fusses and fakes.
> Oh, Wynot, make him bright!"

At once, the illusion of invisibility was dispelled – to the Wizard's eyes, that is – and the spy was revealed as he truly was. And what he was astonished Wilfong to the core of his being. No King's agent this, no member of the murderous Circle of Friends, even if any of them had had the audacity to dabble in Magick. This...*person* was robed and hooded all in black; not one square centimeter of flesh could be seen. It was as if a black hole in space in the shape of a man existed there. The Wizard had to force himself not to stare outright at the fellow and thus alert him to the fact that his invisibility had been a failure. Without breaking stride, he kept walking, all the while casting out his mind in order to catch the other's unaware.

And ran, figuratively speaking, into a wall!

Whoever this spy was, he had – as all trainees in the Order of Wynot had been taught at Level Three, just after learning the art of mind-casting in the first place – raised a mental shield to prevent another Practitioner from reading his thoughts – another *run-of-the-mill* Practitioner, that is, below Level Thirteen. Wilfong the Wizard knew how to crack anyone's mind shield without their being aware of it; furthermore, he could raise one about himself that only another Thirteen could penetrate, albeit with no small effort. If he had had the time, he could have done so on the spot. He had another mission, however, and the "invisible" fellow would have to wait his turn.

Still, Wilfong could deduce something from this less-than-chance encounter. It did not take even a Level Two to realize that the other had to be the mysterious "SC" and that he was trailing the Wizard specifically because, as Wilfong had pointed out in the emergency session of the Inner Nest, "SC" seemed especially interested in him. It was therefore reasonable to assume that this black-robed and –hooded figure would be a fixture in the city for the foreseeable future – ample time to break through his mental defenses and discover his motives for his vile challenge to the Order. For the nonce, it was best that the Enemy still believed he was being excessively clever in his attempts at espionage.

Wilfong's route took him south and west, past the Public Baths for the First Ring (two separate buildings, one for men, the other for women). The lintels of the entrances sported the royal insignia – a bull rampant – amidst a floral display. The Baths were yet another of the public works the Kingdom supported as a convenience to its citizens. Each Ring had a set of Baths and, as one might surmise, each set reflected its surroundings in terms of materials used in the construction. A case in point: the Baths here had been built with imported white marble, the floors covered with mosaic tiles, and the walls painted with intricate murals reflecting Atlantis' long history. In Wilfong's Ring the Baths were of granite with tight-fitting paving stones on the floor and geometric designs on the walls. One supposed that the Middle-Ringers were fortunate in this respect, since the Baths in the Fourth and Fifth Rings were mere brickwork with floors of wooden planks and whitewashed walls, all in need of repair and cleaning. Nevertheless, the system was an improvement over the former mode of public sanitation, that is to say, a trip to the harbor and a quick dip in its frigid waters (though many Fifth Ringers still used that mode). One paid an entrance fee of two bronze coins for which he received two towels, a bar of soap, and directions to the dressing rooms. One spent as much time as he wished (or could spare), soaking in a tub of hot, steaming water.

Minutes later, the Library loomed large ahead of the Wizard in the western section of the First Ring. Its three stories resembled squat cylinders stacked one upon another, each succeeding one narrower in diameter. About the circumference of the lowest story ran a portico punctuated with ornately-carved columns; the bases and capitols reflected the style of architecture prevalent at the time of its construction, giving the building a decidedly archaic appearance. Atop the upper story stood a lesser portico supporting a gilded dome which glistened in the sunlight. The Library had also been built with imported white marble which sent forth its own luster. It was said that mariners needed no lighthouse to find their way into the harbor of Atlantis; all they had to do was to locate the Library's glittering white façade and golden roof and sail unerringly into port in relative safety.

Two streets away, he could hear the murmurings of a large crowd. Frequently, someone would raise his voice in anger, though at this distance, the words were indistinct. At the distance of one street, the voices were clearer, and the Wizard was startled to learn that the angry mob was protesting something inside the Library. The specifics still eluded him, and he decided to scout ahead before charging into an unknown situation. He halted and mind-casted Wembly.

-- It's the damnedest thing, Wilfong [the Conductor responded in an anxiety-filled "voice"]. The protest materialized just a few moments ago. I use the word 'materialized' advisedly. One minute, there was no one on the street; the next, well, you see how many there are. It's as if they all converged on this spot at a given signal.

-- Very queer and strange. What's their gripe?

-- That's just as mystifying. Apparently, someone started a rumor that the Library contains materials which mock the gods of Atlantis. The mob is demanding their removal and destruction in a public show.

Wilfong remained silent for a short while. A myriad of thoughts seethed in his mind. To his knowledge, no one had ever protested the *contents* of the Library. Criticism had been raised during the initial construction on the grounds that so elaborate – and expensive – an edifice was not necessary to store mere books. In the face of the King's will (and a legion of soldiers guarding the property), the opposition had melted away. The idea of a Library *per se* had never been in question; neither had the need to store books regardless of their content. It was a given that Atlanteans could pick and choose whatever they desired and allow others the same privilege. If there were something in the Library which might be offensive to someone (for whatever reason), why, that someone didn't have to read it at all, did he? One of the purposes of the Library was to cater to all tastes.

No longer, apparently. For the first time in Atlantis' history, objections to the contents were being raised. The Wizard could scarcely contain his ire. He loathed censorship of any kind, whether it originated with the State or with the mob. Suppression of free thought was the worst crime anyone could commit against an orderly and informed society; the suppressors said, in essence, that they had no use for an orderly and informed society and that they wished to re-shape it along more restricted, more doctrinaire, more *parochial* lines. Wilfong knew – perhaps more than most – that such restrictive societies were not uncommon; he had heard many tales from the lands bordering the Great Inland Sea where the people were forbidden to read (or even discuss) certain "taboo" subjects on pain of severe penalty. For the most part, those lands were not happy lands as their citizens were ever fearful of misspeaking and bringing down the wrath of the self-appointed "guardians" of thought upon their heads.

Here then lay the gulf between the Kingdom of Atlantis and all others in the Known World: save for the spreading of outright lies, no topic was so "sacred" that it could not be discussed in public. Rational discussion advanced knowledge and understanding; suppression of thought fostered ignorance and superstition. No one worthy of the label "Atlantean" would tolerate censorship. The Library stood as a bulwark against it.

-- Do you have any such materials, Wembly? [Wilfong said at last].

-- I can only speak for my department. There are a couple of comedies written by the early Twelfth Dynasty playwright, Dernylab, in which the central character calls the existence of the gods into question. In the first one, after a lengthy debate, he despairs and throws himself into the sea; in the second, he becomes an avid follower of the local cult and becomes an itinerant preacher. In both cases, public morality is restored. Dernylab was, of course, a satirist, and everyone recognizes – or should recognize – what he was attempting to say. As far as I know, no one other than Wynot ever wrote a *serious* treatise on the subject.

-- And we both know that His writings can't be made public as long as the Dread Edict exists.

-- Yes. The Master demonstrated so clearly that legends of the gods were just that – tales born of ignorance and superstition – and yet, His views would cause such an uproar that the authorities would suspend Atlantean liberties in order to put the torch to His writings.

-- I can tell you that censorship is the least of our worries at the moment. [Quickly, he related the incident at the Gate of Joys.] An evil person with the power of invisibility can cause a lot of mischief.

-- The Cosmos protect us, Wilfong! Or, I should say, *you*. This 'SC' means to strike at you first; for, with you out of the way, the rest of us will be easy targets.

-- Exactly. And, with the Order destroyed, all of Wynot's teachings here will be lost to posterity. Obviously, that's what the Enemy meant in last night's message.

-- Indeed. Are you coming in?

-- I'm not about to let a little thing like a hostile mob deter me. Too much is at stake. I'll see you shortly.

Bold talk, wizard, he thought grimly. *This bunch seems to have doubled in the last five minutes.*

It was only a slight exaggeration on his part. When he had first arrived, there had been perhaps eighty or ninety individuals pacing back and forth in front of the arch which fronted the Library and shouting anti-Library slogans, sometimes in unison, more often not. Now, the crowd had increased to one-hundred-fifty plus, and the sloganeering was even nastier as the larger numbers emboldened the demonstrators. On the whole, Wilfong found the demographics interesting from a clinical point of view. There seemed to be an equal mix from all strata of Atlantean society – shopkeepers and artisans, laborers and farm hands, professionals and entrepreneurs, bureaucrats and slaves, and a smattering of priests from various temples – intermingling in an uncharacteristically egalitarian manner. If any of those were aware of this incongruity, he did not manifest it but instead concentrated on his own role-playing in this little drama. It was, to coin a phrase, very queer and strange.

The Wizard approached the demonstration cautiously but confidently and eased himself through the fringes of the crowd with difficulty. No one challenged his presence. Perhaps they believed him to be just another anti-Librarian. But, as he pushed further on, the feeling that something was wrong here grew. He took a good, hard look at one of the protestors and received yet another surprise.

The object of his examination was a young man of stout build with high cheekbones and a square jaw. His clothing suggested that he was a common laborer. And now that he thought about it, he was sure he had seen the fellow on the piers yesterday – Trimon, wasn't it? The curious thing about him, though, was his eyes; they were glazed over, unseeing. Now Wilfong peered at others nearby. They all wore a stuporous expression; none was aware of his/her surroundings but went through the motions like a puppet on a string. No doubt about it: this crowd was under a Spell of Compulsion!

He glanced about with forced nonchalance. The puppet-master had to be somewhere close by. Ordinarily, an adept Practitioner could control one individual from a fair distance away (though there were obvious limitations, depending on any number of variables). At Level Thirteen, Wilfong could control a single person at ten *stadia*, and he was still working to extend his reach. To control large numbers, however, a low-level operator needed to be less than half a *stadium* away (Wilfong could do it at two *stadia*); the level of control decreased in proportion to the increase of the distance. Even as the Wizard conducted a visual search, he cast his mind out in an ever-broadening sweep.

Aha! he exulted. *There you are, my friend!*

Near the farthest corner of the Library, a now familiar shimmering of the air became visible. With his mind's eye, he observed the human-shaped black figure he had seen not too long ago. He didn't need to cast a counter-Spell to identify the puppet-master; for whatever diabolical reason, "SC" had taken over the wills of more than a hundred-and-fifty persons in order to launch an attack on the Library. The question was, *why?* What had he hoped to gain with this demonstration?

More importantly, what could Wilfong do to counter the Enemy's scheme? What *should* he do? Without a clear idea of what this exercise in control really represented, he could take no action yet; and, while it might be a humanitarian act to wrest these unwilling participants from their compulsion, he risked exposing himself to unwanted attention (and perhaps blame for the crowd's condition). Also, he would reveal to "SC" that he was onto him and put him on his guard. Any counter-attack depended upon keeping "SC" in the dark as long as possible.

In the end, the decision was made for him by inalterable Fate. As he wormed his way through the crowd, coming within a stone's throw of the Library's entrance where he had a clearer shot at the Enemy, he felt a huge hand clap him on the shoulder. Slowly, he pivoted and confronted Trimon. The wharf-rat peered at him with a glint of malice in his otherwise blank face. The Wizard steeled himself for a physical assault.

"What here are you doin', bub?" the large man demanded in a monotone.

"Obviously, I'm going to the Library," Wilfong explained as calmly as he could. "Would you mind removing your hand?"

"Nobody go in can't let."

"And why not?"

Trimon's jaw muscles worked furiously as he sought the proper words to say. The Wizard deduced that the compulsion extended to verbal responses as well; the puppet-master was feeding them into Trimon's brain, and the latter simply repeated what he "heard."

"Uh, un-Atlantean books in there there is, detrimental to family values and common decency."

"*Humph!* If there's anything 'un-Atlantean' here, it's your attitude. Our society is based upon free thought. Now, if you'll excuse me, I have business inside."

He attempted to loosen the other's grip, but Trimon tightened his hold. Wilfong glared at him with his best expression of outrage, a façade for the benefit of the unseen Enemy. Even if this wharf-rat had recognized him from his frequent appearance on the piers, it did not follow that he should express hostility. Wilfong's reputation as a non-threatening, often-amusing, and somewhat sympathetic individual ought to have protected him from violence from the likes of Trimon — one more proof that the fellow was a mere tool, forced into violence by a wholly malevolent creature.

"See here, fellow, if you don't release me at once, I'll be forced to take drastic action."

His assailant laughed briefly and unemotionally. Around the pair, others echoed the pseudo-laugh.

"And what you to me can do do you think, Wilfong?"

Shock upon shock! No one of Wilfong's acquaintances outside of the Order would know, much less use in public, his secret name. He had been born Colxor, son of Tomec, and that was what he was called by any non-Practitioner (and then only in private). "SC" was now speaking to him directly without any need for subterfuge.

The Enemy's mocking tone revealed a supreme confidence in his own abilities (whatever they were), and he was not afraid to reveal himself to the Wizard, even if he employed a cat's paw. Indeed, he appeared to be throwing down the gauntlet and daring Wilfong to pick it up. The latter was all too willing to do just that and take "SC" down a peg or two. Yet, he had to weigh the pros and cons of accepting the challenge here and now. If the Enemy was not going to allow him much choice in the matter, he first had to devise some method of circumspection.

-- Wembly, have you been monitoring the situation?

-- Yes, both visually and mentally. To think that all those people are under a Spell of Compulsion – it boggles the mind!

-- Indeed. Look, I intend to dissolve this compulsion. But, 'SC' won't be standing idly by while I do so. I want you to provide a distraction.

-- Gladly. What sort of distraction?

-- Cast a Spell of Illusion near his position, an image of me pointing at him with one hand and waving to the crowd with the other. Hopefully, that will break his concentration long enough for me to cast my own Spell.

-- Show me his location.

The Wizard formed a picture of the far corner of the Library where the shimmering was occurring and transmitted it to Wembly. The Chief Elder gasped in surprise.

-- The Cosmos preserve us, Wilfong! I might have missed him altogether if I hadn't known where to look. That's the difference between you and me.

-- Don't despair, old friend. Someday, you'll be a Thirteen also. Now, the illusion, if you would.

Wilfong was not optimistic about affecting the mob with the illusion he had in mind. To be sure, all around were far from conscious thought, speaking and acting only as an alien voice in their heads directed them; they would not see the trick nor appreciate the skill behind it. The Wizard wanted just one person to notice it and to be tricked into believing that it was for the larger purpose. Great skill with Magick did not necessarily mean great wisdom; the Enemy could not be all that wise if he allowed himself to be motivated solely by thoughts of revenge. He could be fooled therefore – perhaps only temporarily – by a superior Practitioner.

Had there been any *conscious* Atlanteans on the street at that moment, they might have become alarmed by the "fact" that there were now *two* Wilfongs in their midst. Wembly's illusion had re-created his colleague's image perfectly, right down to the mole on his right cheek. The good citizens of Atlantis might have been further alarmed by the second "Wilfong's" frantic signaling for their attention and pointing at thin air. Ordinarily, such behavior would have invited a visit by a City Guard and a number of embarrassing questions concerning one's state of mind. Since there none present able to summon law-enforcement, no alarm was raised.

The illusion did not go unnoticed by its intended target, however. The Wizard observed a lessening of "SC's" Spell of Compulsion by the blinking of eyes, the stuttering, and the expressions of confusion in those nearby. That was the opening he required, and he acted at once. He placed the tip of his right middle finger against his right temple – a variation of the gesture he had used against the agent of the Circle of Friends – and chanted:

> "There once was a crowd full of drowse,
> Who blocked the door of the book-house.
> They are guided from afar
> By one who's a dark star.
> Oh, Wynot, those sleepers arouse!"

For good measure, he repeated the chant twice more, as much due to the larger number of subjects involved as due to a desire to strengthen its intensity. In the face of a foe with unknown but formidable powers, he was not about to take any chance with weak Spells. If "SC" hoped to renew control over his puppets, he hoped in vain; Wilfong's Spell included a powerful block against further attempts at compulsion. The Enemy could, of course, recruit a new group on which to work his will; but the Wizard reasoned that, once his presence had been discovered, he would slink away to lick his wounds.

And that is exactly what happened. The final repetition of his Spell completed, Wilfong stole a glance at "SC's" position. The illusion Wembly had created was still there, still gesticulating wildly, but the shimmering of the air was not. No trace of the puppet-master remained anywhere in the vicinity.

Meanwhile, the Atlanteans had shaken off the last vestiges of their compulsion. As they focused on their current surroundings, they expressed amazement at realizing where they were, and many loud voices demanded to know (from no one in particular) how they had come to be in this place. The next reaction was shock at learning how many others were in the same predicament. Timon, the wharf-rat who had been gripping Wilfong's shoulder, looked first at the Wizard's grim features, then at the offending hand, and released his hold with a look of embarrassment.

"Gods above! Sorry I am, buddy. Say, Colxor the teacher ain't you? I thought so. Anyways, where I was goin' I must not've been watchin.' Nothin' I don't remember."

"That's quite all right. There was no harm done."

"Uh, right. Well, a job I got to get to. Xenox you protect."

The wharf-rat pivoted and tromped off in the direction of the harbor. His fellow demonstrators also began to disperse, only barely avoiding eye contact with each other. None took particular notice of Wilfong, who remained in place and on guard until the crowd had completely vanished. In a matter of minutes, the street was deserted, and an eerie silence descended. The Wizard gave a final sweeping glance around; satisfied that the danger had passed, he relaxed visibly.

-- Is 'SC' gone, Wilfong?

-- Yes. But we haven't seen the last of him.

-- But why did he choose the Library as a battleground?

-- I can only speculate, Wembly. He probably didn't want me to enter the Library because there *is* a clue to his identity contained in one of your books.

-- Well, I'll have all of the books ready for your inspection by the time you come up. Luckily, the limit of six books per patron doesn't apply to me. You'll have free access to everything I've gathered.

As Wilfong approached the ornately carved main entrance to the Library with its hawk motif (the hawk representing Caxeot, the patron of learning), a sudden gust of wind came up, blowing debris before it. One piece of debris was a scrap of papyrus, and it struck the Wizard full in the face. Moreover, it was still wet from the earlier torrential rain and made a squishing sound when it hit. He suppressed the desire to curse the scrap roundly, ripped it away from his face, and tossed it aside. He had not taken more than two steps when the wind picked the scrap up and sent it flying in his direction. It hit him square on the back of his head and clung there. Now, he did curse, consigning both the papyrus and the wind to the deepest, darkest corner of the Underworld which was the domain of Oconoc the Final Judge, where eternal boredom reigned). He cast it away again – only to watch it twist about in a double loop and swoop toward him.

His suspicions raised, Wilfong seized the scrap with both hands and examined it carefully. To his great chagrin, there was inscribed upon it a two-line message in "SC's" hand. Though there was no addressee indicated, the Wizard instinctively knew the message was meant for his eyes alone. The words read:

> "Question: how many Wizards does it take
> to light a candle?
> "Answer: all of them, if they follow
> Wynot's teachings."

So, Wilfong thought bitterly, *a slap in the face, both literally and figuratively. 'SC' seems intent on provoking me into some sort of rash response. I'll respond, all right, and he'll live to regret he ever threw this challenge at me.*

On a hunch, he re-examined the message for some hidden clue to the Enemy's place of origin but found nothing in that respect. Yet, there was one glaring anomaly; some of the characters were larger than the others. One who spent a lifetime immersed in language noticed such things. When he mentally separated the large characters from the small, he discovered a message-within-a-message. The hidden one read:

> "To Zarel – to Hell."

THE SIXTH CASTING

THE WIZARD AT LARGE

Never one to waste time, Wilfong had selected the Festival of Caxeot to travel to Zarel in search of either Wynot or the reason for "SC's" antagonism toward him. The Festival, which lasted three days, celebrated that god's part in the Creation of the world and his special patronage of the arts and sciences. The usual civil and religious pageantry took place: parades (chiefly of a martial sort); speeches (of a nationalistic bent); rituals of spiritual renewal and re-dedication of temples; more speeches; food and drink (paid for out of royal and temple coffers); contests of skill (mostly of an athletic nature); and yet more speeches. The finale was the Bull Game. The bull was sacred to Atlantis; its fierce image had been carved into every public building in the Kingdom and, in the First Ring, a colossal statue of the animal stood before the Royal Palace as a symbol of its importance to the civil power. During the Bull Game, a prime specimen was first contested by a score of young, naked men and women in a mock battle; the youths leaped over the bull (or tried to), goading it to fury. After the beast had been worn out, it was then sacrificed to the gods in order to ensure Atlantis' prosperity.

The Wizard tried to avoid participating in these events whenever he could and seized on any excuse he could legitimately present. In the current instance, he had sent a message to his Headmaster at the School, begging off joining the School's staff in a group demonstration of piety on the grounds that he had caught a chill from the recent downpour. As a member of the Order of Wynot, he followed a higher teaching; Wynot had spoken out against the folly of putting one's trust in the supernatural and in favor of taking the surer path of putting it in one's own skills for survival and well-being. He had to pay lip service, of course, to Atlantis' gods where necessary but kept the practice to a bare minimum. The idea of living a lie irked him no end, and he would rather have swum the breadth of the Great Western Ocean with blocks of granite around his waist than appear to be full of religious fervor. Since all public functions – and many private ones, including his School – were suspended during festivals to the gods, he had no reason to worry about unexplained absences.

His biggest concern was to keep Murkol moving in the right direction. The Zarelor had greeted the news of the return to his native land with a rapidly-changing string of emotions. First, bewilderment over the suddenness of the trip; then anxiety – he had left under a cloud of enmity and suspicion, and he harbored no great desire to go back, despite the fact that, everywhere else in the Known World, he was a fish out of water – and finally, frustration when his master declared that the stay would be an indefinite one which meant re-packing the trunk he had meticulously packed a few days ago, a time-consuming task at best and a bloody nuisance at worst (although he dared not voice that opinion aloud!). It did not help his frame of mind to have the Wizard look over his shoulder to make certain every useful thing was included in the packing. Although he had done this dozens of times, his master had never been this fastidious as he was this time. What was so different about this trip?

If Wilfong was conscious of Murkol's concerns over the packing, he did not show it. In fact, he had many other matters on his mind. For one, the mysterious Enemy had made a second reference to Zarel, a land which lay far inland from the western coast of the Great Western Ocean and nuzzled the tip of a large, gourd-shaped lake. Why Zarel and not some other land more hospitable was unclear; there was hardly anything about the place which might induce a civilized person to visit it. It was so far off the beaten path that no other Atlantean than Wilfong had ever ventured there; a handful of traders had dealt with people who had traveled to Zarel, and the tales told had not been encouraging. The only reference Wynot had ever made to it concerned the local penchant for complete indifference toward other human beings, and even that had been in passing, a footnote to a lecture the Compleat Sorcerer had delivered on social relations.

And yet, it appeared that an important clue to Wynot's whereabouts might be found there. Of course, "SC" could have been lying through his teeth about the whole matter in order to prevent any of Wynot's disciples from joining him. No matter that the Enemy meant to destroy his Master and his Order, Wilfong was honor-bound to pursue his search wherever it took him, even though he might have to face great personal dangers alone. The need to know overrode all else.

For another thing, the Enemy had evidenced considerable power. What level of Magick he occupied was both problematical and crucial. The Wizard was sure of future confrontations, and it would certainly help if one knew with whom and with what one was dealing. He suspected that "SC" was not about to volunteer that information; he would have to learn by trial and error, all the while fending off one attack after another. He had one slight advantage in that respect, however. From the wording of the messages he had received from "SC," he deduced that the fellow knew many of the Spells of the Order (whether as well as Wilfong was an entirely different matter) and thus could be neutralized by the appropriate counter-Spells familiar to the Wizard. The business before the Library had been a case in point; the attack had been countered handily.

For a third thing, the research in the Library had been mainly a waste of time. Wembly had gathered up all of the foreign-language grammars available – one each for Atlantis' major trading partners – and Wilfong had inspected each one in detail. The Wizard already had a working knowledge of most of the materials; as a teacher of language and as a frequenter of the wharves where all manner of languages was spoken, he could hardly be ignorant on the subject. Nothing he had ever read came near to what language was in the message; whatever language "SC" had been born to, it was not one used in the Known World. Apparently, he had slapped together Atlantean words in the same fashion that he did in his native expressions. Which meant that his origins were as mysterious as Wynot's. Were they both perhaps from the same land?

Though the research had been futile, there was one oddity about the original message which had jumped out at Wilfong like a wild beast when it had been cornered – the spelling of the Compleat Sorcerer's name. At first, he had believed that the Enemy was simply a terrible speller, due to his unfamiliarity with Atlantean. Now that the Wizard had pondered the matter for a while, he realized that that had not been the case. The way "Wynot" had been spelled represented a homonym of another word and thus was a double entendre; moreover, it was a crude slur, suggesting that Wynot was a pedophile. "SC" had much to answer for – if and when Wilfong caught up to him – and this "misspelling" would be high on the "bill of indictment."

After the morning meal of the first day of the Festival of Caxeot, while Murkol cleaned the dishes, Wilfong retired to his *sanctum sanctorum* in order to meditate. So much was on his mind, however, that he could not let go of the mundane world and open up to the Invisible World. Too many extraneous notions kept intruding. In these cases, he would have walked to the Bath in the Third Ring and let the hot steam clear both the pores of his skin and his brain cells. But, all of the Baths were closed for the Festival, and he had no desire to take a long and aimless walk which would give someone a reason to ask him why he wasn't participating in the festivities. Thus, he was relegated to puttering around until such time as Murkol completed his chores and they could then depart for Zarel.

*   *   *

Contrary to popular opinion, Practitioners did not appear or disappear in a puff of smoke reeking of brimstone. Some did, if only to annoy people. Older accounts than this writer has been relying on have said there was a pre-Persecution Practitioner by the name of Oz, who came and went in such an ostentatious (and annoying) manner that no one had to *look* in his direction to know that he was present. In time, he became known as "Oz Shabazz," that is to say, "Oz the Smelly One." Most Practitioners, if they used Magick to travel around, did so in a manner very inconspicuous. There were two advantages of this: one, it gave the Practitioner more credibility if he was seen to use his powers with – and the reader will excuse the pun – an air of confidence rather than of pungency; and two, it gave him more control of a situation if he spent less time in puffery and more on his commission. Both of these reasons furthered one's reputation (and one's purse) immensely.

Wilfong the Wizard was the epitome of inconspicuousness. And, even if he were not, the technique he had learned in the Order would have accorded it to him in any case. It had just been Wynot's way, i.e. to *do* and not to make much ado. Whenever Wilfong used a Spell of Transition, the only side effect was a slight fuzziness in the air where he came and went; it appeared as if someone had set up a filmy veil, then removed it quickly.

Once the Spell had been completed, the Wizard sat down on his trunk and wiped perspiration from his face with a red cloth. Of all the Spells in his repertory, that which could transport him anywhere instantaneously required the greatest amount of energy; and, despite his being a Level Thirteen in the Order, none of his skill came without a price. In the present case, the price was sheer fatigue, particularly since he had not only himself to transport but also another person and his luggage. The catching of his breath was the least of his concerns, however. He needed to take his bearings.

For all practical purposes, the land of Zarel was a swamp, running to all the points of the compass. It had been formed as a "marriage of convenience" between the great lake to the north and the endless plain to the south and west. Thick clumps of tough, tall, wide-bladed grass grew upon islands of (relatively) dry land, while equally tough, woody reeds choked the watery portions. Tiny rivulets meandered in haphazard fashion, at times paralleling each other, at others colliding with each other to form eddies and whirlpools. Upon the grassy knolls and in the waterways, a vast variety of insects, reptiles, fish, birds, and small mammals strove and competed for survival; seldom an hour passed that did not contain some life-or-death drama played out in earnest – and in finality. Surrounding and permeating the whole was the *smell*, the all-too-familiar odor of death and decay. Although the land was called "Zarel" (after some warrior-type) by the local inhabitants, the stench gave it its unofficial name – "Chi-kawgo," the stinking swamp.

In this monotonous expanse of greenery – from the darker hues of the knoll grasses to the paler hues of the reeds to the variegated patterns of thick layers of algae upon the more turgid pools of water – only one bit of contrasting color existed to offset the dreariness. The flora, known locally as the *li-lak* bush, was a hardy growth which held its own against the greater swamp vegetation; a cluster of purple blooms crowned it with stubborn pride. The *li-lak* provided the raw material for the only two industries in Zarel, one legitimate, the other not. The tough fibers of the woody portion of the bush were used to manufacture a primitive cloth for apparel and shelter; many Zarelor farmed it while others gathered the wild variety. The purple blooms were hallucinogenic in nature when chewed and was thus sold to whoever was foolish enough to become addicted to it.

That Zarel was fit for human habitation at all was much to be wondered. Most people, given a choice in the matter, might have selected some more pleasant place in which to be born/live. By their nature, however, Zarelor were suited to this land, for they were a hard-headed – and hard-hearted – lot, and little fazed them, save each other. Moreover, since no one else wanted this stinking swamp (even as spoils of war), they were content to live there and enjoy utter and complete peace. The population numbered four hundred, half of them living in scattered clan-like communities, the other half in the sole city – if Zarelon could be dignified by that term – located on a particularly large knoll in the northern part of the territory.

So as not to attract undue attention, Wilfong had transited himself and Murkol a full *stadium* from Zarelon, a tactic which had both its advantages and its disadvantages. The chief plus was that the pair had the opportunity to spy out the land and learn if anyone was around who might remember them from the Wizard's previous visit; the chief minus was that they had to walk to the city, through the tough grasses and over hidden sinkholes, a difficult task even for the average Zarelor (who was, when all was said and done, a hulking brute akin to a beast of burden) and a test of one's agility for all other mortals. Wilfong turned to Murkol to direct him to pick up the trunk and come along, but no reply was received.

The servant was nowhere to be seen – at least, not at once. Instead, the Wizard allowed himself to be guided by a series of soft moans. He found Murkol huddled in the fetal position behind the trunk, clutching at his belly. The man's normally swarthy face was noticeably paler. Wilfong shook his head ruefully; he had forgotten the effect transitioning had on Zarelor. Still, there was nothing he could do about Murkol's predicament except wait until the cramping subsided.

While he waited, he extended his senses to reconnoiter the area. Presently, he discovered that, after a fashion, he and Murkol were not alone in this district and that, after a fashion, they were. At the side of what passed for a road in Zarel – actually a wide track where the grass had been beaten down by the continuous passage of humans and/or beasts – two Zarelor sat. Both were staring at him. Yet, whether they were *seeing* him was a moot point. The stupefied expressions on their faces and the purple stains around their lips spoke eloquently of the incapacity to recognize the things of this world. For all they knew, the pale-skinned, slightly-built stranger who had suddenly appeared before them out of thin air was merely part of the *li-lak*-induced state of intoxication. The Wizard thus paid the pair little heed; he would have no trouble from them for several hours, by which time he hoped to be safely behind Zarelon's walls.

After a short while, Murkol ceased his moaning, clumsily scrambled to his feet, and apologized profusely for his lack of ability. Wilfong waved his humility aside and ordered him to pick up the trunk. Because their environment had made them a hardy race, Zarelor had great strength. Murkol heaved on the chest and threw it up on his shoulder with one swift movement. With practiced ease, he matched his master's pace along the road.

The road was more suitable for a drunken snake than for any higher life form. It seemed to take forever to maneuver around *li-lak* bushes, sinkholes, and exceptionally large clumps of grass, and Wilfong had to halt after a quarter of a *stadium* to catch his breath and to re-orient himself. He had seen no other sentient creatures so far, but he had *heard* plenty of *non*-sentient ones as they hissed and chirped and barked and clicked out warnings to the trespassers. His only fear, however, was to be set upon before he had a chance to cast a Spell of Protection, whether the attacker was sentient or not.

A few minutes after resuming the march, the Wizard met a third Zarelor on the road, traveling in the opposite direction. Moreover, he was riding a large, shaggy-haired quadruped – locally known as a *bofflu* –which was native to the plains to the west of Zarel and served as both transportation and cargo-carrier. The rider halted only because his way was blocked by the pedestrians, and he stared long and hard at the strangers, particularly the non-Zarelor. It was clear that he had never before seen a smaller human being with pale skin and thick curly hair and beard, and he was trying to make up his mind as to his best course of action. Since Zarelor were notoriously rude, he might have been expected to push the newcomers aside and continue on his way. Yet, he was uncertain how this odd-looking fellow would react, and so caution won the day.

For his part, Wilfong stared only because he always had trouble distinguishing between individual Zarelor. Though he hated to admit it, because the admission seemed chauvinistic, all Zarelor looked alike to him, and he had to force himself not to turn around to assure himself that Murkol was still behind him.

For a long moment, both parties engaged in a staring match, yielding neither courtesy nor the right-of-way. The Wizard chose to concentrate on a tattoo on the rider's left cheek, a stylized image of a reptile, and tried to remember which clan it represented. There weren't all that many clans in Zarel, due to a small population base; but it was important to know which was which, since the knowledge dictated how to deal with each one. In the present instance, the Serpent Clan was the rudest of the rude, and one provoked its members at one's own risk. Nevertheless, Wilfong was determined not to back down from a country bumpkin.

It fell to Murkol then to break the impasse, since he was more versed in the local customs. He pushed past his master and performed the traditional greeting ritual by pinching his nose with thumb and index finger.

"I give greetings, friend," he intoned in Zarelot, the sounds of which imitated boulders colliding with each other.

Apprehension in the rider gave way to formality, and he pinched his own nose.

"I give greetings, friend. Be you from afar?"

"We be. I return to the district of my birth and bring a friend to help me celebrate my homecoming."

The rider peered once more at the Atlantean. His facial expression left no doubt that he thought the weird-looking stranger was not any sort of a "friend." The Wizard smiled broadly and insincerely. He would rather move on and be in Zarelon before nightfall than stand in the middle of a swamp exchanging starchy formalities with this lout whose sincerity matched his own.

"I give greetings, friend," the rider acknowledged Wilfong at last, listlessly.

"I greetings give, friend," the Wizard responded in clumsy Zarelot. "We a long journey are make and your animal to hire wish."

He did not see Murkol wince in chagrin, but he did note the scowl of unabashed hostility of the other. Asking a Zarelor for anything of a material nature was akin to making an insult; this race simply did not part with their possessions to anyone outside of their clan. And the rider saw no clansmen here. Why, the stranger's Zarelor companion had no tattoo on his cheek at all and was undoubtedly an outlaw of some sort! The offer of payment was tempting, of course, since there were few opportunities for money-making in this land, and one took advantage of a situation when it arose. On the other hand, how could he be sure that his *bofflu* would be returned to him? How could he be sure that the strangers would not sell the beast to someone else, someone not of his clan, for a greater profit? It was truly a conflict of interests at work here. In the end, the longer-term interest prevailed.

"Nay, friends, the beast be not available. I have need of it myself. Fare well, friends."

Without further ado, the rider dug his heel into the side of the *bofflu*. The animal, which had been happily munching away on the grass, bawled briefly in annoyance but dutifully shuffled forward, brushing aside the pedestrians in its path. Wilfong was nearly knocked into a sinkhole and had to perform a one-legged dance to avoid an unintentional bath. When he had recovered his wits and his equilibrium, he glared at the retreating figure for all of three heartbeats. Though he had known what to expect from Zarelor in general, he still was not of a mind to be treated rudely by any of them.

The *Chronicles* of Xorzist the Elder in which the most reliable account of Wynot the Wise could be found also included a number of parables allegedly told by the Compleat Sorcerer. "Allegedly," because, unlike other materials, these parables had not been set down in written form before Xorzist's time but had simply been passed on by word of mouth from one generation of the Clutch to the next. The Master Historian took pains, of course, to point out that these stories were only hear-say but set them down in coherent form as part of the "official" record.

One of these parables concerned a boy who had been in the habit of blaming others for errors he himself had committed. No matter the situation, this boy had a ready excuse to deny responsibility; more often than not, he relied on the notion that "evil spirits made me do it." Then, one day, he committed a deed so egregious that even his ingenuity could not satisfy everyone's suspicion. Caught in a glaring contradiction, he was whipped out of town. The moral of the tale, according to Wynot, was that "spirits" tended to go to one's head and that excessive use of them resulted in a Great Lie.

This writer has stated emphatically that Wilfong the Wizard was the Compleat Sorcerer's greatest disciple. As such, it was to be supposed that he would follow his master's teachings to the letter. And he did, as faithfully as he could. He was still a human being, however, not a god, and he was guilty on occasion of exhibiting those foibles which all of humankind possessed; and, while he might be more adept at keeping those foibles at bay, he was not always successful. "Evil spirits" might take him and cause him to do that which he would not otherwise do if he were more in control of himself.

Provoked by the rudeness of another and fueled by a desire for a safe and speedy end to his travels, the Wizard forgot himself and decided to work his will on the rude individual. Thus, he made the gesture relevant to casting a Spell of Compulsion and chanted:

> "There once was a lout from Zarel,
>> Who mistreated a lone infidel.
>>> His beast he does keep
>>> And keep me from sleep.
>> Oh, Wynot, this fellow compel!"

A sharp bark from the rider halted the *bofflu* abruptly in its tracks, and the animal stood in the middle of the road swaying back and forth. Additional digs into its side forced it to reverse course and plod back to the spot where Wilfong and Murkol stood, the one with ill-disguised impatience, the other with ill-disguised dumb-foundedness. The rider slid off the beast, all smiles and friendliness, and held out the reins to the Atlantean.

"The going rate be five *dalas* a day, friend," he spoke in a hollow voice.

"I thee *three* will give," Wilfong replied shrewdly.

"It be a deal."

Wilfong directed Murkol to pay the man. The latter reached into a pouch hanging at his waist and produced three large silver coins which featured a human head on one side and a *bofflu* on the other. He dropped them into the ex-rider's outstretched hand, and the man relinquished the reins to the Wizard. He began whistling some aimless tune, strode off down the road in his original direction, and disappeared into the distance.

Murkol watched in complete awe of his master's power. Wilfong had to nudge him in order to get his mind back on the business at hand. The Zarelor apologized for being such a dunce, tossed the trunk onto the back of the *bofflu* as easily as he might have laid down a tablecloth, clambered aboard himself, and lent the Wizard a helping hand. When Wilfong had settled himself (not an easy task, as he had ridden a *bofflu* only once before), Murkol gave the animal a swift kick and sent it trotting off toward Zarelon.

*   *   *

Symmetry seemed not to be in the Zarelo vocabulary. Or, if it was, it had no virtue. On the other hand, "haphazard" was, and it must have had virtue.

On his previous visit, Wilfong had thought he had entered some nightmare world where the abnormal was the rule, not the exception. Nothing appeared to have changed in the interim in his opinion; if anything, Zarelon looked even worse. From the outside, the city resembled any other urban area: a huddled mass of buildings set in the middle of nowhere, a beacon of order in the general chaos of Nature. This was mere illusion, invoked by the fact that the city lay behind a wall – actually a fence of closely spaced tree trunks trimmed of their branches – and no one could see the nightmare until one passed through the main gate. Then came vertigo....

Picture an architect under the influence of the *li-lak* blossom. His mind twisted and convoluted reality, and nothing was what it appeared to be. He drew his designs according to what he "saw," and the nightmare took its first shape. Street after street, building after building – the whole was less than a collection of blocks placed randomly on top of each other but more than a pile of rubble. Added to this was the equally distorted vision of him who planned the lay-out of the city itself. No street ran longer than two blocks and often ended in a cul-de-sac; no street ran parallel to another and often crossed it at the oddest angles; no street had standard dimensions and often widened or narrowed on the spur of the moment. In such a place, becoming lost and/or disoriented was not only a given but it was also an expectation.

Once inside the gate, the Wizard yielded to Murkol's familiarity of the place and allowed him to take charge of the expedition. The Zarelor had been city-bred and therefore knew the ins and outs as well as anyone. With instructions to "find the best inn in the city," Murkol unhesitatingly spurred the *bofflu* in the proper direction. To the Atlantean's mind, it was like traversing a maze in which there were no clues about the location of the exit; yet, Murkol unerringly maneuvered through a myriad of twists and turns.

No building had more than four stories (most had only two), but the irregular architecture gave the impression that they were all about to collapse with the least vibration and bury the unwary traveler under a ton of brick and wood. The Wizard would have preferred that Murkol keep to the center of the streets for safety's sake, but doing so would have blocked oncoming traffic and created undue problems, the least of which would be further endurance of Zarelo rudeness. Wilfong was overly conspicuous as matters stood, and he did not want both his appearance and his actions to draw attention.

On his previous visit, the Wizard had had no reliable guide. He had come to this land out of curiosity after hearing the amazing tales spun by the few traders to penetrate into the interior of this western continent. He had not expected to be enlightened in any significant way, but neither had he expected to be utterly disoriented. He had had to ask for directions constantly, a task made more difficult by his inexpert knowledge of Zarelot; most of the time, the directions were as confusing as the streets. As a consequence, he remained in the neighborhood of the main gate, never daring to venture too far into the depths of the city. Had it not been for this lack of confidence, he might never have met Murkol; for, during one of his enforced periods of inactivity, he chanced to observe a howling mob chasing the hapless fellow toward the gate in order to drive him out of the city. Out of a sense of fair play, the Wizard had cast a Spell of Confusion over the mob, causing it to disperse in all directions. The grateful Zarelor pledged "eternal shervishe azh a reward for shaving hizh mizherable life." Sometimes, Wilfong regretted having done so.

At length, the Zarelor halted the *bofflu* in front of a three-story building whose structure would (to any *sane* person, at least) be classified as "Early Disaster" but supposedly, to the average Zarelor, be the epitome of "deluxe accommodations." The odd angles and lop-sided projections which predominated in this "hotel" was enough to give anyone a severe case of the blind staggers; yet, Murkol was bubbling with joy for having a rich master who could afford this establishment. Wilfong stared at it dumbfoundedly and was instantly reminded of an urban renewal project he had had to endure in his Ring of the Metropolis – the "before" stage when the old had been razed to make way for the "after."

"This is it?" he asked disingenuously.

"Yesh, Mashter," Murkol replied with a gush, unable to keep the excitement out of his voice. "Thish izh de besht inn in all of Zarel. People from neighboring countriesh try to shtay here if dey can poshibly do sho whenever dey vizhit."

"I'd hate to see the *worst* inn in town," Wilfong muttered under his breath. In a louder voice: "Well, I certainly hope they have a vacancy. I wouldn't want to have to settle for 'second-best.'"

"We sould have no problem, Mashter. De tourisht sheazhon doezh not begin until neksht mond."

"Wonderful. Tell me, what'll we do with the *bofflu?* The Spell I cast will wear off soon, and the beast's owner will come looking for it – and for us."

"I will take it to de gate after we jeck into our room and releashe it. When itsh owner returnzh, he will be sho glad to shee it dat he will forget about ush."

"How resourceful of you, Murkol."

"Dank dee, Mashter. But, I have been doing dis short of ding all my life." He frowned suddenly. "It wazh what got me into trouble dat day we firsht met."

"Oh? I was never too clear on that point."

The Zarelor shifted his weight from one foot to the other in embarrassment, an unusual gesture since, to the more well-bred Atlantean mind, this race possessed no shame at all but behaved however they pleased with regard to the effect their acts had on others.

"Zarelor," Murkol said finally, "have a...cushtom of, uh, 'liberating' de pozheshons of rival clanzh and den re-shelling dem – shometimezh back to de shame people."

"Hmmm. And that day you got caught at it, eh?"

"Yesh. It wazh my firsht job in de daytime, and I did not take enough precausonzh."

"And what's to prevent you from re-selling the *bofflu*?"

"I have learned a new shet of ediksh from dee, Mashter. I have learned not to 'find' dings before dey are losht. And, in dy shervishe, I have food and selter. I do not need to shteal to earn money."

Thank the Cosmos for small favors! the Wizard marveled. *I've made a convert to the higher life. Now, if he'd only stayed* sober...

"I'm pleased to hear that, Murkol. I really am. Now, shall we see about a room?"

If the exterior of the inn gave the wary traveler reason to believe that it would collapse at any moment, the interior was sure to induce claustrophobia. The reception area was no larger than Wilfong's meager quarters in Atlantis; and it was dark and dingy, the only illumination being a single lantern dangling from the ceiling. Long shadows fell on the floor, hiding (partially) the fact that the planks of the floor were warped and, in some places, cracked and splintered. Moreover, the walls and ceiling did not form right angles – geometric perfection seemed not to be in great demand in this land – and they gave the room a closed-in feeling. The sole pieces of furniture were a long table and a stool in the far corner, and both pieces looked well-used. On the table, innumerable scraps of papyrus and several well-worn quills lay scattered. A potted *li-lak* bush in full bloom cowered in the near corner and appeared none too healthy; even so, the flower's slight odor penetrated the general mustiness of the place.

"Deluxe accommodations," indeed! Wilfong mused. *This hotel might be better suited to the wharf-rats of the Metropolis.*

The pair were alone in the reception area. The mess on the table suggested that the innkeeper (or his employee) had left in a hurry for an indefinite period of time. Wilfong, however, did not care to wait any longer than he had to and wanted to expedite matters.

"How do we get service around here?" he asked Murkol.

"We shignal for it, Mashter."

Whereupon the Zarelor stepped up to the table and thudded it with his huge fists several times. Seconds passed, and no response seemed imminent. Murkol banged the table again, now longer and louder. Presently, the expected service materialized in the form of a burly individual with a tattoo of a *bofflu* on his cheek. Except that he was shorter than most Zarelor, he might have been Murkol's twin brother. Also, he was not dressed in the *li-lak*-bark clothing worn by most of the locals but in something resembling cotton. The Wizard speculated that he had bartered for it with a trader from the coast of the Great Western Ocean, though what he had had to offer in exchange for such a luxury item, Wilfong couldn't begin to imagine.

The "concierge" gazed upon the newcomers – particularly the Atlantean – with the typical Zarelo expression, one he might use at discovering he had just stepped in something unsavory.

"I give greetings, friends," he murmured ceremoniously, though his face remain unchanged.

"We greetings give, friend," Wilfong shot back, his own demeanor just as rigid as the other's. "We a room seek."

"We have rooms," the concierge declared in a tone which suggested that he regretted the fact. "How long a stay do you plan?"

As long as it takes to get really sick of this hovel, Wilfong thought evilly, *say until sunrise.*

Aloud: "I not certain be. I a room for four nights will take. After that, who can say?"

Was it the Wizard's imagination, or did the concierge's face brighten just the slightest at the prospect of rooming a long-term guest?

"The rate be thirty *dalas* a night for a double."

"*Thirty?*" Murkol yelped. "That be a tourist-season rate, *friend.*" To Wilfong, he whispered: "He izh trying to jeat dee, Mashter."

"This correct be?" Wilfong demanded in his best outraged manner. "The tourist season *next* month begins. I the *off-season* rate want, or I my business elsewhere will take."

The concierge was torn between cupidity and loss of a prime customer. Perspiration formed on his forehead.

"Very well, friend. The rate be *ten dalas* a night. In advance."

Murkol dipped into the money pouch again and produced four gold coins which bore the same human head as the silver coins on the obverse side but a *li-lak* bush on the reverse. He plunked these on the table, all the while glaring nastily at the concierge. The latter deftly scooped up the coins and deposited them in a box underneath the table. Then he took up a fresh sheet of papyrus and a quill and looked at his new guests questioningly.

"Your names, friends?"

"Wilfong and Murkol," the Wizard replied dryly.

"Wil – wil-fon," the other struggled with the foreign name and wrote it out phonetically in the Zarelo script. He had no problem with Murkol's name. "And your home address?"

"Atlantis," Wilfong replied in deadpan.

The concierge peered at the Atlantean as if he believed he was being the butt of a colossal joke, then shrugged and wrote simply "a foreign land." Underneath the names, he inscribed the current date (in the Zarelo calendar) and the amount of money paid. At the top of the sheet, he set down another number. Along the bottom quarter of the sheet, he re-wrote all of the numerical information; he used the edge of the table as a makeshift knife, tore off the quarter section, and slid it across the table. The remainder of the sheet went into the box underneath. He then twisted around on his stool and selected a big iron key from a rack on the wall which held three score of keys. This was placed on top of the "receipt" with studied casualness.

"Room #41," he said in a monotone. "A fine view of the city. Fare well, friends."

Wilfong snatched up the key and the receipt and silently moved toward the stairway at one of the side walls. Murkol heaved the trunk onto his shoulder and fell into step.

The Wizard nearly changed his mind about staying at this inn the instant he laid eyes on the stairs. They were the ricketiest structure he had ever had the displeasure to see. The steps were as cracked and splintered as the floor boards, and the support posts appeared worm-eaten. Perhaps they would support his weight as slight as he was. But Murkol with the trunk on his shoulder? Unthinkable! Yet, he cared not to give the concierge the satisfaction of thinking that his "deluxe accommodations" were too much for the foreigner. He swallowed hard, gingerly negotiated the first step, found that it would hold his weight, and proceeded to the next one. Each step gave off a creak guaranteed not to re-assure him. The still louder creaking behind him sent shivers up his spine, and he envisioned his and Murkol's falling through the boards and crashing to the floor below. One agonizing step after another, he finally arrived at the next floor. He had only two more flights of stairs to negotiate. And the creaking seemed to grow louder the further he ascended!

THE SEVENTH CASTING

THE WIZARD AT EASE

Given the circumstances, a "fine view of the city" was a gross exaggeration. A view of Zarelon, yes, but a "fine view" depended upon one's perspective.

The one advantage of having a room on the top floor was that the guest was spared having to look at the drab and dreary streets. The one disadvantage was that the guest had to look at the drab and dreary tops of the neighboring buildings, which included most of the city. And, if the topsy-turvy architecture as seen from the ground weren't enough to drive the rational mind to distraction, then seeing it from above was enough to drive it over the line between sanity and insanity. The odd angles and the unbalanced projections were more distinct up there, and they appeared even more treacherous. Belief that the structures would not tumble off their foundations was a testament either to human credulity or to a sense of the perverse.

Wilfong peered out the tiny, grimy window of his "deluxe accommodations" and was inclined to favor the latter explanation. If not for his habit of inspecting any temporary lodgings for any hidden flaws, he might not have had any reason to go near the window at all. A curious sight had drawn his attention there, and he found himself staring at it in horrified fascination.

While the *bofflu* was the largest species of fauna to be found in Zarel, it was not indigenous to the "stinking swamp." That dubious honor went to a winged thing the natives called a *bozzid*. It possessed an oddly-jointed neck, a large, hooked beak, and a wing span of nearly three meters. A carrion-eater, the *bozzid* was reputed to be able to detect dying animals at a height of three hundred meters, whereupon it circled the hapless creatures until they finally expired and then dived to the ground to feed at its leisure. Ordinarily, it inhabited the more barren areas where mortality rates were high.

The Wizard thus was greatly surprised – and greatly disconcerted – to spot several *bozzids* circling high above Zarelon and more of them perched on the ungainly projections of the buildings. He wondered why their presence was tolerated since they lent an ill reputation to the city (on top of its other one!); even if they were acting as unofficial (and grisly) "garbage collectors," still no one should want to be reminded of the more primitive aspects of the natural world, particularly if they were sitting on one's window sill!

He might have watched the flock for the rest of the day had not Murkol collided into him. Whereas he longed for the orderliness of his own apartment where the thought of imminent collapse was not uppermost in his mind, the Zarelor had exuded ecstasy at his "deluxe accommodations" and spent the first few minutes after their arrival touching every object in the room with reverence and tenderness and not watching where he was going. The Atlantean toppled backwards toward the far wall and struggled to stay on his feet. He gave Murkol a glare of disapproval.

"Forgivesht me, Mashter!" the huge man whined. "I wazh sho abshorbed by my shurroundingzh dat I forgot why I am here."

"How could anyone possibly be 'absorbed' by...*this*?" He swept his hand in a broad arc to encompass the room. "I'd use the word 'appalled.'"

The room to which they had been assigned – located in one of the odd corners of the inn – was scarcely larger than the Wizard's kitchen in Atlantis, though it was billed as one of the "VIP" rooms. It might have made even a Hyperborean ill at ease. Straw-filled mats served as beds, covered by thin, moth-eaten blankets. The only real furniture consisted of a low-legged wooden table whose legs were warped from excessive exposure to humid weather and two wooden stools of differing heights. Illumination was provided by a thick, greasy-looking red candle on the table. The room was clean, however, though Wilfong had half-expected it to be knee-deep in dirt and litter.

"How cansht dou shay dat, Mashter?" Murkol protested. "Look! *Fres* shtraw in de bedzh. And an ekshtra-larche candle. At home, we were lucky to have eider shtraw or candle."

"How utterly depressing!" the Wizard muttered under his breath. Aloud: "Well, let's not be gadding about. Unpack tomorrow's clothing."

The Zarelor snapped open the trunk and began removing the two top layers of clothing. One pile for Wilfong was placed on one of the mats, and a second pile for himself on the other. He hummed tunelessly as he worked.

In the meantime, Wilfong checked on the condition of his books of Magick. Riding on that *bofflu* had been exceedingly rough, and he worried that his older books might have been shaken to pieces. To the uninitiated, it might have seemed strange that a Master Practitioner still relied on the written word, and stranger still that he should carry it about with him on his travels. There was a simple explanation, one which contained an important lesson for the aspiring Practitioner. Great Masters of Magick did not become great by flinging words and phrases about in random fashion; rather, they carefully constructed their Spells in order to create the maximum amount of Magickal force. Often, a phrase or a sentence had multiple meanings, and the skillful student attempted to glean them all. The disciples of Wynot the Wise in particular had been taught not to stop learning because their *formal* training had been completed, but to re-read and meditate throughout one's life. As the Compleat Sorcerer's premiere student, Wilfong had taken this maxim to heart and so studied his master's writings repeatedly in a never-ending search for new insights.

Also to the uninitiated, it might have seemed contradictory that the books appeared to be a large and juicy collection of pornography, the sort that invariably found its way into any civilization where public morals clashed with private desires. The Wizard had, of course, cast a Spell of Illusion over his books, not only to protect them from unwitting eyes but also to protect unwitting eyes from *them*. Most of the Spells were extremely potent; in the hands of the untutored, they could wreak unimaginable havoc upon the user and anyone else in his vicinity. Even a cursory glance could determine if a Spell was still in force. Wilfong stacked the books on the rickety table – gingerly – for future reference.

He turned to speak to Murkol, only to discover the Zarelor staring intently out the window. He shifted his own attention and, to his great shock and discomfort, observed a most evil-looking *bozzid* perched on the sill outside. More alarming was Murkol's making clicking noises at it as if it were his pet. Far from being fearful of the human presence, the bird sat there placidly and gazed at its audience with complete indifference.

"Uh, Murkol," the Wizard asked quietly, "is that a wise thing to do? Aren't you afraid it'll try to attack you?"

"Oh, no, Mashter. *Bozzids* never attack humanzh – live onezh, anyway. And shometimezh, we domeshticate dem and train dem azh guardzh."

"*Guards!?!* Most queer and strange!"

"I only wis I had shome *rotsh* to feed it."

The Atlantean conjured up an image of the Zarelo species of rodent, a furry, half-meter-long creature which dieted mostly on grain and occasionally on insects and smaller mammals, and shuddered.

"Personally, I'm glad we don't. But speaking of eating, does this, uh, establishment serve food?"

"Yesh, Mashter, de finesht cuizhine in de shity, azh dou mightesht ekshpect from itsh reputason."

Wilfong refrained from making a caustic comment.

"Uh-huh. Any dish in particular?"

"All de dishezh here are ekshellent, but de inn izh noted for itsh jeezhe."

"Well, we must sample some then. You can finish unpacking later. I'm famished."

Before he exited the room, Wilfong chanced to glance over his shoulder. The *bozzid* was still on the sill, still grimly eyeing the humans. Once, it flapped its wings, and the Wizard hoped it was about to fly away. Unfortunately, the creature was merely shifting its weight to gain a better purchase on its new-found roost. Wilfong shuddered again. He prayed that this was not some sort of *omen*...

Once again, they found the lobby empty. Wilfong indicated that he wanted to place a wake-up call for the next morning. Without hesitation, Murkol moved toward the table and pounded on it vigorously; he counted silently to thirty (the Wizard could see his lips moving) and pounded a second time. Right on cue, the concierge emerged from the back room, looking as bored as ever. He peered at the guests blankly.

"I about a wake-up call ask, friend," Wilfong stated in a monotone.

"A wake-up call be issued to all guests at the sixth hour. It be the custom in Zarel," he added in the tone an adult takes with a backward child.

"I you thank, friend," the Atlantean responded in a barely civil voice. "Now, the dining room open be?"

"Yes, until the first bell."

"Excellent. Which way?"

The concierge gestured vaguely in the direction from which he had come. Wilfong nodded curtly and strode off, wondering idly why the fellow chose to spend his time in the dining room instead of tending to business.

If the Wizard had expected to see anything other than the usual Zarelo clutter in the dining room, his expectations were quickly dashed the moment he set foot in it. Firstly, it was crowded – and not just because of the number of people in it. Though the facility was spacious (by local standards), it had been furnished for a room twice its size. Tables and chairs of all sizes and styles (mixed, of course) had been jammed together like lily pads in a pond; there was barely enough space for a body to pass between them. Wilfong marveled at the Zarelo preference for making oneself uncomfortable. The odd sizes of the furniture required one to fold up like a tent in order to sit down. He had little difficulty in that regard; at a height of a meter-and-and-three-quarters, he could squeeze in at any table. Zarelor, on the other hand, had either to hunch over their plates or to loom above them.

Secondly, the noise was horrendous. Talking, cursing, shouting, belching, and passing gas could be heard, all at once and all at high volume. Wilfong was put in mind of the hog pens he had once visited in a field outside of the Metropolis during slopping time. Added to the human sounds were the rattle and clatter of tableware and utensils, the scraping of chairs and tables as they were pushed about by careless diners, and the creaking of furniture being tested to the limits of their endurance. The cacophony was entirely nerve-wracking.

And thirdly, if all of the above were not sufficiently distressing to the cultured mind, there were the odors – food odors, body odors, and the general mustiness which seemed to be a permanent fixture in all Zarelo buildings, commingling freely and heavily to assault the olfactory nerve with the force of an avalanche. Not even Lymatan's stank this bad on its worst days!

The whole was enough to spoil the Wizard's appetite. If not for the growling of his stomach, he might have been tempted to turn about and flee incontinently.

Judging by the size of the crowd, he could have sworn that the whole of the city were taking their dinners here. They all couldn't be guests at the hotel – there weren't that many rooms. Therefore, the majority were city residents taking advantage of the "finest cuisine in the city." Yet, he did spy a just-vacated table, albeit on the far side of the room. Murkol saw it at the same time and launched himself toward it like a herd of hungry *bofflu*.

The Zarelor pushed and shoved and squeezed and pirouetted through the clutter with practiced ease, eliciting a host of gripes, curses, and half-veiled threats from those whom he accidentally – and not-so-accidentally – jostled. The Wizard followed in his wake like a piece of flotsam in the undertow of a large ship, noting that Murkol preferred to take the shortest route possible rather than zig-zagging through the melee, even if it meant incurring undying enmity from this rough-and-tumble bunch. He had seen the much smaller Hamilton do this at Lymatan's, almost as if daring someone to take exception to his tactics. Apparently, this sort of behavior was the norm here, for verbal repartees were as far as anyone was willing to go.

The pair arrived at the targeted table a scant second before another party approaching from an oblique angle. Murkol seized a chair, thus staking his claim on the territory, and stared defiantly at the also-ran. The latter glared back for a few seconds, then shrugged and pushed off in search of another opening. Murkol waved to his master to be seated. Wilfong did not hesitate.

"Tell me, Murkol," he murmured as soon as he had caught his breath, "would you have fought that fellow over this table?"

"Oh, no, Mashter. While it may sheem dat we Zarelor are very warlike, we do not akshually fight all dat much. At leasht, not over trivialzh shuj azh sheating arranchements. And *never* in Zarelon."

"Why not?"

"Azh dou knowesht, we are divided into clanzh. Each clan hazh itsh own territory, and often dishputesh arizhe which cannot be shettled by negosiason. Den we fight -- bitterly shometimezh. Long ago, however, Zarelon wazh declared 'neutral territory' for de shake of providing a shafe plashe for negosiason. If we do fight here, we do not have clan backing and musht shuffer any conshequenshezh alone."

"Speaking of clans, why haven't you got a tattoo on your cheek like everyone else?"

The Zarelor fell silent and drooped his head.

"Ah, but I'm prying into matters that don't concern me. Forgive me, Murkol."

"Dou dosht not have to apolochizhe, Mashter. It izh dy right to know everyding about dy shervantsh." He paused and took a deep breath. "My clan dishowned me. Dey shaid I wazh behaving...un-clan-like. De detailzh are unimportant. Dey forshed me to remove my tattoo and ran me off. Dat izh how I came to be in Zarelon in de firsht plashe, engaging in...criminal aktsh. I – I am a wordlesh creature, Mashter, and I am forjunate to have a good and kind mashter azh dou."

"Um, well, you're not as worthless as you think." He glanced around at the melee. "How do we get service here?"

He was not startled this time when Murkol began to hammer the frail-looking table with both fists. Obviously, there was only one way to gain attention in this land. Although he himself would have been loath to emulate Murkol, he supposed that the custom had its advantages, not the least of which was being heard over the general din.

Presently, a server sidled up to the table to take their order. The Wizard gasped in amazement to discover that it was the concierge. At least, he believed it was the concierge, since he had trouble telling Zarelor apart. The fellow was wearing the same clothing; on the other hand, it could have been the standard uniform. In any event, if it were the same person, doing double duty, it would explain why he was frequently absent from the "front desk." He still wore diffidence like a second face, peering at his new customers in studied boredom. He remained long enough to slap two dirty, dog-eared pieces of papyri before them and then was gone to tend to some other business.

Wilfong picked up his papyrus and examined it. It was less than a menu but more than a mere list. He wrinkled his nose at the grime on the sheet which adhered because of a film of grease. He quickly let it drop and eyed Murkol, who perused the bill of fare hungrily.

"I'm not familiar with these, uh, dishes, Murkol. I'll let you do the ordering."

"Dank dee, Mashter. I will get dee shomeding which will remind dee of Atlantish."

And what could that possibly be? the Wizard wondered. *I haven't seen or smelled anything even remotely resembling what I could order in even the* meanest *Atlantean inn.*

"Very good. I suppose we must catch the server's attention again in the, uh, usual manner?"

Murkol smiled broadly and thudded the table again. He was not alone in this task, for several other diners had acquired a desire for service. Scattered across the room, a half dozen table-beaters set up a nerve-wracking staccato which hammered the mind as well as the furniture. Nor did anyone cease his part of the beat until the server appeared at his table. Wilfong realized – when he could think at all over the steady drumming – that, in the event of these multiple "requests," one had to keep at it lest one be ignored altogether.

Eventually, the server re-appeared from the kitchen, bearing several trays expertly balanced on his arms. As he unloaded his burden and/or made inquiries, the racket diminished proportionately until the only pounder left was Murkol. Through all of this, the Wizard maintained a forced stoicism, calling upon his mental reserves to nullify the senses-numbing clamor (abetted by his rumbling stomach). When he had shed himself of his load of trays and taken more orders, the server pulled up at Wilfong's table and stared questioningly at the pair. Murkol and he exchanged the usual amenities, and the former pointed to two items on his menu. The other nodded, snatched up the menus, and steamed toward the kitchen. Wilfong was about to utter some pithy comment on the local version of "customer service" but was overwhelmed by a fresh round of table-beating. He grimaced in resignation and retreated within himself again.

After the space of what seemed like an hour, the server returned and carelessly plopped two grimy-looking wooden bowls upon the table, sloshing some of their contents in the process. The Wizard caught his breath at the sight; the dark yellowish liquid in his bowl had the appearance of freshly-churned butter and the aroma of freshly-laid dung. A wave of nausea passed over and through him, and he quickly muttered a Spell of Healing. Murkol expressed his usual concern over his master's distress.

"What izh de matter, Mashter? Art dou ill?"

"No," Wilfong lied, "just tired. I guess our trip took more out of me than I first thought." He peered at the yellow glop in the bowl. "What is this?"

"De shoup of de day – cream of *crot*. De *crot* izh a wild root which growzh in de dryer parts of Zarel. It izh one of de shpesaltiezh of de houshe."

Whereupon he seized his own bowl with both hands, raised it to his mouth, and slurped its contents down with great relish. The Wizard searched for a spoon or some other artifact of higher civilization and found none. Obviously, one was not needed in these circumstances. The protests of his stomach warred with the protests of his sensibilities, and his stomach won. He shook his head in resignation, took up his bowl, and sipped at the thick liquid. To his great surprise, it tasted better than it smelled; it was an artful blend of vegetables, cream, and a variety of herbs and spices. Immediately, he dispensed with his veneer of civilization and gulped greedily at the soup; however, he had not the stamina of Murkol, who had finished off his bowl at one draught, and required three swallows to consume this "first course." Such was his hunger that he had been able to put the clamor around him completely out of his mind.

No sooner had he downed the soup than the server returned, dropped a medium-sized platter on the table, and moved off toward other appointments. What he left behind were two pewter mugs (cracked) and a pitcher filled with a greenish, thin liquid and a brown lump of *something* the size of a human head. The latter appeared and felt like potter's clay; compared to *its* aroma, the cream of *crot* smelled like the finest perfume. Wilfong nearly gagged, his senses overriding temporarily the rational part of his brain. He looked weakly at Murkol for a description of this "course."

"Wine, Mashter," the Zarelor gestured at the pitcher, "made from a common flower hereaboutsh, de *dandlin*. It izh mosht potent. And here" – he pointed to the brown lump – "izh de jeezhe I told dee about. It izh made from de milk of de *bofflu*."

With both hands (Wilfong observed that knives were not required either), Murkol broke off two fist-sized chunks of cheese and placed one in front of his master. The latter wrinkled his nose in disgust; the distasteful odor seemed to increase in opposite proportion to its distance. Meanwhile, Murkol gleefully bit off a huge mouthful and chewed noisily; he also poured himself a large measure of the *dandlin* wine into their mugs and drained half of his at one draught. With a great effort, the Wizard broke off a small piece of the *bofflu* cheese and brought it up to his mouth.

Just as he was about to pop it in, he spied out of the corner of his eye a most incongruous sight: a bit of papyrus sticking out of the main mass of the lump! Disbelief spread rapidly across his face. He blinked several times and looked again. The thing was still there; he had not imagined it. He threw his morsel of cheese on the table and exclaimed:

"By Wynot's flame-red beard! What the devil is *that*?"

"Mashter!" Murkol cried out, dropping his own cheese. "What hazh upshet dee?"

"Is this the 'secret' of your excellent Zarelo cheese? Refuse in the vats?"

The Zarelor picked up the lump and eyed it carefully, his hairy ears twitching in surprise. He pulled the cheese apart with little finesse, scattering bits and pieces over the table and onto the floor, and extracted the papyrus, a smooth, clean product of superior workmanship, folded neatly in fourths. Inscribed on one section in a crabbed hand was Wilfong's name.

"Mashter! It izh a *meshache,* addreshed to dee!"

"*What?* Here, let me see!"

He snatched the papyrus out of Murkol's hand and glanced at the inscription. His heart sank at once. The handwriting was all too familiar. The nefarious "SC" had made contact in this far-off place!

Was it another taunt? A challenge to a duel? Or simply some annoying harangue in which the Enemy wallowed in self-pity and loathing for all that was decent? Whichever, the Wizard was most reluctant to read it. Tremulously, he unfolded the papyrus and read:

"To Wilfong the *phtrx*:

There once was a wizard from Earth,
Who knew not the how of his birth.
He's nothing but slime,
And his life is a crime.
And I will show him what he's worth.

Sinladen Crotchgod"

A storm gathered on the Wizard's face, and his features clouded over until they were a black void. Lightning flashed furiously from where his eyes used to be. A rumble of thunder issued from the region of his mouth. In the surrounding area, the air pressure dropped precipitously, and the temperature followed in its track. Wave after wave of unfettered force poured out of his very being and reverberated throughout the dining room. Eaters and non-eaters alike paused in their activities, shivered in fear, and craned their necks to see what was causing them so much discomfort. The storm expanded and passed through the walls of the inn and into the night. Outside, a *bofflu* bawled in sudden fright. The fury peaked in one gigantic blast as the Wizard roared out his rage and struck the table a board-splitting blow with both fists. The papyrus which contained the vile message instantly burst into flame, and its ashes scattered in all directions. The scent of sulfur hung thickly overhead. And, as quickly as it had materialized, the storm abated, and Wilfong relaxed.

Immediately, he noticed two things. The first was that all eyes were upon him. Whether they were seated or standing or had been moving around, every single Zarelor – even the diffident concierge/server – was glaring in a concerted show of extreme horror. What made the tableau so extraordinary was that most of this race tended to ignore disturbances if they could – unless the disturbances impinged upon them personally – and that their penchant for rudeness served to establish a social pecking order. That any of them – much less a whole roomful – should sit up and take notice of someone's temper tantrum (for that was what it had been) suggested that, here at least, the individual had overstepped the bounds of "social grace." No matter that the individual was a foreigner and thus could not be expected to understand local customs – this crowd was prepared to subject the transgressor to the highest level of humiliation possible.

Wilfong, quite aware of his status in Zarel, tried to make himself as small as possible. When that failed to halt the unrelenting and concentrated scrutiny, he switched gears and uttered a Spell of Forgetfulness:

> "There once was a crowd of Zarelor,
> Who were all full of the why for.
>   They just want to know
>   The reason for my show.
> Oh, Wynot, cause remembrance no more!"

In the twinkling of an eye, all faces went blank for a few seconds. Then the diners returned to their interrupted affairs. The Wizard breathed a sigh of relief.

The second thing he noticed was Murkol's absence. He gazed around the dining room anxiously – perhaps a futile gesture since he couldn't tell one Zarelor from another – but saw no sign of his servant. He frowned. The Spell he had just cast couldn't have caused the fellow to vanish; and, as far as he knew, his tantrum hadn't contained any Spells at all. So, where could Murkol be this time?

"Murkol," he called out softly. "Where are you? Can you hear me?"

"Here I am, Mashter," a small voice rose from the floor, followed by the Zarelor's head. His normally swarthy face was deathly pale. "I shcrambled under the table to get out of de way, jusht in cashe dou shaid shomeding dou shouldn't."

The Wizard blushed a deep scarlet.

"I *was* pretty awful, wasn't I? I do apologize for my behavior. I guess I still have a long way to go toward self-control. Of course, it's not every day I'm called a...*phtrx*."

"I never heard dat word before, Mashter." He resumed his seat. "What doezh it mean?"

"It's from a very archaic language. Some say the language was the forerunner of Atlantean. The word refers to, ah, one who suffers from incontinence. Whoever wrote that message did so in a most unflattering way. I could have chewed this table into sawdust." He saw the anxious look on Murkol's face and held up his hand in conciliation. "Don't worry. I'll behave myself from now on."

The Zarelor gazed at the table disconsolately. The cheese and the wine had gone the way of the offending papyrus – burnt to ashes. And a hint of brimstone lingered in the air.

"Sall I call for de neksht course, Mashter?"

"Only if you're still hungry. Personally, this little episode has ruined my appetite. I think I'll return to our room and meditate a while."

*　　*　　*

Wilfong lay flat on his back on one of the sleeping mats and was now focusing on the large candle squatting on the rickety table for his meditation exercise. After the outrageous episode downstairs, he required extraordinary physical and mental discipline in order to recoup his equipoise, and this position in his current state of mind was the only way to do it. Once he had settled in (or as settled as he was likely to get in this environment), he cleared his mind of all extraneous thoughts.

What had he learned since arriving in Zarel?

A good deal, actually, and the information was carefully filed away in various mental compartments for future reference. He had learned that the mysterious "SC" had either followed him to Zarel or gone on ahead in anticipation of his taking the bait. In the first instance, the Enemy was capable of tracking a Practitioner who had cast a Spell of Transition no matter the latter's destination. That was Level Ten ability which re-enforced the idea the Wizard had originally formed about the fellow.

In the second instance, and more ominous, "SC" was capable of some Level Thirteen material, the most intricate part of a Practitioner's training whereby he appeared to violate the laws of Nature and bend the Cosmos itself to his will. Placing one object inside of another, i.e. the papyrus in the cheese, without destroying the immediate surroundings in a cataclysmic explosion was a difficult and delicate operation, and only the most skilled Practitioner could accomplish it. Wilfong himself had performed the trick only sparingly, as there was little call for it; it was still a needful thing to know when nothing else in his repertoire would do. How far along into Level Thirteen the Enemy had progressed was mere speculation; perhaps the Wizard had but a slim edge or perhaps he had none at all. And perhaps "SC's" abilities had given him the courage and the confidence to embark upon his mad scheme.

One other piece of information Wilfong now had: a name. "SC" stood for "Sinladen Crotchgod." Whether it was a real name or just a pseudonym was unimportant; what *was* important was the linguistic clues the name could provide toward the discovery of the Enemy's true identity, his place of origin, and perhaps his motivations. Outwardly, one's name reflected one's environment; parentage, location, occupation, or physical description were all sources of names. Inwardly, however, one's name reflected one's personality, that is, how one perceived oneself. While no one had ever been able to choose his own birth name, one could always add to it or manipulate it in order to satisfy some inner longing. Sometimes the process occurred on the conscious level, sometimes on the subconscious level; however it occurred, the end product was similar – a name which fitted one's personality as a good pair of sandals fitted the foot.

"Sinladen Crotchgod" had selected, wittingly or otherwise, a name which reflected *his* inner self. In retrospect, that was how each member of the Order of Wynot selected his/her secret name, though each had followed a traditional pattern of choosing one which began with a "W" in honor of the Founder. Foreign as those names were to Atlantean sensibilities – not to mention the vocal cords! – they nevertheless singled out the member as someone special.

Atlantean beliefs had no concept of "sin," i.e. transgression against established codes of morality meriting divine punishment eternally in a place of torment. Atlantis did have a moral code, of course, handed down from one generation to the next; to violate any of its precepts invited immediate corporal punishment by the civil power. Theoretically, transgression was supposed to be dealt with by the gods in their own fashion, but no one in living memory had ever heard of such an instance. Except on religious holidays, the entire subject of morality was given little thought; then, the priests rattled on about one thing or another. The Wizard knew of other cultures which did entertain the notion of "sin"; and, like most of his colleagues, he considered those societies to be rather backward. Wherever this Sinladen Crotchgod called home, its populace apparently subscribed to the "eternal punishment" theory, and he had taken a name which suggested that he was full of "sin."

There were two ways to look at this odd name. First, the Enemy actually believed in its connotations; and it was reasonable to assume that he was rebelling against his nature and that, by succeeding, he would purge himself of his "sins." How destroying the Order of Wynot and its membership (and the Founder, if possible) fit into that scheme remained a mystery; but fit in it did, and Wilfong had to stop him at all costs. Or, second, "SC" was being entirely satirical and using this name as a psychological weapon to confuse and misdirect any who would oppose his scheme. By planting false clues, all information about him would be rendered suspect – a very clever tactic, indeed, one which the Wizard would not put past a foe who so far had played a devious game. Wilfong was more inclined to accept the second interpretation, especially in light of the second half of the name.

"Crotchgod," my foot, he mused. *Just whom does this fellow think he's kidding? There's nothing so dangerous as an enemy with a twisted sense of humor. That kind* never *plays by the rules, his or anyone else's.*

It was time to call in some "re-enforcements," and to file a Field Report with the Order's official Librarian, a task he viewed with extreme distaste.

In the main hall of the Library of Atlantis, consisting of mosaic tiles set in the floor, was a map of the Known World (and a few places on the fringes), accurately (as far as it was possible with the available data) depicting all the lands from the west coast of the Great Western Ocean to the east coast of the Great Inland Sea, from the Great Glacier forty-five degrees north of the equator to the Great Desert in the northern part of the southern continent. Much care was taken to update this colossal map as new information arrived periodically which involved tearing up whole sections of the floor and re-laying it with fresh colored tiles. Often, thanks to the Kingdom's ever-expanding trade, the "official" map became obsolete, sometimes only months after an update; in these cases, smaller, hand-painted maps were available on a rack at one wall of the hall, reproduced every year. These necessarily depicted only specific regions, and one had to consult them all in order to gain a full view of the whole world. The average researcher pragmatically requested one or two at a time, and even then he had to correlate them with the central map.

At the fringes of the Known World, details were obviously sketchy, and one had to employ a good deal of extrapolation. One such fringe area in Wilfong's time lay to the northeast, between the Great Inland Sea and the Lesser Inland Sea. It was called "Cimmeria" by civilized peoples and something quite unpronounceable by its inhabitants. North of it was the Great Glacier, and further east was the Great Unknown. Because Cimmeria was so close to a wall of ice, it was perpetually cold, and its inhabitants were accustomed to wearing lots of animal furs to stay warm. The legendary geographer Lavid, who had undertaken to visit every land mentioned by any explorer of note, wrote of this frozen place that he knew not which was the icier, the ground or the hearts of the Cimmerians – a dour lot which went about with perpetual frowns (perhaps frozen in place?). Needless to say, Lavid's visit there was short-lived; he stayed just long enough to observe the handful of local landmarks in preparation for his map of the country. In the intervening three centuries between Lavid's day and that of the Wizard, very little had been added to his original drawings.

Only one Cimmerian had ever enrolled in the Order of Wynot (and, to the best of Wilfong's knowledge, none had ever joined any other Order): one Zondar by name, the dourest of that dour race (in the Atlantean's humble opinion). In fact, Zondar had joined at the same time as Wilfong; but, because the latter had been such a quick study, he had advanced through the training at a rapid pace while Zondar plodded along. Eventually, at Level Ten, the Cimmerian reached the limits of his Magickal skills and was forced to retire to his native land without ever having had the opportunity to take a secret name. Still, his was the most eidetic mind anyone had ever encountered, and he could absorb and recall almost instantly vast amounts of information, both important and trivial. As a consolation for his failure to complete the training, he was offered the post as Librarian of the Order by which the amount of paperwork could be greatly reduced and the secrecy of the organization maintained.

The Wizard was probably as sober an individual as they came. Yet, next to Zondar, he was the picture of merriment. The Cimmerian could not get the starkness of his country out of his soul, and he was constantly grumbling and griping about everything under the Sun. Nominally his "classmate," Wilfong could never warm up to him; Zondar's peevishness grated his nerves like no other could, and he was always pleased to put distance – physical and psychic – between them. As much as he hated to admit it, the Order's Librarian was the only one he actively disliked, and he never bothered to conceal his feelings – much to the chagrin of his fellow Elders.

The Wizard braced himself for the contact and cast his mind out toward the frozen North.

-- Hello, Zondar.

The silence of the tomb echoed through his mind.

-- Zondar?

Somewhere in the Cosmos, an insect hiccupped.

-- Zondar, are you asleep again?

-- Mmmf.

-- Zondar! Wake up, you lazy lout!

-- Huh? Whozat?

-- It's Wilfong.

-- Yeah? Well, *burf you*, Wilfong!

The Wizard was not surprised at the outburst of profanity. The Order's Librarian frequently peppered his speech with "colorful" expressions and would have been right at home in the wharf district. Zondar's best retorts were reserved for his favorite whipping boy; from the beginning of their acquaintance and progressing steadily as Wilfong outpaced him in the training, the Cimmerian's acrimony knew no bounds, and the pair could scarcely carry on a civilized conversation for more than a minute. Wilfong counted to twenty before daring to speak again.

-- That was not called for, *colleague*.

-- Neither was waking me up in the middle of the burfing night. What the hell's the big idea?

In his haste to obtain vital information, the Wizard had forgotten the time differential. While it was early evening in Zarel, it was the wee hours of the next morning in Cimmeria. He really ought to apologize, though he was loath to do so.

-- I'm sorry to wake you up, but I've got an urgent request to make.

-- Well, ain't that just burfing grand? I'll have to talk to the burfer who sets the clocks and have him synchronize the whole burfing Cosmos for your convenience. Whattaya want?

-- I'm turning in my first Field Report for the Order. Also, I need some information.

-- Shit! That means I have to get out of my nice warm bed, go over to my desk, pick up my quill and a sheet of papyrus, and wait while you think of what you're going to say. [A yawn followed.] Do you know how cold it gets here?

-- Yes, I do. You complain about it all the time.

-- Hell's bells! Why couldn't I have been born in some warmer climate?

-- Just luck, I guess. Can we get on with it?

In his mind's eye, Wilfong could picture the rotund Zondar carelessly tossing aside all of the heavy bed covers which covered him, rolling himself out of the oversized bed like a hog from a mud wallow, waddling over to his work area, and cursing a blue streak all the while.

-- OK, ready to receive.

-- Wilfong, OW-13, to the Inner Nest: Special Field Report #1, in the Year of Our Master 278. I arrived in Zarel with no initial incident. But, half an hour ago, the Enemy who calls himself "SC" revealed his presence here to me. I have reason to believe that the original message was sent to lure me into the open and that "SC" intends to challenge me to a duel of Magick and to defeat me as a first phase in his plan to destroy the Order. Naturally, I am proceeding with the utmost caution. Wilfong out.

A long silence followed. Then:

-- That it?

-- Yes. Why?

-- Oh, I thought you might want to send a message to that little Level-Ten cutie you met the other day. Whatshername? Winona? I hear she had your wheels spinning, and you had *her* wheels spinning.

While not a resolute bachelor, the Wizard had simply not given all that much thought to women and marriage. As a student, he had succumbed to lustful impulses on occasion and might have continued to do so as an adult had not the teachings of Wynot entered his philosophical environment. As he explored the wider world that the Compleat Sorcerer offered to all who would follow him, Wilfong began to devote his life to seeking out that world. He had never considered himself a celibate by any means but indulged in sex less and less as he moved up through the levels of Magick.

And, truth to tell, as his mind opened up to ever newer vistas, he had decided that most women were not worth the effort. With the exception of the handful of women in the Order, most were nattering bundles of trivial pursuits. If he were to seek companionship now, he wanted a woman who hold her own in a lively conversation as well as in bed. Did Winona fill that bill? Certainly, she possessed a sharp, incisive mind. Only time would tell if she were also a sexual creature. Still, he had to admit that, yes, she had "spun his wheels" during that session at the Temple; and, if she found him attractive too, despite the fact that he was at least fifteen years her senior, so much the better. It was an avenue worth exploring.

Assuming, of course, that this business with the devious Sinladen Crotchgod did not prove to be his undoing. By the end of the current cycle, there might not be anyone in the Order left alive to pursue. Intriguing as Winona was, he had other priorities.

-- *Humph!* [he groused] That's the trouble with mind-casting. Unless you deliberately block out everybody around the clock, they all know your business as well as you do. If the lady is interested in a relationship, we'll have one; and, in due time, we'll mate and raise lots of little Practitioners.

-- Ain't love just burfing grand? Shit! If *I* met a broad like her, I wouldn't dance around. I'd quit the damned Order and drag her off to some warm place, like that Meshica south of where you are now.

-- No doubt. But, we're getting off-track here. I want you to find out all you can about the name 'Sinladen Crotchgod.'

-- Is that a person or a burfing disease?

-- It may turn out to be both. How soon can you get back to me?

--Two days?

-- Too long. Make it one.

-- Hell's bells, Wilfong! If you wanted the information tomorrow, why didn't you say so?

-- If you must know, I'm under orders to give you some leeway. Actually, I'd like the information now.

--I just bet you do. You think I can work burfing miracles?

-- Of course. You *are* the Librarian, aren't you?

-- Very funny, burfer. All right, I'll get back to you tomorrow – at a *decent* hour. Now, if it's all the same to you, I'd like to go back to bed. I'm freezing.

-- Certainly. Good night, Zondar. Pleasant dreams.

-- *Burf you*, you –

Wilfong broke off the contact at once and spared himself a profane tirade. He was much too tired to endure more than the barest minimum of Zondar's peevishness. Had he been a lesser creature than he was, he might have been tempted to break into the Cimmerian's dreams and fill them with nightmare creatures. It would have served the fellow right to confront huge, writhing snakes and slathering beasts with twenty-centimeter fangs for starters. He constrained himself and concentrated on his priorities.

Now he sent a mental probe into the ether to determine if Sinladen Crotchgod were physically in the vicinity. He doubted that the Enemy would allow his mind to be scanned, but even detecting a powerful mind shield would be proof of his presence in Zarel. It would not do to have him run free without being "tagged."

The probe proved to be negative insofar as "SC" was concerned. All the Wizard picked up was a myriad of lines of low-level mental static, emanating from the barbarians of Zarel who seemed content to spend their lives just existing. From another point of view, the probe had been an exercise in frustration, and he was hard-pressed to determine which was more dangerous – the lack of a tell-tale sign or the lack of animus.

He stifled a large yawn. All in all, it had been an eventful – and trying – day, and it was beginning to catch up to him. He didn't think he'd need a Spell of Somnolence this night; he was ready to sleep for a week or two. Murkol was no doubt in some tavern at this very moment, downing enough of the local brew to float a battleship, and he'd stagger back to the inn at some unholy hour – *noisily*.

To top matters off, the last conscious impression he had before dozing off was the *bozzid* on the window sill, peering at him malevolently.

THE EIGHTH CASTING

THE WIZARD AT PLAY

The following morning, Wilfong awoke early but did not rise immediately. For one thing, his "bed" in these "deluxe accommodations" was barely protection against the hard cold floor. He had tossed and turned for half an hour before falling asleep in an effort to find some comfortable spot. Inevitably, the primitive nature of the bed created a host of aching joints and muscles; and, every time he made a move, a spasm of pain prompted him to remain still.

For another thing, he puzzled over the fact that he had not remembered what he had dreamed. That he had dreamed was a given. Wynot had taught that all sentient creatures dreamed but that some were more able to recall their dreams and had then demonstrated a technique for total recall. If Wilfong could not remember the contents of his dreams, he was in danger of losing valuable (albeit hard-to-translate) insights. And he needed the maximum input – whatever its source – now more than ever.

A scant two meters away, the large bulk of Murkol loomed like a small mountain. Yet, this mountain moved; the rhythm of his breathing provided a familiar anchor for the Wizard's temporary disorientation. And the mountain made noise – in the form of loud, rattling snoring.

How is it that I haven't noticed his snoring before, he thought, *and how annoying it is? Very queer and strange.*

Presently, he decided to rouse himself and work out the kinks in his body before they became ingrained. Inasmuch as a small number of movements created a number of small pains, he risked all on a sudden large movement and sat upright. Instantly, a sharp stabbing reverberated throughout his nervous system, and he gritted his teeth to prevent himself from crying out and waking the whole inn. Happily, he discovered that the effort was the worst of it; the shift from a sitting position to a standing one resulted in only a dull throbbing in the lower back. Once on his feet, he began a set of stretching exercises designed to restore muscular efficiency.

On the table rested a bowlful of brackish-looking water, an "amenity" the management provided all the guests. The Wizard splashed some in his face (and noted an oily odor) and toweled off with one of the gray pieces of cloth stacked next to the bowl. Now, he peered out the window. Dawn was breaking over Zarelon; the sounds of night creatures (human or otherwise) were yielding to those of day creatures. He was startled to see the *bozzid* still perched on the window sill. It too greeted the new day in its inimitable fashion by flapping its wings and squawking loudly. The bird eyed the man balefully as if sizing up a possible breakfast, squawked again, and flew away with little effort. Wilfong watched it go with a sigh of relief, then left to attend to his ablutions.

When he had returned from the privy (a small room at the rear of the inn containing a single pit over which one squatted), he found Murkol awake. The Zarelor excused himself to the privy and returned a half hour later.

"What are dy planzh for today, Mashter?"

"We're going to the neighboring land of Kank-ki to search for the one called 'Sinladen Crotchgod.'"

Murkol gaped at the Atlantean in surprise.

"Really, Mashter?" he breathed. "Kank-ki izh a hotbed of gambling. Many go dere to sheek rijezh."

"It sounds like just the place the Enemy would use as a base of operations. Well, we will be going there as soon as you hire a *bofflu* for transport. Now, let's get some breakfast."

139

Breakfast, obtained in the same fashion as the evening meal, consisted of a heaping plateful of scrambled *bozzid* eggs, a bowl of thick, lumpy porridge, two chewy biscuits, and a few strips of meat from swamp boars. As before, the appearance and smell of the dishes provoked a desire to fast for a month; yet, the stuff was palatable and filling. The Zarelor might not like you at all, but they fed you well. The food, coarse and dry, had to be washed down with liberal amounts of *dandlin* wine which seemed to be the only beverage available. (Murkol had warned against drinking the local water, but the Wizard, having already seen it, needed no such warning.)

*　　*　　*

The land of Kank-ki lay roughly south of Zarel and served as the transitional zone between the swampland and the prairie to the west. To reach it, however, one had to follow a road as serpentine as some of the creatures which inhabited the area. Most of the roads which led away from Zarelon were more or less well-traveled and thus well-delineated; sometimes, however, they tended to disappear into the wilderness only to re-appear further on. Whoever was unfamiliar with the quirks and idiosyncrasies of the local terrain found himself going around in circles and increasing the odds of his becoming hopelessly lost or set upon by predators (human or otherwise). One spent as much time *looking* for the roads as traveling upon them, Curiously, it had never occurred to the Zarelor to post signs, either of direction or of warning, in order to ease the traveler's way. Perhaps the difficulty of travel gave them something to complain about (their chief pastime, it seemed).

Wilfong thanked the Cosmos for having the foresight to hire a *bofflu* for this trip. When he and Murkol reached the end of the island upon which Zarelon was sited, a wide, watery gulf loomed before them, reed-choked and foul-smelling, and it proved to be as deep as it looked. Even the *bofflu* was reluctant to step into the murk, and Murkol had to kick it several times to inspire it. Into the water it plodded, bawling with indignity and discomfort. The Wizard watched in alarm as the waterline crept steadily up the beast's side until it had nearly reached the riders' feet. On foot, Murkol would have had no trouble wading across, but the Atlantean would have found himself up to his neck in water.

Because this was the Wizard's first venture outside of Zarel, the Zarelor felt obligated to provide him with a running commentary on the fauna and flora of Kank-ki, the outstanding physical features, the local history and customs of the inhabitants, and anything else he thought his master needed to know. His master listened with one ear and observed the countryside with one eye. His mind was elsewhere. He had not revealed to the trusting Murkol the reasoning behind this journey to Zarel's neighbor, as he did not think it would have enlightened him one iota.

The Wizard was following a linguistic clue cleverly planted in the last message from Sinladen Crotchgod – the one in the cheese. Upon later reflection, he had stumbled across a play on words which only a student of language would have recognized; and, since the Enemy knew a great deal about this particular student of language, it stood to reason that he had used that word-play deliberately in order to tantalize and to lure Wilfong further into the open. Despite the obvious risk, the latter was obliged to take the bait and see what developed next.

In that message, written in ancient Atlantean, the word "slime" had appeared. From his admittedly limited knowledge of Zarelot, he had recognized the homophonic word "gamble." The clue was unmistakable: he was to go where gambling took place, i.e. the land of Kank-ki, where the locals wagered on everything and anything, where one required a keen mind to avoid being fleeced. He would have preferred to be anywhere else than on the back of a recalcitrant *bofflu* slogging through a stinking swamp where the inhabitants raised rudeness to an art, but he had little choice in the matter. A gauntlet had been thrown down in a game of monumental stakes, and he was the only one qualified to pick it up.

As soon as the gulf of water had been successfully forded, the pair traversed the next stretch of dry land which Murkol called the "Blue Island" because of a profusion of indigo-colored, bell-shaped flowers which covered the landscape like an immense carpet. The Zarelor also said that the flowers were used during festivals and had no other use so far as anyone knew. Wilfong stared at him curiously. Had he heard correctly, that the Zarelor held *festivals*?

Presently, they arrived at the sole village in this district – though using the word "village" was being quite charitable. The Wizard would have used the term "tent city" instead. A motley collection of animal hides stretched across poles more aptly described the place; the makeshift shelters appeared as though the smallest breeze could blow them all away. Each "house" measured three meters at the base and three high and resembled a cone; a flap at the base served as an entrance while another at the apex was obviously a smoke hole. Wilfong had seen similar structures before during his travels to the north of the Great Inland Sea and so was not too surprised by the "architecture." The village numbered half a score of these tents, haphazardly sited in an area where the indigo flowers had been uprooted and cleared out.

As the travelers approached, the villagers emerged from their tents and stood about, eyeing the newcomers coolly. On their cheeks was a tattoo of a fish-like creature. None of them – men, women, and children – looked like they had bathed recently, and none wore anything except a lengthy piece of animal hide draped over the shoulders and tied at the waist. Even in a land of barbarians, there were *degrees* of barbarism; the dichotomy between urbanity and rurality held true here as it did elsewhere in the Known World. Except for the band of children who squirmed and wiggled to get a better view of the strangers, these peasants blocked the road and waited expectantly.

Murkol halted the *bofflu* a few meters from the motley group and stared back at them.

"Why are stopping here?" Wilfong whispered anxiously. "We must get to Kank-ki by nightfall."

"And we will, Mashter," the Zarelor whispered back. "It izh cushtomary to greet everyone on de road. It izh considered bad manners not to do sho."

The Wizard snorted derisively. "Bad manners" in a country where bad manners were the rule rather than the exception? What next?

Any further conversation was cut short when one of the men – easily the dirtiest and scruffiest of all – stepped forward and place his hands on his hips.

"We give greetings, friends," he grumbled.

"We give greetings, friend," Murkol responded.

"Be you from afar?"

"We be from Zarelon and seek our pleasure in Kank-ki."

At the mention of the name, the headman spat on the ground.

"Few pleasures be there, friend. *Ruination*, mayhap. Our village be poor because of sharpers from Kank-ki."

Wilfong surveyed the village once more and blinked several times. How wealthy had this collection of hovels been *before* its "ruination"? It looked to be poor since its foundation. How did these peasants measure wealth anyway?

"Your companion," the headman continued, cocking his head at the Atlantean, "from his appearance certainly be from very afar, aye?"

"Aye. He be a visitor to our fair land from a land to the east and would see the sights."

"*Umf!* If you be off to Kank-ki, the sights may blind you. Keep one hand on your purse at all times."

"We shall. Good day to you, friend."

"Good day to *you*, friend."

Though the amenities had been attended to, the headman remained where he was, firmly planted in the middle of the road, glaring balefully at the travelers. With a soft *humph*, Murkol reached into the money pouch, brought out a silver coin, and tossed it to the fellow. The latter caught it without looking at it – giving the Wizard reason to believe that this was a well-honed skill – then examined it carefully. Still, he did not step aside. Murkol tossed him another silver coin which was snapped up with equal ease. Apparently satisfied, the headman nodded curtly, turned, and lumbered toward his tent; the others followed him hungrily. Murkol kicked the *bofflu*, and the pair moved quickly off.

"Highway robbery!" Wilfong exclaimed as soon as they were out of earshot. "Outright extortion, that's what it is!"

"No, Mashter," Murkol ventured to contradict him. "A toll for pashache drough de villache. Every clan doezh it. It keepsh de money shirculating. Beshidezh, it *wazh* a poor villache, and de shilver will buy dem shuppliezh for de coming winter."

"Winter is six months away. Even *I* know that. At these rates, they won't be a poor village for long."

The Zarelor shrugged, not wanting to debate the matter in a seeming show of disrespect. The Wizard, however, was not yet willing to let go of the argument.

"I suspect that, because we could afford a *bofflu*, we were easy marks. Would we have been charged a toll if we had been on foot?"

"Perhapsh," came the weak response, "if we were not dreshed in fine clodezh."

"Ah, ha! Payment of whatever the market will bear, is it? That fine fellow back there would be right at home with street urchins in the Metropolis. Remind me not to take this road back to Zarel."

"Yesh, Mashter."

After a few more kilometers of island-hopping, the terrain became less and less watery. The swamp was yielding to meadows. At some indeterminate point, Murkol steered the *bofflu* to the southwest. Soon, clusters of trees began to appear; some of them were mere stands, while others were small forests. The grass was taller now, coming up to a man's knees. Predictably, it threatened to obliterate the makeshift road. Wilfong was pleased to note that the odor of the prairie had overtaken that of the swamp, a sweetness he preferred to all other odors. Perhaps the journey would be pleasant after all.…

*   *   *

The village of Loth – the lone community in these parts – popped into view without warning. The travelers rounded a bend in the road near a medium-sized clump of trees and stumbled into it. In truth, it was difficult to distinguish the village from the forest; the one had been built within the other to form a nearly continuous whole. The dwellings of the Lothians – a far cry from those of the toll-demanding Zarelor

– had been constructed from felled trees; the logs crisscrossed at the corners to prevent the collapse of the walls, and the chinks between the logs had been filled with mud to keep out drafts. Thatch formed the roofs which were pitched at an angle so that rainfall would not collect and seep through to the living quarters below. Smoke holes were clearly visible at both ends of each building. It was an excellent camouflage, the Wizard judged; any enemy force coming this way would scarcely see the village until the Lothians had mounted a counter-attack. *He* certainly had not expected it to be where it was. Murkol had, however, but then he had known where to look.

No one was hiding from an enemy this day. All of the villagers seemed to be out and about, engaged in one mundane task or another. The men were transporting game animals or firewood from the forest to appropriate depots; the women were tending gardens or washing clothes or chasing after their children; and the children were playing games or chasing/fighting with each other. The bustle reminded Wilfong of similar scenes in Atlantis, only on a smaller scale.

With the appearance of the travelers, all this activity came to a screeching halt as one and all turned to gawk at the newcomers. Whispered exchanges and not-so-subtle gestures spread like wildfire. The children – whose curiosity knew no bounds – began to trail after the *bofflu*, staring in wide-eyed wonder. Wilfong imagined that none of them had ever seen an Atlantean before and tried not to be too self-conscious. By the time Murkol had halted the beast at a predetermined spot (or so it seemed), perhaps the entire village had gathered around them, the adults with as much curiosity as their offspring.

In sharp contrast to the Blue Islanders, the Lothians were better dressed. They wore the same styles of clothing currently on display in Zarelon – no animal skins here but cloth dyed in even gaudier colors than in the city. The Lothians were also cleaner than most Zarelor; they appeared to have mastered the art of hygienics for whatever reason, but the Wizard was not about to debate the question. Was it too much to hope that they would be less surly as well?

One singular part of the villagers' appearance fairly leaped out at him. To a man, woman, and child, they wore a crown of flowers on their heads. And no two individuals possessed the same color arrangement; rather, the crowns had all the marks of personal identification. Wilfong had seen similar floral adornments in his travels; but, by and large, they had been part of some religious ritual, not of everyday dress. He recognized the purple of the *li-lak* bush and the yellow of the *dandlin* and even the blue of the flowers of the Blue Island, but the others were unknown, though he was sure that Murkol could provide that information – at length – if he were curious enough to ask for it.

The travelers waited a few moments to be recognized and greeted. Then one of the men wearing a medallion around his neck stepped forward and did a most amazing thing – he *smiled*. The Wizard nearly fell off the *bofflu* in shock. After suffering so much indignity until this moment, he had been quite unprepared for a display of genuine friendliness. This fellow easily stood a head higher than the average Zarelor which made him appear more hostile to the cautious stranger, but his broad grin instantly dispelled any negative thoughts Wilfong might have harbored. And there was neither fear nor suspicion in the Lothian's eyes, only an open show of welcome to travelers on the road. If the whole village were of like mind, why, Wilfong just might come to enjoy himself there!

"The village of Loth welcomes thee, gentlefolk," the huge man boomed.

"We thank the village of Loth," responded Murkol, "and pray for its continued well-being."

"Alight, and rest thyselves. Thou wilt find relaxation and refreshment aplenty here. The village of Loth welcomes all travelers, no matter whence they come."

This last remark was obviously aimed at the Atlantean, and it was not lost on him as he was still reveling in the idea of encountering friendly folk in this gods-forsaken wilderness. The folk of Kank-ki might be ethnic cousins to the Zarelor, but that was as far as the similarities seemed to go. He acknowledged the welcome in his halting Zarelot, smiled back, and slid off the *bofflu*.

Immediately, the children gathered around him, tugged at his Atlantean clothing, and examined his person minutely. Some of the adults made gestures suggesting they would like to do the same thing until they caught themselves and looked away in embarrassment. Except for the children – who were nearly as tall as he – the Lothians towered over him as the trees behind them towered over the village; and yet, he sensed no animosity on their part – only wonderment at this marvelous stranger in their midst. The Wizard flashed broad smiles all around and patted the heads of the younger children (who giggled incessantly and skittered away). He didn't particularly care for children in general (perhaps one more reason why he had remained a bachelor), but he could warm up to *these* youngsters readily enough. They had as much openness of attitude as their parents, an endearing and pleasant quality in anyone, regardless of age.

"I be called Funkol," the Lothian spokesman was saying. "I be Speaker for the village."

"I be Murkol, formerly of Zarelon, now in service to my Master, Wilfong of Atlantis."

The Atlantean gave his servant a sharp look over the use of his secret name. The Zarelor had been warned about such indiscretions many times before. Still, he would not chastise Murkol in public but wait until they were behind closed doors.

Funkol turned to the Wizard, perplexed.

"At – at—lan –" He shook his head in confusion. "That be a new name for me."

"It very far to the east be," Wilfong explained, "beyond what my people the Great Western Ocean call."

"I have heard that there is a sea in that direction" – he shrugged and grinned foolishly – "but I be an ignorant man and know little about these things. Even so, thou art welcome in the village of Loth."

He clapped Wilfong on the shoulder, nearly knocking him to the ground with the blow. Then he invited the travelers to accompany him to the nearest of the log houses. In their wake trailed young and old alike, determined to learn as much as they could about this interesting (if odd-looking) stranger. And, as he walked, Wilfong observed all that *he* could about this place.

As far as humanly possible, Loth had been laid out in an orderly fashion. It was not set in concentric rings as was the Metropolis, but neither was it the madhouse of Zarelon. Instead, it had a chessboard pattern where each building occupied its own space and lay equidistant to those on all sides. In between the houses were either open spaces or occasional trees. Along the east-west axis of this "grid," one observed five rows of buildings alternating with four of emptiness; along the north-south axis were five columns of houses and four empty ones. Well-worn pathways snaked from one structure to another. The dwellings measured approximately twenty meters long by ten wide and five high, and none of them varied from these dimensions. Each had a door at either end, and the long walls were punctuated with windows at regular intervals.

The Wizard was properly impressed. He had not believed that anyone on this continent was capable of ordered architecture – not after having seen the topsy-turviness of Zarel. Apparently, in the matter of construction as well as that in attitude, the Lothians preferred to distance themselves from their northern cousins. It was a most refreshing change.

Inside what the Speaker labeled the "Visitor's Center," the travelers encountered the communal half of the building, an open space filled with several rows of tables made from sections of logs bracketed by chairs fashioned from tree stumps. No other furnishings were discernible. Opposite the entrance was a second door which led to the other half of the building. To its left hunkered a huge fireplace (unlit at this season); to its right, on the wall, hung a large tapestry done in earth colors, depicting a hunting scene. Funkol led Wilfong and Murkol to a table, bade them to sit, and shooed away the villagers.

"Normally, we charge a modest fee for food and drink – which is only fair. If, however, thou dost participate in the games we operate, there is no charge."

"About these games," Wilfong remarked glibly, "I have heard. The village of Loth for them renowned be – even in far Atlantis."

Now we'll see, he thought wickedly, *how far a little white lie goes.*

"Aye?" Funkol now resembled a child who had just been granted his fondest wish on his birthday. "Thou dost us great honor, Master Wiffon. And, in return for thy kind words, thy first meal shall be complimentary, whether thou playest the games or no. In addition" -- he reached into a pouch at his ample waist and pulled out five wooden discs the size of a *dala* – "please accept these free gaming tokens, in case thou dost participate."

"For thy generosity, we thee thank, Master Funkol." He took the tokens and gave four of them to the now-happy Murkol. "We will about the games decide, once we refreshed be."

"Of course, of course," the Speaker said, rubbing his hands together eagerly. "I'll fetch a server who will take thy order."

On reflection, the Wizard was most grateful not to have had to order his meal by pounding on the table or endure the service provided as if it were a great imposition. A few moments after the Speaker had departed, a young woman entered the Visitor's Center, smiling warmly. She was not entirely unattractive, and he was put in mind of a younger sister to Lymatan (if the giantess had one). The woman carried a tray containing a pitcher and two mugs manufactured, Wilfong noted with no small astonishment, from hammered bronze. From the pitcher emanated the aroma of *dandlin* wine. The server set the tray on the table gracefully, filled both mugs to the brim, handed the guests a menu, and sauntered saucily away and through the door to the second half of the Visitor's Center. Wilfong watched her most appreciatively, then turned his attention to the bill of fare. Because of his limited knowledge of the local cuisine, he again deferred to Murkol's judgment.

The server returned shortly, carrying a large wooden bowl full of fluffy, white, irregular-shaped pieces, and placed it gently in the center of the table. Murkol's eyes lit up like twin candles. He seized a huge handful of the stuff – he called it "puffed *con*" – crammed it into his mouth, and chewed noisily. The Atlantean was content to pick up a single piece and put it cautiously into his own mouth. To his great delight, the *con* was quite tasty – although a bit on the salty side – since it had been liberally covered with rich, creamy butter made from *bofflu* milk. Soon, he too was gobbling it up without regard for the forthcoming meal. The server took their order and disappeared into the back again.

Thereafter, the food arrived in a steady flow. Salad, soup, entrée, side dishes, dessert — each course timed so that no more than a few minutes' interval lay between the ending of one and the beginning of the next. Moreover, the food looked and smelled as delicious as it tasted — a lesson the Zarelor had yet to learn. On top of which, he had drunk more *dandlin* wine than he should have, and it was making him giddy. But the best part of the meal was that it occurred in blissful silence (save for Murkol's happy sounds); no one pounded on the tables for service or shouted at the top of his voice or made rude body noises. When he had forced the last morsel into his mouth, Wilfong knew he had eaten a MEAL; he was as stuffed as a holiday goose, and he daren't move lest he burst at the seams.

The server made one last appearance in order to clear the table of empty dishes. But, before she departed, she deposited a small reddish-white disc in front of each diner. The Wizard peered at his dubiously. To the unspoken question, Murkol said:

"It izh a confekson, Mashter, made from de *pepmin* plant. It aidzh dicheshtion."

So saying, he popped his disc into his mouth and began sucking on it. Wilfong shrugged and followed suit. The thing was sweet all right but not excessively so. It was the other quality which stimulated him: a flavor he had tasted only once before. On that occasion -- a celebratory dinner hosted by his mentor upon his graduation from scribal school – certain herbs from the eastern end of the Great Inland Sea had been served at the end of the meal. They had been more pungent, however, filling his sinus cavities with their taste and provoking his salivary glands; further, as the dissolution trickled into his stomach, the stuffiness he had experienced moments before dissipated. And so it occurred in this barbarian land. He had never thought to ask the name of those herbs, but now he realized they had to have been this *pepmin*. If he had had a mind to operate a business, he might have made a fortune selling this confection to the rich-food-eaters of Atlantis.

"That was a splendid meal, Murkol! Especially since it was free! Now, whom do we see about lodgings?"

"I will ashk de Shpeaker, Mashter."

The Zarelor rose and lurched out of the Visitor's Center, belching heartily every step of the way. Wilfong was left to contemplate the events of the day. Unfortunately, he was interrupted by another villager. Since Lothians resembled Zarelor pretty much, he had as much difficulty distinguishing them as well, and he thought it was Funkol to answer his questions about rooms for the night. This Lothian, however, was not the hulk the Speaker was, only an "average" villager. Still, like Funkol, he was all smiles as he approached the Wizard. Curiously, he wore a pendant consisting of three blue feathers.

A badge? Wilfong wondered. *Not likely, since the Speaker had been wearing a medallion.*

"I give greetings, friend," the newcomer declared cheerfully.

"I greeting give," the Atlantean responded in a cautious voice.

"If it pleaseth thee, sire, I would invite thee to join in one of our games."

"What sort of game in mind you do have?" Wilfong asked warily.

"A game of chance and of skill. It tests thy powers of observation and of reasoning, yet is not complicated at all."

"Hmmm. This game me show."

The fellow withdrew from his waist-pouch three small wooden cups and a bright red spheroid the size of a pea and laid them on the table. He lifted up each cup for Wilfong's scrutiny and set them down in a row; he then raised the center cup, placed the spheroid underneath it, and replaced the cup.

"Now, sire, I will test thy skills."

Rapidly, the gamester maneuvered the cups, changing their positions seemingly in random fashion. When he had completed his shuffling, he smiled broadly at the Wizard.

"Tell me, sire, under which cup is the red *mobbel*?"

Wilfong was thunderstruck. Just with whom did this oaf think he was dealing? This "game" was one of the oldest ruses in the Known World, designed to part fools from their money; and there was always a fresh crop of gullible persons who thought they could beat the trickster at his own game. Wilfong had seen this set-up countless times on the streets of the Metropolis – in the marketplace, on the wharfs, at the

Arena, wherever crowds of people with a few coins in their purses gathered – and in foreign cities as well. He knew how the "game" worked better than most, and he had always declined to play, preferring to spend his hard-earned money on utilitarian items, thank you very much.

The ploy was simple: first, allow the victim to make a few easy "lucky guesses," thus boosting his level of gullibility; then increase the wager to "make things interesting"; finally, manipulate the equipment so that a couple of "unlucky guesses" are inevitable. Having been "lucky" once, the victim continued to play in order to change his "luck." Countless fools had spent themselves into financial ruin and social disgrace by playing this game, and still they persisted.

And, now, without so much as a by-your-leave, one of these tricksters was presuming to intrude upon the Wizard's privacy and draw him into a game of "chance." If this fellow knew that Wilfong was as well acquainted with this game as he was, he would have packed up immediately and sought out some gullible person to trick. Wilfong had been trained in the art of prestidigitation – it was part of Level Two in the Order – and he knew how to track moving hands/objects. Thus, when he was asked to locate the red spheroid, he knew exactly where it was. For dramatic effect, he made a show of attempting to make up his mind and then pointed at the correct cup.

"Thou be-est correct, sire," the Lothian exclaimed as he raised the indicated cup to reveal the spheroid. "Thou hast a keen eye. Wouldst thou care to try again?"

The Wizard nodded and allowed a false expression of eagerness to play across his face.

"Mayhap thou willst wager a *dala* on the outcome?"

Wilfong produced the wooden token given him by Funkol and laid it on the table.

"Ah, that be a five-*dala* token. But, no matter, sire, the wager be for one *dala*."

The gambler proceeded to shuffle the cups again, making a grand show of it in order to give the impression of complex maneuvering. Wilfong concentrated on the spheroid's location, all the while assuming a look of perplexity. He too made a show of it when the manipulation had been completed by rubbing his jaw and scratching his head in a struggle to make a correct guess. He then pointed at the correct cup in a manner which suggested sheer randomness. The Lothian confirmed his "lucky guess," fished a silver coin out of his pouch, and handed it over. The Atlantean took back his token and let the coin stand for the next wager.

The cups were rotated again, this time at a dizzying speed. But, to Wilfong's trained eye, they crawled at a snail's pace. He won again and, for the next round, bet both coins. The trickster's face remained as neutral as a cat's, but his eyes betrayed his glee at hooking yet another victim. The Wizard won the next round as well, doubling his winnings which he kept on the table. The Lothian's imperceptible smile was a clue that some trickery was about to occur.

The trickery was not long in coming. An untrained person might not have noticed the switching of spheroids, pressing the original one between two fingers and dropping its replacement out of the sleeve of the trickster's upper garment. But Wilfong took it all in as if it had been done in plain sight. What his new piece was supposed to do was not immediately apparent; further observation would ferret out its secret.

Again, the cups were moved around. The Wizard now cast his mind out and saw the surface of the table as if the cups had suddenly become transparent. At once, he spied the new spheroid attaching itself to the interior side of the cup under which it had been placed. He nodded knowingly; the *mobbel* had been coated with some sticky substance. No matter which cup was now lifted, only an empty space would be revealed, i.e. an "unlucky guess." As soon as the trickster lifted the selected cup (the correct one), the Atlantean reached out, snatched it out of his hand, and turned it over. The startled Lothian's eyes bulged at having his ruse discovered.

"The wager pay, if thou pleaseth," Wilfong demanded. "Then thy cheating self out of here take, or grave consequences suffer."

With a dark scowl, the gambler dipped into his pouch and withdrew the proper number of coins. He threw them angrily on the table, scooped up his equipment, and stormed out of the building. The Wizard chuckled and pocketed his winnings. He wouldn't be troubled by that one again!

Murkol returned soon afterwards to announce that the Speaker had offered to put them both up in his own *kabban* at a charge of one *dala* per person per night, a lower rate – he claimed – than usual. Wilfong followed the Zarelor out of the Visitor's Center. They turned left and walked to the neighboring building. Inside, they discovered a different arrangement. The first section was an open communal space, but it was only half as large as its counterpart in the Center; it was called locally a *pala* in which a number of cushioned chairs had been set. Another huge fireplace occupied a similar position as in the Center. This space was reserved for family activities and for receiving guests. The inhabitants of Kank-ki were as clannish as Zarelor, organizing into extended families of two or three generations, and each *kabban* held a complete clan. The rooms beyond the *pala* were bedrooms – including two dormitory-like rooms, one each for unmarried men and women – a nursery, and a communal kitchen. The occupants of a given *kabban* shifted constantly as births, deaths, and marriages added to or subtracted from a given clan. Once a clan filled a *kabban* to capacity, a second one was constructed to take the excess numbers. As it happened, the Speaker's children had all been females who had long since been married off, and there were now empty bedrooms. Funkol had seen an opportunity to put the unused space to work and seized it.

The headman welcomed the travelers to his "humble house" and introduced them to the few family members who remained and were sitting in the *pala*. All of them greeted the pair cordially but declined to engage them in protracted conversation. It was just as well, for Wilfong was in no mood for small talk; he was here on business, and any talking he did would be to further his mission. Tomorrow, he intended either to confront Sinladen Crotchgod or to seek clues to Wynot's whereabouts, whichever situation developed first. He suspected the former was more likely to occur, and therefore he wanted to get as much rest as possible for the coming ordeal.

He and Murkol passed through the *pala* and found themselves in a narrow corridor which bisected the main portion of the *kabban*. At the other end was another door which led to the kitchen. This area consisted of eight rooms – four to a side – apportioned to the various sub-groupings within the extended family. Funkol led his guests down the corridor, halted before the second door on the right, opened it, and ushered them in. As he lit a lantern, Wilfong quickly scanned the room. To his mild surprise, he discovered that the beds were "bunked," that is to say, stacked one on top of another. The last time he had seen bunked beds was when he happened to peek into the slaves' quarters on Pier Eight. Yet, these beds appeared to be more comfortable than those of the slaves; and, certainly, they surpassed the quality of the mats in Zarelon. Two stacks of three beds each (making for a tight fit on the highest ones) occupied opposite walls. The wall opposite the door contained portable wardrobes. A small table with four chairs, all sturdy-looking, sat in the center of the room.

Wilfong sent Murkol out to tend to the *bofflu* and fetch the trunk. From his winnings from the cup game, he paid Funkol for their first two nights' lodging. Before departing, the Speaker reached into his waist-pouch and extracted a thin, flexible piece of tree bark ten centimeters to a side. At the top of one side, the image of a bird's head had been stamped; below it, wording in the local language – half of which the Wizard could only guess at – filled up a third of the tree bark. On the remaining space was bold-script Atlantean writing.

"I nearly forgot, Master Wiffon. While thou wert at dinner, this arrived for thee by *pijin* from Zarelon."

"For me? But I no one told where I was going."

"Perhaps someone overheard thee discussing it with thy servant. I am an ignorant man and know little of these matters. Good night, sire."

When the Lothian had departed, Wilfong peered at the message with increasing ire. The handwriting told him all he needed to know about the sender. His only consolation was the possibility of obtaining another clue as to "SC's" plans. The message read:

"To Wilfong the *phtrx*:

"There once was a wizard in Zarel,
Who forgot how to cast a Spell.
    He's just a big sap;
    He's fallen into my trap.
Now, I'll break him in two, by Krell!"

The Wizard did not fly into a rage this time. He had learned his lesson. The vile epithet, now repeated, no longer held power over him. An insult, overly used, soon lost whatever force it originally possessed. Besides, he was becoming quite accustomed to receiving outrageous messages from Sinladen Crotchgod. He re-read the thing so as not to miss any nuances or double meanings, then closed his hand around the tree bark. He smiled as the bark crumbled into powder.

He now had another important clue in the reference to "Krell," who was one of the principal figures in Hyperborean folk tales. Why else would the Enemy have bothered to mention that name if not to suggest a direction toward which to bend his search. Crotchgod was leading him on a merry chase, to be sure, but he had to follow the clues, no matter where they led him. Something in the legend of Krell would surely point the way. Wilfong had only a nodding acquaintance with Hyperborean folk legends; therefore, he was obliged to rely on the one person he knew to have such knowledge. In any event, Zondar was supposed to have other information for him at this time.

As a precaution, he stuck his head into the corridor and glanced in both directions in order to ensure that there would be no interruptions from well-meaning strangers. He saw no one, closed the door, and cast his mind out.

-- Hello, Zondar.

-- Mmmm?

-- It's Wilfong again.

-- Well, *burf!* I was just about to call *you.*

-- Do you have the information I requested?

-- Yeah, but you won't like what I have to say.

-- When have I ever? Well?

-- I've searched all the records, all the literature, all the oral traditions, and I couldn't find one mention in the Known World – even at its fringes – of the name 'Sinladen Crotchgod.' It's as if someone simply made it up.

-- That's fairly obvious. What about mythic origins?

-- Nope. I drew a blank there too. No such person.

-- How frustrating. I'll have to –

-- Hold on! I ain't through yet.

-- Eh?

-- You know what an 'anagram' is?

-- Of course I do. It's a word or phrase formed from the scrambled letters of another word or phrase. I sometimes use one in my classes to demonstrate word origins.

-- Well, ain't that just burfing grand! Anyway, just on a hunch, I cross-referenced the name by anagramming it into several other words. You'll be surprised by what I came up with.

-- I'm sure I will be [the Wizard grumbled impatiently].

-- 'Sinladen Crotchgod' becomes *sel rahcnot gniddoc.*

-- Which means?

-- Which means 'old bone crusher' in Hyperborean, one of the more pleasant epithets of Krell the Mighty.

-- *Krell!* Did you say 'Krell'?

-- Dunno what else the burf I said. Does that ring a gong?

-- Oh, indeed it does. [He related the incident of his last communication from the Enemy.] That was the other reason I called you – the legends of Krell. Something in them will provide the next clue to this puzzle I have to solve.

-- Hmmm. There's all sorts of legends about old Krell, none of 'em I'd recommend as burfing bed-time stories. And too many to tell in a single sitting. I've got written copies of all of them somewhere around here. How's about I gather them up and transit them to you?

-- Excellent. How long will it take?

-- Not long. D'ya mind if I have my dinner first?

-- If you must.

-- Thanks a burfing heap! Anything else?

-- No. Just send those materials as soon as possible.

-- Yes, *sir*, your burfing High-and-Mightiness! Your wish is my burfing command.

The Wizard broke contact quickly, lest he say something he would regret later on. Of all the people in the Known World with a perfectly eidetic mind, why did it have to be someone like Zondar?

Murkol returned with a big bowl of puffed *con* under one arm and the trunk on the opposite shoulder. Wilfong stared at him incredulously. Hadn't the fellow had enough to eat not two hours before? The Zarelor set the bowl on the table and then lowered the trunk gently to the floor. His hands now free, he grabbed a gigantic handful of *con* and nearly inhaled it. As he munched noisily (and not bothering to wipe the excess butter off his hands), he threw the latches of the trunk and began to remove two sets of clothing for the next day. The Wizard groaned inwardly. At least, his books would be free of contamination! When the task was completed, Murkol regarded his master questioningly.

"Willsht dou need me anymore, Mashter? I want to play shome gamezh here."

"Very well. But leave the money pouch here. Use those tokens Funkol gave us." He reached into his own pouch. "And you can have mine as well."

"Dank dee, Mashter."

"Oh, by the way, there's one game you shouldn't play. It's run by a fellow with three blue feathers hanging from his neck. He's a cheat."

"All de gameshters wear dat shign. It dishtinguisezh dem from ordinary Lodianzh. Cansht dou be more shpeshific?"

"Yes. He uses three wooden cups and a red *mobbel.*"

Murkol chuckled heartily.

"So, old Fussol izh shtill around, izh he? And up to hizh old tricksh. Why dey let him shtay in de villache izh beyond me."

"Then you know whom I mean?"

"Yesh, Mashter. None of the localzh ever bodder wid him. Dey know he jeatsh. He izh left to prey on de new people who vizhit."

"*Humph!* One would think he'd give this village a bad reputation. Well, run along then. I'll spend my time studying."

The Zarelor departed with the bowl of *con*, cheerfully gorging himself.

As for studying, the Wizard did precious little of it, because his mind kept wandering. Mostly, it wandered toward speculation about what he would find in the materials Zondar had promised him. It was all he could do to stop himself from pacing the floor. It was going to be a long time until the morning came, i.e. the Cimmerian night.

THE NINTH CASTING

THE WIZARD AT ODDS

Having retired early, Wilfong awoke with a start in the middle of the night. He had detected a disturbance in the room, and it was not the non-stop boisterousness emanating from the *pala* (which was enough to wake the dead in several surrounding lands). The village of Loth was, by no stretch of the imagination, a city, but at night it sounded like one. Cities since the first one had been built always had their "night life" wherein the "pleasures of the flesh" (both licit and illicit) could be enjoyed to the fullest. Even in the most puritanical society, for every taste there was a market; and, for every market, there were scores of "entrepreneurs" to provide the taste – if one knew where to look. Loth, while far from the beaten path, emulated a city in one regard, with its gambling parlors – its only real economic activity – which drew people far and wide who wished to forget temporarily their worldly cares in favor of the chimera of instant wealth.

They did so loudly too and forced the Wizard away from his studies and to an early bed. But *they* did not rouse him from sleep.

Neither did Murkol's snoring. The Zarelor had lost all of the tokens given him in short order, consoled himself by consuming a barrel of *dandlin* wine (free to all players), staggered back to the Speaker's *kabban*, and instantly passed out. He sounded like a thousand saws cutting down a thousand trees, but his racket was inconsequential to what really disturbed Wilfong.

He sensed that someone else was in the room – unlikely as it seemed – and that this someone was searching for something. It has been said that soldiers and spies slept with one eye and one ear open and maintained a constant alert. The same may be said for Practitioners of Magick under the threat of the Dread Edict. The era of the Great Persecution had taught a hard lesson – to those who survived to profit by it, at least – and only the foolhardy and the over-confident failed to set wards against the approach of the King's agents. Adept as he was, even Wilfong took several precautions; in fact, *because* of his adeptness, he took precautions, as his loss to the Order of Wynot would have been catastrophic. Thus, while both of his eyes and ears were closed, part of his mind remained on alert for danger from whatever quarter. And, when the intruder entered the room, mental alarms had sounded, and he came out of the sleeping state immediately.

He did not open his eyes just yet, however. Instead, he cast out his mind to scan the darkness. Only those who possess "mental vision" can accurately describe the sensation, though not in terms a non-Practitioner can understand. The difference between it and physical vision was the difference between seeing an object with the naked eye and seeing it through a veil. All the details were crystal clear, and no shadows or tricks of the light existed to fool the observer. The Wizard could identify every single object in the room as if he had been in broad daylight. Thus, the intruder stood out in marked contrast to everything else; and, compared to him, even the shadows seemed bright.

The figure wore a hooded robe of some dull, black material which covered him from head to toe and which seemed to absorb the available light as a sponge absorbed water. Wilfong needed no introduction. It was the same black-garbed individual at the Library, who had manipulated the mob only days before. Sinladen Crotchgod, for whatever reason, had decided to make a "personal" visit.

But what the devil was he looking for? He darted from one part of the room to another with quick, jerky movements as a spasmodic person would. Under the table, on top of a wardrobe, at the door, in a corner near the ceiling – he gave the impression of one in search of an elusive thing, always within reach of it but never able to grasp it. He ignored the "sleeping" figures altogether, perhaps considering them no great obstacle to his prowling. Was he so cocksure of himself then? The Enemy had to know where he was and what one of the room's occupants was capable of. It was time to get some answers.

Some four centuries before Wilfong's time lived a Practitioner named Magetat, who was reputed to be the greatest living magician in the Known World (which was much less than in later days). In those glorious pre-Persecution days, when consultations were openly available, Magetat was much in demand because, it was said, his Spells and Potions were the most effective in their results. Like other Practitioners, he seldom revealed the secrets of his success, relying mainly on carefully worded allusions and parables. Yet, curiously, he did write a short treatise (which this writer has read several times in order to sort it out) on the nature of Spell-casting. He described four score of the more important Spells in regards to their shape, color, and rate of motion. It may astound the non-Practitioner to learn that Spells have these properties since one cannot see a Spell *per se*, only its consequence.

Yet, Magetat claimed – rightly so, as other Practitioners have discovered on their own – that, while no Spell can be seen on the *physical* plane, it can be seen (if one was a Practitioner versed in the techniques) on the *ethereal*, i.e. mental, plane. In his treatise, he categorized each Spell in ascending order of complexity and by its "physical" properties; and he went on to explain the reasons why Spells have these properties and what occurs when two or more Spells are combined. Like Wynot much later, this worthy person disappeared into the mists of Time with no record of his passing. Some have said that he now shares the same plane of existence with the Compleat Sorcerer and that they spend their days debating the nature of Existence itself.

Wilfong maintained minimal brain activity on the conscious level in order to lull the Enemy into a false sense of security. From deep within his subconscious, however, he formulated a mental probe designed to penetrate the mind of another and to discover all that the target knew of himself and of the external world. Practitioners would have "seen" a pink, fuzzy globe approximately five centimeters in diameter oozing from the Wizard's forehead. This occurred, it must be emphasized, on the mental plane and so remained invisible to normal sight. The sphere wafted gently across the room as a flower's spore might be carried on the wind, destined to strike the forehead of the target and seep into his mind. According to Magetat, this apparition should have disappeared from mental view, to be replaced by a shower of pink sparks emanating back to the sender, each spark carrying a vital bit of information.

These consequences unfortunately did not occur. Against a non-Practitioner, yes; against this particular intruder, no. This intruder was another Practitioner with the ability to repulse a simple mental probe. Subsequently, the pink, fuzzy globe merely bounced harmlessly off its target's mind-shield and dissipated into space. Wilfong was, of course, aware of this eventuality and so had not been relying solely upon one simple probe. In point of fact, that probe had been a decoy; and, while it was drifting lazily toward Sinladen Crotchgod's brain, the Wizard was conjuring up a second and more formidable probe – verdant in color, egg-shaped, and rotating upon its vertical axis – and sending it whirling tangentially. Thus, while "SC" was engaged in fighting off the first probe, the second should have approached and re-formed itself into a string of pale green arrows which would penetrate the consciousness more easily. That was the theory.

What actually happened was that, in the instant the first probe had been rendered impotent, the Enemy ceased his frenetic activity and drew himself up to his full height of a meter-and-three-quarters. He spun about, stood rigidly in the far corner of the room, and fixed Wilfong with a pair of glowing, crimson eyes, the only part of him which was visible in the robe's hood. Half a moment later, the second probe struck and penetrated for the space of a heartbeat before it too was rejected. Yet, in that brief contact, the Wizard received three distinct impressions. The first was of a young man (somehow vaguely familiar) seated before a more recognizable figure – Wynot himself – undergoing a vigorous interrogation; the second was of the younger man's shaking his fist at Wynot, hurling vile invectives and not-so-subtle threats at him, and storming out of the Presence in an absolute rage; and the third was a glimpse of an unrolled scroll with the words (written in a barely legible scrawl) "Phase One complete – commencing Phase Two" written on it.

Strange that the Master had never mentioned this incident to any of his disciples, Wilfong mused. Perhaps He had planned to before events overtook Him. It might have been very helpful to have had His thoughts on the subject. These few fragments hinted at the reasons for Sinladen Crotchgod's enmity toward and assault upon Him and His Order, but they did not tell the whole story.

Still, there was no time to ponder them now. Wilfong's probes had exposed his awareness of the Enemy, and the latter was staring at him intently. The Wizard had to give him his full attention. His original opinion of "SC" had been that of a "black hole" in the space-time continuum, a vague, human-shaped void which could not be discerned. Now, the more he peered into that so-called "void," the more confirmed he was in that idea. Both physically and psychologically, Sinladen Crotchgod represented the gravest threat to the concept of *kosmos*.

-- Aha! [boomed a sneering, nasal "voice" inside Wilfong's head]. You *are* awake!

-- Yes, I am [the Wizard sneered right back], no thanks to your clumsy tramping about.

-- And you actually thought you could probe my mind? A puerile effort!

-- Perhaps not. I did learn a thing or two.

-- I doubt that very much. I'm disappointed in you, Wilfong. I thought you'd be more inventive.

-- Oh, I haven't yet begun to fight, Sinladen. I may call you 'Sinladen,' mayn't I?

-- Call me anything you please, old thing. It makes no difference as to your fate.

-- An unusual name, 'Sinladen Crotchgod.' Did you make it up yourself?

The crimson eyes glowed more fiercely for a second or two at the deliberate slur. The Enemy's mind shield slipped ever so slightly (for which Wilfong was hoping), and out leaked a brief picture of a smug, self-centered individual filled with unimaginable malice. The

Wizard suppressed a shudder and gave thanks to the Cosmos when "SC" regained his composure. Despite the Atlantean's desire to pick the other's brain, he thought it a mistake to tap too deeply into that cesspool of hatred and revenge on a sustained basis; unless taken in measured amounts over a period of time, the raw emotions which featured inside that skull could conceivably overpower even a Level Thirteen.

-- No more unusual than 'Wilfong the Wizard,' as you like to call yourself. Personally I never did approve of Wynot's encouraging his followers to adopt pseudonyms.

-- At least, I call myself what I am, and not what I'd like to be.

-- My dear chap, let's dispense with the insults, shall we? We need to talk.

-- About what?

-- About how you're going to cede all of your powers of Magick to me.

In spite of himself, Wilfong burst out laughing and continued for a full fifteen seconds. Part of his brain, however, remained focused on the Enemy in case he should try to take advantage of any supposed mental lapse and work some mischief. Another part monitored the snoring Murkol; it would not do to wake the Zarelor and have him react in a manner they both would soon regret. Happily, "SC" moved not a muscle – mentally or otherwise – and the servant merely shifted in his bed. Wilfong wiped tears from his eyes with the sleeve of his robe.

-- Sorry about that, Sinladen, but your remark was quite droll.

-- You think so? Well, we'll see how 'droll' it is when I begin stripping you of your overrated wizardry. First, I'll relieve you of your books. I know you carry them about wherever you go.

-- Indeed? You seem to know a great deal about me, though I can't say we've ever met.

-- Oh, but we have. You just don't remember the occasion. I try to learn everything I can about my opponents.

-- And why are you opposed to me?

-- Why, you're Wynot's 'greatest' pupil, don't you know?

-- That's hardly an answer.

-- By destroying you, I destroy Wynot's finest product, and my reputation will be enhanced for all Eternity. No one would dare oppose me. Also, by destroying you and adding your powers to mine, I'll be strong enough to face the 'Compleat Sorcerer' himself and defeat him once and for all.

Wilfong grimaced. Sinladen Crotchgod was truly insane if he believed he could accomplish such an act. No other Practitioner in the short history of humankind had possessed the knowledge and skill of Wynot; others may have boasted of their prowess, but the proof lay in the deed and not in the word. And Wynot's many deeds were a matter of public record prior to his disappearance in the face of the Great Persecution. Certainly, no one in his own Order (including the sole Level Thirteen) entertained the idea of defeating the Founder. On the subject of duels of Magick, Wynot had been strangely silent – perhaps his reputation had served to frighten off any would-be challengers – and thus there were no recorded instances of such duels. Given his repugnance of violence, it was inconceivable that he would have participated in any in the first place.

Moreover, the Enemy was doubly insane if he thought Wynot's "greatest pupil" planned on standing idly by and allowing anyone to carry out this mad scheme. Even if Wilfong had to sacrifice himself in the process, upholding his master's honor took priority.

-- Even *I* can't destroy the Master. What makes you think you can?

-- Sheer desire, old thing, sheer desire. That's the difference between you and me.

-- Does revenge have anything to do with it?

Sinladen Crotchgod's crimson eyes seemed to glaze over as if he were lost in thought, and he remained silent for a space. Now the Wizard sat up in bed (as much as he was able to since he was sleeping on the bottom bunked bed) in order to have greater freedom of movement should "SC's" actions necessitate it. Presently, the other spoke.

-- Wynot the 'Wise' once refused to teach me. [Wilfong recalled the scene in his Master's study which he had extracted from the Enemy's memory.] Oh, he presented any number of eloquent arguments against my admission to his precious Order, but it all came down to one factor.

-- And that was?

Another pause. The ebony figure began to pace back and forth. The Wizard wondered if he could send another probe while Sinladen Crotchgod was distracted. Suddenly, however, "SC" flung his arms into the air and shouted:

-- He had the utter gall to deem me 'unworthy'!

-- Perhaps he knew something about you that you weren't willing to face. He taught us all to face our demons and to defeat them.

-- Don't try to analyze *me*, Wilfong! You don't know how. Neither did Wynot, but that didn't stop him from doing so. I was forced to learn Magick on my own over a long period. [Another pause.] It may interest you, old chap, that, under different circumstances, *I* might have been his 'greatest pupil' instead of you. Now, I'll just settle for your demise.

-- I must say that you're refreshingly candid, Sinladen. And not a little naïve too.

-- Don't flatter yourself. I have the utmost confidence in my abilities.

-- As much as I have in mine? We'll see.

The Wizard hoped he *sounded* as confident as he wished to portray himself. He didn't *feel* very confident at the moment. All too obviously, sooner or later, he'd have to face off against this fellow; everything the Enemy had done up to this moment had pushed and pulled him toward just such a confrontation. It galled him no end that he could have been manipulated so easily. Yet, Sinladen Crotchgod had known all the right things to say, and the Wizard had been obliged to investigate his claims, knowing full well that traps and snares lay ahead. "SC" had evidently planned for this moment very carefully and was fairly spoiling for a fight; he would not relent until one of them was dead.

Wilfong understandably dreaded any such eventuality. He'd like to live a long and fruitful life as a matter of preference. Moreover, his demise would lay open the entire Order to an assault the likes of which it could not hope to withstand, even if they all acted in concert. Even if he should prevail, it was not likely he'd come out of this with a whole skin. Therefore, it was imperative that he learn the limits of the Enemy's "might."

He mentally reviewed all that he already knew, point by point. Mind-to-mind communication was a rudimentary skill; no one was admitted to the Order unless (s)he possessed the ability beforehand. Wynot had taught that telepathy was the linchpin of Magick, that it could not be practiced without having a higher brain function. Novitiates were still trained in mind-casting in order to make more efficient use of this talent. Use of the poetic form in which Spells were cast occurred during Level Two (at which time the pupils learned to cast very simple Spells). How "SC" had obtained the form was still a mystery, though Wilfong could have made some shrewd guesses in that department. Transiting one's physical self from place to place –often called "teleportation" – was taught at Level Four; the students absolutely had to master that technique before they could move on to other subjects. Hypnotic compulsion of the sort which had occurred at the Library came at Level Five. Yet, Sinladen Crotchgod had had difficulty in controlling the crowd for any length of time; therefore, he had not mastered all of the techniques of that level. The erection of mind shields occurred at Level Ten. Again, the Enemy had had difficulty maintaining his.

Wilfong concluded that "SC" had learned whatever skills in Magick he possessed by piecemeal (as he had hinted) and that, if he had any weaknesses at all, they would derive from a lack of a cohesive, step-by-step approach to Practitioning. The partial success of Wilfong's mind-probe testified to that. Thus, if he cast enough differently formulated Spells, one or two of them ought to overwhelm Sinladen Crotchgod's defenses and defeat *him* "once and for all"!

But where to begin?

Begin by ejecting the impudent fellow out of my room – if I can – and work from there.

While self-transiting was relatively simple, transiting another person was not – particularly when the other person did not wish to be transited. The transiting Practitioner generally had a clear picture in his mind of where he wanted to go or where he wished another to go; the latter presumed prior consent. Resistance required additional energy output to overcome it. And a *Practitioner's* resistance was a formidable barrier indeed! Still, Wilfong was determined to try.

Consulting his mental catalog of Spells of Transition, he found two which were very powerful when combined. Softly murmuring, he chanted:

> "There once was a prowler most fey,
> Who dared not to show up by day.
> He sneaks about in my room
> And spreads a terrible gloom.
> Oh, Wynot, send him away!"

On the ethereal plane, Spell #1 materialized as a puce-colored hexahedron spinning rapidly upon its horizontal axis. Spell #2 was a navy-blue sphere which floated up and attached itself to one of the apexes of the hexahedron. Instantly, the latter screwed itself into the former until all that could be seen of it was the apex jutting through it. When the two had conjoined, they shot off and bore down upon their target; as soon as they reached it, they would create a vortex around the target, suck it in, and displace it to another location of the Spell-caster's choosing, the co-ordinates of which were usually implanted during synthesis.

The Wizard's expectations were quickly dashed. Just as the Spell was close to forming the vortex, Sinladen Crotchgod uttered a counter-Spell; his mental protective shield was given two extra layers of protection, halting Wilfong's materialization in its tracks. And the shield began to glow. In the blink of an eye, it turned cherry-red. The Spell of Transition disappeared with a soft *pop!*

"SC" was not finished yet. He spread out his arms, and his protective shield expanded like a balloon. Before Wilfong could react, he was being pressed against the wall, trying to breathe. At some other time, he might have admired this Level-Eleven skill; just now, however, he was trying to avoid asphyxiation. Though it seemed like ages, the horrendous pressure lasted only two seconds of real time, then was released as suddenly as it had commenced. Wilfong gasped for air as an evil chuckle rang in his mind.

-- Was that the best you could do, Wilfong the Washed-up Wizard?

-- Of course not [the Wizard replied with false bravado]. I was merely testing you.

-- I see. And did I pass?

-- I'll reserve judgment for a later date.

-- Don't make it too much later, old thing. I'm going to make you squirm a bit before the end comes. Rest assured that your days are numbered. Well, enough of these pleasantries. We'll meet again when you least expect it. Toodle-oo, Wilfong!

Sinladen Crotchgod traced a gray line down the length of his body. Immediately, the left side folded over onto the right side, creating a half-silhouette. He folded twice more until all that remained was a long, thin, inky mark hanging in mid-air. In a matter of milliseconds, that too vanished.

I must admit, Wilfong mused as normal breathing resumed, *the fellow has style – which makes him all the more dangerous.*

He attempted to go back to sleep, but his mind was too full of conflicting thoughts and resisted the will to relax. In the deafening solitude, he let his consciousness wander where it will in the hopes that his mind would eventually tire and allow sleep to return. Invariably, thought returned to the one subject which ever pre-occupied the hearts and minds of the Clutch: the whereabouts of their Master.

Those who had walked and talked with Wynot while he remained in Atlantis were nearly as revered as the Master himself. Yet, in their own writings, they considered themselves poor indeed; for, without the Presence, they were like children without parents, and their one goal had been to live forever in Wynot's estate (wherever it might be). And this goal they bequeathed to subsequent generations over the course of two-and-a-half-plus centuries. First, Wynot had to be found. Searching for him became all-consuming for the members of his Order; a minimum of ten hours in each training cycle were required for all Level Elevens and above in casting out their minds across Space and Time searching for the least little clue which would point them in the right direction. So far, no one had been able to take the first step along that elusive path.

Until now.

Until Wilfong had had his incredible dream.

Perhaps it was due to his being the only Practitioner to achieve the complex Level Thirteen that Wynot called out to him via his subconscious. Or, perhaps it was because the Compleat Sorcerer had deemed this moment the proper time to put into motion the next phase in some Grand Plan he had devised long ago. Whatever the truth of the matter, contact had been made, and that was encouraging in itself. No matter that, in response to the alien call, the Wizard found himself in the middle of a barbaric territory following cryptic clues. No matter that he might be running around in circles and wasting his time. The Prime Goal superseded all other considerations.

What particularly interested the Atlantean was the fact that, though *he* had not met Wynot in the flesh, he had met someone who had. And the occasion of that meeting had not generated ineluctable joy but bitterness and eternal hatred. Wilfong's one link to his Master was a foe who had vowed to destroy everything he held dear because of some personal grudge.

By Wynot's ragged toenails, he'll do so over my dead body!

Which was a distinct possibility.

*   *   *

Eventually, Wilfong did fall asleep – but not for long. Dawn arrived shortly after Sinladen Crotchgod's visitation, and the sounds of the village awakening to the new day stirred him out of his all-too-brief slumber. He yawned and stretched and yawned again. On the other side of the room, Murkol still snored, as oblivious to the early morning noises as he had been to the night's sinister confrontation. While excessive drinking made some people belligerent and others silly, it made Murkol drowsy; and the more he drank, the more he slept.

Wilfong clambered out of bed, stretched a second time, dressed, and re-checked his books. After last night's encounter, he was taking nothing for granted. Although everything seemed to be order, he re-enforced the wards and departed.

The aromas of breakfast assaulted him the moment he set foot in the corridor. Unfamiliar odors, to be sure, but not unpleasant, not like those which had assailed him in Zarelon. A steady stream of traffic flowed through the corridor as women of all ages carried platters and bowls and pitchers of exotic foodstuffs from the kitchen to the *pala*. Men of all ages bore water and firewood from outside to the kitchen, and children of all ages skittered back and forth, playing silly games and/or teasing one another and generally making nuisances of themselves. Wilfong had to duck and dodge several times on the way to the privy and back again to the *pala* in order to avoid being bowled over.

As soon as he entered the common room, he found himself part of a large crowd. Not only were Funkol's extended family in attendance for breakfast, but the Speaker seemed to have invited half of the village to join him. A dozen extra tables had been set up to accommodate the surplus diners, and nearly all of them were fully occupied. The Wizard stood at the inner door, blinking in confusion, and became a party to two more near-collisions. A yelp of surprise from the second would-be collider brought the Speaker's attention. The huge man excused himself from a small knot of villagers with whom he had been engaged in animated conversation and came to the rescue of his foreign guest.

"Ah, Master Wiffon!" he boomed. "Thou be-est in time for breakfast. And why not? Thou be-est paying for it, after all. Heh-heh-heh."

Funkol was wearing the colossal smile of the day before, and Wilfong wondered if it had been painted on. How could anyone – except an idiot – smile so much? Was he perhaps a "connoisseur" of the *li-lak* flower? The Speaker clapped his guest on the shoulder with such force as to send a shock wave throughout the Atlantean's body.

"I thanks for the invitation give, Master Speaker," Wilfong retorted, rubbing his bruised shoulder. "At first, I thought I an important affair had interrupted."

"Nay! There be some of the revelers from last night's games who were waiting until daylight before returning to their own homes. Sad to say, there be highway robbers aplenty these days."

The Wizard nodded knowingly, recalling his own experience at the dingy Zarelo village.

"Very sensible. I myself the roads to be treacherous know. Where I may sit?"

"Thou be-est my special guest, Master Wiffon, and shalt dine at my table. And, while we eat, thou shalt tell us all about thy land of At – At –"

"Atlantis."

"Aye, of course. Come then, and I'll introduce thee to the others here."

Breakfast was a hearty affair. Wilfong could not believe that a simple folk like the Lothians had the ability to set a magnificent table and that only the aristocracy of Atlantis could afford to do so. Certainly, he had never taken such a meal, even at his graduation from scribal school; his dietary needs were deliberately subsistent due to his limited economic status. Funkol explained that, once one got away from the wetlands, the soil was suitable to grow a variety of crops in abundance; and what the people of Loth did not grow themselves, they either bartered with others or used the revenue from the games to purchase any needed foodstuffs – a most equitable arrangement, he declared in ebullient tones, which kept money circulating and everybody relatively happy.

Though the Wizard did not recognize any of the dishes before him (with the exception of a platter of small loaves of bread and a bowl of freshly churned butter), they were delicious and filling, and he let his appetite be his guide. Meanwhile, the Speaker's other guests at his table – introduced as the other officials of the village – plied him with a host of questions about Atlantis. Despite his poor grasp of the local language, he fielded the questions reasonably well, taking care not to boast overly much so as not to offend his hosts. Long after breakfast had finished and the dishes cleared away, the Lothians continued to make inquiries, and he had to beg off so that he "might take my morning constitution." Funkol gave him leave but broadly hinted that there might be further interrogation later on. Wilfong sighed heavily and quickly left the *kabban*.

Once outside, however, any thoughts of privacy soon dissipated. At his appearance, the curiosity-seekers, young and old, gathered around, slowly and shyly at first, then more boldly. And always, the children were in the vanguard. The adults asked pretty much the same questions their leaders had, although they might not have been as eloquent or subtle in their phrasing. Still, Wilfong did his best to satisfy them even as small children poked and pulled at him in order to determine if he were a real person. On a whim, he produced a coin from his pouch and held it up for all to see; then, with a pass of his hand, he palmed the coin and gave the impression that it had disappeared. A chorus of gasps of wonder circled the crowd and sufficed to tell him that he had succeeded in fooling them.

"A magician!" a post-pubescent girl exclaimed. "He be a magician!"

"Hoo-rah!" cried a teen-aged boy. "Please, Master, show us more!"

In response, Wilfong stretched out his hand toward the girl who had "identified" him, placed it behind her ear, and let the palmed coin "magically" appear there. More reaction in the form of "oohs" and "aahs" ensued. Even the adults present seemed stunned by his simple acts of prestidigitation. Thinking quickly, he performed a few more tricks, using the materials at hand, and he had the crowd cheering wildly. On a subconscious level, he was bemused by their attentions; these people would quite possibly recoil in horror if they were to discover what he was really capable of doing. In some cases, ignorance truly was bliss!

Once more, he had to beg to be excused on the grounds that he required a rest in order to "recharge my magical powers." Reluctantly, the Lothians yielded – after first extracting a promise to give them another performance later on – and gave him a boisterous send-off. He wondered idly if he ought to charge a fee for performing "magic tricks"; after all, it seemed to be in the nature of these folk to seek payment for everything they did. Or, he could "work" for his and Murkol's room and board while they remained here, a good deal on the face of it. He would certainly raise the issue to Funkol at the earliest opportunity.

Surprisingly, the Wizard had never walked through a forest. He had seen any number of forests from afar and talked to many people who had visited forests; but, he himself never had the time to make such journeys. To be sure, Atlantis possessed no native forests to speak of; the central and largest island was mostly plains bisected by a mountain range. Still, a world traveler like the Wizard ought to have taken advantage of the lands which did boast of large forested tracts of land. Somehow, more interesting sights had taken precedence.

No more, he decided. *This last part of my explorations of the natural world has been neglected long enough.*

The forest of Loth loomed before him, and he had no ready excuse to avoid it. He plunged into the arboreal depths which comprised the "backyard" of the village. Some of the species of trees were familiar to him – oaks and pines and poplars – but most were not. Each species had its own domain, isolated from all others. Why that should be, he could not say – another question for the Speaker. What pleased him the most, however, was the *quiet* of his surroundings; the soft soughing of the wind in the branches was the only steady sound he heard. Occasionally, he heard the chirp or bark or hiss of some wild creature. The forest literally generated peacefulness, serenity, and relaxation, a suitable environment for meditation. Later, he would test that theory. For now, he just wanted to luxuriate in the stillness and in the heady aroma of leaves and sap and bark, allowing them to seep into his mind and drive out all extraneous thoughts.

It was a faery world into which he had wandered, and he had little desire to leave it any time soon.

It has been said that nothing lasts forever, and so this unique, enticing experience came abruptly to an end.

Wilfong had taken an oblique path through the forest and so emerged from it at a point northeast of the village. In the distance, he observed the furthest fringes of the "stinking swamp." Nearby, a solitary *bofflu* sedately munched at the tall prairie grass. The beast did not bolt in fear at the appearance of the human intruder, and the Wizard had to assume it was one of the domesticated animals used for labor and transport. He paid no more attention to it than it did to him, even when it snorted suddenly as he was passing within two meters of it.

He had taken no more than three steps past the animal when he felt something wet and warm on his back. He whirled about and discovered that the *bofflu* was urinating on him in a strong, steady stream. He immediately jumped out of range.

"By Wynot's hairy mole!" he thundered. "You foul thing! I'll drop you down a volcano!"

"Oh, please, kind sir," the animal replied in a child's voice in Atlantean, "don't harm me. I was only doing what comes naturally."

Wilfong's heart nearly stopped. Was this dumb animal actually *speaking*? He now ignored the pale yellow liquid soaking his robe and the powerful stench which arose from it in order to examine the *bofflu* more closely. The latter returned his gaze with an utterly stupid expression. The Wizard stroked his beard with no small amount of perplexity.

"Is something troubling you, kind sir?" the beast asked innocently.

"There's no way an animal can speak," Wilfong reasoned aloud, "least of all in a tongue foreign to its surroundings. Therefore, someone must be speaking through it."

"Score one for the wizard!" The voice now took on a more familiar sneering tone. "Give him a prize – a *booby* prize!"

"*Sinladen Crotchgod!* I should have known."

In response, the space about the *bofflu*'s head shimmered as a mirage does in the desert and was replaced by a large black circle. The faint outline of a hood appeared in the circle; and, within the hood, two crimson eyes gleaned and sparkled with unabashed glee. The Enemy chuckled evilly.

"How did you like your bath, Wilfong?"

The Wizard said nothing and did not trust himself to say anything in light of this disgusting attack on his person. Instead, he formulated a mental probe similar to the second one he had deployed the night before – with one major change. In place of the verdant egg, he created a yellow one which he knew was even more potent. He hated wasting his time and energy in wresting control of a non-sentient creature from "SC," but he had to prove (to himself, at least) that he wasn't entirely helpless in the face of the greatest threat he and his Order – and perhaps to the very concept of *kosmos* – he had ever known. From previous experience, he knew that Sinladen Crotchgod's ability to control minds was shaky and could be easily broken.

This new probe revealed that control over the *bofflu* was even more tenuous than that over the crowd at the Library. Was this because a non-sentient, relatively alien brain was involved? Or was it because the Enemy was so cocksure that he did not bother to establish a more solid link-up? No matter – if Wilfong the Wizard could excel at anything, it was mind-control, sentient or otherwise.

Sinladen Crotchgod was aware of the probe, of course, and he attempted to counter-act it. Unfortunately for him, he did not have a solid surface against which to press Wilfong and so force the air out of his lungs. A new tactic was necessary. Thus, a black cube, a meter on all sides, materialized directly over the yellow egg. The Wizard smiled to himself; he had used just such a defense when he was a novice and knew from bitter experience how useless it was against this probe. The yellow egg collided noiselessly against the black cube and infiltrated it without any loss of velocity. "SC's" eyes burned brighter while he watched the probe boring down on his puppet. Now, a violet pyramid formed near the *bofflu's* head, rotating lazily upon its vertical axis. Wilfong recognized it as a Spell of Paralysis, and a fairly inept one at that. Here was another weakness in the Enemy's armor.

Wilfong conjured up a counter-Spell in the shape of an inverted magenta pyramid. After sending it on its way toward the violet pyramid, he created a large brown disc, a half meter in diameter, and impregnated it with blood-red polka dots; this Spell was designed to sever the compulsion. As he launched it, the anti-paralysis Spell came into contact with its opposite number. For a fraction of a second, the two mystical objects danced around each other like a pair of birds in courtship; then, the counter-Spell crashed into the other, producing a coruscation of violet sparks and streamers. The invisible (to non-Practitioner eyes) battle continued until the violet pyramid had been completely obliterated. In the meantime, the probe and the anti-compulsion Spell shot unerringly toward their target.

Sinladen Crotchgod was working at a disadvantage, since he had not a cohesive grasp of Magick, and Wilfong was well aware of that fact. The latter was in the vicinity of the battle whereas the former was not. It was a truism that, in the metaphysical realm as well as the physical one, consequences occurred in reverse proportion to the distance between sender and object. Therefore, the Enemy could not effectuate his Spells with maximum efficiency. Knowing this, Wilfong cast his Spells unmercifully.

The yellow egg and the brown disc disappeared inside the *bofflu's* skull with little resistance and came into contact with a peach-sized black sphere which surrounded the motor area of the creature's brain. Tiny flashes of light arced across the surface of the sphere like hundreds of exploding firecrackers. The disc sliced through the sphere, and the fireworks increased in intensity; soon, the thing was reduced to the size of a grain of sand. Meanwhile, the egg focused on "SC's" mind-shield; and, when it made contact, the shield was weakened. The dark circle which had replaced the *bofflu's* head blurred. It seemed too that the Enemy's eyes were dimming.

"Damnation!" Crotchgod roared. "You win this round, my friend. But I'll not be stopped – not until you're just a bad memory!"

The dark circle winked out of existence with a loud *pop!* Released from the control of its tormentor, the animal bawled in protest and galloped away toward the west.

To say that the Wizard was enormously pleased with himself would have been an understatement. He had needed this little victory in order to dispel the black mood which had been a constant companion since he first learned of the existence of Sinladen Crotchgod and his monstrous scheme. Rather than remaining on the defensive and withstanding whatever the foe could throw at him was not in his nature; now that he had drawn blood (so to speak), he knew that he could hold his own, come what may. Yet, he was ever mindful that he had won only a *battle* and that the *war* would continue until one of the combatants had been utterly defeated. He still had to maintain his guard – especially since it was abundantly clear that the Enemy preferred sneak attacks over face-to-face confrontations – and work on a strategy which would win the war.

With this newest threat checked, Wilfong became aware of a more immediate problem: his urine-soaked robe was beginning to stink horrendously!

THE TENTH CASTING
THE WIZARD AT STUDY

Even though he had been mobbed by curiosity-seekers not an hour ago, Wilfong was now the object of rejection. And he did not blame anyone for keeping his distance; he would have avoided himself too, if he could. As the temperature of the day rose, so also did the intensity of the foul odor which hung about him like a rancorous shroud; and, whenever any Lothian chanced to come within smelling distance, the stench pummeled him with the force of a hammer blow. More noses wrinkled than the Wizard could count. He maintained a brisk pace all the way to Funkol's *kabban*, stopping for nothing or no one, and sighed in relief when he entered his room. He wasted no time in shedding the soiled robe and tossing it aside. He hadn't planned on contracting for laundry service, but now it seemed imperative.

Murkol, who had still been sleeping, awoke with a start and, upon spying his sour-faced master, sprang out of bed. He too displayed his disgust at the malodor by making a hideous face but wisely refrained from making a comment. He quickly dressed and awaited any orders. They were not long in coming.

"Find me a laundress, Murkol. I wouldn't want our host to give us the boot just because we were a bit unsanitary."

"What happened to dee, Mashter?"

The Wizard gave a brief recounting of his confrontation with Sinladen Crotchgod. Although the Zarelor tried not laugh at his master's misfortune, a wry smile peeped through, instantly to be replaced by a more somber expression. If the Atlantean took any notice of Murkol's less than serious mien, he preferred to ignore it.

"Dou weresht lucky," the servant observed, "dat dou didsht not shtep in any *bofflu* sit. Dat shtuff izh very meshy, and de shtink shtayzh wid dou for dayzh."

"I'll keep that in mind the next time I go for a stroll. I don't need to –"

He was interrupted by an incongruous sound, the tinkling of chimes emanating from the far corner of the room – incongruous because no such objects existed there. The pair turned in that direction just in time to see a small chest materialize about a meter above the floor. Whatever force held it in mid-air was now released, and it crashed to the floor with a bone-jarring thud. Wilfong shook his head with mortification. Trust Zondar to be disruptive!

The Wizard stepped over to the chest and picked it up. It was still warm from its transition from Cimmeria, and he quickly set it on the table. The chest had been manufactured from cedar wood and held together with strips of bronze; even the hinges and the knob on the lid were of bronze. The wooden surfaces had been painted with the likenesses of mythological beasts, some in repose, others in a threatening stance. As soon as the chest had cooled off, Wilfong opened it eagerly. Inside were half a dozen scrolls wrapped with a yellow ribbon. He removed one, unrolled it, and nodded with pleasure at what he read there.

"Well, I'll be busy for a while, Murkol. If anyone asks for me, say I'm meditating and don't wish to be disturbed. That won't be too far from the truth."

The Zarelor acknowledged the command and departed, taking the soiled robe – at arm's length! – with him. Wilfong took up the scroll again and began to read.

*   *   *

Tarry a while, wayfarer, and I shall speak to you of Krell the Mighty and his curse upon the Earth.

Sit closer to the fire. My tale is a lengthy one, and the night is cool. Help yourself to food and drink. I have plenty for both of us.

Ah, where shall I begin? Well, at the beginning, of course.

First, I must tell you that Krell had many names in his day. Perhaps you have heard of some of them in your travels. Amongst my people, he was called sel rahcnot gniddoc, *'Old Bone Crusher' (I will say why shortly). To the yellow-skinned folk in the east, he was the 'Thunderer." The tribes who dwell on the shores of the Lesser Inland Sea called him variously the 'Crooked One,' the 'Great Bull,' and the 'Trampler.' Other names I have heard, but you see the pattern. Krell was feared by all who witnessed his fury.*

How did he come by the name 'Krell,' you may ask? Once, he was a human being, like you and I -- nay, do not laugh, my friend! It is true! – and he had human parents who gave him a human name (which he seldom used during the peak of his power). To be sure, he was much larger in stature than most Hyperboreans – even as we are unusually larger than most human beings – and thus he was a very powerful person. Nonetheless, he was human – in the beginning.

Bend your ear closer, wayfarer, for I must say this next part in a whisper, lest the sound of my voice carry across Space and Time and fall upon unfriendly ears. Can you hear me? Good. I must tell you quite frankly that 'Old Bone Crusher' was an imbecile. *Perhaps he had been born that way, or perhaps he had been dropped on his head in his youth. It is enough to say that he was not at all intelligent. It is true that, later on, he acquired intelligence; yet, much of what he did in the later years of his existence reflected his earlier level of mentality.*

But, I am getting ahead of myself.

I see you are shivering, my friend. Sit closer to the fire. There, that is better.

Krell was born in the mountains in the east of Hyperborea. When he was old enough to handle a pick, he, like his father and his father's father and so on for many generations, went into the mines to dig for the black metal we call zelz *(and which people in the south call 'iron'). There, he toiled away into manhood. And, because he was unusually large and strong, he gained a reputation for being the fastest, most productive miner in all of Hyperborea. He could dig out so much zelz as all others combined. Not that being the best miner improved his temper, mind you. Oh, no! If anything, he was more belligerent than ever. Many a man required extensive medical attention if Krell took it in his head that someone had wronged him; the number of dead men at his hands could be counted twice on both hands, and then some. As you might guess, most gave him space aplenty.*

We Hyperboreans have a saying, wayfarer. 'Dig no deeper than one's height.' Ah, you have heard it before? Then you know that it is a caution against over-ambition. The saying arose, in point of fact, from what happened to Krell one fateful day; for afterwards, his ambition grew until it had reached monumental proportions and led to what he later became.

I must point out here, my friend, that there are several versions of that extraordinary event, and one will believe what one will believe. I shall tell you the most popular version (though that in itself does not make it truer). I myself am indifferent to the matter, being only a simple trader who must maintain good relations with all I meet.

Let me refill your cup. The wine is good, yes? It comes from the South, along the shores of the Great Inland Sea, where wine-making is an art.

One day, Krell went into the mines at the break of dawn as was his habit, going down the deepest shaft where he had been working the day before. Many hours did he labor without pause until he had dug enough zelz to rival the output of a score of men. Only then did he rest a while and drink some beer. At that moment, he spied a most curious object half encased in the zelz he had already dug. It was a globe as big as one's fist, metallic (though of a metal no human eyes could recognize), silver-colored, smooth and cool to the touch, and highly polished. To Krell's simple mind, it was a pretty thing, something to impress the womenfolk, and he set to work freeing it from its zelzac prison.

As soon as he had freed it and held it in his hand, it began to sing to him. Ah, do not scoff, wayfarer. Did I not say that this was only one version of the tale? Many other versions are even more fantastic. The thing sang in a foreign tongue, but somehow Krell understood every word. It sang of great wisdom and great power, of the ability to change his form or that of any other creature in the blinking of an eye, of the ability to bend men's wills to his own, of the ability to move mountains without touching them, of fabulous places and peoples never before imagined, of the true nature of the Cosmos and even Time itself. All this Krell heard, and he was filled with wonder.

And, woe! he was filled with unholy ambition.

A simple miner who knew nothing beyond mining for zelz and drinking and whoring and brawling, he nevertheless understood that he lacked power to change his life so that he might be better than he was. He understood that this pretty bauble promised him power beyond imagining. And so on that fateful day, he asked the singing globe to give him power. Thereafter, he was no longer Krell the miner and the son of a miner; now, he was Krell the Mighty, the Old Bone Crusher, who walked the Earth like a god, conquering all who stood in his way.

Of these conquests, I will not speak, for the telling would take many days. I have my business to conduct, and I know you also have a mission to attend to. Besides, I count myself a gentle man and so find tales of blood and rapine very distasteful. Suffice it to say that Krell lived up to his awful reputation.

Let me instead tell you of his transformation into an immortal being which in turn led to his colossal battle with the itinerant magician whom many called 'Wynot the Wise.'

With each use of the singing globe (which he labeled the 'Orb of Power'), he lost more and more of his humanity. Neither knives nor spears nor arrows could penetrate his flesh. Fire could not burn him. If he fell from a great height, he always landed on his feet, as a cat does, with nary a broken bone. He could breathe underwater and so could not drown. Neither poisons nor noxious fumes had any effect upon him. The Orb of Power had given him protection against all danger, and he went into battle with absolutely no fear of death.

The more Krell used the globe, the more he wanted to use it. It was an addiction, one which transformed him into something more than human.

In the course of his conquering, his enemies – past, present, and future – realized that he could not be defeated by purely physical *means. Therefore, they turned to magic. To this purpose, all who claimed to be a dabbler in the mystic arts were recruited (sometimes involuntarily) to use their knowledge and skills to counteract the terror which Krell wreaked upon the Earth. I need not tell you, my friend, that all of their efforts met with utter failure.*

For the Orb of Power had the means to defeat magical weapons as well as physical ones; it neutralized every spell and incantation employed against it with its own spells and incantations, and many a magician perished in the process. In the end, Krell stood even more undaunted and crossed over the final boundary between mortality and immortality.

For several ages, that was how matters stood. All of Hyperborea went about their business in a state of abject fear, not knowing if or when the Old Bone Crusher would visit his brand of terror upon them on a whim. Much tribute did he exact from his 'subjects' – precious metals and stones, food and drink, women, the finest works of art that craftsmen could produce – and woe to them who did not give him full measure. Most dreadful of all, this new 'god' required a human sacrifice, ten each from every land he had conquered, five males and five females, all virgins, every year. What became of these unfortunates, no one can say. They were delivered up to the place of sacrifice; one moment, they stood there in mortal fear, and the next, they vanished from the face of the Earth. And perhaps it is best, my friend, that we do not dwell upon their fate.

Then, one day, the gods – the real gods – sent us a savior. Some say that Wynot the Wise came from the stars; others that he came from another dimension. It is futile to speculate on such things. It makes my head hurt! Certainly, Wynot (probably not his true name) never spoke of his origins but focused all of his energies upon the defeat of Krell and the end of his terror. By all accounts, this itinerant magician was extremely powerful, more so than any other magician who had ever lived; and, it was rumored, he possessed powers identical to the Orb of Power or he had an Orb of his own by which he could summon colossal energies. Time and again, he demonstrated his abilities and left no doubt in anyone's mind that he could deliver us from evil.

As to the matter of why he wished to defeat Krell, he was less tight-lipped. He simply claimed that great power requires great responsibility; without responsibility, no one deserves power. And, because Krell served only himself, he was undeserving of the power he possessed. Wynot said that it was his duty to oppose the Crusher. Most amazing of all, he did not ask for a reward for his services (though he could have had anything he wanted); for him, Krell's defeat was reward enough.

Long before the appearance of Wynot on the scene, Krell had retired to the same mountains wherein was his birthplace, relying on well-paid hirelings to oversee his collections of tribute and the enforcement of his decrees. Here, he built a mighty fortress, using slave labor from a score of lands. This fortress – known to us as the 'Maw of Krell' –was as solid as the mountains themselves for, in truth, it was carved out of the very rock of those mountains. Inside and out, it was festooned with the tribute Krell had demanded so that travelers would know that a powerful being dwelled therein. So secure did the Crusher believe himself to be that he never posted guards at the gates of the Maw but relied on the Orb to sound a warning of danger. Thus, when Wynot approached the main gate to issue his challenge, no human barred his path.

Is your cup empty again, wayfarer? Drink your fill, for I have a goodly supply.

As I was saying, Wynot stood before the Maw of Krell and bade the tyrant to show himself. Now, it is true that Krell had long before lost all aspects of humanity – save one. He never backed down from a challenge to his authority, and the challenge made by some upstart stranger (of whom he had heard all the rumors of his powers) was more than his lust for blood would allow. He vowed in a fearful voice that he would smite this fool and eat his bones for supper. Within the hour, the two faced each other before the main gate, the one radiating pure hate, the other calm and serenity.

I must confess, my friend, that, at this point, the tale takes on elements of the truly fantastic since it has been handed down to us for a hundred generations and each telling has no doubt been embellished. But, I recite it to you just as I have heard it, adding or subtracting nothing.

Wynot and Krell stood face to face in absolute silence, attempting to stare each other down, and neither moved for the space of two days. All around them, however, were the most horrendous thundering and lightning, earthquakes and avalanches. Parts of the mountains, including Krell's fortress, crumbled into dust; rivers ran dry; fields and pastures were scorched black; the sky itself turned blood-red; and no one could see the stars at night. And still Wynot and Krell maintained their rigid stance. At the end of the second day, Old Bone Crusher fell to his knees, totally exhausted. Then did Wynot step forward and remove the Orb of Power from his neck. This he *flung into a mighty crack in the Earth — some say it lies there still — and placed a curse upon the place. Another spell changed Krell into a gigantic boulder. Legend has it that, if only one human being sheds a tear for him, he will rejoin the world of the living. It is safe to say that he will be trapped forever.*

You have no doubt seen the boulder in question, wayfarer, when you entered Hyperborea. It bears a face on one side, a most wicked-looking face, and it serves as a warning to all to take heed of the one who is imprisoned therein.

There you have it, my friend, the whole story. You may believe it or not as you wish. It is all the same to me. I can only tell what I know. Believability is in the hands of the gods.

Safe journey to you, wayfarer. Perhaps we shall meet again.

*   *   *

Look, I wuz dere. I seen da whole boifin' t'ing!

But, yez gotta gimme some boifin' pertection, or I ain't sayin' another boifin' woid ta nobody. I want safe passage out o' da country, some money ta set meself up some'eres, an' absolutely no use o' me name. Dat ain't too much ta ask, eh?

OK, then, it's agreed? Dese two guys behind me are witnesses. Yez try ta double-cross me, dey know some'un who knows some'un... But yez get da boifin' pichure, eh?

Anyways, like I wuz sayin', I seen da battle between Lord Krell an' dis Wynot boifer. Damnedest t'ing I ever seen too. Yez mIght not believe some o' the story — or any of it, fer dat matter — but I don't give a flyin' boif. I seen what I seen.

Yez already know I wuz on Lord Krell's staff. Ha! Big boifin' deal! I wuz a 'sanitary engineer' which means I got to clean up all o' da boifin' horse shit 'n' chicken shit 'n' pig shit 'n' every udder kind o' shit dere is. All day long — nuttin but boifin' S-H-I-T! For which I got da usual ration o' bread 'n' beer — plus whatever else I could swipe out o' da boifin' kitchen.

Nacherly, due ta me less-dan-exalted position, I wuzn't too privy ta Hisself's bizness. Us down-belowers get some boifin' rumors now 'n' den;

and, oncet in o' while, some'un sees sumpin an' passes it along. Udder wise, da big boifers don't take us inta deir confidence. Dat's why I wuz surprised when woid came down from one o' da soivin' wenches who overheard talk between Hisself an' some o' his lootenants. She said dat Hisself told 'em ta expect some boifin' magician, name o' Wynot any day 'cause da boifin' Orb predicted it. Yez know dat whatever dat Orb said had ta be true; it wuzn't never wrong.

Da lootenants – not bein' very boifin' bright in da foist place 'cause Hisself di'n't want no smart boifer around ta make 'im look bad – dey got real scared 'cause dey had heard about dis magician an' what he could do. Hell's bells! All o' us down-belowers had fer dat matter. People from da valley who brung us our supplies wuz full o' stories about how Wynot did dis 'n' did dat 'n' generally had dose boifers eatin' out o' his boifin' hand. Anyways, da lootenants wuz all in favor of desoitin' da Maw before dis magician arrived an' put da Evil Eye on 'em. At which pernt (da wench claimed), Hisself just laughed an' turned dem boifin' cowards inta stachoos wit' a wave o' his hand. Yez kin believe dat or not, but I've seen some extra stachoos in da main hall an' damn if dey di'n't look familiar.

So, us down-belowers got togedder a lottery – one krob each – da winner bein' da one who came close to guessin' da day when Wynot would show hisself. An' before yez ask, no, I di'n't win. I wuz off by a boifin' week!

I wuz haulin' out a load o' boifin' pig shit da day Wynot arrived at da main gate. At first, I di'n't pay 'im no nevermind, 'cause people wuz allus showin' up at da gate fer one t'ing or anudder. An' dis raggedy-ass boifer di'n't look like no boifin' magician. Looked more like a tramp, lookin' fer a boifin' hand-out, he did.

Yeah, I know, how many magicians have I seen? More'n yez know, bub. An' doncha t'ink a foist-class magician woulda dressed fer da part, just ta let da boifin' rubes know who 'n what he wuz, eh? I t'ought at da time dat, if da mudderboifer wuz lookin' fer a hand-out, he coulda had all o' da boifin' pig shit he ever wanted! Heh-heh.

Well, I got ejacated real fast when dis 'tramp' started yellin' at da top o' his verce. 'Krell!' he sez. 'Krell, yez craven coward! Dis is Wynot da Wise! Come out an' face me – if yez dare!' I sez ta meself, 'Yeah, right, mudderboifer. An' I'm Beulah da Beautiful.'

Dis went on da whole boifin' day. Wynot would wait five minutes, den repeat hisself, an' wait five more minutes. Me, if I'da been Hisself, I'da been in dis boifer's face da second or t'ird time he challenged me, ready ta squash 'im like a boifin' bug. I reckon dat's why I'm a 'sanitary engineer' an' not some up-above boifer, eh?

Well, finally, near sunset, Hisself decided he'd heard all the boifin' shit he cared fer, an' he charged out da main gate ta give Wynot what-fer. It wuz a sight, I wanna tell yez. Dere wuz Lord Krell, drawn up to his full height o' t'ree meters, all muscle 'n' sinew, his bald head glistenin' like dew on da grass. And dere wuz Wynot, just shy o' two meters wit' a mop o' red hair an' a beard ta match. Dey wuz starin' at each udder like a snake looks at a mouse. I di'n't know what the boif wuz gonna happen, but I knew it wuzn't too boifin' smart ta be out in da open. I dumped me load o' pig shit an' ducked behind a boulder.

An' not a boifin' moment too soon, lemme tell yez! Hisself made da foist move; he touched da Orb (which he allus carried around his neck) an' chanted. Lessee, how did dat go? Oh, yeah.

> *"Oh, Orb! see my enemy, see him now!*
> *He makes a noise like a fatted cow.*
> *His name is Wynot, and he's a blot.*
> *Shower him with great pain and distress,*
> *And chase him away from my address!"*

Now, get dis: dat boifin' Orb starts glowin' — all bright 'n' white, it did. It hurt me eyes ta look at it. Da glowin' grew 'n' grew 'n' grew until dere wuz nuttin where Hisself wuz standin' but dis great big ball o' light, brighter'n da Sun itself. I almost shit me boifin' britches!

Did dis bodder Wynot? Not on yer boifin' life! He just stood dere wit' his arms folded across his chest, grinnin' like a boifin' idiot. If he expected sumpin ta happen, he sure di'n't show it. Suddenly, a ray o' light shot out o' da Orb an' split da air; an' where it stopped, a huge black sword appeared. Da sword zoomed toward Wynot like it wuz t'rowed at 'im. An' damn if da mudderboifer di'n't smile even more!

Just as dis sword wuz halfway between Hisself and Wynot, da magician made his own move. He flung out his arms wide an' chanted hisself. It went like dis:

"There once was a bald-headed chap,
Who caused such a horrible flap.
He conjures up a sword
That looks like a board.
Oh, Cosmos! fling it into a gap!"

Yeah, dat's exactly how he said it. Boifin' weird, eh?

Well, weird or not, it done da trick all right. Dis big hairy hand formed in front o' Wynot; an', just as da sword zeroed in on 'im, da hand grabbed it an' gave it a heave over da boifin' mountain. Far as I know, it's still flyin'.

Da next t'ing Hisself created wuz an army o' spiders – big, black, smelly boifers wit' fangs as long as yer thumb. I like ta shit me britches again! Dese spiders crawled over ta where Wynot stood an' formed a circle around 'im. An' what did dat boifer do? Why, he just t'umbed his nose at Hisself! Den he reached under his raggedy-ass clothes, brung out a handful o' red pebbles (dey looked like rubies ta me), spat on 'em, an' whispered sumpin I couldn't hear. He t'rowed da pebbles at da spiders – one at a time – an' when a pebble hit a spider, dat spider crumbled inta dust wit' a sound like some boifer fartin'.

Say, yez got anyt'ing ta drink around here? All dis talkin' is makin' me dry.

Water? Yez got ta be boifin' kiddin', eh? Well, hell's bells! No! Wait! Don't take it away. I guess it's better'n nuttin.

I hope yez don't mind me skippin' over most o' da details. Da boifin' battle lasted two days, y' know, an' much of it went pretty much like I described da first rounds. Hisself and Wynot t'rowed one spell after anudder at each udder – I di'n't know dere wuz so many in dis woild – wit'out needer havin' much effect on da udder.

Da sichuation di'n't last, o' course. Toward da end o' da second day, Hisself began ta tire, an' da boifin' Orb di'n't glow as bright as before. Each spell he conjured up took more 'n' more time ta come inta bein', an' many times he repeated hisself as if he had run out o' original idears. Boifin' Wynot, on da udder hand, still looked bright-eyed 'n' bushy-tailed, makin' nasty faces at Hisself an' castin' even weirder boifin' spells by da minute. It di'n't seem like he'd ever run out o' boifin' t'ings ta say.

Just before sunset on da second day, Hisself went slack-jawed an' fell ta his knees. I also noticed da Orb had stopped glowin'; fact wuz, it sputtered out like an old fire. Da look o' panic on Krell's face when dat glow died wuz a t'ing no one in livin' memory had ever seen; since he had depended on dat boifin' Orb so much, he wuz boifin' lost wit'out it. At dat pernt, I reckon even I coulda knocked 'im over if I'd had a mind to.

But I wuzn't gonna leave me hidin' place until I wuz boifin' sure da boifin' battle wuz over. When da reality o' his sichuation finally sunk in – an' I swear dis is true, so help me all o' da boifin' gods o' Hyperborea – Hisself cried! Hell's bells! He blubbered, if yez want da boifin' trut'. He begged Wynot fer moicy. Imagine dat! Da Old Bone Crusher – beggin' fer moicy!

Wynot, who'd been pretty boifin' nonchalant up ta den, got all serious-like, an' his face went so boifin' grim dat it woulda frightened a boifin' stachoo. Slowly, deliberately, he walked up ta Hisself an' removed dat dead Orb from his neck. He held it above his head an' recited anudder weird chant:

> *"There once was an Orb so fell,*
> *That it seduced a lout like Krell.*
> *It corrupted him through and through*
> *And caused him great rue.*
> *Oh, Cosmos, send the thing to Hell!"*

Den he t'rowed da boifin' Orb as far as he could. I seen it disappear some'eres inta da mountains.

As fer Lord Krell hisself – I should say da former Lord Krell – Wynot laid a hand on his head, chanted again, an' turned 'im inta a big boifin' rock. Yez don't believe me, mudderboifers? Well, yez kin go out dere an' see fer yer boifin' selves. No never mind ta me. Big boifin' rock wit' a human face – dat's what's left o' da Old Bone Crusher. An' good boifin' riddance to 'im, I say!

Whattaya mean, watch me tongue? It's not like sumpin boifin' nasty is gonna happen ta me, eh? I kin speak freely now. 'Sides, a guy's gotta look out fer hisself, don't he? Yez don't know how many boifers down in da valley hate our boifin' guts, just 'cause we woiked up here. Long live da revolution, eh?

Yez got any more boifin' questions? I'd like ta get da boif out o' here before some mudderboifer who ain't heard da news takes it inta his head dat Krell-people are still boifin' fair game.

Hey, what da boif yez doin'? Aw, no! Double-crossin' mudderboifers! Boif yez! BOIF YEZ ALL!!!

* * *

There was more, but the colossal breakfast Wilfong had consumed was by now fully digested, and he was experiencing a bowel movement. Without another thought, he headed straight to the privy.

Like everything else in the village of Loth, the outhouse had been constructed from whole logs and planks and resembled a miniature *kabban*. Inside, one found accommodations for half a dozen people at a time. Wilfong wondered idly if the Lothians allowed the mingling of the sexes here or if they announced their intent before entering. As sturdy as the privy was, the Wizard had trouble getting comfortable. At home, he had been accustomed to either porcelain or lacquered wood upon which to sit; here, however, the planks were strictly rough cuts, and he feared picking up splinters. Consequently, he was not prepared for an incoming mind-cast.

-- Hey, Wilfong!

"What the devil?" the Atlantean muttered.

-- Wilfong, are you there?

Wilfong grimaced. Leave it to Zondar to break in at the most inappropriate moment. Was he trying to get even for having been awakened in the middle of the Cimmerian night?

-- What do you want, Zondar?

-- Am I interrupting anything?

-- If you must know, I'm relieving myself.

-- Yeah? By all the gods of Creation, you're human after all. Ain't that just burfing grand?

-- Are you through joking around? What d'ya want?

--Damn, but you're touchy today.

-- I have good reason to be. Sinladen Crotchgod has made two assaults against me since we last communicated.

-- No shit (excuse the pun!)? He's not wasting any time, is he?

--No, and I'm sure those incidents were just a preliminary. Now, for the third time, what's on your mind?

-- Um, well, have you read the material I sent you?

-- Some of it. Why?

-- I came across another scroll while I was tidying up after that transmission. A single sheet of papyrus, actually. I have no idea where it came from.

-- That's very queer and strange. I thought you knew where everything came from. What's it about?

-- That's the damnedest thing. There's only two short sentences on it. 'I have the Three. Follow me.'

A long silence ensued.

-- Hey, Wilfong! You didn't fall asleep on me, did you?

-- Eh? No, no. I'm still here.

-- What the hell's going on?

-- That message   did you quote it word for word?

-- Of course. I'm the burfing Librarian, ain't I?

-- And in what language was it written?

-- Well, that's another funny thing, Wilfong. This sheet of papyrus is fresh out of the mill, but the language is late-Thirteenth Dynasty Atlantean.

-- Really? The Master walked the streets of Atlantis at that time.

-- By all the gods of Creation, d'ya mean *Himself* wrote this?

-- I can't say for sure. It would seem so, though.

-- What's the message mean?

-- I'm afraid I can't tell you just yet. This message is only for Elevens and up. Someday, all of the Clutch will be advised of its meaning.

-- Well, ain't that just burfing grand? OK, you're the boss. I'll follow orders.

-- I'm glad to hear you say that, Zondar. Now, stand by for my next report to the Elders.

The Wizard tersely relayed what information he had gleaned in the past centi-cycle and added a personal warning to all of the Order to take particular note of any unusual activity, no matter how trivial it might appear. From his recent experience, he knew that the Enemy disguised his attacks with innocuous acts; anything out of the ordinary could well be a prelude to another assault, and keen observation might just prevent incalculable damage, individually and collectively. He also recommended that all Elevens and Twelves put themselves on immediate alert status and perform a mental sweep of the entire Known World in order to locate the Enemy's headquarters.

-- *Holy shit!* [Zondar exclaimed as soon as the transmission was completed]. I've seen mental sweeps by four Twelves any number of times, and once I saw an eight-man job. But, *all* of them – plus the Elevens? That's enough burfing juice to turn the Cosmos inside out!

-- Better *we* do it than Crotchgod does. At least, we'd want to restore the Cosmos later on. That madman is bent on revenge, and he'll destroy Space and Time to achieve his goal.

-- Well, ain't that just burfing grand?

-- Isn't it, though? Well, that's all I have for now.

-- No *personal* messages?

-- Good-bye, Zondar.

-- So long, Wilfong. Don't take any wooden *dalas*.

Impertinent scoundrel! the Wizard grumbled. *He takes far too much advantage of my good nature.*

*   *   *

The Three!

Of course, Wilfong recognized the message instantly. Upon hearing it, he experienced a thrill up and down his spine. His breath caught in his throat, his heart skipped several beats, and his eyes unfocused. For a brief time, the world stopped in its tracks. It was only with the greatest effort that the Wizard snapped out of the temporary trance those fateful words had induced in him.

The Three!

Wynot the Wise had established his Order long ago so that the powers of the mind could be developed in a more rational and progressive fashion. Most Practitioners who had founded other Orders did so merely to enrich themselves and to shelter their followers from the Dread Edict; they taught very little beyond passing on the "tricks of the trade" with which they were familiar. The Compleat Sorcerer, however, wanted his disciples to explore new dimensions of thought and reality.

To that end, his curriculum followed a step-by-step progression where each lesson built upon previous material and became the basis for future lessons. The novitiate rose through the levels of instruction at his/her own pace until (s)he had arrived at his/her unique level of incompetence. Pragmatically speaking, (s)he had to complete ten levels of formal training before (s)he could be considered a full-fledged member of the Clutch; Levels Eleven and Twelve made him/her eligible to become Elders. Level Thirteen involved independent training which all Twelves dabbled at as they could; in it, the Twelves learned alternate ways of viewing the Cosmos and of operating within it, and they were always cautioned not to embark upon this path unless they were absolutely mentally prepared to accept what they discovered there.

Toward the end of Level Eleven training, the student was exposed to Wynot's treatises on the fabled "Three Grand Spells of the Cosmos," the mastery of which permitted a Practitioner to become One-with-the All and exist (so it was claimed) as pure energy. The Three had been a favorite topic in any number of writings set down through the ages (most of which this writer has read with varying degrees of comprehension). Mostly rooted in ancient folklore and even older superstitions, they allegedly were formulated by the Most High in the Beginning of the World and held out to a bedazzled humankind as a goal to work toward if humans aspired to be gods themselves. Each Order had its unique variation of the origins, the nature, and the consequences of the Three; yet, none had ever had the ability to pursue The Dream. Even Wynot seemed to have been stymied in his personal pursuit (though he was much closer to that goal than most Practitioners) and always encouraged his followers to persevere. His theory was taught to the assiduous Elevens and Twelves, but only a Thirteen was actually expected to discover the method of incorporation.

Now, allegedly, Wynot the Wise was proclaiming that he had finally acquired the Three, mastered them, and become One-with-the-All.

The Wizard could hardly contain his joy at receiving this message. In his mind's eye, he envisioned the Master trodding along a seldom traveled path, discovering among the ruins of some incredibly ancient but long-extinct civilization a fragile scroll written in an obscure language, spending an age in its translation, spending additional ages in learning its secrets, and testing and re-testing the validity of what He had learned. It must have been a glorious moment when He realized the true nature of His find and a *supremely* glorious moment when He was transfigured and became a god.

Now the Compleat Sorcerer was calling to His disciples – those who were able to comprehend the Summons – to follow Him into that hallowed realm. Wilfong could scarcely imagine its happening to *him*. It seemed, on the face of it, a colossally impossible task and an equally colossally impertinent act, his striving for godhood. But, Wynot, Who knew more than most sentient beings, had opened the gate, so to speak, and transmitted a definite invitation. Therefore, it must be both possible and pertinent. And the dream which had come to him days before had to have been his *personal* invitation, serving to re-enforce the magnitude of this personal message. The Master knew about him, knew how quickly he had mastered His teachings, and knew how worthy he was to follow in His footsteps. It was enough to render a lesser mortal senseless.

As gratifying as it was to dwell on such ethereal ideas, Wilfong could ill afford to do so for any great length of time. Before he could travel down the path toward Oneness-with-the-All, he first had to clear away the obstacles in the path, the foremost of which was the evil scheme of Sinladen Crotchgod. He thus needed a clear head in order to formulate a definite plan of attack.

Gingerly, he removed himself from the rough-hewn privy and returned to his room. But, as he reached for the handle of the door, Murkol burst into the corridor from the common room. He wore a grin broad enough to split his face in two.

"Mashter!" he exclaimed breathlessly. "Comesht shee what de villacherzh have done for dee!"

Puzzled, the Wizard followed his servant back the way the latter had come. As they passed through the common room, those Lothians who were still present smiled hugely and waved at him with great enthusiasm. The Atlantean returned the greetings, though for the life of him, he was at a loss for this sudden show of popularity. Once outside, he spotted a small crowd gathered around a sign which had not been there three hours before. Murkol herded him toward the gathering, nearly dragging him in the process. Upon spying him, the villagers broke into spontaneous applause.

"Here he be!" one young man shouted. "Our star performer!"

Even as they parted to allow him to approach the sign, many hands tugged at his sleeves or slapped his back. He turned to the Zarelor.

"Would you mind explaining all this?" he muttered.

"De shign, Mashter. Readesht de shign."

Wilfong now peered at the make-shift poster, hastily lettered but still legible. In large block letters, his name (or the Lothian rendition of it) jumped out at him; and, whereas the remainder of the words had been rendered in blue, his name stood out in red. He had to read the words twice before he could make sense of them. He was left dumbfounded. The sign read:

A Limited Engagement

WIFFON THE MAGNIFICENT

Performing Amazing Feats
Of Magic and Legerdemain

Performances at 6 & 9

Admission: $5 (Adults)
$2 (Children)

"By Wynot's crooked teeth!" Wilfong swore. "Whose idea was this?"

"Dey shay dou agreed to perform tonight, Mashter."

"A *small* performance, for the benefit of the children. I certainly didn't agree to some – some *circus act*! Where's Funkol? I want to talk to him!"

He did not have to search at all. The Speaker of the village, ever at the center of all activity in his community, had spotted him first and was steaming toward him, the picture of ebullience and optimism. Even the Wizard's grim expression was not sufficient to erase the grin which stretched from ear to ear. Funkol slammed to a halt and clapped his Atlantean guest heavily on the shoulder.

"Master Wiffon! I be pleased to catch up with thee. We have to finalize tonight's program."

"Me pardon?" Wilfong yelped. "What *program* this be? I nothing of it know."

"Why, the very program thou didst announce earlier today. In Kank-ki, when one announces a thing, it be as good as done. Surely, thy servant explained this to thee?"

"I for a *paying* audience did not agree to perform. Only the children I thought to entertain."

"Thou didst? I was given to understand that thou wouldst give a general performance. There must have been some misunderstanding."

"I should say so!"

"Oh, but, Master Wiffon! Surely, thou wilt change thy mind. Most of the arrangements have already been made, and word of the event has been sent throughout the land." His eyes took on a lost-little-boy look. "So many people – so many *children* – will be greatly disappointed." Now his face took on a sly appearance. "We will be happy to cut thee in for a share of the profits – say five per cent of the net? – and provide *free* room and board while thou art in Loth."

Wilfong pondered long and hard. Given a choice between making a public spectacle of himself and breaking a promise (the consequences of which he had failed to think through completely), he supposed the former carried the least amount of negativity. It wasn't a matter of performing in public *per se* which bothered him – he had "entertained" in Atlantis in front of selected audiences at Lymatan's on many occasions – but, rather, it was being taken advantage of by a sharper looking to add to the village's (and his) treasury. Money-hunger seemed to permeate this land like a fog; no one did anything without attaching a price tag to it. The Lothians could teach Atlantean merchants a thing or two about profiteering!

Well, he could play that game too. If Funkol wanted him to perform like a trained animal, then he damned well was going to pay for it.

"The deal seven-and-a-half per cent make, and *as scheduled* I will perform."

"Agreed," the Speaker replied unhesitatingly. "Oh, this will be a splendid event! Loth will shine tonight!

"Now, we must know thy needs, Master Wiffon. In the way of props so that we can allot sufficient space for the stage and seating area. We must know if thou wilt supply thine own costume, or if thou wilt require one to be made; if the last, then we must have some idea of its appearance. We will be holding the performance in the Visitor's Center, of course, and that brings me to the next item of business...."

THE ELEVENTH CASTING

THE WIZARD AT LENGTH

Wilfong the Wizard dreamed.

i am walking along the streets of my home town. on either side, i see familiar buildings, familiar monuments, familiar signs.

i am in no particular hurry. i am just out for a pleasant stroll. all is well with the world.

i have been down these streets many, many times, and, while i recognize most of the landscape, i notice significant changes. often when i walk these streets more than once, the differences are never the same ones twice; always the scene re-forms into something new.

now, i enter an area i have not been in before, far from the central city. it is a residential area where the streets are paved with a strange sticky substance which clings to my sandals when warmed. Thus, i avoid walking on the streets and keep to the adjacent walkways separated from the streets by strips of grassland and constructed from a mortar-like substance. the houses in this district are all made of wood; curiously, they all appear identical, row after row of them like the spots on a leopard. some attempt has been made to alter their sameness through the use of color, but there seems to have been a small range of hues from which to choose.

to my utter surprise, i spy a chariot traveling along one street. it is unlike any chariot i have ever seen, for nothing draws it, neither horse nor ox nor mule nor any other beast of burden. the chariot moves by itself, powered by some magical force, the nature of which is beyond my simple brain to comprehend. and, moreover, the chariot is not open but enclosed on all sides, and its passengers sit upon benches within facing forward. as the vehicle passes by, i hear an ominous growling issuing from it. it is drawn by some beast after all, but the beast is invisible! *it is a great wonder to behold!*

the passengers of this marvelous conveyance stare at me, even as i return their gaze. i do not have to be a natural philosopher to realize that they have never seen anyone quite like me (nor i them). yet, they do not stop to make inquiries of me as i have experienced elsewhere in my travels but continue on their way.

whether by chance or by design, i spot several more of these magical chariots. at one point, two of them meet at an intersection and are on the verge of colliding. one of the vehicles never slows down but instead actually speeds up. the second one halts suddenly, making a noise like some tormented soul, and the invisible beast which draws it brays in protest.

i continue to walk, marveling at what i have witnessed thus far. as i have theorized before, two possible origins for these wonders arise: (1) i am in the city in its future self, or (2) i am in the city in another dimension. either of my conjectures is fantastic on the face of it, but what else am i to make of the familiar yet unfamiliar?

at length, i approach a much more re-assuring sight: a great house constructed of good, honest stone. it is three stories high, possessing many windows and doors, rivaling any of the buildings in the central city. surely, a wealthy merchant dwells within. a fence surrounds the estate; it is not made of stone but of metal, specifically the black metal known as iron. *the house stands amidst a wide, well-manicured lawn upon which many trees and shrubs grow. a wide walkway, constructed of bricks and paving stones traverses the lawn from the main gate to the front door of the house. parallel to the walkway is an even wider swath of the black sticky substance for the use of the chariots.*

the main gate stands open, invitingly. i am eager to enter this house and meet its master; yet, i have not been specifically invited. as i stand there debating whether i should proceed, the front door swings open, and a figure appears there. i recognize him instantly; it is the man with my face again! he walks toward me at a measured pace, neither smiling nor frowning. he halts before me and signals me to follow him. as i fall in behind him, his/ my face begins to age as before.

we do not enter the house, however (i am not a little disappointed), but go around toward the rear of the estate. there, i see another familiar sight: a pedestal with a carved owl perched upon it. i am dumbfounded and turn to my guide for an explanation. he says not a word but walks on until we are standing beside the pedestal. he twists the owl-figurine sharply, and immediately a trap opens up in the ground nearby. a rough-hewn stair leads to the bottom of the revealed cavity. my guide waves toward it. my body trembles as i descend into the pit.

unlike a similar subterranean chamber i have visited many times before, this one has no other exit; it is merely a hole in the ground leading nowhere. puzzled, i crane my head upward to question the man with my face, only to discover that he is gone and that i am alone there.

without warning, the hole is filled with a bright white light, one which i have experienced once before. and, when the light fades and normal vision is restored, i realize i am no longer in the hole.

rather, i am in the great metal cave wherein Wynot the Wise dwells.

i am filled with unimaginable joy! to be once again in the presence of my Master is as much as i can bear, and i am close to swooning.

as before, the golden-yellow carpet stretches out into the distance toward the nether end of the cavern. the figures clad in gray again line both sides. the nearest one (the pig-faced one) again smiles its inhuman smile with its inhuman face and salutes me in the customary fashion. i return his greeting. now, i begin the long, slow walk along the carpet, greeting each member of that Company in its turn. i am completely at ease.

then i am reminded of where i am and of Who resides in this place. a wave of humility washes over me, and i approach the great throne more contritely; and, when i have halted before it, i am as abject a thing as ever was created. i gaze cautiously at my Lord and meet His ancient eyes which project Harmony and Wisdom everlasting. He smiles at me and salutes me. i do likewise. then i throw myself to the ground.

"o, Wynot!" i murmur. 'great art Thou, and lowly am i! strong art Thou, and weak am i! wise art Thou, and stupid am i! o, Wynot, may Thy glory

shine forth forever and ever! bless me, Thy humble servant, and guide me down the path of Harmony and Wisdom!'

'arise,' the Lord commands.

He looks into my face as if to discover some flaw there, either of design or of function. i feel His eyes penetrate my body – my soul – and i fear that i am not worthy in His sight. i am greatly relieved when He smiles yet again.

'it's…wilfong, isn't it? you've been here before.'

'yes, Master, once before.'

'we didn't have much of an opportunity to chat, did we? i had some pressing business to attend to. perhaps we can make up for lost time now. but, first, i'd like to show you something interesting.'

the Master snaps His fingers, and i hear a slight metallic noise above my head. i look up at the ceiling and observe a sphere of silvery metal a meter in diameter descending to the floor. it halts two meters above the floor and hovers in mid-air, glowing with a pale green. the Lord speaks to it in some arcane language, and a ray of green light issues from the sphere and bathes the floor with an eerie luminescence. to my great astonishment, an image forms where the light strikes the floor, slowly at first, then more quickly as the Master speaks again in the unknown tongue. my breath catches in my throat as i recognize the image presented. it is the metropolis of atlantis – all five rings with their various architectures, the wharf district, and the surrounding fields and pastures. if i look closely enough, i can make out the building in which i live. it is mid-morning, for the streets are filled with people engaged upon some errand or another or on a sight-seeing tour. though i hear no sounds, my imagination can easily supply the babble which must surely be occurring.

yet, what is most amazing about this marvelous sight is the fact that I am viewing it as if i were suspended in the air high above the ground or i were riding on the back of a gigantic bird!

now, this 'magic eye' zooms toward the ground, toward the wharf district. i see the work crews loading and unloading the steady stream of merchandise. i can actually pick out familiar faces. yes, there is my 'drinking companion,' hamilton, barking orders at his crew; undoubtedly, he is creating fresh obscenities with which to shower those driven souls. the 'eye' swings over to pier eight, and i spot the slave ship still in the harbor.

there is no activity at this time beyond a skeleton crew making repairs and resupplying for the outbound journey. the 'eye' lingers only momentarily, then hurries on to the warehouse where the slaves are kept temporarily.

on the city side of the warehouse, between the building and the outer wall, a small crowd gathers. the semi-naked females are being paraded before potential buyers prior to their being auctioned off. the slaves are, to a woman, defiant toward both their foreign captor and their would-be atlantean masters. yet, i see in their faces the fear of what sort of future they will have when their 'usefulness' is at an end. i recall my lessons on the subject in Temple and shudder. i am not viewing humankind at its noblest.

i steal a glance Wynot. He too is grim-faced; His eyes are as hard as stone. what, i ask myself, would He do if He were present in the flesh at that place?

'nothing has changed in atlantis,' the Lord says abruptly, 'since I walked its streets. what say you, wilfong? do you see any hope for improvement?'

i swallow compulsively.

'there is always hope, Master,' i whisper, 'as Thou hast taught. But, i fear we must wait a time before the minds of men are unclouded and they realize the folly of their ways.'

'my sentiments exactly. observe, pupil. i will show you yet another wonder.'

the scene of the wharf district winks out as if a shadow has passed over it. the silvery globe glows again, and now a blue ray of light shoots forth. the image it produces is beyond comprehension. i spot the moon, not as a silver disk in the night sky but as a huge grayish-white worldlet, dotted with hundreds (perhaps thousands) of craters of all sizes and shapes, crisscrossed by mountain ranges which dwarf those on earth. the 'magic eye' which had flown over atlantis now hovers over this pockmarked landscape nearly at the same height. some obscure atlantean philosopher had once speculated on the nature and habitability of the moon, but i realize now that he had largely let his imagination run wild. were he to observe what i was observing, he would have known that everything he had ever said on the subject was mere fantasy.

as i watch the 'eye' roam over the surface of the moon, my own eye catches sight of an unusual object high above the 'eye's' position. it is descending slowly to the surface while – here, i gasp with disbelief – a huge fire issues from its lowermost parts. the nearer the thing comes to the moon, the more details I can make out. it appears to be metallic, but no metal I have ever seen glistens as much as this sort does. the object is as big as a house; yet, this 'house' has 'legs' and 'feet' – spindly legs, and feet like platters – arranged like the appendages of a beetle. atop the object are various protrusions studding its surface in several places. on one side, a red-white-and-blue configuration adorns the object, resembling the pennants i have seen in my travels to represent one kingdom or another. apparently, this strange visitor bears the sign of its origin.

if I were not a faithful devotee of the teachings of Wynot but retained the popular superstitions of the day, i should judge that i am witnessing a manifestation of the gods of creation. whatever else this object is, it is clearly a construct by flesh-and-blood creatures, though what kind of flesh-and-blood fills me with awe and not a little fear. perhaps it belongs to one of the race of Beings who are represented along the golden-yellow carpet.

the object settles gently on the surface of the moon, and the fire it had been belching out sputters away into wisps of smoke. and now it just sits there, silent, unmoving for several long moments.

the 'eye' drifts closer to the thing, and i see in great detail all of the protrusions on its body. there are small cylinders and globes and cubes. a disk attached to the cone which tops the object rotates back and forth a quarter of a turn, the only apparent motion.

more long moments pass. abruptly, a section of the object opens up like the drawbridge of a castle. i spot movement inside. to my great astonishment, a man-sized and man-shaped bulky figure appears in the opening, clambers down a short ladder, and then drops the remaining distance to the ground. the 'eye' zooms in on this newcomer. there is something familiar about it....

then realization hits me like a hammer. this figure who dares to walk on the surface of the moon resembles many of the Beings who line the carpet behind me. is it akin to any of them?

there is, however, one significant difference between this new being (now hopping about as if he were a frog!) and the Company in the cave. the insignia he wears is similar to that which adorns his vehicle, but none of the others have such an insignia. i can only conclude that this hopper is of a separate allegiance than the devotees of Wynot.

shortly, a second figure (similarly garbed) emerges from the object and joins its fellow creature in hopping about. is this a religious ritual they are performing? or are they merely expressing joy at being where they are? it is both fascinating and perplexing.

another silent command from the Lord causes the image to fade away. but i continue to stare at the empty space, completely entranced. not until the Master clears His throat for my attention do i break off my reverie.

'there is more, much more, pupil,' Wynot says softly. 'i have shown you but an infinitesimal part of the greater reality of Space and Time. once you have opened your mind to this greater reality, you will know what I know. do you believe that, wilfong?'

'if Thou hast said it, Master, then i must believe. yet, even if Thou hast not, the proof' – I gesture at the place where the miraculous images had materialized – 'was before my eyes. only a fool denies the evidence of his eyes.'

'but, i could be deceiving you with illusions.'

'to what end, Master? i saw only things of a benign nature. true, that what i saw was strange to me at first sight, but not inexplicable, given some thought.'

'very good, wilfong. that is the answer i expect from my disciples. do you remember my admonition at our last meeting?'

i rack my brain to recall that incident. it had seemed so unreal. slowly, however, memory returns to me, and i nod my head.

'yes, Master. Thou didst say, "where I go, few can follow. if you would follow Me, take the One True Path toward Harmony and Wisdom and be One-with-the-All."'

'correct. and do you know where the path lies?'

'faithful adherence to Thy teachings, keeping an open mind, and looking beyond oneself.' i hesitate to speak further, for it might seem impertinent. but, Wynot, sensing that i do wish to add something, gestures by way of encouragement. i swallow hard and say: 'Master, Thou hast said that Thou hadst found the Three. i think this is the final step, is it not?'

'it is. And you will find Them in your own time. be of good cheer, wilfong.'

He salutes me, and i Him. He touches His left temple with His left thumb. a blinding flash of white light envelopes the throne, and Wynot is gone. once again, i am alone.

nevertheless, i am also filled with infinite joy. for the Lord had found worth in me and had shown me wondrous sights not given to lesser mortals. and He had promised me that i shall be with Him forever in due time – a desire i hold greater than life itself.

i turn and walk the length of the carpet toward the hole in the ground which had gained me entrance to the cavern. when i reach the other end, as expected, another flash envelopes me, and i find myself sitting on the lawn of the great house next to the owl statuary. it is night now, and the streets are illuminated by brilliant globes atop tall poles which are spaced at regular intervals. if not for the presence of the stars in the sky, one might have been tempted to believe it was still daytime, so great was the light from those globes.

on the streets are many more of the strange chariots drawn by invisible creatures. they too possess globes of light to find their way in the dark. i return home with both a sense of wonder and renewed hope in the rightness of my course.

*   *   *

Instantly, Wilfong awoke, for two reasons.

The first was that the dream he had just had had been so vivid, so vibrant, so...*realistic* that it couldn't have been a dream at all but rather a real event in which he had actually participated (though he had no idea how he had done so). Many of his dreams were similar in nature, although they were often more symbolic than this one had been. This one had contained very little symbolism; all of the objects seemed authentic, even if they were strange-looking to his way of thinking. No doubt about it: he had been in a real place, speaking to Wynot in person.

The Master had deigned to teach him personally!

Truly, he was blessed among all of the Clutch. Only that first generation of disciples could boast of such blessedness. Yet, at the same time, he felt much humbleness, for the Compleat Sorcerer had also been displeased by the lack of progress humankind had made since he had worn flesh. Though Wilfong had been under no obligation to assume guilt for the things others did, he did, on behalf of his fellow creatures, because all of the members of the Order should have been doing their utmost to advance the principles of Civilization and could not. All the more reason to apply himself more vigorously in the future.

The second reason was more mundane. While the various elements of the dream remained fresh in his mind, he needed to verify them. To achieve this required that he return to Atlantis at once. If even some of the elements proved to be actual events, he could extrapolate the rest. Moreover, he would come close to realizing the true nature of dreams and thus profiting from them (philosophically, of course) in the pursuit of his goals. He doubted he could verify his being in the presence of Wynot, however; where the Master was at this moment was far from Wilfong's point in Space and Time.

The Wizard had no intention of transiting back to Atlantis. His corporeal absence would be hard to explain, even by the faithful Murkol. There was sure to be an inquiry, and no one would have been able to report having seen Loth's prize guest depart physically. More gullible villagers might well believe he had left by "magical" means; the Speaker, on the other hand, struck Wilfong as the sharpest card in Kank-ki, and he might not be so easily fooled. Prestidigitation was one thing Funkol understood well. The powers of a Master Practitioner were quite another matter. And Wilfong was not prepared to reveal his true self to any non-Practitioner, and certainly not to some barbarian on the fringes of the Known World!

No, the visitation had to be a purely mental one. So long as his body remained in Loth, the ploy of his having to meditate before the night's performance gained strength. Thus undisturbed, he could cast out his mind and use 'inner vision" to scan the streets and buildings of the Metropolis.

He sought a more comfortable position on the bed, found one, and relaxed both physically and mentally. Quickly, he called up to the conscious level a Spell of Far-Seeing and chanted:

> "There once was a place of great sheen,
>   A city which may never have been.
>   To it I must fly
>   In the twinkling of an eye.
>   Oh, Wynot, send me unseen!"

His body slumped as consciousness left it, and his mind raced towards home.

Only a minute or two may have passed from the time Wilfong awoke and the time he cast his Spell. Therefore, he expected to see much the same scenes in his mind's eye as he had seen in the dream. He was not disappointed. Following the same course that Wynot's "magic eye" had taken, he floated unseen over the Metropolis' wharf district and hovered above the notorious Pier Eight. The auctioning of the slave women was now in progress; the bidding was taking longer than usual because the bidders were spending more time ogling the scantily-clad females than making bids on them.

What concerned the Wizard more than the loose behavior and the immoral trade – if only on a superficial level – was how the auctioneer was being allowed to conduct this business on an alleged festival day. All businesses were required to close on festival days, so that the Most High could be honored (even if only with lip service). Wilfong suspected some favoritism and/or bribery at play here – he certainly didn't care about such matters as "blasphemy" – but he had neither the time nor the inclination to pursue the question.

And now, he spotted a familiar face in the crowd of oglers: none other than his lunkhead of a student, Zorpac. Instead of tending to the religious obligations (if indeed he entertained any at all) or studying his lessons, the worthless fellow was engaged in idle pursuits. But, then, what else was new?

Wilfong resisted the temptation to approach Zorpac and play a prank on him – which the latter might ascribe either to an "evil spirit" and thus become even more witless than he already was or to his neighbor and thus pick a quarrel with him. Either scenario would have caused him great public embarrassment and/or censure and certainly *private* censure from his sire. But the Wizard had no time for pranks and so let the moment pass.

Having verified what could be easily verified, he departed the wharf district and zoomed toward the Second Ring of Atlantis. As he passed over familiar sights, he observed with bemusement the activities of his fellow Atlanteans as they (to one degree or another) paid their respects to the Most High. This day was the second day of the Feast of Caxeot, and that meant a long, slow, and ponderous procession throughout the city by throngs of devotees, led by the priests and acolytes of the god. Since Caxeot was the patron of learning, Wilfong was not surprised to see the Directors of the various Academies and Schools at the forefront of the procession. Each delegation wore their distinctively colored robes with a grand show of egotistic splendor (how would the gods regard this bit of human vanity?).

The order of march had begun in the First Ring, at the temple dedicated to Xenox (as he was the Lord of Creation), from whence it moved on to the temple of Caxeot, where many prayers would be offered up asking for the god's blessings on the people and the Kingdom of Atlantis. Thereafter, the line would wind its way past the temples of the other gods in the Atlantean pantheon in the order of their importance after Xenox and finally to the Royal Palace, where another host of long-winded prayers would be said. In between stops, the mob sang many hymns of thanksgiving and praise, punctuated by a spate of "spontaneous" prayers for additional blessings on Atlantis. Once all of the stations in the First Ring had been visited, the procession would move into the other Rings and exhort the parade-watchers to join them. Eventually, it would return to the temple of Caxeot for a final round of prayers and hymn-singing.

Most of the participants lining both sides of the streets were non-Atlanteans, either foreign tourists or alien residents. Devotees of their own gods (or of none at all, as the case may be), these individuals had been drawn by curiosity to witness the rituals of the indigenous population who claimed to be the most advanced race – by whatever standard of measurement – in all of the Known World and to be either disgusted or amused by them as the spirit moved them. Naturally, few (if any) of them were persuaded to join in the procession; rather, on occasion, a catcall or a jeer was shouted (anonymously!), the more so as the line marched toward the lower end of the Metropolis' socio-economic spectrum. The presence of the City Guards walking in step with the parade on either side served to keep the catcalls and jeers to the barest minimum and/or prevent any retaliation on the part of Atlanteans who may have been slighted by the "blasphemy."

When Wilfong caught up with this outpouring of religious fervor, it had neared the end of its circuit of the Second Ring and was about to pass into the Third Ring. At that moment, he spied yet another familiar face: Wembly. Behind the ranks of the priests and acolytes of Caxeot, behind the ranks of the academicians and scholars, trod the personnel of the Library, all in their blue and white splendor. The clandestine Chief Elder of the Order of Wynot was putting on a mighty show of devotion, but one versed in reading non-verbal signals (as most members of the Order were) would have recognized that Wembly's face and eyes displayed a completely different set of emotions. The Wizard could well sympathize with his friend but still thanked the Cosmos for not being down there himself. Now, he descended closer to the procession until he hovered just above Wembly's right shoulder.

-- Let's show a little more enthusiasm here, shall we?

Wembly's step faltered at the sudden "voice" at his side, and he surreptitiously looked left and right to see if anyone had noticed his clumsiness. Suppressing a frown, he replied:

-- Wilfong? What's the big idea?

-- Sorry about that, old friend. But, you looked *so* absorbed in what you were doing.

-- I should have been an actor instead of a scholar. I've managed to fool my superiors for years with my shows of piety. The Cosmos take these self-righteous frauds!

-- I concur. I have to go through the same song-and-dance at my School. By the way, that's my Headmaster just in front of you.

-- Really? I swear, he's on the verge of self-flagellation. Has he always been like that?

-- As long as I've known him. He claims to be setting an example for the rest of the staff. It takes all of my will power to keep from laughing out loud. Or screaming. Or both.

-- If Wynot hadn't taught us how to deal with this sort of tomfoolery, we'd soon be the 'guests of honor' in the Square of Contemplation.

-- Too true. And speaking of the Master, I had another vision only a short while ago.

The Wizard related the whole fantastic incident quickly and waited for Wembly's reaction. It was not long in coming.

-- By all the gods of Creation, Wilfong! What a marvelous experience! Excuse me, old friend, I didn't mean to use one of Zondar's pet expressions. It just sort of slipped out.

-- You're excused – as long as you don't use his *other* pet expression.

-- I won't. [A pause.] The Master has truly blessed you, Wilfong. To my knowledge, none of the Clutch beyond the First Disciples has ever been instructed by Him personally since He left us. Of course, since you're our first Thirteen, it's only logical that He should take a personal interest.

-- It's all very humbling, Wembly. And yet, at the same time, it's very exhilarating. I look forward to the day when I can sit at His feet and receive more of His instruction.

-- You'll be sorely missed.

-- Thank you. And I'll miss you as well. Now, I must dash. I have one more stop to make before I return to my body. Farewell, old friend, and keep a stiff upper lip!

The "one more stop" was the Temple of the Order of Wynot – or, more precisely, the private estate under which it lay. Curiously, though the Wizard had visited this noble dwelling in his capacity of private tutor to the scions of the Lord of the manor, he had done so only at night. Consequently, he had never seen it very clearly; it had been just a dark silhouette against the night sky. He now desired to see it in the daytime and to compare its appearance with that of the house in his dream. He departed the religious procession (now passing through the Gate of Laughter into the Third Ring) with a sigh of relief at having been spared the ordeal of participating and hastened to the opposite quadrant of the First Ring.

It may be fairly said that, having already witnessed a number of eye-opening and/or mind-numbing sights, the like of which neither he nor any other living human was ever likely to see again, Wilfong had perhaps become immune to future shock. Therefore, he was not disappointed when he saw no magic chariots on black-substance streets. He was pleased, however, to discover that, with the exception of the building materials used – limestone here, a mortar-like substance there – the actual house and the dream house might have designed by the same architect. And where here were fences of stone and gates of wood, there were fences and gates of iron, but placed in the same configuration. Even the landscaping, down to the last shrub and blade of grass, was identical. Wilfong circled the estate three times to verify all the details. Proof he had sought, and proof he had found,

Wherever in Space and Time he had been during his dream, it paralleled his own reality in most of the essential elements. It was entirely possible, were one to view the matter objectively, that the "dream" world had been reality and his world the "dream." Or that both were "dreams" and that some *third* world was reality. Or that both were reality, and there were worlds without number existing side by side, separated from each other only by a heartbeat.

The Wizard already knew how to cast a Spell to take him backward and forward in Space and also in Time. It seemed only logical that there existed a Spell to take him *sideways* in Space and Time. Apparently, he had done so while in a trance. Could he travel thus consciously? Were the Three the key to such travel? Here was a course worth pursuing, for – since he was thinking along these lines – it was entirely possible that Wynot the Wise originally resided on one of those alternate worlds. It certainly would explain some of His cryptic remarks.

That, however, was for another day. Once he had dealt with Sinladen Crotchgod, he could devote as much time as he needed to the conundrum. In the meantime, he had a "magic" act to perform.

He was about to utter the counter-Spell to whisk himself back to Loth when a movement on the yard below caught his eye. The figurine of the owl on its pedestal had just rotated half a turn. Immediately, the secret entrance to the Temple slid aside. To say that Wilfong was alarmed was putting it mildly. Who in the world was in the Temple in broad daylight? Not Wembly, who might have had good reason to visit it at any time, because he was busy playing the hypocrite elsewhere in the Metropolis. This was a huge breach of security, to say the least!

Imagine then his complete and utter shock to discover the identity of the person emerging from the hole in the ground – the young disciple known as Winona!

But, before he had a chance to mind-cast and to interrogate her, the Level Ten straightened up quickly and whirled about in surprise. She stared intently at the spot where Wilfong would have been had he been there in the flesh and frowned.

-- Master Wilfong? Is that you?

-- Yes, it is, Winona. Did I startle you?

-- Um, a bit. I hadn't expected you to be here. Why *are* you here?

-- I might ask you the same question, my dear. As a member of the Inner Nest, I may come and go as I please. You, on the other hand, are still subject to a few restrictions.

-- I know, Master. But I'm following orders. Master Winsley requested me to come here and retrieve a document for him.

-- Winsley, eh? Most queer and strange that he didn't come himself. What document was it?

-- The message the Elders received from Sinladen Crotchgod, laying down his challenge to the Order. Master Winsley said he wanted to examine it further.

-- Does he think he missed something the first time he read it?

-- He didn't say. Have I done wrong, Master?

-- No, no. Carry on. I *am* curious though. Why did he request *you* for this task?

-- He claimed I showed the most promise of all of the teaching assistants.

-- Well, he's certainly right there.

-- Thank you, Master.

-- I daresay you've shown a great deal of promise. Since my encounter with the Enemy, I've had to maintain my mind shield on a constant basis. Theoretically, no one except another Thirteen should have been able to penetrate it. Yet, you detected me in my disembodied form and knew who I was. How did you do it – and so easily?

-- I – I can't say. I've always been able to penetrate any mind shield I've encountered since childhood. One of the reasons I joined the Order was to learn the *why*.

-- Amazing! You'll soon be a member of the Inner Nest at this rate.

-- You flatter me, Master. And yet, I –

Winona flushed and fluttered her hands.

-- What is it, my dear?

-- If I may be so bold as to say it, I would be pleased to join the Circle of Elders. Not that I'm ambitious, mind you. Oh, no! The Master taught us well in that respect. If I were in the Circle, I'd be eligible to study at your feet and try for Level Thirteen.

-- Indeed? A very noble goal, Winona. But, I sense some other motive on your part.

-- I – I am…afraid to speak of it aloud, Master. It's…personal.

-- Hmmm. "Personal," eh? I think it best we let it rest there before we're both embarrassed. I will say, however, that *you* flatter *me*.

-- It's how I truly feel – if I may be so bold, Master.

-- Thank you, Winona. Now, I'll let you carry out your mission. I must return to my body and rest. Farewell.

-- Farewell, Wilfong.

The Wizard hadn't intended to extend his mental journey so long. Consequently, the drain on his store of energy had been greater than usual, and he was now quite exhausted. He lay on the bunked bed very still so as to conserve himself.

Something nagged at him, however, something he was too tired to identify at this time. Something Winona had said. It was like a mental feather which tickled and couldn't be brushed away. He'd deal with it tomorrow. Right now, he needed another nap.

THE TWELFTH CASTING
THE WIZARD AT WORK

Instead of a much-needed nap, Wilfong received a sharp knock on the door. Whoever it was was being persistent about it too. As he mumbled under his breath briefly, he slid out of bed, padded to the door, and flung it open, ready to give the disturber a piece of his mind. The Speaker of the village stood before him, radiating anxiety.

"I regret this disturbance, Master Wiffon, but this urgent message just arrived from Zarelon by *pijin.*"

And how do you know it's urgent, my friend? the Wizard pondered. *Did you read it? And, if so, why?*

Wordlessly, Wilfong took the hastily folded piece of papyrus and scanned the message. The words practically jumped off the page at him.

> "There once was a phony magician,
> Who sullied an ancient tradition.
>   His act is devoid
>   And one to avoid.
> Don't cheer – send him to Perdition!"

He smiled wryly and crumpled the sheet into a small ball. One eyebrow on Funkol's forehead shot upward.

"Be there a reply, Master Wiffon?"

"Nay, no reply. This from an…old friend be, wishing me well tonight."

"Ah, excellent. Well, I have a few more details for the performance to attend to. Until tonight then."

The huge man charged off, leaving his guest alone with his thoughts. And many varied thoughts now coursed through Wilfong's brain. For one thing, there seemed to be no end to the insults from Sinladen Crotchgod, all designed to keep him distracted from the real attack. For another thing, "SC" had left yet another clue in this newest message; that it could be a false trail was not without the bounds of possibility since the Enemy had already led him a merry chase so far. The alleged clue was the word used for "avoid." It was not the verb form at all but the noun "void" preceded by the mark used as an indefinite article. The Wizard did not believe Crotchgod's grammar was all that faulty, given the nature of the previous messages. No, again he was being extremely clever. The phrasing had been deliberate, and Wilfong was obliged to follow through on it.

Which, naturally, led to a third thing: the Void itself. As a philosophical concept, it had not been a topic of wide discussion; apparently, most of the wise men of Atlantis had better things to debate, or else they were completely puzzled by the subject. Wilfong had read a treatise by the philosopher Lytonol (who, it was claimed, had lived for over two centuries), titled *A Void in the Space/Time Continuum, or a Void in Philosophy?* and written a century before the Wizard's time. It had undertaken to collate and analyze everything spoken or written on the subject. According to old Lytonol, it had been a difficult task; the literature, sketchy as it was, was bad enough; but tracking down lines of thought in folklore, old-wives' tales, and pseudo-serious oral traditions had occupied the better part of fifteen years. The sage had been sure there was more but, he said, discovering it all would have left him no time to actually write the treatise!

Theoretically (Lytonol claimed), the Void existed, not so much as a "place" in this or any other space/time continuum – which would be a contradiction in terms in the first place – as it did as a state of mind. It "existed" (in so far as the concept of Existence could be used in this context) *outside* the bounds of Space and Time and thus could not be accessed through either physical or mental means. He offered many protracted (and convoluted) arguments in defense of this view, but the gist of his theory lay in the notion of being/not being; that is to say, if a place *is*, one could go there by *being there*, and conversely, if a place *is not*, one could get there by *not being anywhere*. If one is not anywhere in Space and Time, then *ipso facto* he is in the Void. Therefore, the trick was to stop thinking of being anywhere. That accomplished, the transition (unlike physical transitions) was instantaneous. And one could remain in the Void as long as he did not think of being elsewhere. This, Lytonol admitted, was a very subtle difference, yet a difference all the same.

As a post-script, the sage had disappeared without a trace. The popular story making the rounds was that he had transited to the Void and forgotten how to leave.

Wilfong had had to laugh to himself when he first read Lytonol's treatise. It had borrowed heavily from what Wynot had written a century and a half earlier. In point of fact, the Compleat Sorcerer had originally suggested the technique of transiting to the Void by means of not thinking of being somewhere; he had often spoken of his own experiences there (though no one really understood how "nothingness" could be experienced) and encouraged his disciples to experiment with the technique as soon as they had achieved Level Twelve. It became an integral part of Level Thirteen training – that area of the curriculum reserved for mastering the "impossible." i.e. "contravening" natural law. Wilfong had struggled long to discipline himself sufficiently to slip in and out of the Void with ease – the sole instance in which he had any difficulty in his training at all.

The question now forming in the Wizard's mind was, did Sinladen Crotchgod also know how to travel to the Void? That he had mentioned it in the first place strongly suggested he did. If so, *why* had he mentioned it? Was he waiting for some Level-Thirteen Practitioner to show up and ambush him for the purpose of stealing his abilities?

Another line of thought then entered his head. Since the only other person known to have mastered the technique was Wynot himself, was

He also in the Void? Was He waiting for one of his disciples to join Him there? That would certainly explain the Master's recent cryptic remark, "Where I go, few can follow."

Many questions, few answers. To seek answers, one had to take the obvious step. He might be playing into "SC's" hands again, but his skills had protected him so far. And, for what he now had in mind, he was going to need every iota of skill he possessed.

First, he required silence – total, absolute silence – so that he would not be distracted. Since he was not likely to have it in his current circumstances, he had to go to the one place in Loth he knew was quiet. He slipped out of his room, checking diligently to assure himself that he was not being observed (by *human* eyes anyway), exited by the rear entrance of the *kabban*, and hastily walked to the forest. When he had judged himself to be at the center, he climbed the nearest tree and inched his way along the first limb he came to; when he reached the point where the limb began to tremble under his weight, he carefully wrapped his legs around the limb and remained still.

Second, he required concentration – total, heavy concentration – in order to effect the transition. Thus, he cast his mind out, searching for all sources of possible distraction; he found only one – a female thrush chirping a warning to all and sundry not to approach her nest and its clutch of eggs – and spoke to it gently, requesting a period of silence and receiving it grudgingly.

When all the world was dead still, he gathered up his remaining mental energies and focused them upon one central theme – not being anywhere. With a single point of bright light as the sum total of his universe, **Wilfong the Wizard**
   -- did not think of the forest
   -- did not think of the village of Loth
   -- did not think of the world
   -- did not think of anywhere
Wilfong the Wizard thought of –
Nowhere
And he was in the Void.

*   *   *

SPACE:

The fabric of all being, in all possible directions. A great land mass upon which all living things crawl from one point to another. An infinite stretch encompassing Totality.

TIME:

An inexorable flow, surging forward, ever forward. A great wave which throws all living things upon the beach of Being, and then carries them back to Nothingness. An uncaring flood which leaves Totality in its wake.

SPACE:

A challenge to some, an obstacle to others. A measure too short or too long, according to the journey planned. A thing to be desired or to be shunned, as the mood dictates.

TIME:

A precious commodity to some, a heavy burden to others. A measure too short or too long, according to the goal projected. A thing to be seized or to be rejected, as the mood dictates.

SPACE:

Men ask themselves: can it be owned? Can we divide and subdivide it, buy and sell it as we will? More germane, can we exploit its boundless riches and thus gain infinite wealth?

TIME:

Men ask themselves: can it be controlled? Can we make it run forward or backward, make it stand still as we will? More germane, can we free ourselves from its bonds and thus gain immortality?

*   *   *

SPACE and TIME were no more.

*   *   *

Wilfong the Wizard finds himself in a great VOID where no sun shines in radiant glory nor electron hisses in rapid orbit, where no living creature encounters another nor thought hums in greeting from one mind to another.

He sees, smells, hears, tastes, touches NOTHINGNESS. He stretches out his consciousness, and still there is the VOID, an infinite ebony blanket.

He knows he is now In-Between-Reality.

As long as his will maintains a rigid control, he does not exist as men understand Existence.

Therefore, he is free to construct a new Reality of his own design.

He marshals his energies and creates, pixel by pixel, a life-sized image of Wynot the Wise and projects it onto the "screen" which is the VOID itself. It is, he knows, an imperfect image, for the only representation of his Master currently available is an idealized portrait created by zealous disciples. All who had known Wynot in the flesh had not considered accurate images of Him as a necessary part of His legacy. Out of second- and third-hand descriptions, then, had come the pertinent features of His Person: the flame-red hair and beard, the shoulder-length, bowl-cut hair, the bulging eyes, the large ears, the paunch, the perpetual slouch. All had thought Him to be an odd, unprepossessing character – until He put His awesome mental faculties to work.

The Wizard works at a casual pace in order to render the construct as realistic as possible. (Of course, he has all the "time" in the "world"!) When the task has been completed, he salutes it in the traditional manner. He relaxes then, allowing his subconscious mind to merge with his conscious mind, and scans his extensive mental catalog of Spells for the precise one which will serve his present purpose.

He finds three such, none of which individually is powerful enough to accomplish what he wants to do but which when combined will. Two of the Spells contain elements which will negate each other and thus will reduce their effectiveness. But the third Spell, in combination with two-thirds of the first and one-quarter of the second, will work admirably. In fact, Wilfong believes he has invented an entirely new Spell. But he does not stop to congratulate himself – time enough for that later (if there is a later) – and acts to assure that there will be a later. Now, he splices the desired elements into the main sequence and in the proper order, quickly re-checks the new synthesis for correct pronunciation and nuance of inflection, and conducts a few "dress rehearsals" of the new Spell. When he thinks he is ready for the actual Spell-casting, he concentrates on his construct.

Best to focus on one part, *he thinks.* I'll conserve energy that way.

He contemplates "Wynot's" navel as his focus point and sends out into the VOID in an infinity of directions a tight beam of mental energy designed to reach out and touch another mind (if indeed another mind is present in the VOID), to signal to that mind that communication is desired, and to exchange glad tidings of Harmony and Wisdom. If the Master is truly here, He will surely receive this signal, recognize it for what it is, and respond accordingly.

The construct crosses its "eyes."

The Wizard is, naturally, momentarily startled. At first, he thinks it is just his imagination because he is concentrating so hard on his Spell. Still, he diverts a tiny fraction of his attention to inspecting the construct and verifies that its "eyes" are indeed staring at each other. Is this perhaps a side effect of the particular combination of Spells he had just formulated? Or is it a distortion due to the tremendous energies being generated? Whatever the reason, it is not only a distracting sight but also an unflattering one, for it makes his Master look like a buffoon.

The question arises, does he dare take the time and energy to restore the image to its original appearance? It would mean having to halt the mind-casting and then begin again from the start. Wilfong hates to waste time and energy if he can possibly help it. Yet, the change in the image, beyond its obvious annoyance, will not otherwise interfere with the Spell. Therefore, he can perhaps ignore it and continue the project.

The construct sticks its "tongue" out.

The Wizard blinks in amazement. Since the "eyes" are still crossed, this new image is now more than that of a buffoon; it is a buffoon who wishes to call undue attention to himself. Wilfong begins to think that there is something dreadfully wrong here. The first distortion – if that is a proper description – may have been a random event. The second one certainly is not; it is now a major problem, a systems break-down which will have untoward consequences if not checked. He seriously considers terminating the construct and re-forming it.

The construct thumbs its "nose."

Had the Wizard been in a real place with a solid surface beneath him, he might have leaped to his feet in indignation over this latest distortion. Since he is not, he remains in a fixed position. His mind, however, seethes with outrage. The construct is so ludicrous-appearing that any concentration on the task is virtually impossible.

Just as he is about to dissipate the image and create a fresh one, all of the distortions disappear, one by one, until only the original image is left. He breathes a sigh of relief; the strange effects have been temporary after all, due perhaps to the fact that the Spell used was a new, untested one.

Then the construct grins from "ear" to "ear" — a great moronic grin typical of one who has lost his wits and seen the world as a tragic farce.

-- Just what in all the Hells of Creation is going on here? *[Wilfong exclaims in exasperation].*

-- How did you like my improvements on your artistry, Wilfong?

-- Sinladen Crotchgod! Why am I not surprised?

-- None other.

-- Who else would have had the audacity to pull a stunt like this?

-- Who else, indeed? Except, perhaps, Wilfong the Washed-up Wizard?

The construct vanishes, pixel by pixel, with a slow hissing sound like air escaping from a balloon. In its place, a narrow, vertical band appears, a line so black that even the surrounding VOID seems like a sun-lit room by comparison. The line unfolds three times, and the hooded Enemy reveals himself in all of his malevolence.

-- Are you happy to see me, Wilfong?

-- Most assuredly, *no!* What's on your evil little mind this time?

-- Oh, all sorts of things, all guaranteed to give you major fits.

-- *Humph!* Your mere presence is enough to do that.

-- *Tsk, tsk.* You're not behaving very wizardly today.

-- Persist in your nefariousness, and you'll find out just how 'unwizardly' I can be.

The Wizard ponders his options to counter the menace of "SC." A force field is useless because there is nothing in the VOID against which to pin the fellow. How is he at withstanding a Spell of Stasis? A chill runs up and down Wilfong's spine as he remembers his *first experience. The senior teaching assistant in his Eighth-Level training session had put him in stasis as punishment for a breach of etiquette; he had been suspended for two weeks of objective time and fallen behind in his studies (and an irate employer demanded an explanation for his unannounced absence). Only his ability as a quick study had prevented his being washed out of the Order in disgrace. Since then, he had been the very model of civility toward his fellow disciples – with one notable exception.*

Wilfong considers where he is and with whom he is dealing. Spells of Stasis have four levels of effect, depending on how long one wished to maintain the effect. The first level remains in place for an hour; the second, for a day; the third, for a week; and the fourth, for a month. He decides that a level-two Spell is sufficient. Grimly, he chants:

> "There once was a fellow of ill will.
> Who gave me a tremendous chill.
> His manner is crude;
> His speech is quite lewd.
> Oh, Wynot, make him stand still!"

Since nothing else exists in the VOID, mental energy is visible there. It has long been a truism amongst Practitioners that what is in Reality is not in the VOID and what is in the VOID is not in Reality. No one has ever been able to prove/disprove this theory empirically – even old Lytonol had been open to debate – but the idea has seemed so sensible that it has gained the status of an axiom. Thus, in the VOID, the impossible becomes possible, and vice versa.

Consequently, the Wizard's Spell produces a mauve, meter-long cylinder rotating about its horizontal axis. A second one joins it, then a third and a fourth. Soon, a dozen of them form a circle three meters in diameter, and they begin to link together by yellow beams of light. The whole now spins about its center, moving faster and faster until mauve and yellow blur into each other. Wilfong sends it toward the Enemy, who has been observing this activity with bored fascination.

Whether Sinladen Crotchgod recognizes a Spell of Stasis is moot. He merely assumes he is under attack and responds in a predictable fashion. He conjures up a handful of cherry-red globules, five centimeters in diameter, and flings them against the array of cylinders. The globules bounce harmlessly off and turn to pink dust. "SC" then produces a handful of violet globules; and, when they strike the cylinders, they burn holes in some of them. He chuckles evilly and throws handful after handful of violet globules; quickly, the cylinders resemble termite-ridden logs which will crumble away at the slightest touch.

Upon seeing his original Spell countered, Wilfong calls up three more of the mauve arrays. These, however, are freckled with orange spots. The Enemy continues to manufacture his globules, but they have a lesser effect on the new arrays and do not corrode the cylinders as much. Hastily, he creates a thick, meter-long, green arrow and sends it flying. The arrow is designed to disrupt the yellow beams of light and thus scatter the cylinders hither and yon, but it fails to do so. In desperation, he manufactures a colossal orange cylinder in order to engulf the mauve ones and crush them.

Wilfong has anticipated this counter-Spell, because he would have used it had the roles been reversed. Even while Sinladen Crotchgod activates his orange cylinder, the Wizard creates a yellow cross and flings it into the wake of the mauve arrays. The cross positions itself at the forefront of the arrays; instantly, the yellow beams of light grow thicker. When the orange cylinder reaches its target, it is rendered useless as the thicker bonds hold it fast; instead of cracking the offense, it is itself cracked and disintegrates.

With the last defense breached, the mauve cylinders loop about the hooded figure. All of their internal activity ceases, and so does the external activity of their victim. Until the Spell wears off, "SC" is capable of only thought; no Spell of his own will free him.

-- You tricky bastard! You think you're so damned *clever!*

-- That's why they call me 'Wilfong the Wizard,' don't you know?

-- *Hah!* This Spell won't hold me long.

-- It'll hold you long enough for me to learn what I want to know.

-- And what do you want to learn, if I may be so bold as to ask?

-- Why the Master rejected you, of course.

-- I could have told you that.

-- *Your* version of the story, Sinladen, but not the real one. Wynot never refused admittance to the Order to anyone who was qualified – until you came along. Somehow, He found you objectionable. I hope to find out why.

-- And then?

-- Ah, well, now *you* squirm a bit. Be seeing you, my friend.

*   *   *

Several schools of thought existed in the Wizard's day concerning traveling through Time. At one extreme, it was said to be impossible under any circumstances. Time was not a *place*, the argument went, and therefore could not be traveled as if it were a road between cities. Rather, Time was an *experience*, each moment of which could be indulged in only once, and one must not presume to go back and forth at will. Besides, there was the "Paradox of Time" which stated that, if it were possible to travel back and forth, it was also possible to alter the past and thus change the future; and, since any alteration might preclude the future existence of the alterer, he could not have existed so that he could alter the past. At the other extreme, the prevailing view was that there existed an infinity of time lines created by significant events, and a traveler could move along a particular time-line but could not jump from one to another. No matter how far back he went, he would always find himself on a line which detoured him around a given significant event, and therefore he would not be able to alter history.

Wynot the Wise in his teachings had fallen on the "possible" side of the question, but with a slight variation. He claimed that, yes, it was impossible to travel through Time *physically* because of the Paradox. But, it was possible to do so *mentally*; that is to say, one could send one's consciousness back and forth along a given time-line or across the infinity of time-lines and explore both the Past and all possible Futures without fear of altering any of them. In his Order, one section of the Thirteenth Level had been reserved for learning the technique for casting a Spell of Time-Transition. There was one caveat, however. A Practitioner may not remain at any one temporal point for more than one hour; due to the elasticity of Time, one risked a build-up of mental pressure which led to insanity.

As it happened, Wilfong did not need to cast a Spell in order to make a journey in Time. Had he been on the physical plane, it would have been necessary. But, he was in the VOID, which was neither here nor there; to be some*when*, all he had to do was to think it.

Thus, he thought of a specific point in Time.

And he was there.

*   *   *

"There" is the very first Temple of the Order of Wynot, established when the Compleat Sorcerer had walked amongst men yet had to conduct his teachings in private. Before it had been discovered by the King's agents and burnt to the ground, it had been an old converted warehouse in the western quadrant of the Fifth Ring of the Metropolis; it had originally belonged to a weaver who stored his spools of yarn there (remnants still lay scattered about) and who abandoned it due to space limitations. In the fore of the building, a furniture-repair shop is in evidence – one of the First Disciples owns and operates it – and several pieces in various degrees of disrepair await the craftsman's attention. In the back, behind a false wall, is the Temple proper, a small labyrinth of "classrooms" – actually sections of space divided from one another by thick curtains made from the former owner's left-overs. In the farthest corner, Wynot has established his "office"/study where he writes up the curriculum and lesson plans, establishes training schedules, raises funds for expenses, administers the day-to-day affairs of the Order, and – when he has the time – thinks arcane thoughts.

The study now is the epitome of organized chaos. Scrolls and books and odd scraps of papyrus layer every available surface, often several times over. The Wizard, when he first surveys this area, is reminded of his own *sanctum sanctorum*. Talk about walking in the Master's footsteps!

Wilfong's vantage point is just to the left of the small writing table (which also serves as Wynot's "desk") and midway between the floor and the ceiling. Had he been there in the flesh, he might have been mistaken for a spider dangling from one of its strands of webbing. The position has been deliberately taken, for he wishes to have a panoramic view of what will shortly take place here – the confrontation between the Master and Sinladen Crotchgod. He knows he has the correct time period because the image derived from his brief probe of the Enemy's mind had been superimposed in bright red numerals with the specific date of the event as though it had been burned into "SC's" memory for all time. Observing the actual scenario rather than relying on distorted versions of it will provide the Wizard with insight into the motivations of both parties; thereafter, he can deduce a weakness in the Enemy he can exploit.

Presently, Wynot enters his study. Wilfong's breath catches in his throat. Other than the two dreams he has had, this is the first time he has seen the Master in the flesh. He is immediately filled with awe and reverence, joy and adoration, and a great wave of Harmony and Wisdom. Thrill after thrill courses up and down his spine like scurrying insects, and he is close to swooning. Yet, he manages to collect his wits and examine Wynot dispassionately for future reference. The Founder appears to be shorter in stature than extant descriptions suggest, and Wilfong ascribes the difference to awe-struck exaggeration. The Compleat Sorcerer had been a philosophical giant in his time, and so to his disciples he had been a physical one as well. Otherwise, the physical features jibe with past accounts.

Wynot looks haggard on this day, but that is to be expected in those hectic times of renewed enforcement of the Dread Edict against all Practitioners. *Not* to be worn down would have been the greater surprise, since the King's agents had been encouraged to concentrate their efforts upon the most notorious of the "criminals."

He sits down at his cluttered desk and picks up several papyri seemingly at random. After a brief examination of each, he carelessly tosses them aside. Now, he takes up quill and a fresh piece of papyrus and begins to write in his familiar scrawl. Wilfong shifts his vantage point ever so slightly so as to read over the Master's shoulder. He is disappointed to learn that the writing is in an entirely unfamiliar language and returns to his original position. Wynot pauses frequently and gazes in the distance, lost in thought, then resumes his work, his left elbow propped up on the desk and his head against his left hand.

Abruptly, Wynot peers at the hour-glass which sits on a shelf above him and nods enigmatically. He then glances in Wilfong's direction and smiles impishly. The Wizard is startled momentarily and nearly loses his concentration. Has the Master actually detected his presence here? Had He anticipated this visit? Obviously, Wynot knows much more than he does. Since completing the Thirteenth Level, Wilfong had always had the impression that he had been taught only a fraction of his Master's knowledge and that his training had been merely a preparatory course for the real instruction to come. Or perhaps the Wizard is reading too much into the odd gesture.

He has no time to ponder the matter, however, for the curtain which separates the study from the remainder of the Temple parts. A hooded figure walks in.

Sinladen Crotchgod has finally arrived.

If Wilfong has been nonplussed by Wynot's apparent detection of his presence, he is shocked to the core of his being when the Enemy throws back his hood and reveals his true likeness. Until now, the Wizard had never seen it; Crotchgod had always hidden it, perhaps out of shame, perhaps out of desire for some dramatic effect. Now that it has been revealed, the Atlantean is beside himself with confusion.

Sinladen Crotchgod wears his face!

How can this be? Is he dreaming again? He recalls the image of his "guide" who had led him to the portal to the cave of metal which had been Wynot's home/base of operations/headquarters, the man whose face kept ageing and de-ageing. Had that been "SC"? Or had it been a construct created by Wynot as a puzzler for Wilfong to solve?

If so, then *who* – or *what* -- is this creature who now stands before Wynot, scowling fiercely, not showing the least bit of deference to One who is far above him in wisdom? Is it yet another construct? If Crotchgod is a mere construct, what purpose does he serve in his supposed war against the Order?

Wilfong's mind is all agog, and he seriously considers returning to his own time so that he may meditate and sort things out. He cannot, of course; he has expended too much energy to cut short his mission without learning anything. Meanwhile, the drama before him unfolds as it is meant to. In a daze, he observes and hopes either of the actors will provide some clue to shed light on this conundrum.

"So," Wynot mutters to "SC," "you've come back, eh?"

"Did you think otherwise?" the Enemy responds with his characteristic sneer.

"I'd hoped you'd have taken the hint the first and second times that you're not the sort of material we're looking for."

"I've got potential – hell, I've even demonstrated what I can do so far. I've been Practitioning on my own, but I can go only so far. This Order is the best there is for further development, and I want to be a part of it."

"I know. What you've failed to explain, however, is *why* you want to develop your abilities. So far, all I've heard are vague remarks about 'stretching one's horizons' and 'exploring the Unknown' and so on. You haven't been very specific about your goals."

"Isn't what I've said enough?"

"Not for me. Anybody can say those things. It takes a genuine seeker after Harmony and Wisdom to articulate exactly what he seeks."

"And you think I'm not a genuine seeker?"

Wynot heaves a great sigh and stares in Wilfong's direction again.

"I'd hoped to be diplomatic about this," he resumes, "but you leave me no alternative. So, I'll be blunt, Chuckie. I've reviewed your original petition, re-examined your interviews, even pondered over the demonstrations you've given. On the whole, it's all very impressive. But, I sense a disturbing element in your personality, something I suspect you're holding back for personal reasons. You strike me as being overly ambitious, eager to exploit new knowledge for personal gain. This is *not* what I teach in this Order. I teach selflessness, charity, and humanitarianism. You're not any of those things, and I couldn't trust you to be anything but what you are."

A long silence follows. Wynot regards Crotchgod coolly, calmly. The Enemy scowls darkly, his fists clenching until his knuckles are white. Suddenly, he jumps to his feet.

"Damn you, Wynot! Damn you and your self-righteousness! How dare you judge me! You're no better than I am – except you have a happy, sappy following."

The Compleat Sorcerer smiles mirthlessly and examines his fingernails.

"Well, you've just proved my point. Beneath that veneer of civility lies the beast, ready to vent his rage on whoever crosses him."

"A 'raging beast,' am I?" Crotchgod roars, drawing himself up to his full height and raising his fist. "I'll show you rage."

"I hope you're not going to try Magick here," Wynot says quietly. He places his left index finger against his left temple and whistles sharply. Immediately, "SC" clutches at his throat, unable to breathe properly. The Founder negates the Spell, and Crotchgod gasps compulsively. "That was just a sample, Chuckie. Now, I think you'd better leave – while you can."

Crotchgod has regained his composure – and his rage. He glares at Wynot with murder in his eye.

"You haven't heard the last of me, *phtrx*. I'll learn what I need to know on my own if I have to. Then I'll be back, and we'll see who's the master and who is not."

"Do your worst, Chuckie. I'll be waiting for you. Now, get out!"

Sinladen Crotchgod storms out of the study, mumbling dire invective under his breath.

Wynot smirks, casts another glance toward Wilfong, and *winks broadly.*

Perplexed to the *n*th degree, the Wizard wills himself after the man with his face. He hopes to learn something of his plan for revenge, something which will aid him in the upcoming battle. But, he receives a fresh jolt. Sinladen Crotchgod is stomping past a group of novitiates, gesticulating wildly and shouting curses; yet, no one takes any notice of him but goes about his business as if the Enemy is not there. Wilfong knows why *he* is unseen. Why the other remains so is a large mystery. "SC" continues on into the section of the building which is the furniture-repair shop and past its craftsmen and apprentices. Still, he is disregarded.

When he exits the building, he *disappears!*

Already shocked to his core, Wilfong fights off a wave of dizziness. For a brief moment, he wonders if he has tarried too long outside of his own time-period and is experiencing the first stage of madness. A check of his internal "clock" tells him that such is not the case. Therefore, the disturbance must be wholly psychosomatic. He has prided himself (perhaps overly much) on his being able to take anything in stride, to look at each situation calmly and rationally, to resist the normal human urge to panic before an extraordinary event. This day, however, his vaunted stoicism seems to have deserted him, as enigma piles upon mystery and mystery piles upon conundrum. He has to believe there is a *rational* explanation for what has occurred. He cannot be going mad. In order to meditate on this matter, he requires the absolute silence of the VOID.

Once again, he clears his mind (not an easy task this time now) and does not think of being anywhere.

*   *   *

Wilfong may or may not have returned to the same point in the VOID that he had left. Since the VOID is nowhere, the notion is moot; there are no signposts to mark one's location, and one point looks like all other points. In any event, it is of little consequence: what matters is interaction with In-Between-Reality.

Wilfong may or may not have dwelled in the VOID for a second or a century. Since the VOID is nowhen, that notion too is moot; no clocks exist to marks one's passage, and one moment looks like all other moments. In any event, it too is of little consequence; what matters is interaction with In-Between-Reality.

The Wizard meditates long and hard on recent events. He replays each incident in minute detail. Each gesture of the actors, each inflection in their voices, even each change of facial expression is scrutinized, bit by bit, until he knows them as well as he does his own mannerisms. And he comes to but one conclusion:

The scene in the Master's study had been staged, *from beginning to end. It had been a remarkable piece of Magick — yet child's play, apparently, for the Compleat Sorcerer — for the specific purpose of sending a message to one Wilfong the Wizard. Consider the correlation between the images of the "guide" in his dreams and of Sinladen Crotchgod of the past. Consider the planted messages which had led him from one location to another. Then consider the increasingly complex "attacks" against him by the Enemy. It all suggests — what? Nothing more or less than a test — a test of Wilfong's abilities under fire, of his devotion to Wynot and the Order, of his capacity to advance beyond his present level of Magick and be One-with-the-All.*

The convincing argument lies — as it has all along — in the language employed in the staged scene, waiting for the discerning mind to interpret it correctly. Wilfong realizes that, in the same manner that the name "Sinladen Crotchgod" is an anagram of the Hyperborean epithet sel rahcnot gniddoc, *so also is the name Wynot used to address the Enemy: "Chuckie." It can be anagrammed into the Atlantean word for "seeker" which word had been used repeatedly throughout this drama. More precisely, it means "seeker after truth" which has always been the ultimate goal of the Order of Wynot. Moreover — and herein lies the true cleverness of the Master — "Chuckie" is a homophone of the Atlantean word for "future." This explains more than anything else the meaning of the images in his dreams; the wondrous sights could have derived only from the future. Clearly, the Compleat Sorcerer has told his disciple exactly where he must go.*

The puzzle solved at last, the Wizard relaxes and luxuriates in his new-found wisdom. Yet, he cannot rest upon his laurels, for there is still one loose end to tie up before he can resume his Great Quest. The drama has not run its full course; Sinladen Crotchgod — regardless of his true nature and origin — remains a viable threat to the Order and must be dealt with once and for all. It is a bothersome task to be sure, given what is now known, but there is nothing to do for it but to play the game to its inevitable conclusion.

Therefore, he thinks of being somewhere.

And he is there.

THE THIRTEENTH CASTING

THE WIZARD AT WILL

Zarelon had not been this chaotic – or so it seemed to Wilfong as he peeped through the curtain on the make-shift stage.

Kank-kians (and a few disreputable-looking Zarelor) flocked into Loth's Visitor's Center by the scores, young and old, male and female, all jabbering excitedly in anticipation of the evening's entertainment. The local method of public relations was obviously very efficient, for it had drawn an audience from far and wide. One could tell from the style of clothing – and often the *color* of the clothing – who were town folk and who were country folk; the former wore the gaudiest styles and the brightest colors, while the latter had to make do with frayed and faded apparel.

So far as the Wizard could determine, however, no class discrimination was evident here of the sort one could see every day in Atlantis. Each person greeted one another like a long-lost relative. And, he reasoned, that was probably close to the truth. In small communities, most of the inhabitants were related either by blood or by marriage; and where they lived and what occupations they filled was more of a matter of choice than of necessity. In any event, this particular crowd had heard about the presence of a magician in Loth (a strange-looking one at that), and they came because either they were interested in new forms of entertainment or they were curious about the stranger.

The first performance of "magic" drew mostly children, from toddlers to teenagers. Thus, Funkol had requested Wilfong to adapt his "act" accordingly. He had not, on the other hand, placed any restrictions on the second performance in which the audience would be mostly adults (after the children had been sent off to bed), hinting that the magician could be as risqué as he wished. The Wizard had no problem with the request as he had already planned to do different tricks for each performance. Still, he was a bit miffed at the lack of prior consultation in setting this show up and was not about to be any more elaborate for the sake of making the Speaker look good in the eyes of his community; the extremely short notice had caught him without the props he usually employed at Lymatan's, and he had had to spend some time after returning from the Void in running hither and yon seeking appropriate materials. No, Funkol would have to be more co-operative in the future if he wanted some kind of "super show." Wilfong was willing to put on a *good* show for the children because he had made a promise to them, and he always kept his promises to children, regardless of adult expectations.

Though no more seats were available, people continued to pour through the doors. Only a fifth of the common room of the Center had been given over to Wilfong's stage; the remaining space had been crammed with wooden benches, as close together as human comfort would tolerate in order to accommodate the maximum number of bodies. Zarelor had nothing on Funkol in this respect, and the Wizard wondered how much he was making from the admissions he was charging; no doubt the free room and board and the percentage allocated to his "star performer" were a mere fraction of the take. Next time Wilfong visited (assuming, of course, he was foolish enough to make a return trip), he'd demand a larger percentage. Why should the Speaker get all the profit when Wilfong was doing all the work?

And it *was* work, what he was about to do. To the average person, it might seem like "magic," but it wasn't. It was simple prestidigitation and illusion; and using distraction and hand-manipulation, he could fool entire audiences into believing he was a "great magician." The trick lay in the skill of the manipulator, and that required a lot of work.

"Magic," Wynot had declared long ago when he was in a whimsical mood, "is nothing but sleight-of-hand and mumbo-jumbo." None of his disciples had ever heard of the expression "mumbo-jumbo"; but, in that context, they deduced that it meant a group of nonsense words and phrases which lent an air of authority to control the credulous. "Magic" in this sense was quite different than Magick which Practitioners performed; the former was meant to amuse the gullible and/or fortify authority (particularly religious authority), whereas the latter endeavored to seek rational answers for what was so far from ordinary experience as to boggle the average mind. Yet, Magick obeyed natural law as much as anything else; its principles had just not been clearly articulated. Wynot had always impressed upon his followers that what he taught was *not* "magic" but a higher form of natural law in which the mind could affect its environment in predictable ways. He had demonstrated – and down the years, his Order had passed on – those principles, using arcane techniques to manipulate the external world.

The Compleat Sorcerer had used the simple act of making fire as an example. Once upon a time, humans did not know to make fire as they had no understanding of its principles. They discovered fire only by accident. Now, one struck a flint against a rock, created a spark, and ignited combustible materials. No one thought it extraordinary because the principle behind fire was now common knowledge. Someday, he declared, one would take a short stick, one end of which was coated with certain chemicals, scrape it against an abrasive surface, and – through the heat of friction – produce fire. Such a thing might be viewed as "magic" to those amongst whom one dwelled, only because they did not understand the principle involved.

When one cast a Spell, say of Transition, one set in motion certain energies in order to produce the desired effect. Those energies would produce no other effect – the realization of which was at the heart of understanding the nature of natural law – thus avoiding throwing the world into chaos, disorder, and unpredictability. Wynot knew the principles behind his Spells well enough to be confident in their use and to teach them to others whom he had deemed both worthy and capable. And, because the average person did not understand the principles involved, they would hold Practitioners in great awe/fear/loathing and react accordingly.

So it was for Wilfong. Not for nothing did he call himself a "wizard" (but not in public!). Far more than a mere conceit, it was the Truth. And so, this "magician" – real and pretend – stood poised to flummox yet another crowd.

Presently, the Speaker strutted onto the stage, very much full of himself (in Wilfong's humble estimation). He raised his arms for silence, and the jabbering audience immediately quieted down.

"Fellow Kank-kians and honored visitors!" he boomed. "I be extremely pleased so many could attend tonight!"

I'll just bet you are, the Wizard thought derisively. *More people means more loot in your pocket.*

"The village of Loth be known far and wide for its great entertainments. Indeed, we pride ourselves on presenting a variety of artistes who are nowhere else to be seen. Tonight is no exception, my friends.

"Tonight, we have the rare privilege to present to thee, as part of his world tour, a limited engagement of a master of magic, a crafty conjurer, a sensational sorcerer of the first water who will delight and amuse, bedazzle and confound."

What a load of ox-droppings!

"Good friends, here from Atland be – *Wiffon the Wizard!*"

Wilfong took a deep breath, waited until the curtain across the stage was retracted halfway, and then tossed out a handful of pinkish powder. The simple chemical compound ignited when it came into contact with oxygen and produced a loud *whoosh,* a brilliant white light, and a cloud of red smoke with a slightly pungent odor. He had spent two hours before the evening meal concocting this compound and was pleased when it caused the expected reaction. The audience squealed with shock and awe, and all necks were craned toward the stage.

Before the smoke cleared away, Wilfong hastened to center stage to give the impression that he had appeared by "magic." The crowd saw now a figure standing before them in all his "wizardly splendor." Actually, he was wearing a spare robe upon which had been sewn by one of the women in Funkol's household pieces of multi-colored cloth in a number of geometrical shapes, e.g. red pentagrams, green crescents, blue circles, and yellow crosses. For good measure, he had also added the characters of the Atlantean alphabet which he thought was as arcane to these simple folk as anything else. In the back of his mind, he wondered idly if he should fashion a permanent costume; as long as he was being billed as a "great magician," he might as well look the part.

When the audience had recovered from this spectacular entrance and recognized the trick for what it was, they broke out in a noisy response. Clapping, whistling, hooting, foot-stomping, and babbling amongst themselves erupted from all parts of the room; the loudest response came from those few who had already witnessed a demonstration of the Wizard's "magic." He waved to as many as he could in acknowledgement and tugged the cheeks of several children who were sitting on the edge of the stage – a grandfatherly gesture in imitation of his own grandfather who had taught him the art of prestidigitation in the first place. The cheek-tugging elicited a paroxysm of giggling from the youngsters.

Now he raised his arms for attention and got it instantly. He smiled in gratitude. At Lymatan's, he would have had to wait for several minutes before the raucous crowd settled down. Enthusiasm was one thing, but obnoxiousness was quite another.

"Good evening, good friends," he declared in his best stentorian voice. "I for this warm welcome thee thank. I the world over have traveled, and in no other place such a delightful audience have I seen." *A little white lie, but flattery goes a long way – most of the time.* "This my first visit in the lands west of the Great Western Ocean be – which, of course, *east* of here be" – loud guffaws punctuated the air – "but I thee assure it not the last will be."

To this hint of future entertainment, the audience vented another enthusiastic round of applause as if to encourage just such a plan.

"Yet, I here not to make speeches be, but to make -- *MAGIC!*"

So saying, he swung his arms down and up in a wide arc. On the downstroke, he let fall into his hands two bouquets of the local flora which he had previously concealed in the sleeves of his robe. On the upstroke, he flourished the bouquets for all to see; the movement was so rapid that it seemed as if the flowers had appeared "magically." This was the foundation of prestidigitation: moving the hand faster than the eye could follow. The act of illusion worked along the same principle. Wilfong flung the flowers into the audience and silently chanted a Spell of Disintegration; the flowers turned into sparling dust and showered an *ooh*ing and *ahh*ing crowd.

For the next fifteen minutes, he pulled various objects out of "thin air," popped a string of eggs out of his mouth, threw a cloth over "empty hands," and produced birds and small mammals in quick succession. He ignited more of the pinkish powder here and there on the stage in order to "materialize" and "de-materialize" several items he had carefully secreted prior to the performance. His grandfather had taught him many tricks of this nature, and he had created a few of his own over the years. A third of his repertoire was reserved for the first show – simple tricks principally for the amusement of younger people. Another third was held in reserve for more mature audiences. The remainder consisted of card tricks which he thought were not appropriate in these circumstances. Loth, noted for its games of chance, might not appreciate the skills of one who could manipulate cards at will.

At one point in the first act, Wilfong halted suddenly and shook his head vigorously. Then, he stuck a finger in one ear, made an expression of pained surprise, and dug furiously. The children snickered insanely. When he had built up enough suspense, he cocked his head to one side and began pulling a crimson scarf out of his ear. Amidst further giggling, he made another comical face, this one of exaggerated exasperation, and pulled out more colored scarfs. The children squirmed in their seats with uncontrollable fits of laughter. Subconsciously, the Wizard noted with pleasure that many of the adults also shared their offspring's sense of wonder; apparently, they had never seen a "magic" act in their lives. In all likelihood, he could have repeated these tricks endlessly and not tire this lot out. As a finale, he gathered up the scarves, tossed them into the air, and chanted a different Spell of Disintegration. The scarves "disappeared" in a multi-colored flash, and the audience whooped their approval. Once more, he held up his hands for silence.

"I a volunteer to assist me need. Who will help?"

A dozen hands shot up at once, all belonging to the younger set. Wilfong cast his mind out and caught a strong, pleading thought: "Me, me! Oh, please, choose me!" He zeroed in on the thought and was not too surprised to learn that it emanated from the post-pubescent girl who had been the first to identify him as a "magician." He searched her mind and discovered her name. Grandiosely, he placed his fingertips against his temples and closed his eyes.

"I a name see, one who most desires to help. The name I see with the letter 'P' begins." A ripple of gasps spread though the audience, punctuated by one sharp squeal of joy. "The name be – the name be – *'Puckol'!*"

The lone squeal transformed into a cry of triumph, and the one "chosen" jumped to her feet, grinning from ear to ear. Puckol, about twelve or thirteen years of age, was tall and lanky like most Lothian children; she wore her ash-blond hair in braids and disdained the local practice of wearing footwear. Her round, elfin face was covered with freckles. She was beside herself with glee and stumbled over many pairs of feet on her way to the stage. After what seemed like a lifetime, she clambered up and approached the "magician" with a rapturous expression on her face.

Not that I need one in this place, Wilfong mused, *but I'd hazard to guess I've got a friend for life.*

He placed a hand on Puckol's shoulder and declared:

"Puckol a brave lass be, the Mystic Powers to face. A round of applause her give."

The audience responded enthusiastically in appreciation of one of their own. The girl blushed inordinately.

"Puckol," the Wizard announced when the applause had subsided, "in a round of mind-reading me will assist. Into the audience I her will send; at random, one person she will pick, and from that person for a personal item ask. *At no time must she to me the item reveal.* I in her mind it will see and it identify."

The Atlantean had seen this trick performed hundreds of times throughout his travels in the Known World. It seemed that every society, no matter what its level of development, harbored a host of tricksters who bamboozled whomever they could by claiming to possess "mental powers" for the benefit of potential clients. "Mind-reading" was the commonest of those "powers," the purpose of which was to locate hidden/lost items of value. Generally, the tricksters employed trained assistants who used pre-arranged code words; given the proper codes, the "mind-reader" knew exactly what was hidden/lost as surely as if he were looking directly at it. To true Practitioners, these charlatans gave Magick a bad name.

Wilfong, of course, had no need to resort to such trickery since he really could read minds as if they were open books. And he intended to do so here, though he had to act circumspectly. Most humans detested Practitioner and charlatan alike and would do great bodily harm if they discovered either one.

He now turned his back to the audience and, for good measure, had Puckol blindfold him in order to convince everyone that he was not peeking. In his mind's eye, he was right beside the girl as she went into the crowd to pick out a likely target. She stopped before the Speaker himself who immediately removed his badge of office and handed it over. She held the badge high in the air.

"Master Wiffon," the girl announced, "I have something in my hand. What is it?"

The Wizard again placed his fingertips against his temples and pretended to concentrate.

"An image in my mind is forming," he replied shortly (and truthfully). "I see – I see – a metal object, I think. Yes, it metal be. The image sharper now is becoming. The object – *gold* – be. A disc of gold." The audience *ooh*ed loudly. "There words on the disc be inscribed. The words say -- Why, me bless! The disc to the Speaker belongs! It his badge be!"

"Thou art correct, Master Wiffon," Puckol breathed, as equally impressed by this feat of "wizardry" as her fellow Lothians.

The audience broke out in a thunderous ovation. Some (including the Speaker) even rose to their feet in honor of the performer. Wilfong turned briefly to acknowledge the response, then directed his wide-eyed assistant to seek out another item to be identified. Once more, she meandered through the assembly; dozens of people now pressed her to select them and attempted to place personal items in her hand. In a moment of supposed cleverness on her part, she pulled off a ring on her own finger and held it up for all to see.

"What do I have in my hand now, Master Wiffon?"

Wilfong smiled to himself. He had seen her attempt at subterfuge as clearly as anyone in the room. He peeked into her mind and discovered that the ring was a gift from some young man of the village, a token of affection – and perhaps more than that someday. The Atlantean mentally raised an eyebrow. The age of consent must be quite low in these parts.

After the requisite *hem*ing and *haw*ing, he identified the item and "guessed" the nature of its importance to its owner. Puckol blushed furiously, even as she concurred with the "guess." After a few more demonstrations of "mind-reading," Wilfong begged to go to the final part of his act.

At the Wizard's signal, Murkol brought out two crates and set them on the stage a meter-and-a-half apart. Wilfong then placed the girl in a hypnotic trance (easy to do, he opined, with a primitive subject) and caused her body to be as rigid as a log. With Murkol's help, he laid her across the crates, head on one and feet on the other. Nothing supported her body. The audience *ahh*ed in wonder. The Wizard swept his arms over Puckol's body to suggest she was not being held up by wires. At a nod from his master, the Zarelor pulled away the crate which held the girl's feet. She remained rigid, seemingly unsupported at one end. The crowd *ooh*ed heartily.

This trick was usually performed with thin wires placed at strategic points; and, in order to "prove" that no supports existed, the "magician" passed his arms over and under the subject in a manner which effectively avoided the wires. No such trickery existed here, however, for Wilfong had whispered a Spell of Levitation prior to Murkol's removing the crate. He nodded a second time, and the Zarelor removed the crate under Puckol's head, leaving her to "float" in mid-air. The crowd *ahh*ed vociferously. Finally, Wilfong mimed the act of lifting a great weight; immediately, the girl began to rise toward the ceiling, slowly, steadily.

The entire audience was on its collective feet, shouting, hooting, and whistling raucously, the adults as much as the children.

Wilfong bowed low. He had this lot firmly in the palm of his hand. With a grand gesture, he mimed the act of pulling on a rope, and Puckol's body descended to its former position. Murkol replaced the crates, and the Wizard brought his assistant out of her trance. Though confused by the thunderous applause, the girl nevertheless acknowledged it with grace.

What happened next was definitely *not* on the program. As Wilfong was taking his bows, Puckol made a tiny mewling sound and stiffened. She turned toward the Wizard and slapped his face. It was problematical who was the more surprised – Wilfong, Murkol, Funkol, or the audience. The latter, still on their feet, gasped in shock and exchanged worried glances. Funkol was beside himself with fear of having his Grand Plan go suddenly awry. Murkol was close to fainting. The Atlantean stared at his assistant in disbelief for all of two seconds, then noted the blank expression on her face and the glassy look in her eyes. An outside agency had taken control of her, and Wilfong didn't need to be a wizard to identify it.

-- Crotchgod! What are you up to?

No *verbal* response was forthcoming. Instead, Puckol raised her right foot and stepped on Wilfong's left foot. The Enemy's ability to manipulate his human puppets was limited; but it did cause pain, and the Wizard winced. The audience murmured in confusion. Funkol wrung his hands. Murkol began crying.

"Alarmed do not be, good friends," Wilfong called out through clenched teeth. "This all part of the act be. You soon enough shall see."

Brave words, wizard, he thought, willing the pain away. *You'd better come up with a really creative explanation this time. It won't be easy, now that 'SC' had decided to make a public spectacle of me.*

-- Oh, Sinladen! Come out, come out, wherever you are!

Still, the Enemy did not respond directly. Puckol leaped into the air abruptly, spun three times, and landed on the toes of one foot. She bent forward, arms outstretched perpendicular to her body, and raised the other leg straight out behind her. The picture – ludicrous as it seemed when one considered the lack of physical grace of most Lothians – was that of a dancer going through her warm-up exercises. Wilfong gaped unabashedly.

Now, the girl spoke in a somber, monotonous voice – *in perfect Atlantean*:

"There once was a wizard of old,
Who thought he could put me on hold.
He's an idiot, I think,
And makes a big stink.
And I will soon cause him to fold."

For good measure, she repeated the verse in the local language. The rhythm was uneven due to the change in vocabulary and grammar, and the rhyme scheme failed altogether. Even with his imperfect grasp of Zarelot and related tongues, Wilfong yielded to a pained expression, partly because of the vulgarity of the recital, but chiefly because of its public airing.

To his great relief, however, the crowd responded exactly as he supposed Crotchgod wanted them to respond – with laughter. Originally confused by the apparent pointlessness of what was occurring on the stage, they now believed their "star performer" and his assistant were putting on a comedy act featuring slapstick and self-effacement. It would never have occurred to them that, if Wilfong had chosen Puckol at random, a pre-conceived routine on stage had to be impossible; it also would never have occurred to them that, if Puckol had been chosen beforehand, their "mind-reading" act was a complete fraud. Rather, they responded to the moment, and the moment – unexpected as it was – was a funny one.

Their reaction was the Wizard's only consolation. He didn't have to worry about their panicking or his having to come up with an explanation of odd behavior. The scene was ugly enough now that "SC" had picked this most inopportune time to intrude. Wilfong's task was two-fold: keeping the audience unsuspecting and getting rid of the intruder. He had no problem doing either, given a little effort; doing both simultaneously would tax his abilities considerably.

Which led him to conclude that, although he understood the nature and purpose of Sinladen Crotchgod, the fellow was as much a threat as ever. The Enemy was operating from some pre-programmed agenda, devised centuries ago, and that agenda had yet to run its course. The test Wynot had posed would be over when he, Wilfong, successfully passed it. Clearly, he had to defeat the instrument of the test in a contest of Magick, or he would be doomed to encounter Crotchgod again and again as long as he lived.

How then did one defeat the creature of the Compleat Sorcerer? One would have to be as knowledgeable and as skilled as Wynot Himself – a remarkable task, even for a Level-Thirteen Practitioner. On the other hand, would the Master have devised a test impossible for a disciple to pass? No, He would have made it just difficult enough to challenge one's skills. Wilfong needed to find a final solution that was well within his mental grasp and yet not so commonplace as to render the test totally meaningless. There had to be one last confrontation, but not here in front of an unsuspecting and easily frightened band of primitives. He had to convince "SC" to meet him elsewhere.

In the meantime, he assumed the same ridiculous pose as that of Puckol, except that he stood on the opposite leg. He faced the girl and began to create comical faces. The audience howled with delight and resumed their seats. Funkol breathed a huge sigh of relief. Murkol stopped crying.

"So, I stink, eh?" Wilfong ad-libbed. "Well, this take! And that!" With each "this" and "that," he made a new face. "I will wager thou me not equal canst."

The challenge was as much for the Enemy's benefit as it was for the crowd's. The Wizard was gambling that the former's ego -- artificially implanted though it was – would react in a predictable fashion. It had to be soon, though, for Puckol was now hopping around on one foot while still in the "spread-wing" position. Wilfong grimaced. This sort of activity would surely injure the girl's body as well as her mind. He had to get Crotchgod out of her as fast as possible since the Enemy didn't care a whit what happened to his cat's paws so long as they produced results.

The Wizard started with the tried-and-true by casting the same counter-Spell he had used to release the *bofflu* from its Spell of Compulsion. "SC" was ready for him this time, and the counter-Spell bounced harmlessly off a fortified shield.

-- You didn't think you'd get away with that a second time, did you? [Crotchgod sneered].

-- It worked once, didn't it? And I'm still dealing with the same inept clod I did before.

-- 'Inept clod'? Why, you insufferable...*phtrx!* I'll show you who's 'inept'!

Good. Get mad, won't you? Make mistakes. Then I'll have you right where I want you!

He consulted his list of redundancy Spells and selected a pair of them. The first consisted of two globes – one red, a meter in diameter; the other blue, twice as wide – attached to each other by a thin white rod no thicker or longer than one's little finger. He set this array spinning about its common center; the globes wobbled back and forth as the motion of precession gained some momentum. Lazily, it careened toward Puckol. Crotchgod's original defense, a large violet pyramid, changed colors to an indigo and inverted itself. Wilfong raised his eyebrows in surprise; this was a new wrinkle. Ordinarily, inversion of a construct resulted in the opposite effect one desired. Which meant "SC" had some devious scheme in mind.

How devious soon became apparent as the red and blue globes picked up speed that they were not supposed to have. They bore down on the pyramid like a runaway chariot. Just before the moment of impact, the Enemy re-inverted the pyramid and changed its color again, to alternating bands of violet and indigo. The globes collided with their target and ricocheted off into space. Wilfong nodded in grudging admiration; his nemesis had learned some new tricks while in stasis. The fellow ought not to rest upon his laurels, however, because the attack had only just begun.

Charlton Clayes

After the first Spell had been dispatched, Wilfong fashioned a second one. It was a bit more complicated (the more so as he had never had the occasion to use it) and required many precious milli-seconds to bring it into existence. Outwardly, it resembled a swarm of mosquitos – lemon-yellow mosquitos with large black heads – a hundred of them flying in random orbits. At his signal, the swarm sped away toward Crotchgod's pyramid. He wished he could see the Enemy's reaction just then; this Spell was as unorthodox as they came (it had been part of the Level-Thirteen curriculum labeled "miscellaneous Spells," a hodge-podge of truly *weird* conjurations). The "mosquitos" formed a ring around the pyramid, then swooped down upon it, their black heads pecking at it as they passed. Again and again, they attacked until nothing was left of the pyramid.

Try as he might to bolster its strength and/or eradicate the pests, "SC" had no counter-Spell to equal the assault. When the "mosquitos" had done their work, the familiar brown disc – now mottled with purple – dived toward the Spell of Compulsion surrounding the motor-control section of Puckol's brain. Once more, the Wizard had the advantage of proximity. Hadn't Crotchgod learned even that much during his previous encounter? The disc smothered and absorbed the black sphere in an instant.

When she had been released from her hypnotic trance, the girl became aware of her unusual and awkward position, panicked, and fell to the stage like a collapsed puppet (which, in a sense, she was). The audience, thinking this was all part of the act, roared with laughter, further deepening her consternation.

-- *Damn and double damn!* [the Enemy shrieked]. I'll bring this building down on your head!

-- And what will that accomplish – besides killing some innocent people? Your gripe is with me, not them.

-- So?

-- So, let's be done with this petty sniping. If you want the chance to destroy me, I'll give it to you.

-- Is this a trick?

246

-- No trick. I propose a duel, out on the plains where no innocents can be hurt – no holds barred. If you're half the Practitioner you claim to be, you'll accept the challenge.

-- No holds barred?

-- None. Just you and me, using everything we have.

-- When?

-- The day after tomorrow. That should give us both plenty of time to prepare ourselves. I, of course, need no preparations. You, on the other hand, will need all the preparation you can get. I want to be fair about this.

-- Fair? *Burf you*, Wilfong! I don't want your burfing pity. I'll be there – with bells on.

-- Excellent. Begone, Sinladen!

Like a vacuum created by a rushing wind, the presence of the Enemy was displaced by an eerie silence. Yet, the Wizard had no time to wonder about his exit; his immediate concern was Puckol. She was just now picking herself up off the stage, her face still full of confusion and disorientation. She stared blankly at Wilfong, then at the cheering crowd.

"Wh – what happened?" she whispered.

"Um, well, I, uh, thee hypnotized and silly things made thee do."

"Oh, gods!" she yelped, clapping her hands over her face. "Is that why they're laughing?"

"Yes. Dost thou anything remember?"

"No. As soon as I returned to the stage, a strange…feeling came over me. The next thing I knew, I was standing here looking like a fool."

"The act nevertheless a huge success was. See how they cheer you."

To further re-assure the girl, the Wizard faced the audience and bowed low several times in rapid succession. Puckol made a half-hearted attempt to acknowledge the applause, embarrassment now replacing confusion. Wilfong signaled for silence.

"Good friends, for thy appreciation of my humble abilities, I thee thank. My great privilege thee it was to entertain. Most of all, to Puckol for her invaluable assistance, I many thanks give."

And he bowed low to her, causing her even more embarrassment. Yet, she smiled broadly at her new-found notoriety. Now, Funkol climbed up on the stage.

"The village of Loth likewise thanks *thee*, Master Wiffon, for providing us with marvelous entertainment. I will remind the audience that the second show will start in two hours. Good evening to thee all, good friends."

What a huckster! the Atlantean mused. *He just had to get the last word in.*

By twos and threes, the murmuring crowd got to their feet, and most actually left the building. The remainder stood around in small groups, chattering excitedly with friends and strangers alike. Puckol was joined by a pack of teenagers who showered her with praise and adulation over her "stardom" and asked many questions about her experience. Whenever anyone chanced to look his way, Wilfong saw nothing but awe. He nodded by way of acknowledgement even as he listened to the Speaker drone on about his opinions concerning the first performance.

"Master Wiffon," the huge man concluded, "I think that last part clinched the entire act. May I hope that thou wilt feature more of the same later on?"

"I shall see. I some new tricks up my sleeve – the pun please excuse – have which not for children's consumption be."

"Excellent, excellent!" He clapped his hands together. "Oh, what an evening this be! Excuse me, Master Wiffon, but I must consult with the Elders."

No doubt to plot your next money-making scheme. But, don't count on me to puff your ego up, my fat friend. This will be a very short 'tour'!

With the departure of the Speaker, several of the villagers took the opportunity to approach the Wizard, to a person timidly. The eyes of the children in the group were bright and shining – which pleased Wilfong immensely – while those of the adults expressed cautious pleasure.

"Pardon me, Master Wiffon," one mother ventured. "I, uh, would be honored if – if thou wouldst put thy mark on this." She handed him one of the advertisements Funkol had posted all over Kank-ki and Zarel. "As a *soofnir* of thy visit."

Wilfong was mildly surprised by the request. He had never heard of the notion of attaching one's name to one's creation; the artiste was recognized by his/her unique *style*, and no other identification was necessary. He who did ask for such recognition was perceived as an arrogant and self-serving person, not as a serious artiste at all. Apparently, these Lothians saw things differently. Perhaps they required constant assurance that the artiste was what (s)he claimed to be.

Well, when in Atlantis, etc., etc. He accepted the advertisement and a quill which instantly materialized in the woman's hand and wrote his name at the top of the sheet – in Atlantean characters. All of his admirers stared at the writing in wonder. No doubt they viewed his language as "magical" as himself!

As if a floodgate had been opened, a swarm of people stepped forward, all with papyrus and quill in hand, all insisting that he make his "mark." He regretted at once his having acceded to the original request. Still, he was obligated by a sense of personal honor to treat everyone equally. For the next fifteen minutes, he scribbled on one advertisement after another until he thought his fingers would cramp up. There seemed to be a never-ending stream of *soofnir*-seekers once the word had spread; he even spotted a member of the village council standing in line. If this was the price of "fame," he could easily foreswear fame forever. Attention was one thing, but *too much* attention was quite another. Practitioners must ever be circumspect.

Finally, the last of the seekers was satisfied and departed the Visitor's Center with her "treasure" firmly in hand. Wilfong sat down on the edge of the stage, wearied beyond belief, and flexed his aching fingers. Murkol appeared at his side with a mug in hand.

"I brought dou shome *dandlin* wine, Mashter. I dought dou could uzhe it."

"You thought correctly, my friend." He seized the mug and drank deeply. He sighed and peered at his servant. "This has been quite a day."

"What happened on shtache, Mashter?" the Zarelor asked as he hunkered down beside the Atlantean. "Dat lasht part wazh *not* in dy

249

orichinal plan. And de look on dy fashe – no one elshe shaw it, but I have sheen it many timezh."

The Wizard quickly described the confrontation between him and Sinladen Crotchgod. The more he heard, the more indignant Murkol became.

"My people have a shaying: 'When de *bozzid* fliezh, look for cover.' Dish Crojgod izh shertainly a *bozzid* if ever dere wazh one."

"I heartily agree. That's why I challenged him as I did. It would have happened sooner or later, but I prefer sooner. Otherwise, he'll wear me down with these endless petty attacks."

"I am afraid, Mashter."

"I'm afraid too, Murkol, but not for myself. As immodest as it sounds, I'm the only thing standing between the Enemy and his goal. If I fall, all else will fall. I have to do all I can to stop him, even at the cost of my own life."

"Dou wilt win, Mashter! *No one* can defeat dee!"

"Thank you for your vote of confidence. I am heartened by it." He sighed again. "Well, I must rest now for the second performance. Tell Funkol I don't wish to be disturbed for any reason."

Wilfong had no sooner stretched out on his bunked bed when he heard a low-level humming in his head, the unmistakable sign of an incoming mind-cast. He quickly sat up and cleared his mind. The message was brief – and alarming:

"EMERGENCY! ALL INNER NEST MEMBERS, REPORT TO THE TEMPLE AT ONCE! *Yalc.*"

The Wizard's eyes went wide with trepidation. Had the Enemy decided to attack the Temple directly? Why would he expend energy now when he was supposed to face off against Wilfong the day after tomorrow? Was he that confident in his own abilities? That the message was a genuine communication and not a ruse perpetrated by "SC" was indicated by the last word in the message; it was a meaningless code word devised by Wembly as a precaution against just such ruses.

He wasn't going to get any answers sitting here. The answers were back in Atlantis. So much for any rest he had contemplated. He scribbled a hasty note for Murkol, explaining why he was gone. Then he summoned up a Spell of Transition and de-materialized.

THE WIZARD AT ONCE

Atlantis at sunrise was the greatest wonder of the Known World.

This opinion was borne neither of self-serving propaganda nor of self-centeredness. Even foreigners had proclaimed it so – not as enthusiastically as the indigenous folk, perhaps, but equally as genuinely – and their endorsement (solicited or otherwise) was not without considerable weight in tourist circles which the Kingdom's bureaucrats exploited shamelessly. That this natural phenomenon drew as many artists to Atlantis' shores as ordinary sightseers spoke volumes on the efficiency of both the phenomenon and the bureaucracy.

Picture, if you will, the Sun peeping over the eastern horizon, spreading orange-red flames across the blue-green expanse of the Great Western Ocean, which separated the islands from the rest of the Known World. Ever westward, the Sun's rays crawled as the orb rose higher in the sky, its light glistening off the waves like a million million precious stones. In due time, the sunlight arrived at Atlantis and struck the gray-white granite of the walls of the Metropolis, coloring them a reddish-yellow. The most dazzling effect, however, occurred when the light bathed the pure-white marble of the buildings of State – the Royal Palace, the several Temples of the gods, the Library; those edifices positively *glowed* in the reflected radiance of the Great God of the Sky.

There was one particular moment, no more than a few seconds after the Sun crested the horizon, which epitomized the whole phenomenon, a moment which transformed the Metropolis into an ethereal, other-worldly structure, never to be repeated at any other time of day. Many – native- and foreign-born alike – had braved the elements, the rough crowds, and their own natures to climb to a high place outside of the city in order to catch that moment. It was, they claimed, worth the trouble, a souvenir to be carried in the memory for a lifetime.

Wilfong himself had witnessed the awesome sight – more than once in fact – both in childhood (whenever he could escape his morning chores) and in adulthood (whenever he could escape his teaching responsibilities). His favorite place of viewing was a small rise half a kilometer from the southeastern wall of the Metropolis; from that vantage point, he could watch not only the rising Sun and its effects upon the city but also the waking of the city itself (equally as fascinating a phenomenon as Nature's own, in his humble opinion). Those trips had become less frequent as his adult responsibilities increased, but he always kept future visits in the back of his mind.

At this point in time, the Wizard was not enjoying the Atlantean dawn and was not, in fact, aware that it was occurring. After receiving the urgent summons from Wembly, he transited directly to the Inner Nest's chamber, even though transiting to an indoor location was a tricky business, requiring great precision. His appearance brightened the faces of most of the assembly, but their eyes betrayed their inner fear.

Wilfong noted two anomalies. The first one was that not all of the Elders were present; the thin and frail Winsley was nowhere to be seen. Where was he? Had he fallen prey to the Circle of Friends? Was that the nature of this emergency? It would not have been the first time one of the Inner Nest was taken – as the Honor Roll attested – nor (sadly) would it likely be the last; the King's agents were relentless and creative when it came to carrying out their mission, and even the most adept Practitioner could be tripped up if he let his guard down for even an hour.

The second anomaly was the presence of a tall, lean man with dark brown hair done up in ringlets (a new fad amongst the Atlantean upper class, first seen by Wilfong on the dunderhead, Zorpac), watery blue eyes, and an expression which suggested permanent woefulness. He

253

was Caznat, the owner of the property above which the Temple of the Order of Wynot was located; a minor nobleman, he was the one known sympathizer the Order had in either the First or the Second Ring. Why was he here? He had never bothered to enter the Temple in the past, preferring to remain ignorant of its inner workings on the grounds that he could not testify to what he did not know. His presence here now indicated that a storm of the first water was brewing and that all of the resources of the Order would be required to deflect it.

"Thank the Cosmos you've come, Wilfong!" Wembly exclaimed, rushing to the Wizard's side. "We face grave business today!"

"As grave as what I'm involved in?"

"Yes. The Enemy may be a thorn in our side, but we've had a viper in our midst and didn't know it. Let's convene the Circle, and I'll explain."

Quickly and quietly, the Elders took their customary seats at the table. The empty chair two seats from Wilfong's stood out as conspicuously as a missing tooth, and the two Elders on either side of it cast trepidous glances in its direction. Caznat remained where he was until such time as he was called upon.

"Colleagues and friends," the Head intoned, "let us pay homage to Him Who has brought us to the Truth."

All faced the giant portrait of Wynot and saluted with, it may be said, greater zeal than ever. Even Caznat paid his respects, a remarkable act considering his status in Atlantean society; yet, as a non-Practicing disciple of Wynot, he might also be expected to humble himself in his master's house.

"Gentlemen," Wembly murmured when everyone had been re-seated, "this is the second emergency session we've had this cycle, and I fear for the future of the Order. Until now, we've had to deal with only external threats. We now have an *internal* one as well, a traitor in our midst."

Immediately, an uproar filled the chamber. All but Wilfong and Wembly exhibited various degrees of shock and outrage, skepticism and terror. Two Elders actually rose from their seats in order to effect an escape; the remainder exchanged glances of suspicion. Wembly squirmed in his chair waiting for the storm to blow over, while the Wizard merely stared into the distance, mulling the number of consequences this revelation had generated. It had brought to the forefront of his consciousness a thought which had nagged at him since his mental journey of the previous day. Some additional facts would clarify the matter, although he was beginning to suspect the true nature of this emergency.

In due time, the other Elders shouted themselves hoarse and, having expressed themselves sufficiently, sheepishly shut up and sat down.

"If you're quite through," the Head said irritably, "with your histrionics, let's be a bit more constructive. We waste valuable time while the Enemy creeps about, doing his dirty work."

At the mention of the word "Enemy," Wilfong perked up his ears.

"Are you suggesting 'SC' has something to do with this?"

"Ah, perhaps it was a poor choice of words, Wilfong. I was speaking metaphorically."

"I thought as much. You're really talking about Winsley, aren't you?"

If Wembly's announcement had produced a furor, then Wilfong's remark had double the effect. The clamor arose anew, and more than two Elders were ready to bolt the chamber. Even the Head was stunned and moved his mouth wordlessly for several seconds. The Wizard remained nonplussed. Presently, all had become rational again and collapsed wearily in their seats.

"Indeed, I do, Wilfong," Wembly whispered. "But how – how did you know?"

"An incident occurred yesterday which bothered me, and I couldn't resolve it until now when you brought up the idea of an internal threat." Tersely, he related his encounter with Winona at the Temple. "I had not mentioned Crotchgod's name in any of my reports to the Inner Nest. Yet, Winona knew it, and she had gotten it from Winsley. And, you'll recall, he handled the original message first – which, I think, means he probably had something to do with its writing."

"Mere conjecture, Wilfong," Wofford muttered from the end of the table. "We must have proof of Winsley's alleged treason."

"Wembly?"

"Proof you shall have, Wofford. That is why noble Caznat is here – to bear witness. Noble sir?"

The tall, lean Atlantean approached the table and bowed deeply.

"I thank thee, Masters, for allowing me to stand before thee. I too bear evil tidings. As thou dost know, I am a low-level member of the Royal Court and, as such am frequently ignored by the higher levels – so much so that I can sometimes go about in the Palace as I please.

"Yester evening as I was strolling through the back halls, hoping to drop a word or two of advice to one of the King's Ministers, I spotted thy missing colleague, Winsley, in conference with a captain in the Circle of Friends. Neither of them took notice of me; otherwise, I might have been detained on the spot. Thus, I overheard a good deal of their conversation. Winsley, I must tell thee, was offering to name names and to lead the King's agents to this place.

"Naturally, I became alarmed. For not only art *thou* in danger, Masters, but I also and my family. My cousin, the Queen, will not be able to prevail on my account. The King will surely include me and mine in his awful punishments. I cannot say how much time thou hast before the Circle of Friends mount their assault, but I would not delay any counter-measures thou hast at hand. Even now, I am taking steps to spirit my family out of Atlantis."

A stunned silence ensued for the space of a minute. But the threat of a third noisy eruption existed under the surface. Having said his piece, Caznat sat down and awaited the inevitable questions stemming from his shocking report.

"You're absolutely certain," Wilfong spoke up first, "that it was Winsley, and not someone who resembles him?"

"Absolutely, Master Colxor. I have seen all of thee on the grounds enough times to recognize thee in any circumstances."

Mentally, the Wizard winced at the use of his real name. Caznat was perhaps the only person outside of the Order who possessed that information, only because he knew Wilfong in his public persona as a teacher of writing. Though the noble was not likely to divulge that information to any other outsider, most Practitioners preferred to be addressed by their assumed names while in Temple.

"How was he behaving?"

"Pardon me?"

"Was he nervous or self-confident? Conspiratorial or under duress?"

"Nervous, I should judge, yet not under duress. I think he behaved as any normal citizen would in the presence of a member of the Circle of Friends."

"If there is no doubt remaining on that point," Wembly declared, "then we ought to form a contingency plan. Naturally, we can't rely on precedence. This location was the *original* 'contingency plan' against the last royal assault on the Order. It seems we must 're-invent' ourselves, so to speak."

"Well put, Wembly," Wofford agreed. "I suggest we emulate the noble Caznat and evacuate the Metropolis."

"Some of us have families, Wofford," the Elder known as Wulford protested. "They'll not understand the reason for a sudden re-location. Moreover, all of us moving out of the city at the same time may raise as much suspicion as the whisperings of a traitor."

"Would you prefer a knock on the door in the middle of the night, Wulford?" Wofford retorted hotly. "Or an ugly scene in public?"

"Neither, of course. But –"

"*But*, our personal safety is paramount. I say, damn the neighbors' suspicions! Let's gather up our families and get out of the city. And I also suggest we inform the lower levels of the Order that they should prepare themselves for evacuation."

"I'll see to that as soon as we adjourn," the Head said softly. He leaned back in his chair and stared at the ceiling. "The Cosmos preserve us! What a sad state we've come to."

"If thou hast no further need of me, Masters," Caznat said. "I shall take my leave and attend to my own affairs."

"Of course, noble sir," Wembly responded. "And you have our eternal gratitude for your devotion to our cause."

"Let us hope, Master Wembly, that we live long enough to devote ourselves further. Farewell, Masters."

He bowed deeply, then pivoted and marched out of the chamber.

"In order to facilitate the warning to the membership, I suggest we each contact an equal number of students. And –"

"Excuse me, Wembly," Wilfong interjected. "Before you set this plan in motion, may I suggest an alternate course of action which – if I am not being overly boastful – only I am qualified to handle?"

"What do you have in mind, Wilfong?"

"Seeking out Winsley and neutralizing his threat before he can do any real damage."

A wave of gasps rippled across the table.

"Is that wise, Wilfong?" Wofford blurted out. "You'll be the first he'll direct the Circle of Friends to the moment you confront him."

"Oh, he won't know I'm anywhere near him until it's too late." The Wizard pursed his lips. "Besides, I'm not entirely convinced that Winsley is acting of his own volition. Something – or someone – else is involved."

"Do you believe he's being controlled by Sinladen Crotchgod?" Wulford asked.

"I'd put even money on it, Wulford. But I won't know for sure until I investigate. I'll need an assistant, however, and I'd like to request Winona."

"Winona?" Wembly exclaimed. "But, she's only a Level Ten. How much help will she be?"

"The girl has a sharp mind," the Wizard replied, smiling as he recalled his previous encounter with the young woman. "I suspect she'll be sitting at this table in the near future – assuming, of course, we have a future. Also, Winsley has used her for his own purpose and won't suspect her. Don't worry, my friends, I'll be constantly monitoring her activity."

"Well, do whatever you think best, Wilfong. The Cosmos knows you're the best qualified to act. And may the Master watch over you."

*   *   *

The Library of Atlantis appeared much as it did when Wilfong had visited it four days ago. Except, today, the usual hustle and bustle was not present. Today was the third and final day of the Festival of Caxeot, and the Library was still closed so that its employees and patrons had no excuse to forego their religious obligations. Hardly a soul was in sight for several streets in all directions. The Wizard had chosen this place for the entrapment of the traitorous Winsley, because he needed absolute secrecy; otherwise, the operation would have become public knowledge to the detriment to the Order. At the moment, he was standing in the shadow of a column on the Library's portico, using both physical and mental vision to scan the area.

Before arriving here, he had first cast out his mind to Winona. The young woman was both surprised and pleased that he had contacted her and honored that he had chosen her for such a delicate task. She was so profuse in her thanks that he had to interrupt her quite brusquely in order to communicate his desires. His instructions to her were to go directly to the Library without stopping for anyone or anything; once there, she would receive further instructions. It was a credit to her training and loyalty to the Order that she obeyed at once.

While waiting for Winona, Wilfong again cast his mind out, this time to search for Winsley. As he had told the Inner Nest, only he could perform this task; as a Level Twelve, Winsley could detect and block any mental probe except that of a Level Thirteen. The traitorous Elder would not be able to resist (as the Enemy had discovered to his chagrin), and his mind would reveal every secret it harbored. Wilfong had no intention of reading Winsley's mind, however; he merely wished to locate the fellow as a prelude to the trap he was planning to set.

In an ever widening circle, his mental dragnet – a reddish-orange cube spinning clock-wise on one of its apexes – ranged across the Metropolis. A special Spell that Wynot had hidden in his writings like some grand puzzle, awaiting the mental ability of someone like the Wizard to discover, it could locate and track any Practitioner and neutralize his protective shield. Wilfong could have used it most effectively against Crotchgod, but he hadn't wished to reveal too many of his abilities all at once if he could rely on tried-and-true Spells instead. In the present instance, however, time was of the essence, and subtlety had to be shelved.

Five minutes after the creation of the Spell, the Wizard had his man. Winsley, ever an early riser, was wandering through the streets of the Third Ring in an easterly direction. In his mind's eye, Wilfong "saw" the surrounding area as clearly as the Elder; the probe also allowed him to use Winsley's eyes as much as the Elder could. The Gate of Tears was fifty meters ahead. Winsley stopped short of the Gate and stood before a bakery, an anxious look on his face. Instantly, Wilfong knew why the man was there; the baker was reputed to be a relative of one of the members of the Circle of Friends. The Elder was clearly meeting with someone in the Circle in order to keep his promise to divulge all he knew about his erstwhile colleagues. The Wizard had not acted a moment too soon.

Winsley peered furtively all about him, then whistled shrilly. A few seconds later, a figure materialized at the doorway of the bakery and stepped into the morning light. Wilfong smiled to himself. It was Aloxam, who had trailed him several days ago and whom he had put under a Spell of Compulsion (to the fellow's great embarrassment). Wordlessly, the agent strolled off toward the Gate of Tears with Winsley in tow.

In order to deal with the traitor, Wilfong had to part him from his overseer. Though he was now acting at a distance, the task still posed little difficulty, considering with whom he was dealing. He relaxed and chanted:

> "There once was a spy in the royal pay,
> Who sought to work in a treacherous way.
> He corrupts one of our own
> And casts the first stone.
> Oh, Wynot, send him a vision most fey!"

Mentally, he observed the effect of his Spell. One moment, the agent was trudging along in smug self-confidence, perhaps thinking of the reward this little coup of his would garner. The next moment, he stopped dead in his tracks, turned to look at Winsley, and screeched at the top of his voice. What the Wizard had done was to hide the Elder behind an illusion; the agent now believed he was in the presence of a demon out of Atlantean mythology which rendered its victims limb from limb in order to suck out their bone marrow. In reaction to the illusion, the agent bolted down the street as fast as his legs could carry him, leaving behind a very bewildered Winsley. The latter whirled around to see what had panicked the man so; he saw nothing but an empty street, and his level of apprehension rose appreciably. And, when a few locals, aroused by the blood-curdling scream, called out in challenge, he retreated in the direction from which he had come.

Wilfong's timing was impeccable. No sooner had the first phase of his plan been accomplished than he spied Winona nearing the Library. He signaled to her, and she picked up her pace. When she stepped onto the portico, they saluted each other.

"Wilfong," the young woman said breathlessly, "I came as quickly as I could. How may I assist thee?"

The Wizard did not need to be told of her haste to get here. Her disheveled appearance spoke volumes. The ringlets of her hair which she favored had lost their shape because she had not attended to them this morning, and so her tresses fell to her shoulders in long tangled strings. Her robe was rumpled from rapid dressing; to Wilfong's decidedly inexpert eye when it came to women's fashions, it seemed as if she had put it on *backwards*. Despite the outward signs, he still considered her very attractive. Her inner self shone through to mesmerize and to tantalize him. Was this what it was like to desire a woman beyond all reason? He had to fight to dispel the carnal instinct; too much was at stake to yield to thoughts of physical pleasure.

Quickly, he updated her on recent developments. In other circumstances, a Level Ten would not have been made privy to the discussions of the Inner Nest; only when (s)he had completed Level Eleven would (s)he be allowed to sit in as a non-voting member in preparation for the day when (s)he was formally sworn into that august body. The circumstances of the present situation, however, called for Winona's having all the facts if her co-operation were to be secured. Besides, the Wizard felt instinctively that he could trust her with this knowledge. Yet, as he related the facts, Winona reacted with horror (and not a little disgust) at this treachery and wrung her hands at the thought that she might have abetted Winsley in it. Reflexively – and perhaps not so reflexively – Wilfong placed his hand on hers as a gesture of comfort.

"You're not at fault, my dear. Winsley took advantage of your trust in the Inner Nest and used you as a pawn in his nefarious scheme."

"I thank you for that. I couldn't live with myself if I thought I had betrayed the Order."

"There's no danger to us at the present. I've bought us some time." He described the incident at the bakery which brought a smile to her lips. "What we must do now is take Winsley out of the picture as well so that the Circle of Friends can never contact him again."

"What do you want me to do?"

"Call out to him mentally and ask him to come here at once. I can't do so, because he'd become instantly suspicious. He won't suspect you and will walk right into the trap I've prepared."

"What shall I tell him when I contact him?"

"You're a bright girl," he replied, smiling. "You'll think of something."

Again reflexively – and not so reflexively – he squeezed her hand. And quite in the same spirit, she placed her free hand on his for the space of a second or two. It was a most rapturous moment – until both realized where they were and what they were about. Hands were withdrawn rapidly, and the moment passed into history.

Winona then relaxed and cast her mind out. Wilfong uttered a Spell of Far-Seeing and "traveled" along with her in order to monitor the proceedings. He noted with some interest that mind-casting seemed to come naturally to her, for she had not bothered to focus her mental energy. Her mind-cast had been formed and transmitted in the same millisecond, smoothly and effortlessly. That was a good sign. The Order certainly needed minds like hers both to protect itself and to expand on its mission. As the Wizard had suggested, she might become an Elder in a short time and perhaps join him at Level Thirteen, sharing the cosmic experience open to those of that rank. It was lonely at the top, and companionship would be most welcome...

-- Master Winsley [Winona called out as soon as she had made contact], it is I, Winona, Level Ten.

Wilfong "saw" the surprise on the Elder's face as he recognized the incoming signal. He "saw" the standard mind-probe issue from Winsley's mind, speed back along Winona's signal, and impact that portion of her mind she had left open to a probe. He "saw" the expression of relief as the other re-assured himself of the signal's authenticity.

-- Winona, what's wrong? Why are you contacting me?

-- Oh, Master Winsley! There – there are soldiers at the Temple, and – and I don't know what to do. You're the only one I've been able to contact.

-- Really? That *is* ominous. Where are you now?

-- At the Library. I was hoping Master Wembly might be there, but he isn't.

-- What about…Master Wilfong?

-- As far as I can tell, he's not even in Atlantis. I – I just don't know what to do!

During the course of this exchange, Winsley had issued another, more complex probe, one designed to burrow deep under the conscious level of Winona's mind and to uncover secret thoughts. Wilfong viewed this with a certain smugness. The Elder was reacting exactly as he had been taught. Fortunately for the sake of his plan, the Wizard had taken precautions to safeguard secret thoughts. A Level Ten would not have withstood the sort of probe now on its way, and her duplicity would have been revealed instantly. Wilfong had extended his own mind-shield to block out Winsley; moreover, he had re-enforced the story Winona had concocted with a few selected false images. Now, he "watched" confidently as the probe struck the young woman's mind, examined the false images, and sent them back to the Elder. At the other end of the "line," he "saw" a look of satisfaction spreading over Winsley's face as the latter swallowed the bait.

-- Stay where you are, Winona. I'll be there in a few minutes.

-- What if the soldiers come here?

-- You're a Level Ten. You should know how to protect yourself. There's no need to panic.

-- Thank you, Master Winsley. I'll be waiting for you. [She broke off contact and turned to Wilfong]. "How did I do?"

"You should have been an actress, my dear. You'd have gotten an award for that performance." He chuckled in spite of the gravity of the situation. "Now we'll see if *Winsley* can find a need to panic."

Not far away, from the direction of the Temple of Xenox for this Ring, trumpets sounded to announce the call for morning prayers and begin the third day of the Festival of Caxeot. After prayers of dedication and supplication, the Bull Game was scheduled, followed by the Grand Sacrifice to the Most High. Immediately, a chorus of bells – small bells and large, iron bells and bronze, single bells and clusters – clamored from all parts of Atlantis to hurry worshipers along. This mighty carillon seemed to go on forever but actually lasted only fifteen minutes. It touched a sympathetic chord in Wilfong, who had been born and raised in the Metropolis and therefore was accustomed to the melody of the bells. Though he now eschewed the old gods in favor of the teachings of Wynot the Wise, he could not entirely suppress residual feelings the bells induced. When the bells ceased their tolling, the trumpets sounded once more to announce that the Kingdom was ready for celebration.

"Wilfong," Winona whispered, "I see Winsley now."

"Good. Step out into the open where he can see you."

She moved out of the shadows of the portico and waited for the Elder with what she hoped was a convincing exhibition of anxiety. The Wizard uttered a Spell of Invisibility, amended so that it was limited to only Winsley, and observed the latter as he approached. He "read" in the other's mind only apprehension and worry. When the Elder spotted Winona, he slipped on a false smile of confidence and hurried to her side.

"Master Winsley!" she gushed. "Thank the Cosmos you've come! I was so worried…"

"There, there, child," Winsley soothed, patting her hand in a not-so-fatherly manner. "Have no fear. Together we'll puzzle this matter out." He glanced around furtively. "First, we must get away from this public place. The Festival of Caxeot is resuming, and the streets will be full of people."

"Where shall we go?"

"Ah, I have a place not far from here. We'll...be safe there. Come along, child."

Surreptitiously, Winona glanced over her shoulder to appeal silently to Wilfong. The Wizard gestured her to go with Winsley. She nodded imperceptibly and accompanied the Elder down the street. They stayed close to the buildings in order to remain as much out of sight as possible. The Wizard retained his partial Spell of Invisibility and dogged their heels. He had no fear of raising suspicion; he was just another festival-goer on his way to one temple or another.

As it happened, he had a fair idea of where Winsley was headed. It was a basic rule of the Order of Wynot that a member's private life was just that – private – and that no other member had the right to pry. (There was no rule, however, preventing any member from confiding in another member or in the entire Order if he so chose.) The one exception to this rule was if a member's private life impinged upon his duty to the Order; in this instance, he was expected to disclose as much information as necessary to resolve the conflict.

Winsley's proposal to take Winona to a "safe house" created around certain mental images which Wilfong "saw" via the high-level probe he had maintained all this while. Although he had a wife and four children (none of whom suspected what he was) with whom he lived in the Third Ring, he also had a mistress whom he kept in the Fourth Ring and who worked as a sewer in the garment district. It was to this latter dwelling that he was taking Winona. What, Wilfong mused, would the mistress say to that? Would she rise up in a rage as a "woman scorned" and make Winsley's life miserable? On a more subjective level, the Wizard hoped so; it would serve his errant colleague right. Moreover, he did not appreciate the manner in which the Elder was regarding Winona. It struck him as very lecherous...

The garment district lay in the northern quadrant of the Fourth Ring, and that by design, for the herds of sheep which provided the wool for cloth inhabited pastures north of the city. It was thus just a short distance between the cloth-making facilities and the sewing workshops. As might be expected, the district was also one of the grimiest and rundown. So long as the product was forthcoming in steady streams and in desired quantities, little regard was given to environmental or safety concerns. Large numbers of workers crowded together, laboring from dawn to dusk (and often beyond) in squalid conditions; most of these were either slaves or immigrants (depending on the nature and/or the generosity of the owners of the businesses). Little outdoor traffic existed here; those who were on the streets earned their living in less reputable enterprises, preying on anyone who seemed to have a fat purse. Even the City Guards did not patrol the district on a regular basis and yielded their authority to whomever could control/intimidate the rabble; and, in times of civil unrest (which was frequent), they appeared *en masse*.

This day, not even the preying class were on the streets. On High Holy Days, all businesses were required to close so that all citizens – managers and workers alike – could attend the religious/civil ceremonies. And the King strictly enforced that edict at the prodding of the priesthood. Employers grumbled mightily since a shut-down meant lost profits, and employees grumbled also since it meant lost wages. Both classes absented themselves from the ceremonies if they could; they attended only if they were coerced into and/or rewarded for participation or if they were actually true believers in the Most High.

Wilfong had little reason to visit this district in the ordinary course of the day. He did so once a week at night, because one of his private pupils lived here; payment was usually something in kind since his client had little money to spend on "frills" such as learning to read and write. Thus, to some in this Ring, he was recognizable and left alone – most of the time.

The Wizard eventually found himself in front of a woolen-robe factory whose upper floor consisted of a warren of small rooms which housed the sewers. Winsley's mistress occupied one of those rooms, and he and Winona had just passed through an adjacent alleyway to gain access to a stairway at the rear of the building. Wilfong contacted the young woman.

-- Stall him somehow. *Don't* go into the building if you can possibly help it.

-- Very well, Wilfong. I'll tell him I've turned my ankle and have to walk slower.

-- Excellent, Winona. You're becoming an expert at subterfuge. I'll catch you up in a few seconds.

Just as Wilfong prepared to cross the street and enter the alleyway, he was arrested by a familiar gruff voice.

"Colxor! What in the names of all the gods are ye doin' here, *boyo*?"

The Wizard turned slowly around. Hamilton, the diminutive crew-boss from the wharf district, was steaming toward him and displaying all of his teeth (what were left of them), and he was not tracing a straight line. It was clear that he had been "celebrating" the Festival of Caxeot early – with a liter or two. Even so, one drunken Hamilton was a better worker than five sober Atlanteans any day. Despite his inconvenient appearance, Wilfong had to smile in return.

"Ham, my friend. What brings you so far from your usual haunts?"

"Ah, well," the short man replied, winking broadly, "I met this…lady recently, and she tendered me a warm invite, if ye catch me meaning." He squinted at the Atlantean. "And you?"

"I confess, Ham, that I'm here for much the same reason."

The crew-boss' bushy eyebrows shot up like twin signal flags.

"Are ye now? Oh, and won't that break our poor Lymatan's heart. Despite her *blarney*, she's got it terrible hard for ye, *boyo*. You really ought to give her a work-out."

"Um, well, I'll take it under advisement. Look, I, uh, mustn't keep the lady waiting" – now *he* winked broadly – "if you catch *my* meaning."

"Right ye are, laddie-buck. Say, whyn't you collect her, and then we'll go to my lady's place, and the four of us can celebrate the High Holy Days together."

"I don't think that would be a good idea. My lady is, um, particular about such things."

"*Bosh!*" The wharf-rat seized Wilfong by the arm and began steering him in the direction the Wizard had been going. "How often do we get a chance like this?"

Wilfong grimaced. Winona was counting on him to intercept Winsley before the latter grew suspicious and escaped the trap they had set for him. There was only one recourse, although Wilfong hated to fall back on it. It was a dirty trick to play on a friend (even one as rough as Hamilton), and someone might be watching. Still, he needed to be free of all encumbrances quickly. In a whisper, he chanted:

> "There once was a fellow I just met,
> Who caused me to worry and fret.
> He makes me delay
> A trap I would lay.
> Oh, Wynot, make him forget!"

Almost immediately, the Spell of Forgetfulness blanketed Hamilton's mind and scrambled his memory. The short man's eyes glazed over momentarily, then recovered their usual steely gaze as he took in his present surroundings. At that instant, he realized he was gripping someone's elbow, blinked in confusion, and released the grip as if the elbow was a hot iron. He stared at the Atlantean sheepishly.

"Uh, 'scuse me, citizen. I, uh, musta got turned around somehow." He scratched his head. "Dunno what I'm doin' here in the first place."

"Well, there's no harm done, friend," the Wizard murmured.

"Yeah. Well, may Xenox watch over you."

"And you," Wilfong responded softly as Hamilton staggered off aimlessly.

Later, he would correct the damage he'd done by restoring his friend's memory of everything that had occurred – except his meeting with the Wizard. Now, he had a rogue to snare.

He hurried down the alleyway and spotted his quarry and Winona midway up the crudely constructed wooden stairway. The young woman was faking a limp in order to slow their progress. Wilfong marveled at her ability to adapt to changing circumstances. He took a deep breath, canceled his Spell of Invisibility, and cried out:

"Winsley! Stop where you are!"

The Elder pivoted, gasped in shock, and shrank against the wall of the building.

"Wilfong? What are you doing here?"

"I know what you've done, Winsley. The game is up."

"I – I don't know what you mean."

"Would you prefer I tore the truth out of your mind for all the world to see? You know I can do it easily."

The Elder worked his mouth for a space, but no sounds came out. Perspiration dotted his forehead, and his breathing grew ragged. Abruptly, he slid down the wall, slumped on the stairs, and covered his thin face with boney hands. Great muffled sobs filtered through his fingers. Wilfong shook his head in disgust. To think that a member of the Order of Wynot had come to this state – why, it outraged one's principles!

"Oh, Cosmos!" Winsley wailed piteously. "Please, Wilfong. I – I had no choice. I had to do it."

"'No choice'? How can you of all people say such a thing? One of the first things the Master taught us was that each of us can choose his own destiny if his will is strong enough. Explain your lack of 'choice.'"

"He – he blackmailed me. He threatened to tell my wife about – about –" He gestured vaguely toward the warren above him. "He would have too, if I hadn't co-operated."

"'He'? Who is *he*?"

Without warning, Winona issued a half-stifled cry. Her body became rigid, her face went blank, and her eyes glazed over. The Wizard stared at her incredulously. The young woman opened her mouth mechanically.

"Guess who?" a sneering voice spilled out.

"Crotchgod!" Wilfong roared. "What's the meaning of this intrusion? Couldn't you wait until tomorrow?"

"Oh, I intend to honor our duel. But, I wanted to wear you down some more."

"What's your connection with Winsley?"

"I'll let him tell you." Winona's body turned stiffly. Her arm raised up and fell with a stinging blow on the Elder's skull. "Answer him, worm!"

Winsley swallowed compulsively.

"I – I was the one who placed the first message in the Temple, just before Wembly arrived to make up the training schedule for the next cycle."

"Yes, of course," Wilfong declared. "It had to be you, since Crotchgod knew we would turn it over to our most adept psychometrist for examination. And, of course, you 'discovered' nothing of any use to us." He regarded the Enemy's newest tool and seethed inside. Outwardly, however, he remained calm. "I presume you also had Winsley contact the Circle of Friends and have them assign one of their members to follow me around."

"Right," "SC" replied smugly. "And now, you can worry if I've gotten to other Elders."

The Wizard frowned. In that regard, Crotchgod was correct. If he had been able to ferret out the weak spot of one Level Twelve in the Order, conceivably he could find other weak spots. And the damnable thing was that Practitioning was not involved at all; the "weapon" had been the oldest in the annals of humankind, and its use required only willfulness – which Crotchgod had in quantity.

"Well, forewarned is forearmed, you know, Sinladen. Now that I know what to look for, I can counter anything you do."

"Brave words, Wilfong. Perhaps I ought -- *Damnation!*"

As Wilfong stared in amazement, Winona's eyelids fluttered briefly, and her eyes became unglazed. Her face became less blank, and her body lost its rigidity. She peered about warily.

"Winona?" Wilfong asked cautiously, hopefully. "Are you all right?"

"Yes, Wilfong," she breathed. "Was that…creature the one who calls himself 'Sinladen Crotchgod'?"

"It was indeed." He now regarded her with fresh admiration. "Tell me how you were able to reject him."

The young woman sat down on the stairs, leaned wearily against the building, and stared off into the distance.

"He took me by surprise and, before I could react, he was in my mind. But I was able to retreat and gather up my strength, waiting for the proper moment for a counter-attack. His control, I discovered, was erratic, mostly because of his inordinate boasting. So, I hit him with everything I had." She smiled sweetly. "He never saw it coming; he was too sure of himself."

"His greatest weakness, I can tell you. Well, Winona, you've applied your training splendidly your first time in the field. And you've exhibited the last lesson in Level-Eleven training. You'll soon be ready for Level Twelve."

"Will you train me personally, Wilfong?"

The Wizard hesitated before answering. He found himself in a quandary and had to think matters through. During this exercise, the young woman had altered her attitude toward him. First, she had stopped calling him "*Master* Wilfong" but used his code name in a more informal manner; and second, she had expressed an ongoing interest in *personal* training on his part. Was she as attracted to him as he was becoming to her? Any close relationship between them could complicate the functioning of the Order, or even compromise it. On the other hand, if they were both part of the Inner Nest…

"I could," he replied cautiously. "But that's a matter for the future. Right now, if you're up to it, we ought to return to the Temple and report our activities."

"Wilfong!" Winsley whined. "What's to become of me?"

"You're free of Crotchgod for the time being, but not of your betrayal of the Order. You'll stand before the Elders and confess your guilt. After that, who knows?"

*   *   *

The Wizard gave his report in two parts. The first centered on the more immediate events concerning Winsley. As he waited for his colleagues to absorb this new information and react, he noted their varied expressions. Some of the Elders registered relief over having averted a major crisis; others registered disgust at the sad state of affairs which had engulfed the Order. Comments were not long in coming. One faction – the minority, led by Wofford – was in favor of expelling Winsley from the Order; another – the majority, led by Wembly – sought to rehabilitate him on the grounds that he had not acted of his own free will. Wilfong chose to remain neutral.

So heated was the discussion that no one (except Wilfong) paid any attention to the presence of Winona, who, as a mere Level Ten, ordinarily would not have been allowed into the chamber of the Inner

Nest. When all was said and done, then Wilfong stepped in and offered a compromise: Winsley would suffer a quasi-parole with a review at its end; in the interim, he would be suspended as an Elder and placed in a special training program overseen by Winona. That last part elicited another heated exchange; but, in the end, Wilfong prevailed by reason of his superior training. Winona briefly touched his arm as a gesture of thanks for this tremendous honor.

Once this matter was concluded, the Wizard launched the second part of his report – and, in his mind, the most important part – which dealt with the events occurring prior to the capture of Winsley. As he described his adventures in the Void and in the past, all of the Inner Nest registered awe exponentially; none remained in a non-agitated state, and two of them were close to swooning. In the corner of the chamber, Zondar, who had been specially summoned in order to record the proceedings, grimaced frequently. When Wilfong finished speaking, a long silence permeated the room like a thick fog.

"Unbelievable!" Wembly finally rasped, obviously expressing the general opinion of the others. "What have you concluded, Wilfong?"

The Wizard rubbed his jaw. He had an answer, but he didn't know how the Elders would receive it. It just seemed too fantastic on the surface. Yet…

"As incredible as it sounds, I believe that this entire business with Sinladen Crotchgod has been a very elaborate test, designed by Wynot Himself, to evaluate my worthiness to join Him (wherever He is). The Master created Sinladen Crotchgod and set us both on a course leading to the upcoming duel of Magick. My defeat of the so-called 'Enemy' will be my price of admission into the Master's exalted Company which I had seen in my dreams."

"And you think that the Master planned all this before He disappeared two-and-a-half centuries ago? *Unbelievable!*"

"Did anyone – past or present – really understand His purposes? Wynot showed us only what we needed in order to stimulate our natural abilities, and that was but a fraction of what *He* was capable of. I must confess that I am truly humbled by this affair."

"Well, ain't that just burfing grand!" Zondar piped up. "Imagine: the great Wilfong the Wizard, showing humility. This *is* worth recording, I'd say."

Wilfong spun around to regard the Librarian, his face reddened by the other's impertinence. He started to jab his finger at the Cimmerian in order to berate him. Instantly, he thought better of it, calmed himself, and mentally berated himself for losing his temper. Now that he was close to achieving apotheosis, he must not allow petty emotions to cloud his thinking. Wynot had devised a Grand Plan for him, and He could just as easily withdraw it and leave His errant disciple dangling in self-reproach.

"I apologize for what I was about to say, Masters," he murmured, bowing toward his fellow Elders. To the Librarian: "Forgive me for every evil thing I've ever said to you, Zondar. I had no right to say them. You're a valuable asset to the Order."

"'S all right, Wilfong," Zondar muttered. "No real harm done."

"What's your next course of action, Wilfong?" Wembly inquired in order to defuse a tense situation.

"Well, Sinladen Crotchgod remains a problem. Even if he's a construct fashioned by the Master, he still has the power to create mischief if he isn't stopped. Therefore, I have to defeat him utterly."

"That'll be a tall order," the Librarian remarked. "Judging by what you've said about him, he ain't nothing to be sneezed at."

The Wizard stood silently for a long while, and his eyes took on a faraway look as he became lost in thought. Around the table, stirrings of concern arose (and Winona at his side gripped his arm unabashedly). Though everyone in the room had a reasonably good idea of Wilfong's mental agility, they had seldom seen him in action. This display of concentration agitated them as much as Winsley's treason had done. Wembly got to his feet and came out from behind the table; slowly, he approached his old friend and gently touched his shoulder.

"Wilfong?" he asked softly. "Are you well?"

Instantly, the Wizard snapped out of his reverie and fixed the Head with a steely glance. The latter winced and withdrew a step as if he had just disturbed a venomous snake.

"I'm fine, Wembly." He smiled then. "Not true, Zondar. Thank you for the idea."

"Huh? Wha'd I say?"

'Colleagues, all our problems will soon be solved. Now, it's back to Loth for the final 'performance.' Farewell."

Still grinning, he uttered a Spell of Transition and de-materialized with a flourish, leaving behind a most perplexed group of Practitioners.

THE FIFTEENTH CASTING
THE WIZARD AT HOME

"Repeat after me," Wilfong instructed Murkol, "*exactly* as I say it.

There once was a fellow dressed in black,
Who pressed upon me his dreadful attack.
He casts out his Spells
From the deepest of hells.
Oh, Wynot, send them all back!"

The Zarelor complied and had his usual trouble with the sibilants in the Atlantean language. The Wizard grimaced at the idea that a Spell of Power could possibly be uttered by such a barbarian tongue and made his servant run through it several more times until he had committed it to memory. This option ran a great risk, since all Spells depended upon inflection and nuance – it had to do with harmonics, Wynot had explained long ago – and one word spoken improperly would not have any effect at best and the wrong effect at worst. Wilfong was not going to turn Murkol into a full-fledged Practitioner; yet, if the Zarelor could cast this one simple Spell half as well as a Third-Level student, he would be satisfied. After all, he needed it (he hoped) for one time only. The only other option was for him to throw his own voice into Murkol's mouth. But he planned to be far too busy when the time came to divert his attention toward awkward ploys.

"I am shorry, Mashter, dat I cannot shpeak dy tongue any better."

"Don't worry, my friend. You speak better Atlantean than I speak Zarelot. You'll do fine. Against the two of us, the Enemy hasn't got a prayer."

"How? I am no shorsherer."

"You don't have to be. Crotchgod won't be expecting any moves from you. So, when you say this simple Spell of Protection to deflect whatever he'll throw at us, he'll be so surprised that he'll be off his guard long enough for me to make my own move." He sighed deeply. "At least, that's what I'm counting on. Actually, anything can happen, but so far he's been quite predictable."

"What *art* dou planning?"

"If I tell you, he will read it in your mind and counter-act me. I'll explain it all afterward – if there is an afterward."

"Don't shay shuj dings, Mashter! Dou art shecond to none!"

"Ah, my good and faithful servant. If your conviction were Magick, victory would be assured. Yet, you may be right. Crotchgod can dish out surprises well enough, but he can't take them. And I'm planning one huge surprise for him."

They were standing on the plain outside of Loth, nearly on the same spot where Wilfong had encountered "SC" two days before. Why he had chosen this place for a duel of Magick, he couldn't say in so many words, but it seemed apropos. The site of his one minor triumph might have bolstered his self-confidence. Still, he did not delude himself about scoring another triumph anywhere; his future and that of the Order of Wynot were clearly on the line, and it behooved him to win or lose the contest in solitude. No human brain which did not belong to a non-Practitioner could possibly comprehend what was to occur shortly nor fathom the consequences of the outcome. Therefore, all contestants were free to use any of the "tricks of the trade" without interference from outsiders.

The easiest course of action for the Wizard would have been to be elsewhere. He could have whisked himself to the other side of the Cosmos or back to its very beginning or to the furthest depths of the Void. Yet, to abandon all that he held dear to the tender mercies of a construct like Sinladen Crotchgod was not in his nature. And, sooner or later, "SC" would find him and gloat, and he would have to fight after all. In addition, his Master would disavow him for all Time to come, and that would be a fate worse than death.

The Sun was just peeping over the eastern horizon, casting its glow upon the verdant prairie and dispelling the gloom of the woodlands. Wilfong allowed himself the briefest smile. It was a good day to die. The primitive peoples he had met on his many travels believed that the world was flat and immobile; if one journeyed far enough, one would fall off the edge and drop into the abyss. No educated Atlantean countenanced such a notion; proof of a mobile Earth lay in simple observation and rational deduction. "Sunrise" was a product of irrational thinking. Still, it was the one of only two certainties on this or any other day; all else was subject to a hundred or more variables.

A few steps away, Murkol fidgeted. If Wilfong manifested apprehension on the mental plane, then the Zarelor was acting strictly on the physical plane. His lips moved furiously as he repeated endlessly the Spell taught to him hastily, and he glanced around nervously for any signs of intruders. The least noise caused him to jump out of his skin and turn him into a jittery mass.

Murkol had been on pins and needles ever since the Wizard departed to Atlantis and right up to the moment he returned. He had had to fend off a horde of well-wishers and signature-seekers and to make excuses to Funkol in the meantime. All were disappointed, of course, not understanding why the "great magician" needed a rest before his second performance of the evening. And, when the "great magician" had returned, there were the preparations to be made for the performance. He had had little time to catch a decent breath, least of all take a cup of "cheer."

After the performance, fresh hordes assaulted the Atlantean. And the Speaker begged and cajoled until Wilfong agreed to two more performances the following evening, and the whole maddening scene re-played itself down to the last detail. And, just before retiring, Murkol had been told that he must awaken well before dawn, crawl out of a warm bed, creep out of the *kabban* without disturbing the household, and wait for the Enemy on the plain. From his standpoint, the events of the next couple of hours was going to be strictly anti-climactic!

The seconds seemed like minutes, and the minutes like hours, and still Wilfong and Murkol waited.

He's trying to destroy my equipoise, the Wizard concluded. *He thinks he can defeat me by sheer exasperation. Well, it won't work. I won't let it work!*

Wilfong had no doubt that Sinladen Crotchgod would appear. In the first place, the fellow had his own "mission" in life to perform, and he had made it clear that he would not be persuaded from it. In the second place, he had so much pride that failure to show up could be construed as cowardice, and that was the one thing he could not tolerate, either in character or in Practitioning. And, in the third place, he had been stung so many times that revenge would be uppermost in his mind. Yes, he'd appear all right, if it were the last thing he ever did.

And, the Wizard thought grimly, *I sincerely hope it is – even if being here is the last thing I ever do.*

It may be that he allowed these dire thoughts to leak out and spread across whatever plane of Existence Crotchgod now inhabited, for they seemed to produce almost instant results. A solid black line formed in the air not six meters from Wilfong's position. The Wizard pursed his lips as he observed the now-familiar method of materializing and finally the black robe and hood shimmering against the rising Sun. Again, he caught the stench of contempt which radiated in waves like heat energy. From inside the hood, the crimson eyes burned like twin coals. Wilfong put on his best sneer.

-- Well, it's about time. Whatever else you are, you're not punctual.

-- *Humph!* I just allowed you a few more minutes of life, that's all. I can afford to be generous.

-- Brave talk, Sinladen. And do you have deeds to match?

-- Oh, you'll find out soon enough.

Behind the Wizard, Murkol gasped in terror. Even though his master had described the Enemy in vivid detail, this was the first time he had seen him in the flesh; and, clearly, the seeing was more terrifying than the hearing. He nearly fainted dead away.

"Mashter!" the Zarelor whispered hoarsely. "He'zh more hideoush dan dou hasht deshcribed. How cansht dou bear to look at him?"

"Steady on, Murkol. He may be ugly, but that's all he's got going for him."

-- Keep it up, *phtrx*, and I'll not allow you an easy death.

-- If it happens at all, you mean. I intend to be around for a long, long time.

-- By the way, 'old friend,' what's *he* doing here? I don't recall agreeing to a group session.

-- And nothing was said about *not* having others present, as *I* recall. Murkol is an eyewitness, in case anyone questions the validity of the outcome. Or perhaps you don't want any witnesses to your demise?

-- *Humph!* Let's dispense with the puffery and get on to the business at hand, shall we?

-- By all means. First, however, I must tell you that the Master has been exceedingly clever in all this.

-- Wynot? What has he got to do with it?

-- Why, everything, of course. I've come to the conclusion that I'm being tested to see how worthy I am to be His acolyte. You, Sinladen Crotchgod, are part of the test.

-- *I* am?

-- Oh, yes. I don't know who – or *what* -- you are, but the Master created you, physically and mentally. He supplied you with all of your ideas about loss of face and of revenge against the Order. He arranged for you to meet me in mortal combat, probably by a post-hypnotic command.

"SC's" eyes glowed more fiercely than ever and seemed to project from their sockets until they threatened to burn into the observer's own eyes. Further, Crotchgod's robe became awhirl with shifting light patterns as he literally shook with rage.

-- *You lie!* [he exploded, and the vehemence of the denial nearly knocked Wilfong off his feet!]. I'm my own man! *No one* controls me!

-- Sorry, 'old friend,' but I've seen the proof with my own eyes. At first, I was unwilling to believe it too. But, in the end, I had to.

-- What 'proof,' *phtrx*?

-- Observe – and learn.

The Wizard turned ninety degrees and traced a rectangle in the air, his fingers creating a shimmering gold framework, two meters by three. When it was completed, the space within it became milky white and opaque. Wilfong now called upon his memories, specifically those of the events in the past he had witnessed two days before; these he projected onto the opaque "screen." Like a moving picture, the scene between Wynot and Crotchgod played out, followed by a shot of the cryptic remark the Compleat Sorcerer had written in his journal. Meanwhile, the Enemy watched in rigid silence; only the sound of his raspy breathing could be heard. At last, the "picture show" concluded, and the gold-framed "screen" blanked out. Wilfong dismantled his construct and faced his foe again expectantly.

-- What does all that prove? Only that you saw something in the past, more or less as it occurred. It tells me nothing else. Enough of this foolishness!

-- 'Foolishness,' is it? Would you be willing to test that claim?

-- How?

-- By accompanying me to a place in Space and Time where Wynot first hatched His scheme.

-- I think you're stalling, Wilfong, delaying your much-deserved death with empty talk.

-- What have you got to lose, Sinladen – besides your ignorance? We can always fight, but there's no need to.

A long pause. The Enemy's ebony robe again swirled in multi-colored, kaleidoscopic fashion to denote agitation. Then:

-- What exactly do you have in mind?

-- I suppose you'll dismiss this as mere speculation as well, but I believe that Wynot came to Atlantis three centuries ago, not so much from a foreign land as from another time, specifically from the far future when what might seem like 'Magick' to us was as commonplace to the inhabitants of that world as our culture is to us. For whatever reason, Wynot traveled back to His past – our present -- in order to teach us and guide us. He was infinitely wise and put into motion any number of ideas and practices He knew were needed according to His knowledge of history – *His* history, that is. Some of those plans unfolded quickly; others – such as the testing of selected individuals – have yet to be completed.

-- Sheer fantasy! I'm surprised at you, Wilfong, for indulging in utter nonsense.

-- It's not nonsense, Sinladen. I know where the Master is, and I can take you to Him – if you still want to confront Him after all this time.

-- How do I know this isn't some sort of trick?

-- You don't. Still, as I've said, what have you got to lose?

-- All right, proceed. And be careful what you do. I'll be watching you every second.

-- I certainly hope so.

The Wizard then chanted a Spell of Transition:

> "There once was a speculative man,
>   Who hatched a monumental plan.
>   He decides to climb
>   The ladder of Time.
>   Oh, Wynot, give him a hand!"

*   *   *

"What place is this?"

Wilfong and Crotchgod stand at one end of a vast cave lined with metallic paneling which glistens even in the subdued light. The ceiling and floor are also metal and, except for a long, richly embroidered, golden-yellow carpet which stretches the length of the cave, creates the illusion of being one solid piece. The walls are adorned with rows of equally richly embroidered tapestries, but no other decoration is present.

The Practitioners have materialized at the exact spot on which Wilfong had found himself in his two dreams, at one end of the carpet. Crotchgod stares down its length and attempts to discern what lies at the other end. As the Wizard already knows, it is a futile effort.

Lining either side of the carpet are the tall, robed Beings with their odd, spherical headgear, standing stiff as statues – Wynot's Honor Guard, whose purpose is to greet all visitors to the Master's Holy of Holies. Crotchgod, ever suspicious, eyes as many of them as he can see and issues low animal growls in reaction.

"This is Wynot's Grand Temple," Wilfong replies. "Here, He directs the activities of all of the lesser Temples He has established throughout the Cosmos."

"So you say."

"I've been here twice before, in my dreams. It's all very familiar to me."

"*Humph!* If I'm supposed to be Wynot's 'creature,' then why isn't it familiar to me?"

"I had hoped that the familiarity of these surroundings would have triggered some recall. Either the Master created you somewhere else or He provided you with false memories."

"Bah! This is all meaningless! Where's Wynot? I want to see him."

"The Honor Guard will indicate when we may approach the Master. In the meantime, show some patience, will you?"

As if in response to Crotchgod's impatience, the first Being in the left-hand row turns toward the pair. Slowly, deliberately, it removes its headgear. "SC" utters a short shriek of terror at the sight of the Being's "face." Wilfong sucks in his breath; even though he knows that most of these Beings are far from human, he has not seen this "face" before. The head is lumpy and misshapen like a piece of clay with which a sculptor has only begun to work, and it is gray-colored like clay with wisps of black hair sprouting from it, mostly at the top. Its eyes are two black beads imbedded deep within the clayish lump. One protrusion has what appears to be nostrils, and beneath that is a slit which may be a mouth. This latter feature is upturned in the manner of a human smile, but little else suggests that the creature is friendly. Wilfong swallows hard. Beside him, Crotchgod quivers in multi-colored ferocity.

The Being now salutes in the manner of the Order of Wynot, and the gesture serves to restore the Wizard's mental equipoise. He responds accordingly and even attempts a smile of his own (though his heart is not in it).

Immediately, the Being in the right-hand row removes its headgear, and Wilfong relaxes. He has seen this member of the Honor Guard before; it is the pig-faced Being who had greeted him on his first and second visits here. A whimpering sound issues from Crotchgod. The second Being salutes, and Wilfong returns the greeting.

Both figures signal to him and "SC" that they are now permitted to march down the golden-yellow carpet. The Wizard has little trouble moving forward, because he is eager to be in the Presence. Crotchgod is glued to the spot.

"You're not going down there, are you?" he barely whispers.

"Of course. It would be bad manners not to. Come along, Sinladen; you said you wanted to see the Master. If these creatures had meant to harm us, they'd have done us in at the start."

"Maybe they're waiting for orders from your 'master.'"

Nevertheless, the Enemy moves forward in short, jerky steps. As the pair pass each set of Beings, these remove their headgear, revealing still other alien visages, and salute. Some of the Honor Guard are as close to human-ness as the Atlantean; the rest have clearly evolved along much different lines. Yet, none of them exhibit ill-will but regard the visitors with equanimity.

Once again, Wilfong marvels at the scope of Wynot's Master Plan. If non-human creatures exist, then the Master has traveled, not only to the past and the future but also to an infinite number of worlds which populate the Cosmos. Imagine: human beings are not the only intelligent beings; other forms inhabit Space and Time, subject to those passions and experiences which rule humans. Imagine: the Compleat Sorcerer is more than a *human* prophet; He is a prophet to the Cosmos, seeking His disciples where He may. Is He then on a par with Atlantis' fabled Most High? Truly, there is a Great Mystery here!

At last, the pair arrive at the golden throne. To the Wizard's dismay, it is empty. He glances left and right but sees no sign of Wynot. Now he discovers that the Honor Guard has departed. He and Crotchgod are quite alone in the cave of metal.

"Well?" says the Enemy, returning to his old sneering self. "Where's Wynot?"

"I don't know. I'm sure He'll appear eventually."

"Huh! He's afraid to show his face, that's all. He knows how powerful I've become, and he's in hiding." He flings his arms high into the air and spins around a couple of times in order to encompass the entire chamber. "Show your miserable self, Wynot!" he shouts, and his words echo faintly in the distance. "Prove to me that you're not a big, fat *coward!*"

Wilfong is horrified. Never in his wildest imaginings could he ever conceive of saying such vile things about the Master! He reaches out to seize Crotchgod's arm, thinks better of it, and instead waggles his finger at the ebony figure.

"Don't be rude. Remember where you are."

"I'm in the house of a *phtrx*, that's where I am! A *phtrx* who's scared shitless and won't accept my challenge!"

The Wizard is about to admonish his companion a second time but is interrupted by a somber voice behind him.

"Is that any way for a guest to speak?"

The pair both whirl about in astonishment. Surrounding the golden throne is a milky-white haze which sparkles and glitters like a million million fireflies. Soon, within the haze, a human shape coalesces and becomes vivid. It is Wynot, who now slouches upon the golden throne with his arms crossed. His face is appropriately grim; yet, a trace of bemusement in his eyes can be discerned. Wilfong sinks to his knees abjectly and bows his head. "SC" merely stands rigidly, his crimson eyes glowing fiercely.

"Get up, Wilfong," Wynot commands. "Kneeling is for slaves, and you're not a slave." The Wizard scrambles to his feet and gazes reverently upon his master. The latter regards him warmly even as he ignores Crotchgod. "So, my faithful pupil, you've figured it all out, have you?"

"Yes, Master. And I must say that it was a grand scheme, designed to challenge all of my skills." He flushes at his boldness and casts his glance at the floor. In a hushed tone: "But, of course, that was the whole idea, was it not?"

"A test wouldn't be worth the effort if just anyone could pass it."
Now Wynot acknowledges the Enemy's presence with a nod in his
direction. "Why did you bring *it* here?"

"I believed I could convince him of his erroneous ideas and therefore
avoid actual conflict."

"You were supposed to best it in combat, not to *convert* it, Wilfong."

"But, Master, didst thou not once say that a former enemy makes
the best ally?"

"Did I? Hmmm. My memory's not what it used to be. Be that as it
may, however, I intended that you should defeat him. The test is still in
effect, pupil." The Wizard expresses remorse. "I may be long-lived, but
I'm not immortal. Someday, I'll be gone, and I need someone to take my
place and stand up to the evil which still remains in the Cosmos. You,
my most worthy disciple, must learn to fight on many different levels."

"Hey, you two!" Crotchgod shouts. "Haven't you forgotten
something? Don't talk like I'm not here."

The Compleat Sorcerer regards him and smiles wryly.

"I guess I'd better shut him off for a while." He gazes off into the
distance. "Command code 31-C – close program."

"SC" disappears on the instant. Wilfong goggles in amazement.

"Master! What hast thou done to him?"

"You wouldn't understand, Wilfong. You must continue your
training before all things will become clear to you."

"How much more is there to learn?"

"A great deal more. What you have been through up to this point
is but the First Phase of Discipleship. Shortly, I will send you the
first lesson plan of the Second Phase. When you have completed all
of the lesson plans, then you will be a True Disciple, and I will show
you wonders never dreamed of." He snaps his fingers, and the "magic
eye" descend from the ceiling. "Before I send you back to your own
continuum, I want to show you something important."

Wynot utters something incomprehensible and, as before, a spear
of green light issues from the sphere. A picture forms, and once again
the Wizard views Atlantis from a great height. The "magic eye" circles
the Metropolis lazily, dropping lower and lower with each orbit until

people can be easily seen. Most are gathered in small knots and stare into the sky; they point and gesticulate agitatedly. Fear and terror are written large on their faces. Though Wilfong cannot hear what is being shouted, he makes a shrewd guess. They are not looking at the "magic eye" or giving any sign that they *can* see it; they are looking at something beyond it, higher up.

The sphere now spins upon its axis and the view shifts toward the heavens to reveal what the Atlanteans have been watching in stark horror. Wilfong also registers shock. A colossal fireball is descending from the heavens at an enormous velocity. The primitive races call such objects "shooting stars" and assign dire consequences to their appearance; the more educated, however, label them "meteors," large rocks which fall to Earth and burn up in the atmosphere. Yet, the Wizard has never seen one this huge. It appears to be the size of the Moon. If so, then it will not burn up completely, and the remnant will strike the Earth a tremendous blow, perhaps causing significant damage and loss of life.

The sphere soars high above the Earth so that the whole of the island-continent can be seen. The fireball slams into the Great Western Ocean only a hundred kilometers southwest of Atlantis. Instantly, a great explosion occurs as the all of the kinetic energy of the meteorite is transformed into heat and light. The brilliance of the explosion dwarfs that of the Sun, and Wilfong, though he is far removed from the cataclysm, instinctively shields his eyes. The blast produces its primary effects: a shock wave of huge proportions which manifests itself in two forms – hurricanes and tidal waves, both of which race toward Atlantis like twin battering rams.

And there is a third form, invisible until it actually strikes its target. The shock wave has created the king of all earthquakes, and a giant crack in the Earth develops, splitting the main island into three parts. The tallest buildings in the Metropolis – the Royal Palace and the various temples of the Most High – rock back and forth violently until their foundations are torn asunder and they collapse into heaps of rubble. From the central crack, tributary cracks are born, splintering the island further. Gouts of molten material spew up from the bowels of the Earth and flow through the streets like rivers of fire. Further tremblors crumple the walls between the Rings of the city and buildings of modest height, including many mansions of the upper classes.

Horrified beyond belief, the Wizard witnesses death on a mass scale. Atlanteans, in small groups and large, are either buried beneath the rubbles or scalded by the magma or pulled into the cracks. No one – young or old, male or female, native-born or foreign, rich or poor – is spared a hideous death. The catastrophe is all-encompassing and all-consuming, and he is grateful that he cannot hear the screams of the dying.

Now, the hurricanes and the tidal waves put in their evil appearances and strike Atlantis with fell intent. Buildings which had been weakened by the tremblors fall before this fresh assault. Worse, the water of the ocean makes contact with the fire of the Earth, producing awesome explosions. Geysers of steam and debris shoot into the sky like obscene fountains and fall back to Earth to create secondary effects. The continent is literally shaken to pieces.

In one vast, final spasm, the ruined Kingdom heaves up into the sky like ocean spray, then falls back and sinks beneath the waves. Not a trace remains to indicate that a mighty civilization once existed there. The "magic eye" circles the area, still steaming furiously. The last tremblors subside, and the hurricanes and tidal waves spend themselves in the far reaches of the Great Western Ocean. All is deathly still.

All is still in the cave of metal as well. The spear of green light winks out, and the sphere retracts upward. As it does, Wilfong the Wizard, overwhelmed by what he has just witnessed, succumbs to a torrent of emotion. He falls to the floor, sobbing loudly, and pounds his fists in impotent rage. Wynot regards him impassively. Presently:

"Get up, Wilfong, and face me."

The Atlantean reluctantly rises to his feet. His eyes are reddened, and his cheeks are tear-stained. He stands before his master in a slump as a man utterly defeated.

"What you have seen," the Compleat Sorcerer declares, "is – will be – an actual event. The fate of Atlantis is sealed."

"Wh – when, Master?"

"Not in your lifetime, but some time afterwards. I can't be more specific than that."

"Canst thou not prevent it?"

"I can, but I'm foresworn not to interfere."

"'Foresworn'? To whom?"

"I can't tell you that either – not until you complete the Second Phase of your training." Wynot gazes at his disciple solicitously. "I can, however, erase the memory of this future event for your peace of mind – if you so desire."

Wilfong closes his eyes and replays the horrific scene in his mind. The images are as ghastly and sense-numbing the second time around. Tears trickle anew. He shakes his head.

"No, Master. I shall keep my memories. Perhaps they will stir me to greater effort in all that I do henceforth. Perhaps, through my influence, some few will heed my words, depart Atlantis, and thus avoid" – his voice choked at this point – "the coming catastrophe. Perhaps they will find safe haven elsewhere in the Known World and become great teachers so that others may not have to face a similar fate."

"I hoped you'd say that. That is one of the marks of a True Disciple. Now, my faithful pupil, I'll send you back to Loth. You still have a test to pass."

"Very well, Master. I shall –"

*   *   *

"—attend to it…"

Wilfong's voice trailed away as soon as he realized he was no longer in Wynot's *sanctum sanctorum* but back on the grassy plain surrounding the village of Loth. Unlike the method he usually employed in transiting, that used by his Master was nearly instantaneous; the only noticeable result that a transition had taken place was the absence of the usual dizziness. Truly, he thought with humbleness, he had much to learn before *he* could achieve the level of skill of Wynot the Wise. And he had been privileged to bear witness to the tiniest fraction of that skill – based upon technology in the Master's own continuum which countless as-yet-unborn generations would largely take for granted.

One other "Truth" he had been "privileged" to witness – though it seemed more of a *curse* –was the ultimate destruction of his beloved Atlantis. The Kingdom had its many faults, to be sure, born of ignorance and superstition, but it was still the most advanced civilization ever to exist. That this center of political, economic, and cultural dominance should be utterly annihilated was a cruel act of Fate. And the irony of the situation was just that: a mindless, natural event. Had Wilfong been a superstitious person, he might have believed the destruction to be the will and/or the capriciousness of the Most High – "divine punishment" meted out for the "sins" of Atlantis and its people. As a disciple of Wynot, he had learned that "divine will" simply did not exist, that the Cosmos was without purpose and meaning in and of itself, and that only *human* will gave purpose and meaning to Life. The assured destruction of Atlantis, horrendous as it would be, was one which could not be prevented.

Or could it?

The Master had suggested that it could, though he seemed not to be at liberty to explain how. The *how* of it would be a real feat of Magick; to halt that enormous fireball in its tracks before it struck the Earth required greater forces than his poor brain could imagine. (Perhaps, in the Second Phase of his training in which the Master promised to reveal many marvels, he could imagine. Perhaps he himself could learn the technique!) Yet, Wynot had said that he would not act, due to foreswearing on his part. If this were true, then he was acting on some Grand Plan of the Cosmos whereby the destruction of Atlantis was a necessary part, not to be interfered with until all things had come to pass. What sort of plan permitted such monstrous acts to occur? It was beyond a simple wizard's comprehension.

The Wizard was not entirely powerless in this affair, however. He could prepare some of the more enlightened Atlanteans – particularly the Order of Wynot – for the event to come and perhaps persuade them to migrate elsewhere. He himself was now seriously considering such a move in order to preserve whatever posterity he might sire before the end of his days. On the surface, it may have seemed a gross act of selfishness to abandon one's homeland and leave others to their awful fate; the humanitarian thing to do was to see that the maximum number of people were saved from the destruction. Of course, one must be believed before one could be effective, and no one – not even Wynot himself – could guarantee belief in a sealed future.

In any event, the prime concern for the Order of Wynot was the preservation of knowledge for the benefit of future generations of human beings. In the Master's world-view, knowledge was everything, and its advancement was the noblest of endeavors. If Atlantis had to fall, then so be it. But, its heritage had to survive at all costs.

"Mashter!" Murkol cried out behind him, interrupting his train of thought. "Dou hasht returned! I wazh sho worried when dou and Crojgod dishappeared."

Wilfong eyed him curiously.

"Don't you remember why I left?"

"No, Mashter. Dou wert arguing wid de Enemy and den, in de blink of de eye, dou wert gone!"

The Wizard rubbed his jaw in confusion. Either Wynot had erased a few selected memories from Murkol's mind for reasons of his own, or He had returned Wilfong to a point in Time prior to the latter's decision to transit to His *sanctum sanctorum*. He was about to comment on that mystery when, as if on cue, the black-robed and –hooded figure materialized in the exact spot he had occupied only moments (centuries?) before. And he was agitated. He seemed to be in the throes of an epileptic fit; every move he made was spasmodic and exaggerated. After a moment or two of herky-jerky activity, "SC" became sedate – but only physically.

-- What in all the hells of the Cosmos happened here? [he screeched]. What did you do to me, *phtrx*?

-- Don't you remember?

-- All I know is you were blathering on about Wynot's being in the future. Then some sort of…*fit* came over me, and I blacked out. [A pause]. You used a Spell against me, and I never saw it coming!

-- Then you don't remember traveling to Wynot's Grand Temple?

-- *Humph!* I'd surely remember that. But, no, I didn't. What sort of Spell *did* you use?

-- I didn't use any Spell. It may be that the Master erased some of your memories. After all, you *are* His creation.

-- Are you still doing that song-and-dance? I tell you, I'm nobody's puppet. *Nobody's!*

-- Ah, but you are, Sinladen.

-- *Lies! Lies! Lies! ALL LIES!* Prepare yourself for oblivion, Wilfong the so-called Wizard!

Crotchgod raised his arms to form a "T," his pasty-white hands knotted into fists. His body trembled all over, and the crimson eyes turned ruby-red. Wilfong shook his head sadly. Reason had failed to prevent a nasty conflict. He was forced to unveil Plan B.

First things first, however. He called out to Murkol to repeat the Spell he had taught him not half an hour ago. The Zarelor moved his mouth, but no words came out of it; he was too paralyzed with terror at the Enemy's war-stance to react. At some risk to his own safety, the Wizard turned his back on Crotchgod and slapped Murkol hard. The stinging pain cut through the paralysis, and the fellow hastily spoke the Spell. Instantly, a translucent pink bubble formed around him, shimmering slightly.

Wilfong quickly returned his attention to "SC" – and not a moment too soon. The latter had created a Spell – a gigantic orange cube with blue polka dots – and was sending it careening toward the Atlantean. With only milliseconds to spare, the Wizard threw up his personal force field and deflected the cube away with a resounding thud. Crotchgod pressed his attack with a host of Spells – a red-and-blue hour-glass-shaped concoction which spat white sparks; a red-and-black lozenge which flip-flopped end over end; another orange cube but with *red* polka dots; a pale green inverted pyramid which spun upon its apex – all of which raced toward Wilfong with maddening fury. The Wizard was kept busy countering these Spells with some of his own – a black sphere which turned white every other second; two brown pyramids joined at their apexes, each of which rotated in the opposite direction;

a cloud of red dust; a large green cube which fragmented into hundreds of tiny ones.

Inexplicably, the Enemy ceased his assault and merely stared at Wilfong. The latter speculated that either he had exhausted himself or he was attempting desperately to think of new Spells to employ. Wilfong's money was on the latter guess. In any event, this respite – however long it lasted – allowed him to put Plan B into action. He signaled to Murkol, and the servant hurried to his side. What the Wizard had in mind was definitely a long shot – some might even have called it madness – yet he hoped it was the sort of ingenuity, not to mention surprise, which would win the day. At this point, he had only one roll of the dice, and he had to make it count.

-- Do you now require assistance, *phtrx*? [Crotchgod asked sarcastically].

-- Ordinarily, no. But, in this case, Murkol is a necessary part of my counter-attack.

-- No matter. You're still dead meat. Good-bye, Wilfong the Washed-up Wizard!

"*Now*, Murkol!" the Wizard commanded. "The powder!"

Before the Enemy could summon up fresh Spells by which he hoped would be the final blow against his hated foe, the Zarelor reached into his waist pouch and extracted a handful of black powder his master had instructed him to procure from the kitchen of Funkol's *kabban*. The Atlantean had promised to explain the significance of the substance should he survive this day. Murkol swallowed hard and threw the entire handful into Wilfong's face. The latter flinched and wrinkled his nose, but there was no other reaction. The odd action did, however, cause "SC" to halt his Spell-casting.

-- What are you doing, Wilfong? Have you gone mad?

The Wizard ignore him and instead motioned Murkol to throw more of the powder. The Zarelor complied and sprayed him a second time. Now, there was a reaction; the Atlantean's face contorted into a grotesque mask, and his head bobbed up and down. Excitedly, he waved for more powder. With the third dose, his facial spasms increased in frequency. Finally –

Wilfong the Wizard sneezed!

A school of thought existed which held that the seemingly innocent sneeze was actually an arcane language, millennia old and forgotten by all but the most assiduous Practitioners. If a Practitioner sneezed (it was said), anything may happen, from uttering a death curse to transforming base metals into gold. Most writers on the subject had dismissed these views as sheer fantasy. But Wilfong knew exactly what would happen, and thus he elected to subject himself to a fit of uncontrollable sneezing. Following the categorization of old Xelax, the Wizard produced six Thunderclaps in rapid succession, and the sounds echoed far into the distance. With watering eyes, he gazed in Crotchgod's direction to learn the outcome of his ploy.

Needless to say, the Enemy had been most perplexed by this strange action. Now, at the conclusion of the sixth Thunderclap, he stiffened as a familiar sensation coursed through his body. His crimson eyes blinked like signal lights far out to sea. His image flickered in and out of sight as if passing from light to shadow and back again.

-- *Oh, damnation!* [he wailed]. Not *again!*

In his moment of realization, Sinladen Crotchgod de-materialized with the sound of the bursting of a thousand balloons. An odor of sulphur lingered where he had once stood.

Wilfong heaved a huge sigh of relief, even as he wiped his watering eyes. The ploy had worked beyond his wildest imagining. Before he knew it, he found himself being lifted high into the air as a joyous Murkol expressed his own thoughts.

"Mashter! Dou hasht won! De Enemy izh gone forever!"

The Wizard struggled to free himself from the crushing embrace. When he had succeeded, he felt relaxed for the first time in many days. His plan, unorthodox as it was, had worked remarkably well, and his spirits been lifted immeasurably. The Order would not have to worry about Sinladen Crotchgod for a good, long while (only about the King's agents!). And didn't the day seem brighter all of a sudden?

The Big Question was, would his actions qualify as the sort of ingenuity Wynot had insisted upon? He supposed he'd find out soon enough. For the moment, he just wanted to bask in the glory of it all. He faced Murkol.

"Not quite forever, my friend, but long enough."

"I do not undershtand, Mashter."

"Do you recall my sneezing the other day and your winding up inside my trunk? Well, what happened there was that sneeze triggered the same energies I normally use for casting a Spell of Transition. But, since I was out of control temporarily (so to speak), I couldn't direct the Spell, and whoever was in the vicinity – you in that case – was transited in a random direction. And the greater the sneeze and the number of sneezes, the greater the number of permutations."

"Den, doezh dat mean dat Crojgod may return?"

"Eventually. During transition, one needs to know two things: where he is, and where he is going. If one doesn't know where he is going, he won't know how to get back to where he was. I have no idea where Crotchgod went; and, if I don't know, *he* certainly won't. He'll be a long, long time just trying to figure that out."

The Zarelor hefted his pouch.

"Dish powder, Mashter. What izh it?"

"We Atlanteans call it 'pepper.' It's a spice from a land on the eastern fringes of the Known World – and very expensive too." He grimaced. "Which says something about our 'friend' Funkol. He must be pocketing more than his fair share of the revenues if he can afford pepper. As to its effect, when inhaled, it causes a violent reaction, as you saw. I was counting on it to do the trick; and, since I wasn't casting a Spell *per se*, the Enemy had no defense against it."

"Lucky for ush."

"Not *luck*, Murkol, but good, old-fashioned know-how. It works every time." He sighed heavily again. "Well, let's get back to the village. I'm ready to go home."

The Zarelor cast a sheepish glance at the ground, nervously shifting his weight from one foot to the other.

"Mashter," he whined, "I may have done a bad ding."

"Oh? And what would that be?"

"Funkol dishcovered me in de kijen looking for de black powder and demanded to know why I wanted it. I told him dat dou needed it for reazhonzh I could not ekshplain, and he inshishted upon sheeing dee. I – I made him a promish in order to get rid of him."

"A promise?" Wilfong muttered ominously. "What kind of promise?"

"I, uh, I told him dou would shtay *anodder* day and – and give *two more* performanshezh. Dat sheemed to shatishfy him."

"*Two more performances?* Murkol, whatever got into you? The last thing I want to do is line that lout's pockets more than I already have."

"I am shorry, Mashter."

"The damage is done, I guess. Funkol will get his two performances, but he's going to pay dearly for them. And, if he doesn't come through, I'll make *him* part of the act!"

THE SIXTEENTH CASTING
THE WIZARD AT HOME

Down through the infinite number of corridors of SPACE and TIME, searching, searching, searching for the one which will make a connection, a VOICE travels. At last, it finds the correct corridor. And now, it speaks:

-- DUMB LUCK, *PHTRX!*

Wilfong the Wizard awakes with a start. He casts a glance at the sleeping feminine form beside him and is pleased that she remains undisturbed.

He is disturbed, however. There is a storm on the horizon, and he must prepare himself. He lies awake and traces the pathways the VOICE has taken in order to reach him. Now, he sends his own message:

"There once was an insolent pup,
Who sought to wake me up.
He is most annoying
And positively cloying.
Oh, Wynot, give him bitter herbs to sup!"

Printed in the United States
By Bookmasters